DEN OF THIEVES

Falon slid next to the bandit. His precious cape was draped loosely over the thief's shoulders. He swiped at the cape, catching it in his claws. Then he snatched up the bandit's sword.

"Now!" he yelled at Caissir. The wizard skidded on some spilled wine, and Falon had to jerk him to his feet. The cape trailed behind him, a brilliant flag drawing the unwanted attention of whole tables of bandits. Some of them started stumbling to their feet.

"Move, Caissir! Get your fat mrem tail moving!"

Falon turned to look over his shoulder. A blade was flying at him, a long, heavy blade thrown with the deadly expertise of a practiced brigand. No more than an arm's length away, and aimed perfectly at the center of his chest . . .

GUARDIANS OF THE THREE, VOLUME 3

WIZARD OF TIZARE

Matthew J. Costello

BANTAM BOOKS

NEW YORK · TORONTO · LONDON · SYDNEY · AUCKLAND

WIZARD OF TIZARE
A Bantam Spectra Book / January 1990

ISBN 0-553-28303-0

Published simultaneously in the United States and Canada

Bantam Books are published by Bantam Books, a division of Bantam
Doubleday Dell Publishing Group, Inc. Its trademark, consisting of the
words "Bantam Books" and the portrayal of a rooster, is Registered in U.S.
Patent and Trademark Office and in other countries. Marca Registrada.
Bantam Books, 666 Fifth Avenue, New York, New York 10103

WIZARD OF TIZARE

BOOK
ONE

THE KING OF AR

▲━━━━━━━━━━━━━━━━━━━━━━━━━━━━━━━━━━▲

1

Paralan stumbled through the hallway. The flickering torches set his shadow dancing against smudgy walls.

He pushed past mrem, soldiers, courtiers, guests, and servants . . . their bellies filled with sweet wine and grain-cakes, all of them enjoying the beneficence of the victorious King Talwe!

By the All-Mother, is this what we fought for? Paralan wondered. *To turn the castle into a banquet hall for scoundrels of every stripe?*

He quickly turned a corner and stumbled right into a noisy couple vigorously rutting against the wall. The mrem tumbled drunkenly to the ground, while the she-mrem quickly eyed Paralan, licking her lips, apparently eager to replace her lover with someone with less wine in his gut.

Paralan shook his head.

"Go on playing with someone you're safe with," he grunted, looking down at the mrem, still erect, scurrying to his feet.

More steps, twisting and turning this way and that. In times of battle the mazelike hallways of the great castle would let the king's troops surprise an attacker. But if anything were to happen now, if any liskash were to *now* come from the East, why, they'd simply have to cut their way through the belching hangers-on. The soldiers . . . where were they? And what state of preparedness were they in?

They're probably just as unprepared as I am, he thought grimly, balancing himself awkwardly as he reached some curving stone steps.

It is Talwe who is to blame!

Talwe has allowed all this to corrupt him, soften him, until it has affected all of Ar.

Even before he became king, before he joined with his beloved Sruss to win the throne of Ar, Talwe was too much given to pleasure. There may be no braver fighter in the West. But he loved the sheer splendor *of being king.*

Paralan reached the top of the staircase. The line of rooms beckoned with the boisterous noise of even more raucous partying, more bleary-eyed strangers enjoying Talwe's hospitality.

He walked steadily now, preparing himself for the grim business ahead. He gently smoothed his whiskers.

Then Paralan was at the room, its oaken door shut tight, somber.

Paralan knocked on the door.

It opened a crack.

A small face, with sparkling eyes, looked up at him.

"Thank you . . . for coming. I know that you must be very busy this night."

She was called Feila, a young and beautiful female. She had started out on the cleaning staff, just another servant. But with her striking markings, so golden that she glowed even in the dank hallways, and her eyes such a clear, sparkling blue, like the water of the River Tizare—well, she did not go unnoticed for long.

Feila was beautiful, by the All-Mother, maybe the most beautiful she-mrem in all of Ar!

She opened the door further, just enough for Paralan to ease his bulk into the small room. He looked around at the candlelit quarters, the narrow bed, the small cabinets, and high up, a single window—too high for her to look out at the courtyard.

So this was how one of Talwe's courtesans spent her time when she was not in the royal chambers!

Paralan snorted his disapproval.

"Sit here," she said, pointing at the bed. "Would you like some sweet wine? It's still quite cool. . . ."

He shook his head, again nervously fingering his whiskers. She gave off no aroma of love, no scent of desire. Instead, she radiated fear, a terrible, childlike fear.

And yet, her beauty stirred him.

She came and sat next to him on the bed.

"Are you sure you won't have a cup of wine?"

"I've had more than enough for one night, Feila. I was part of the 'welcoming party' for Talwe's guest," Paralan said with obvious disdain, "before I got your message. I came immediately."

Feila stood up, blocking the lone candle. She was a shadow, and Paralan's face was covered in darkness.

"It's about Talwe. I—"

Paralan raised a hand up.

"There's nothing I can do there, Feila. He has always been one to enjoy females, leaving them when he's had his, er, fill." Paralan winced at his own inept way of expressing the hard facts to Feila. With Sruss away supervising the reconstruction of Cragsclaw, Feila had, perhaps, allowed her hopes to rise. Maybe Sruss wouldn't come back, she hoped. Maybe Talwe would keep Feila close by his side forever.

But Paralan knew his king better than that.

No one would ever take the place of Talwe's beloved Sruss.

Feila took a step closer to him, and rested a graceful hand on his broad shoulder.

"Surely *you* still have his ear . . . he listens to you more than anyone in Ar. . . ."

"Perhaps. But it's not often these days that he seeks my confidence."

In fact, Paralan thought, *Talwe goes against my advice more often of late. Like tonight's welcoming party, throwing open the doors of the castle to a stranger, with only an honor guard present for protection.* Still, they had been through much together, and that had to count for something.

"No," the young she-mrem said quietly. "It's not . . . that."

Paralan raised his eyebrows. "Eh, then what is it?"

"I'm pregnant. I'm going to have Talwe's kit. He has not spoken to me since I told him." Feila sat down. "I'm afraid of what he might do . . . to me . . . to his kit."

"By the All-Mother," Paralan laughed. "A kit! Just what

the young warrior needs. Something to use up all that energy he goes spending around the palace."

But he saw that Feila wasn't laughing.

"Paralan . . . I'm scared. Talwe hasn't said a word since I told him."

He stood up, none too steadily, he noted. "Don't you worry, Feila. I will gladly intercede with Talwe. That overgrown kit should be glad of your news." He leaned close to Feila, smelling the sweet aroma of her scented fur. "Now you've done more for Talwe, and Ar, than Sruss has been able to do. An heir," he whispered into her ear. "An heir! Rest now. I will speak to him before the morrow."

Feila took his right hand in both of hers, still barely unable to encircle it, and she squeezed it hard.

"Thank you. I knew I could count on your help."

"Yes . . . now if you'll just direct me to the way out I'll try stumbling my way past all the rutting couples who litter the hallways."

She laughed, quickly skipping over to open the door. She turned the heavy doorknob and all the party sounds, scented with the smell of spilled ale and wine, came rushing in.

"And remember—don't worry."

And Paralan made his way to the Great Hall where his lord and friend, Talwe, entertained the ambassador from the Far Western Kingdom of Kazeir.

Here, at least, some semblance of order prevailed.

Still the tables groaned under the heavy platters of arbunda, all sliced into every variety of steak known to the butchers of Ar. Servants walked from table to table with large silver goblets filled with the fruity wines native to neighboring valleys.

Two different bands played, one at each side of the hall —so far apart that their cacophonous sounds, the rustic rhythms so favored by Talwe, could barely be heard by each other.

The head table, larger than any Paralan had ever seen before, was raised under the new tapestry that Talwe commissioned when he became king.

Paralan paused a moment and stared at the enormous woven mural.

Cragsclaw!

The battle that was legend in all of the Western kingdoms.

There, in the center, was Talwe, his sword raised high while a pile of dead liskash lay at his feet. And off to the right, there were lines of gleaming chariots, many more than actually attacked them on that fateful day. Archers were letting loose their arrows, while other liskash were attempting to climb the castle walls.

To the left stood Mithmid, seemingly removed from all the action.

That, Paralan thought, was indeed funny.

Without Mithmid's intervention—magically removing the liskash's protection from the winter chill—the cold-blooded monsters would have kept on coming, more and more of them until they would have swarmed over the castle walls.

And there I am, Paralan thought, looking at himself on the tapestry, through the smoke of the scented urns and the dusty haze made by the storm of battle and so many mrem. He was there, right by Talwe's side. "As it ever shall be," the king-to-be had said.

So, he had been true to his word. Paralan was Talwe's most trusted friend. Yet time had worked hard, bitter changes. Many important decisions were routinely made without Talwe spending time walking with Paralan among the leafy fronds of the castle's great fern garden. At other times, Paralan felt that Talwe would consult with him only out of some distant, half-remembered sense of obligation.

More and more of late, Paralan was thinking perhaps it was his time to leave.

Paralan walked through the maze of mrem, up to the dais. He looked at Talwe, who turned and nodded quickly, not interrupting the flow of conversation with his guest of honor.

Paralan studied this guest—this ambassador—a moment, before taking his seat.

There was something that was almost familiar about the mrem, something that had troubled Paralan from the moment he saw him. True, the markings were strange, with the use of heavy dyes favored by the Far Westerners. And the scalp fur was cut in the distinctive wedge shape. Worse, his whiskers were trimmed—a thought that sent a shiver through Paralan.

Still, there was something more disturbing about this guest.

Paralan sat down at his place. His goblet was quickly refilled and a fresh plate of meat put in front of him. But Paralan ignored the food and just watched Talwe in close discussion with this guest, Ambassador Wydnic. They were in close conversation, Talwe and this emissary.

Just what kind of deals were they up to?

Talwe laughed, a hearty, robust sound, and signaled to a servant to refill his goblet. Paralan caught his eye, got up, and walked over to him.

Wydnic was eating daintily from his plate, long tapered fingers poking at the meat, extending a curved claw to pull out an especially rare tidbit.

"Lord Paralan, come sit next to us. The ambassador here was telling—"

Paralan leaned down close to Talwe, whispering to him. "Hold onto your balls when talking to the likes of him, my lord Talwe. One couldn't even grab this one by the short hairs of his whiskers should he wish to make off with the palace silver."

Talwe laughed despite himself.

"Paralan, be civil," he whispered. "He's explaining many good things his kind Western king can do for Ar. Why, do you know that—"

"I'm sure, Talwe. But listen," Paralan said, willing to speak directly to his old friend and fighting companion, "I have come from Feila. She has told me of—"

Talwe's expression completely clouded over. He chewed his mouthful of food as though it suddenly had become distasteful. "I won't," the king said in measured tones that chilled even Paralan, "talk of this now."

Paralan sighed. "But Talwe, she's—"

"Not now!" the king ordered, his voice rising. A hush fell over the head table, then spread to the nearby tables, like a stone making waves, rippling. Heads turned, studying Talwe to see what could have made him break the mood. The shock of hearing him raise his voice to his lord Paralan doubled their confusion.

"Yes," Paralan said slowly, standing right next to the oversize image of himself on the tapestry.

The ambassador looked over, smiled, then wiped his hands on the thick napkin on his lap. "I don't believe I've had the pleasure. . . ." Wydnic said, extending a graceful hand.

"Lord Paralan, my personal lieutenant," Talwe said without enthusiasm, devoid of the special fondness that he usually displayed when introducing Paralan.

I, too, have my limits, Paralan thought. He shook the ambassador's hand.

He looked the ambassador right in his dark eyes.

And Paralan knew that there was something hidden, something false about this Far Western dandy. It was there, in the clear gleam of his eyes, and in his hands, manicured to perfection, but strong . . . assured.

"Ambassador," Paralan said, releasing the hand.

Wydnic held his gaze.

"I have been telling your king that such feasts as this in the West are rare. It can be so dry. Much of our food arrives from the Southern islands. We have learned dozens of ways to cook fish."

Paralan watched Wydnic, watched him, even as he talked, dissecting the slab of steak on his table, extracting the chewy lines of fat like a surgeon.

Yet, Paralan thought, *you have seen more steaks in your day than I have. If Talwe weren't so full of sweet wine, he'd see it, too.*

He looked at his king. "Talwe, I just—"

But Talwe turned and spoke to a servant standing just behind him.

"Tell the dancers that my guest and I are ready."

Paralan shrugged and turned away. There would be time later to plead Feila's case, to make Talwe see that his heir must be protected, recognized, honored. To protect the kingdom.

Paralan took his seat just as the dancers arrived, taking over some hurriedly cleared space. The two opposing bands now struggled to work together, playing an ever-faster rhythm, cheered on by the wild clapping of the revelers. Faster and faster, the dancers, each dressed in a thin green gown, spun around like tops spinning out of control. Faster and faster . . .

And he looked back at his king, who had one eye on the dancers, but was still in close conversation with Wydnic.

There is danger here, Paralan wanted to tell him.

But for now I must wait, watching the dancers spin out their stories of great kings and their great loves.

Chapter 2

▲━━━━━━━━━━━━━━━━━━━━━━━━━━━━━━━━━▲

The ambassador let Talwe clasp his hand tightly.

"We will talk more in the morning, Wydnic, of your kingdom, and Ar."

The ambassador smiled graciously. "I look forward to that, Talwe. I'm sure that this festive night bodes well for the good relations between Ar and Kazeir." He watched Talwe stifle a yawn, and thought, *It's not fatigue that hurries you away, my randy king.* No, the magician could clearly read the drunken flood of thoughts and feelings that gripped Talwe, and it wasn't mere affairs of state that concerned him now.

Wydnic smiled. "In the morning then."

"I shall look forward to it," Talwe said.

And then the ambassador closed the door, and fell against it, biting into his hand, suppressing the laughter. It was almost too easy, to be here inside the castle, at Talwe's right hand.

Too easy!

There had been a moment, during the feast, when he thought he'd lose control. It took clear, almost perfect concentration to keep his mental shield strong and impenetrable. How else could he be there, beneath that enormous tapestry showing the moment of his greatest failure?

Cragsclaw!

He wanted to scream at them. *I was there, too! I almost brought the Eastern Lords their greatest victory. And then*

I, Cwynid, would have ruled the Western lands along with them!

But there had been incalculable factors. Talwe's natural brilliance as a soldier, as a strategist. He had organized an incredible defense of what was an indefensible position. It was more than impressive.

It was, quite simply, magical.

At first Cwynid had suspected nothing more than some ragged beast magic, nothing to stand up against his own powers. But he had gradually felt another power, strong, clear, direct . . . and growing.

Cwynid stepped away from the door. He walked over to the bed, pulling the sheets and rich coverlet back. While it must appear that he had slept soundly, he would not rest at all this night.

He then went and placed a chair near a small dressing table. He sat down, closed his eyes, and began to concentrate. . . .

Yes, Talwe had had powerful help that day, a magic that had trapped the liskash without their magical warmth. They had slowed, some even collapsed in the dirt, cut down like sand rats by the flurry of arrows and the flashing swords.

Cwynid had fought the spell but—from out of nowhere —it had been just too powerful.

The Eastern Lords had not dealt kindly with him after that defeat. He had thought that they might even torture him, or skewer him alive and serve him at one of their ghastly feasts. But one of the elders, a veteran of many battles with the mrem, had come forward.

He's too valuable, the elder had argued. *Let us keep him. There will come a time when we will need him.*

Yes, Cwynid had agreed. *Listen to this wise liskash. I can be of great, great service to the Eastern Lords . . . if only you'll spare my life.*

And despite the loud protests of some of the survivors of Cragsclaw, Cwynid had found himself spared, spared for this. . . .

He placed his hands flat on the table.

I must concentrate, he thought. *To make sure that the contact is there.* He began breathing deeply, the dark room vanishing before his eyes.

And then he was *there.*

Inside one of Talwe's palatial rooms, lying next to Talwe.

Talwe, of course, saw nothing but the supple beauty next to him, gently running her claws over his mottled fur, whispering words of encouragement to him, enjoying him in all his languorous drunkenness as he slowly became hard.

And now Cwynid felt it! There! He was part of her now, smelling the delicately scented air, the still-fruity taste of the goblet of wine next to the bed.

"Come," he could hear her say, "come, my king, and rest yourself inside me."

In his dark room, Cwynid's lips quivered, enjoying the perverse pleasure as Talwe struggled to mount the young beauty.

And there will be others, Cwynid thought, *others to catch the attention of King Talwe, while I remain a friendly confidant, friend of the court . . . until the very throne itself becomes mine.*

Day after day, Cwynid would grow closer to the king, while at night he would whittle at the fraying strands of Talwe's character, hacking into his very spirit, until the king was ready to give himself over to Wydnic's wise leadership.

And then . . .

Cwynid smiled in the dark.

Ar and its king would be presented to the Eastern Lords for retribution.

And, for the moment, the great magic user felt no danger.

Mithmid woke up from his troubled sleep. The hall outside still echoed with the waves of celebrants stumbling from one part of the castle to the other.

No matter, he thought. Before dawn the last of the wine would have been consumed and the food platters would be empty. The harsh light of morning had a way of chasing away even the most persistent and obnoxious guest.

Mithmid turned over, grinding his sleepy head into the fluffy down pillow.

But his eyes blinked open.

Like a cold breeze wafting through a window, he sensed something awry. He sat up and concentrated. A flood of sensations came: the squeals and mewlings of lovers (or strangers), the heavy snores of guests collapsed in dim corridors, the sounds of fights, nasty battles over nothing, all fueled by too much wine.

In the midst of it all—what?

Danger?

Or just the endless waves of so many mrem prowling around at night?

He lay there a moment and then, when the feeling faded, he shrugged and lay down again.

Paralan had to wait for Talwe to wake up.

By the time the king took breakfast the castle had been scrubbed clean, from the lowest storerooms to the upper parapets. The guards were in their assigned positions and some semblance of normalcy and routine had returned.

Paralan strolled back and forth, waiting outside Talwe's chambers, until finally a servant opened the large wooden doors.

"Come in, Paralan," he heard Talwe call out to him. "We can talk while I have some breakfast."

Paralan walked in and found Talwe sitting up in bed—alone. There were platters of fruit, nuts, and sweet cakes, still steaming and warm from the castle kitchen.

"Please, sit. And help yourself. There's no way I'll be able to eat all this food."

"You're feeling all right?" Paralan asked, sitting down on a corner of the bed.

"All right? Oh, last night. Well, I *have* felt better. Still, it was a grand celebration. Ambassador Wydnic was extremely impressed."

"Talwe, I don't have very good feelings about that mrem." Paralan saw Talwe look up at him. Then Talwe spoke, his voice cold and distant.

"There is much his king can do for us, Paralan. Not everyone lives like this." he said, gesturing at the room and the food. "You and I, of all people, should know that. If I can improve trade in Ar, make it easier for the mrem who live here, then I'll do it."

Paralan stood up. "I don't know, Talwe. It's a feeling. I don't trust him. What would Sruss say of all this?"

Talwe noisily bit into an oversize pompa berry, its purplish juice dripping down his chin. He dabbed at his fur, then rubbed his whiskers.

"Sruss is not here, Paralan," Talwe said quietly.

"Talwe . . . last night . . . when I was called to Feila's chambers . . ."

Without looking up Talwe took another bite of the fruit, letting Paralan hang there.

"She asked me to intercede with you. She is worried, about herself . . . about her child."

Paralan watched Talwe clear his food away and stand up. "It is all taken care of, Lord Paralan. In fact, I was going to summon you myself today."

"Summon, Talwe? I thought that you merely had to ask me to see you. Am I to be summoned now?"

Talwe grinned, and put a hand on his friend's shoulder. "Yes," he laughed lightly, "I am forgetting who I'm talking to. But—" Talwe turned more serious "—it was about Feila. I've arranged for her to be adopted by the King of Pleir."

Paralan shook his head. "Adopted? And Pleir! Why that's nothing more than an overgrown Northern village, a barbaric outpost."

"As was Ar at one point, my friend. Pleir's King Yarrou has agreed. And that is what I am going to do with this troublesome vixen," he hissed.

"And what of your kit?"

Talwe glared at Paralan, more and more irritated by the discussion. "Feila's kit will be taken care of by Yarrou. That will be no problem."

Now Paralan came close to Talwe. How could his friend be so *dense?* "It's your heir, Talwe. Your heir."

But Talwe shook his head. He shed his rich sleeping garment, and pulled on a deep blue cape. Then he strapped on his sword, the same sword he had used at Cragsclaw.

He had promised, Paralan knew, that the sword would always be with him. To remind him of the need for constant vigilance. The East never rests, he had told Paralan.

Now it seemed to Paralan to be nothing more than a hollow gesture.

"It is not Sruss's kit. Unless I accept Feila, the kit cannot be an heir." Talwe paused. "And I will not accept her. In fact, I want you to escort Feila to Pleir. You may stay with her to ensure that she is well provided for. I don't expect," Talwe said, raising an eyebrow, "that there will be much for you to do here. At least for a while."

Paralan shook his head. "But Talwe—"

The servant came back into the room.

"Ambassador Wydnic is here, Your Highness," she announced.

"Oh," Talwe said eagerly, turning away from Paralan. "Show him in right away."

Paralan hurried to Talwe's side. "Why are you doing this? The kit is yours!"

Talwe shrugged. "Perhaps. Perhaps not. I'm not ready for an heir. And I certainly wouldn't choose a kitchen helper to be the mother of the next—"

"And since when is *your* background so fabulously royal!"

Wydnic entered the room, his face going wide with exaggerated embarrassment. "Oh, is this a bad time, my lords? Perhaps I should—"

But Talwe shook his head. "No, Wydnic. My counselor here was about to leave. I expect you to leave today, Paralan."

Paralan stood there.

Time changes things, he thought.

There was a time when Talwe wouldn't urinate in an alleyway without mentioning it to his good friend and lieutenant. Now, he thought, *I'm just another "loyal servant" to King Talwe.*

"Yes," Paralan said grimly, "I'll take Feila. But only because I wouldn't trust anyone else in your court to do the job. But when I come back, my king," he said coming right up to Talwe's face, "then we will talk some more. This," he gestured at Wydnic, "is not what I fought for."

Talwe's angry expression matched Paralan's. "Go then," he said quietly.

Paralan turned and walked past the ambassador, forcing him to step aside.

"Oh, excuse me," the ambassador said, turning and watching Paralan leave.

And Paralan's nostrils flared as he passed, sniffing as he

continued out of the room, walking to Feila's chambers. . . .

Almost as if he smelled something familiar . . . disturbing.

And dangerous.

Chapter 3

▲————————————————————————▲

Mithmid sat in his chair in the empty chambers of the Council of The Three. He waited there, in the darkness, trying, over and over, to understand just what it was that disturbed him so.

He heard the heavy door open just behind him, and Eronica, dressed in the silvery flowering cloth that he favored, hurried to him. Eronica, not known to favor such early morning meetings, sat down grumpily.

"Well, Mithmid, what is it that has you so upset on this bright morning?"

Mithmid shifted uneasily in his seat. How could he explain such a vague malaise, an odd disturbance that left no clue to its source?

"It's Talwe. I have been worried. . . ."

Eronica nodded. "And well you should be. If he doesn't spend more time on affairs of state rather than affairs of the heart, well, Ar won't enjoy the fruits of its victory for long."

But Mithmid shook his head. "No . . . Talwe was always like that . . . but he was always able to respond to danger quickly. There is something else at work here, something—"

"Magical?" Eronica added.

Mithmid nodded.

"But," Eronica said, extending his hands, "I feel nothing. The city is free of any magic."

Mithmid stood up, pacing the dull council room. "But that is exactly it. I have only the vaguest of feelings that something is not quite right, but when I probe the king and those around him, there is nothing . . . nothing at all."

Now Eronica stood up, eager to conclude this clearly unnecessary meeting. "So there, you see. There is nothing awry in Ar. But," the older council member said, putting an arm around Mithmid, "I have a thought. Perhaps you are getting some disturbing feelings from someone close to Talwe."

Mithmid turned and gave Eronica a confused look.

"You see, our king's consort, Sruss, has been gone for quite a while. And she will be gone longer still, supervising the workers rebuilding Cragsclaw. Maybe this warning comes from there, from Cragsclaw."

Mithmid shook his head. "I don't—"

"Why not go there, Mithmid? Visit Sruss, and see how she fares. If all seems well, return here. I'll keep a close watch on Talwe."

And Mithmid slowly nodded, agreeing to the plan.

But not believing that it was Sruss who was in danger . . .

Paralan made quick work of telling the terrible news to Feila, ignoring her tears as he stuffed her possessions into two small satchels. And when he didn't stop packing, she beat him, yelling and screaming terribly.

And he let her do it, let her cry out her anger.

"There's nothing that can be done," he repeated gently. "You will be safe and provided for. And so will your kit."

And, Paralan thought, *I'm just the good lieutenant, carrying out my king's wishes . . . no matter how stupid and ill-thought they might be.*

So it was that, armed with grain-cakes and water for the journey, Paralan led the distraught Feila out of the castle to the northern gates and out of the city of Ar.

Look! he wanted to tell her. *See the great market place with its cages of clucking patter fowl ready to be bought for some tangy stew. Look at the great piles of young songomore leaves, harvested for their spicy flavor. Look at the great chunks of arbunda hanging from the butcher's metal hooks.*

Look at them, because who knows when you'll see their like again.

He knew that such delicacies were rare in the Northern villages. Such things might be seen at festival time, and even then only in the richest households.

But Feila looked at none of it. She walked beside Paralan, leaning into him, her tiny body arousing his every instinct for protection. She closed her eyes, trusting Paralan to lead her safely to the road, and her hated destiny.

At first, when they started the gradual climb to the low-lying hills that sat at Ar's northern border, Paralan kept up a steady stream of chatter. The North was different, he breezily assured her. She would surely find someone to be with, someone who would appreciate her beauty. And it was a healthier place, with clear bracing air, laced with the snow and spring flowers of the mountains.

But then she spoke. "Please," she said. "I want to just walk there . . . quietly."

Paralan nodded. He pulled her close, and busied himself watching the tough lowland grass gradually give way to the lush trees and bushes of the highlands.

Each time they stopped to rest—which was often—Paralan tried to get Feila to eat. But she shook her head, taking only a few sips of water before telling him that she was ready to move on.

The first night he found a quiet glade by a small stream. Though it was still warm, Paralan unrolled two heavy blankets. When Feila curled up by a rock and once again refused to eat, Paralan decided to do something about it.

He walked over to her, crouched, and touched her shoulder. "You *must* eat," he commanded.

She shook her head, keeping her eyes closed.

Paralan poked at her again. "You must eat . . . if not for your own scrawny, underfed body, then at least for the kit growing inside you."

And now her eyes opened wide.

"And what of the kit," she hissed. "He's been denied by his father. What does it matter what happens to him?" She sat up, spitting out her words. "If he were to be born now, I would take him and toss him into the stream. It wouldn't matter at all."

"Him?" Paralan said softly. "You know?"

She nodded. "Yes. It's a male."

"By the All-Mother," Paralan said, standing up. "By the

blessed All-Mother, what is wrong with Talwe? This," he said gesturing to her still-flat midsection, "is his heir."

"It's because of Sruss," Feila said quietly.

"Eh?"

"Sruss wants to give him his heir. If she doesn't, then no one shall."

"I should have guessed as much." Paralan knew that Sruss, as brave as any at Cragsclaw, tolerated Talwe and his endless procession of desirable vixens.

But there were some things that could not be allowed.

Paralan came back to her, resting his large hand right on Feila's fur, rubbing right near her teats. "A son," he whispered, expressing no surprise at Feila's beast magic. He had suspected as much.

And, he wondered, *what will be* your *destiny, oh unlucky kit, in the great lands to the north?*

Paralan woke to the sound of Feila's screaming.

"What?" he said groggily, jumping up. He unsheathed his sword and ran over to the spot where she had been sleeping. But she wasn't there.

"Feila!" he bellowed.

He heard her mewling, coming from the stream.

"What is it?" he yelled, running over. "What's wrong?"

She was standing at the edge of the stream, her kilt off. He had no time to appreciate her beauty before seeing what had terrified her.

He started to laugh. "Oh, ho, yes, watch out for that. Best be careful. You don't want *that* taking any bites out of you."

"Wha—what is it?"

"It's a river skud," Paralan said, still laughing. "Perfectly harmless."

He knew that the skud, which looked almost like a tiny liskash, was a fierce-looking creature. It was ugly, with a beaked mouth that looked like it could rip a nasty chunk out of your pelt. But in truth Paralan knew it only gnawed at the stringy plants that grew along the edges of rivers and streams.

Still, most mrem didn't miss the opportunity to quickly dispatch them. They were just too reminiscent of the dreaded armies of the Eastern Lords.

"Here," he said, still chuckling, "allow me."

He brought his sword down quickly on the slimy skud. He sliced it in half, and the bang of his sword echoed in the lush glade.

Feila ran to him. She pressed close. "I've never seen one. I've lived my entire life in Ar. I was so scared."

"There," he said. "It's all over now."

The laughter left his voice as she rested against him, her slim body pressed tightly, her soft fur so close to his own natty pelt. He felt himself stirring.

He gently pushed her away.

"There. Everything's fine," he said brusquely, masking his embarrassment.

She looked up at him. "Thank you."

"Yes. And we'd best be on our way."

Feila nodded sadly, and began to roll up their sleeping blankets. And then, when they started walking on the trail again, he saw Feila dig into one of the packs and extract a large chunk of grain-cake.

At least, Paralan thought with relief, watching her chew noisily on the cake as they climbed the low hills, she was eating. She even started talking a bit, telling him of her father, a tinsmith, and her mother, who died when she was still a kit.

"I was left pretty much on my own," she said proudly, "I was so happy when I got to work in the castle."

Paralan arched an eyebrow. "Talwe always has an eye out for new talent. And his staff has been well trained in his preferences."

The mention of Talwe's name made her grow quiet again.

"I . . . I didn't know what to think. It was all so exciting."

"Yes. Well, you can see where it's gotten you now."

She laughed. "Climbing a hill with a mighty skud-killer."

And Paralan laughed also, enjoying the wonderful sound of her laughter. If Pleir was a good place, and King Yarrou a good mrem, why, Feila would do just fine.

And if not, Paralan thought, *I will be there. . . .*

The hills gave way to rough, rocky land dotted with spiky bushes and the stunted, almost skeletal agora trees.

The easy part of their journey was over, Paralan thought. Their marching would take them up to higher and higher ground, until they reached the first mountains of the great Northern range that girded the Southern Kingdoms. He had heard stories of mrem who went beyond the Northern villages, past the icy mountains, to the great plateau at the top of their world.

Every kit grew up with the myths and tales of the ice folk, and their mysterious towns and tunnels dug right into the ice. Not a harvest season went by that some enterprising showmrem didn't appear in Ar with what he claimed were genuine artifacts of the ice folk. Once, one pudgy mrem had shown up with a kit, its fur a shiny gray.

"A living specimen!" he had claimed.

Except that it wasn't hard to wet one's hand and rub it over the gray fur—revealing a smudgy brown pelt beneath it.

Still, it wasn't hard to believe that the North held secrets, both wonderful and dangerous. Even Paralan, who had seen such lands before, became quiet and thoughtful, breathing hard as they climbed the hill.

He looked over at Feila.

If anything, she seemed more comfortable, almost relaxed. Every now and then she stooped down and picked up a stray flower sprouting, in an unlikely fashion, from the dry, hard soil of the highlands.

It was midafternoon when his reverie was disturbed by other travelers on the narrow hill trail.

At first, the small group of mrem, five of them, sitting by the road, looked as if they might be merchants taking a break from their wearying journey from village to village. But the closer Paralan came to them, the more alarmed he became.

They wore heavy swords sheathed in thick leather, and their throat armor, while not fastened tight, dangled loose around their necks . . . ready for quick action.

And except for the uncorked jug that they were passing among them, Paralan would have said that they were soldiers.

"Steady, Feila. Stay close to me. Say nothing." He looked over at her, the low-lying sun casting her in shades of yellow and orange. "And pull the cowl of your cape up tight around your head."

"But I am so hot," Feila whined, still not aware of the danger Paralan felt.

Then Paralan adopted a cautious, but steady gait towards the sprawling soldiers. His hand rested on his own sword, not in any threatening way, but with obvious implications for any who should choose to look.

They were almost upon them when one of the soldiers, the apparent leader, stood up.

"Ho, there, friend. Why do you hurry so?" The soldier, a plump lout, planted himself right in the middle of the trail.

Paralan's hand closed around his sword, and he debated just drawing it out and taking the first swing. At least, he thought, he'd start the game with the advantage of having one less to deal with.

But what of Feila? Could he guarantee that she would be kept safe, out of harm's way?

He decided to talk his way past the drunken party.

Paralan stopped, and pulled Feila to rest just behind him.

"We're on our way to Pleir, to see King Yarrou. He expects us tomorrow."

The leader turned to his cronies. "Pleir, eh? King Yarrou." He turned back to Paralan and spit into the ground. "King Yarrou. The liar king . . . the thieving king . . . slavemonger . . . murderer."

The other four soldiers all stood up.

Obviously, thought Paralan with painful hindsight, these soldiers were *not* from Pleir.

The burly spokesmrem for the group took a few drunken steps closer. "And what are you bringing to 'good' King Yarrou?" He reached out a hand and flicked back Feila's cowl.

Paralan saw the others shift closer, straining to see the suddenly revealed treasure.

"Oh," the soldier said, "now don't tell me that you're going to bring this beauty, this—" he reached out to run his massive hand over her sleek fur.

In an instant, Paralan reached out and grabbed the soldier's wrist.

"This *prize*," the leader snarled in a whisper, turning to look at Paralan.

Then, as if a carefully rehearsed routine, the soldiers all drew out their swords.

"By the All-Mother!" Paralan yelled. He flung Feila backwards. She went flying into the dirt, rolling over and over.

Well away from this little party, Paralan hoped.

He didn't get his own sword out in time to parry the first blow. But either their skill was wanting, or they had sampled too much sweet wine, for Paralan was able to dodge the first strike.

"Paralan!" Feila screamed.

He turned, and saw one of the soldiers about to drive his sword into his back.

Paralan made a quick backwards swing, a neat arc that caught the attacker in his midsection. Paralan didn't bother turning to see the damage. He pulled the sword sharply to the front, taking the telltale strings of red that dangled from the blade as proof positive that he was now down to four attackers.

All four were then facing him, taking measured steps. Paralan turned his sword, letting its red coat glisten in the late afternoon light.

"Yes? Which one of you is next?"

The attackers seemed hesitant and unsure.

"Give us the she-mrem, and you can pass on your way," the leader said.

"Leave now and I'll let you live," Paralan answered.

"Now!" the leader yelled. Paralan watched the burly leader raise his sword, but it was the other three who charged forward, eyes flaring.

Paralan drove his blade straight into one attacker and he fell forward, spitting blood onto Paralan's kilt. Paralan tried to draw his sword out but now the skewered soldier's weight pinned his blade to the ground.

He looked to his right. A blade was coming right for his unprotected throat.

Paralan leaped backwards, abandoning his own sword.

One charging soldier stumbled forward onto his compatriot's body. Then Paralan jumped onto him, pressing his foot down onto the back of his neck.

It was an easy matter to relieve him of his weapon.

Now there were just two, a younger mrem and the leader, who, with his puffy, bladder-shaped body, didn't seem to pose any threat. Even he seemed to realize that.

With a sick grin, he lowered his sword.

But the other soldier yelled and came charging at Paralan.

"Idiot," Paralan whispered, neatly slicing a deadly opening in his attacker's exposed chest. The soldier's blade seemed to fly out of his hand, followed by a torrent of blood.

The leader started backing away.

"You . . . you had best not go to Pleir. It is a nightmare city . . . a death town."

Paralan just stood there, watching the fat oaf back away. He took his foot off the soldier's neck, and the soldier scurried away like a sand weevil, running on all fours.

"Believe me," the leader continued to call out, nervously fingering his stumpy tail, hoping that Paralan wouldn't bother chasing him, "Pleir is not a place for such a young and beautiful she-mrem."

Then the two survivors turned and ran as best they could, off the trail and down the rocky hill.

And Feila was there, next to him.

"What did he mean, a 'death town'?" she asked.

Paralan put an arm around her.

"Just trying to scare us, Feila. He was just hoping to save his own skin. But come, we've lost some time dealing with the buffoons. I want to reach the next valley before dark. Then, we should be able to reach Pleir by midday tomorrow."

Once again, they started climbing, racing the light as the long shadow of the hill followed them up the trail.

That night, Paralan built a fire, just on the other side of the hill.

It grew cold, and even sitting near the fire didn't keep the chill away. Feila sat all tucked in tight, her heavy blanket wrapped around her.

The wind whistled eerily around them. Paralan had built the fire in a small depression, but still the wind lashed at it, sending the sparks whirling around.

"Not too close to the flames," he cautioned. He sat down beside her. "Any closer to that fire and we'll be having *you* for dinner."

She smiled, her face lost in the mesmerizing dance of

the flames. "I've never felt so cold. Is this what it's like to be a highlander, to always be shivering?"

Paralan laughed. "No, the hills and mountains have their warm season, too. But nights are cold, and most highlanders retire to the warmth of their huts. A warm fire, some savory stew. Maybe a glass of ale or two. It can be very pleasant to sleep like that, with the cold wind swirling outside your door."

"But not this way," Feila laughed. "There's nothing too cozy about this."

"I guess not," Paralan said. And, without thinking, he sat closer to her, fussing with her blanket. He pulled it even tighter around her. "There, that should seal any crannies and keep the drafts away." He let his hand rest on her shoulder. "I wish you weren't shivering. . . ."

She turned to him. "Thank you . . . for today. With anyone else, I might have spent the night being passed around like a jug of wine." She kept her eyes on him.

"They were no problem." He smiled. "I may be out of practice . . . but I'm not *that* out of practice."

She kept looking at him. And he, much to his surprise, held her gaze. His hand left her shoulder and touched her cheek. "The fire makes your fur even more golden."

His hand traced the hollows of her face.

Feila tilted her head, and gently kissed his hand. She reached up and brought his hand down to her breasts.

For a moment Paralan froze. Perhaps this should not happen. This was one of Talwe's consorts, and soon to be the adopted daughter of a friendly king. Perhaps this should not happen. . . .

But, as she pressed his hand against her body, he thought, *She is between two worlds, between two lives.* Her past life had been summarily ended. And the future was not of her own choice.

His hand cupped a breast, and felt the nipple harden under the thin material of her kilt. He lowered his face and kissed her lips, then, he felt her reach down, grasping his erection, working it with a practiced urgency.

She let the blanket slide away.

And as the twin moons slowly crested the nearby mountains, he entered Feila, surprised and excited by the strength and power of her need.

Chapter 4

▲————————————————————————▲

The Captain of the Guard, a tough old soldier whose name was known throughout the city of Ar, stood uncomfortably before his king, Talwe.

And Cwynid watched the scene that unfolded with disguised glee.

First, Talwe accused the captain of a list of offenses, some slight—such as the appearance of certain sentries' uniforms—and others involving the very safety of the city.

Each time the captain tried to defend himself, Talwe snapped at him, his voice bellowing, the pitch rising.

Yes, Cwynid concentrated, *this fellow, this captain, is such a lout, so stupid, so clearly dangerous . . .*

"But King Talwe," the captain started, once again trying to defend himself.

Cwynid pulled the strings tighter. . . .

"You will be quiet! Quiet, Captain!"

The poor mrem just stood there, confused by the whole scene, while Cwynid exercised his growing power over the befuddled King of Ar.

"Remove your sword!" Talwe ordered.

"But sire, I—"

"Your sword," Talwe hissed.

Some wine, Cwynid suggested.

"I'd like some wine," Talwe barked at a servant. Then, he directed his attention back to the captain.

"Your weapon. Now."

And Cwynid watched, fascinated with his own power, as

the captain unstrapped his heavy sword and let it clatter to the floor.

"You are banished," Talwe said, dismissing him, turning away.

The captain seemed to hesitate a moment, and then he slowly shuffled out of the great chamber.

"Some wine, Ambassador," Talwe said, extending a goblet to Wydnic.

"Why, certainly, sire." Wydnic smiled. "Certainly."

"That must be Pleir," Paralan said, trying to sound enthusiastic.

Even with all his experience outside the great cities of the South, Paralan was unprepared for the grim sight before him.

Oh, it was undoubtedly a city. It spread before them, from the bottom of the valley all the way to the foot of the Great Northern Mountains. A winding river, probably leading to the Western sea, meandered along its periphery.

But just what kind of city was this?

It resembled some barren fort or outpost, girded by an enormous wooden stockade. There were clusters of tents outside the city, gray, tattered things, while outside the stockade ragged groups wandered aimlessly about. The fence surrounding the city was dotted with soldiers, their bows clearly ready.

And inside the city, just visible from this hill, what a strange assortment of buildings! They were all jumbled on top of each other, with dozens of smoky plumes leading to the slate gray sky.

It looked, Paralan noted, about as uncivilized a place as he had ever seen.

Feila held his hand tightly. "Paralan . . . it looks . . . so . . ."

"I know." He nodded. Then turning to her, "unfriendly? But don't worry. If everything isn't to your liking inside Pleir you will not stay, no matter what Talwe has arranged."

"There's no chance . . . that you'll—"

He raised a hand. "Wait. Let us meet King Yarrou first. We can talk of other things later."

He led her quickly down the hill. And the closer they got
to the tents, the more alarmed he became. Their inhabit-
ants looked like troops of beggars, a poor and hungry army
with tattered clothing. As soon as they neared the entrance, the tent-dwellers came running up to him, begging
food or gold pieces. Some of the females brought their
young, sick little creatures half near death.

"Paralan," Feila whispered. "It's horrible."

"Yes," he said.

But the army of beggars pulled back when he and Feila
reached the gate.

With good reason.

The guards had their swords out, and they stood close
together, comparing blades and practicing feints.

It was about as uninviting an entrance as Paralan could
imagine. He stopped in front of them. And he waited until
one of the guards paused in their play.

"Eh, what do you want, stranger?"

Paralan walked up to the guard. "I escort someone from
King Talwe of Ar for your King Yarrou."

The guard looked over at Feila. Then he grinned. "Oh,
you do. Then you'd best follow me. Pleir can be a bit
confusing to the first-time visitor."

At this, the other guards laughed. But they cleared an
opening, and Paralan, still holding Feila's hand, followed
the guard.

If the city was dark and forbidding from the distance it
was, if anything, worse seen up close. The buildings,
houses, inns, and merchant's shops were a ramshackle col-
lection that leaned against each other like a crowd of
drunks. The street was dirt, filled with the droppings of
mrem and animal alike. The smell was all but unbearable.

"Look," Feila said quietly, giving his hand a squeeze.

Paralan turned to see what she was staring at.

They were mrem, tearing down the burned-out carcass
of a building. Other mrem were piling new-cut wood beside the wreck.

The mrem were chained together. Their fur bore distinctive hatch marks.

"Slaves," Paralan whispered.

A few guards were laughing, occasionally yelling at a
worker, kicking at another's naked rump.

"What is this place?" Feila asked.

And Paralan just shook his head.

The guards led them through a maze of streets and then up wooden stairs, to a pair of doors flanked by yet more guards. In Ar, such a building might be a charnel house or some bawdy inn. But here, it was the palace of King Yarrou.

The guard led them through some dark hallways, and finally into a large room with a banquet table and a rough, stone floor. It smelled of sweat and ale and—Am I imagining it? Paralan wondered—

Blood.

"King Yarrou will be with you presently," their escort said, and he disappeared through a door off to the side.

They were alone, and Feila threw herself onto him.

"Paralan, I'm scared."

He caressed Feila's cheek, and gently stroked her hand. "I told you that I would be here. I am. And from the looks of things, you'll probably be leaving with—"

The side door opened.

"Well, don't tell me that King Talwe is passing on damaged goods!"

Paralan looked up, releasing Feila.

"King Yarrou?" Paralan asked. The mrem in front of him was tall, dressed like one of his guards except for flashes of what Paralan took to be gold or silver. Paralan also noticed that he was followed into the room by guards, three on each side. It looked more like a small army than a welcoming party.

"I bring King Talwe's best wishes," Paralan said. "He asks that—"

Yarrou came closer, right next to him. "So this is to be my adopted daughter." Yarrou brought his hand close to Feila and pushed away her kilt. "Yes, she looks wonderfully"— he looked up to Paralan, and grinned—"fit."

Feila leaned against Paralan, squeezing his hand tightly. He squeezed back, reassuring her. "I have been sent as an escort and to—"

"Oh, I know. To see that she is safe and content." Yarrou turned, and walked back to his guards. "And who wouldn't be, amidst all this . . . luxury. Why, this vixen will be treated as well as all my other . . . daughters."

The king turned to a guard and mumbled something.

The guard came over to Feila, and grabbed her wrist to lead her away.

Paralan reached out and gave the guard's wrist a squeezing twist to the left. The guard fell to his knees, yelping in pain.

"I said that I was sent to escort Feila, to guarantee that she would be treated properly. I would like—"

Now Yarrou turned, his eyes fixed on Paralan. "You would what? Want to see her chambers, perhaps, or see the lovely gardens she can stroll in while the bastard kit grows in her belly?"

Yarrou caressed Feila's stomach, his hand trailing down. Feila backed away.

"Leave. You've done your assigned task. Go back and tell your king that all is well. That his troublesome wench will be well taken care of—for as long as she takes care of good King Yarrou."

Yarrou laughed, joined by his guards.

Paralan waited until it subsided.

"Then she will not stay. My king has made a mistake—"

Talwe's counselor took a step backwards, pulling Feila with him.

"I'm sorry if we have to disappoint you, but . . ." He paused, making sure that he had Feila held tight and close.

But Yarrou moved also, signaling to his guards.

They drew their swords, and from behind, Paralan heard the door open, the clatter of mrem in armor and swords being unsheathed.

"We have a saying here in Pleir, Lord Paralan. The dead laugh at no jests. Your plans are not mine, I'm afraid."

Then the Lord of Ar felt the swords at his back. He glanced to his left and saw two blades pressing into Feila's shoulder.

"Let her come to me."

Paralan paused . . . and then spoke, quietly, urgently. "Go, Feila."

She turned to him. "Paralan. Don't. I—"

The blades pinched her skin, and she moaned. He felt the blades dig into his own skin, felt the thin trickle of blood. "Slavemonger," he hissed at Yarrou.

"Tell her to come," Yarrou ordered, "or you'll both be dead, including the bastard she carries."

"Go, Feila," he said. "Go, for now."

He watched her stumble forward, he heard her crying, and he saw the heaving of her small body.

Her face, thank the All-Mother, was hidden from him.

"Good. Now that that's settled," Yarrou said, "what of you?" Yarrou put his nose right to Paralan's, and Paralan smelled this ruler, a stench as foul as the odor in the room. "We cannot, quite obviously, send you back to Ar with your tales, now can we? And if I were to kill you it might eventually bring the wrath of your King Talwe upon my fair city. That I am not prepared for. . . ."

Yarrou paused, and rubbed his chin thoughtfully.

"No. I have it. You shall stay, as a guest. Yes, I'll send word to Talwe that you are enjoying my hospitality *so* much that you've decided to stay and see that Feila is nicely settled in. Who knows, maybe I'll suggest that your interest in Feila became more than that of a protector."

The king stepped back.

"If you hurt her, I will kill you," Paralan said quietly.

"Oh," Yarrou laughed, "I have no doubt at all that that's just what you would do. But fortunately my prison cells are even more secure than the walls of my great city." The king gestured to his guards.

"I hope you enjoy your stay. . . ."

Yarrou nodded to the guards behind Paralan, and they circled him, guiding him back out of the room.

And Paralan turned, and glanced at Feila.

He saw her then, her tears running down her cheek.

But the guards pushed him outside of the room, and the heavy doors slammed shut behind him.

Paralan's first thought, on walking around the cell, was that this bleak hole would be the place he'd die.

He saw the desperate creatures he had passed, their arms outstretched, clutching at the newcomer in hope that he'd bring something that would save them.

Or perhaps simply end their miserable lives.

And the smell of the place! That was familiar enough. It was death, the foul stench of decay. The rats chattered as the guards pushed him down the dark corridor. He glanced into one cell and saw a small pile of bodies.

Storage, Paralan thought.

There was a jailkeeper, a bulbous-eyed fellow who stumbled down the corridor as if he were navigating the galley of an overloaded merchant ship in some terrible storm.

Paralan heard the guards who escorted him snickering about the old fellow.

He looked at them.

To try and get away was hopeless. Not counting the jailer, there were three guards, weapons out, ready for any excuse to cut him down.

His only hope was Talwe.

King Yarrou wouldn't risk a full-scale invasion.

And Paralan was sure that's just what Talwe would do if he didn't return soon.

But Yarrou could trick Talwe—at least for a while. Talwe would merely think that his trusted counselor was staying with Feila. He might even think that Paralan was smitten with the pregnant female.

That wasn't far removed from the truth, he admitted.

The jailer finished fumbling with the keys and opened the door to a gloomy cell.

"There you are, nice and clean," the jailer said, starting a laugh that tumbled into violent coughing.

Paralan looked inside. The floor was covered with a blackish scummy layer of—who knew what? Blood? Food? The cot was a layer of dirty straw and the waste hole in the center of the floor looked clogged with droppings and old food.

No matter, he thought.

Whatever happens here, I will live.

I will live, I will escape, and I will kill Yarrou.

And now he permitted himself just a brief, flashing image of Yarrou, skewered on his sword as he twisted it, again and again, wrapping the barbarian's entrails around his blade like strands of hair.

"In!" one of the guards barked, jabbing at him.

Paralan stepped inside, and the door was slammed shut.

"Enjoy your stay," one of the other guards laughed. And they left, once again arousing the horrible pleas and begging of the other prisoners.

Paralan sat down on the cot.

He could almost feel his fur absorbing the soot and stench of the dungeon.

He balled his hands into fists, great powerful fists. He

relaxed his hands. And again, and again, as the day gave way to night, and the night to the new morning . . .

Paralan quickly learned the way things worked in Yarrou's pit.

Food and water arrived infrequently. The jailer would rattle his keys and stumble in, throwing chunks of bread into cells, while he drunkenly made jokes. He'd scratch and pull at his tail, a twisted thing that dangled behind him. If he didn't forget, he'd ladle some milky water into a small trough built right into the cell wall.

But as bad as all this was, it was far worse to listen to the prisoners' mewling and pleading.

After one trip up the aisle, the jailer would quickly leave, ignoring any cells he missed, muttering and cursing under his breath. And he might not return for another couple of days . . . usually finding at least one less mouth to feed.

The first cycle of the moon wasn't any worse than Paralan imagined it to be. He kept track of each day. He exercised, stretching and pushing against the wall.

Then one morning he woke up to find that his fur seemed to be shedding, great tufts of it just falling off. He brushed himself and watched the fur fly off, down onto the floor.

His teeth started to hurt.

His eyes were pained by even the faint glare from the open crosswalk above the dungeon corridor.

One morning he woke up, heard the jailer, and he slid off the now even more soiled cot, and pulled himself up to the bars.

"Here," he croaked, "here," joining the chorus of pitiful voices.

And he stopped . . . and started laughing hysterically.

I've become one of them, he thought. *I'm just like them now.* He could see his own body carelessly thrown on top of a pile of bodies.

He pulled back from the cell door, shivering with the horror of his terrible image. As he shivered, the jailer walked by.

The jailer stopped.

He put down a steaming bowl. A thick loaf of bread. A jug filled with arbunda milk.

Paralan looked at the food. His stomach hurt from the sheer anticipation of looking at so much wonderful food.

The jailer moved on, tossing his small chunks of bread into the cells.

Thereafter, the jailer came every day, bringing bread regularly to all the other prisoners, and hot, nourishing meals to Paralan. And Paralan didn't, at first, question his good fortune. He began to feel restored. After who knew how many moon cycles of just lying on the filthy cot, he began pacing his cell, exercising his once-powerful body.

The terrible keening of the other prisoners also subsided.

It was not long after this remarkable turn of events that he had the dream.

It was unlike any dream he had ever had.

At first, he just saw himself once again back in Ar, strolling its busy streets, sampling the wonderful food found in its marketplaces, enjoying long talks with Talwe. . . .

Then something happened. Dark clouds filled the sky, and cold winds raced through the alleyways, blowing down stalls and sending people scurrying indoors.

He saw Talwe, walking merrily along one of the streets.

He wasn't alone. Right beside him was Wydnic.

Only Paralan could see, quite clearly now, it wasn't Wydnic at all.

It wasn't anyone called "Wydnic."

It was Cwynid.

He had his arm around Talwe, talking to him, whispering into his ear.

Paralan tried to run up to Talwe, to tell him that this was their great enemy from Cragsclaw.

But Talwe just smiled, and turned down a corner. Paralan ran, as one can run only in a dream, ever so slowly, as if the ground itself was struggling to hold his feet still.

Until he came to an alley.

And Talwe lay at Cwynid's feet, his head snapped backwards.

Cwynid turned to him.

He was wearing the crown of Ar.

And in blood, smeared on the ground, on the walls of the buildings, a single word.

Help.

He woke up.

So the Eastern Lords are to have Ar after all! Is that the meaning of this dream? Is there no one to stop it. Where is Mithmid?

Was all this planned? This trip to the north with Feila, this jail cell? All planned to isolate Talwe so that Cwynid could claim power?

But Paralan also knew that the image was a warning. There was still time, if he could get to Ar before it was too late.

Feila sat at the table, and stared at her face in the mirror.

It was a stranger's face, a face limned with pain and worry, a face marked by memories of countless debauched nights.

She picked up a small brush and placed streaks of red into her golden fur. Her eyes were already great dark circles, but she used a tapered brush dipped in a smudgy blackish paste, and made them darker.

Each detail she labored over. Because if Yarrou was not pleased, thrilled, and absolutely titillated by her appearance, he'd just as easily throw her onto the streets.

And she couldn't let that happen.

Lastly, she dabbed herself with scent, a strong, almost overpowering odor that nearly made her sick.

But Yarrou loved it, sniffing at her, biting into the soft fur at the back of her neck, chewing at her as he rammed into her, over and over and over.

Some nights he dispensed her like a gift, giving her to some friend to be played with. And some of them were even worse than Yarrou.

She stood up wearily, her muscles almost quivering in anticipation.

Careful, she told herself, nothing must reveal anything different tonight.

It must simply be another night in his bed.

She walked into his room and awaited the tall king. Feila heard his footsteps, trudging up the stairs. He drank every night, which only made her work that much harder.

She lay on the bed, arranging the kilt so that it revealed small patches of her body in the flickering candlelight.

Yarrou opened the door roughly, slamming it against the wall.

"I'll kill his clan . . . cut them down . . ." he muttered drunkenly, letting his robe slip off his shoulder. "He'll not insult me and get away with it. His clan is nothing more than a pack of thieves."

Yarrou started giggling. "And bad ones, at that."

"Don't worry," Feila said soothingly. "Come here and let me touch you."

He had taught her how to talk to him, the right words to say to excite him.

"Come, my king. Let me pleasure you."

Feila shifted slightly in the bed, and her gown slipped further to the side. She saw Yarrou eyeing her.

"Come," she whispered.

Yarrou loosened his kilt.

She saw that his erection was a halfhearted thing. It would still need much coaxing to cut through the fog of so much wine.

Yarrou came to the bed, stood there. Feila turned over, rolled to him.

He brought a hand down to her back, extending his claws. He traced a line in her back, gentle at first but then harder, digging into her fur.

She ignored the pain, as she worked on him.

Ignored the pain, as she had every night, struggling to keep Yarrou pleased . . . struggling to keep herself alive.

"Yes, my king," she whispered.

Yarrou grunted and sat down on the bed.

"Won't you lie back?" she suggested.

Yarrou stretched out on the bed.

"There," Feila said, "that's much better, isn't it?" She turned, taking off her gown. And she mounted him, as he lay there, eyes half closed, biting into her soft fur with his powerful hands.

She talked to him, told him things to keep his mind on her, on her young body. . . .

While her left hand dangled down to the side of the bed. She dug around under the mattress, feeling for something.

"Yes, my king," she hissed throatily.

Her hand searched, but found nothing.

Feila felt panic. Where could it be? She had placed it so carefully, practiced with it. What had gone wrong?

Then she stretched forward, and her fingers felt the

delicately carved handle. A fingertip touched the blade. More pain, but sweet, laced with hope.

"Yes," she said one final time.

She brought the knife up silently, and plunged it down.

On the first stroke, Yarrou opened his eyes. Then he tried to scream. But she brought the blade up, tearing a cruel line from the chest up to the soft flesh of his throat.

His scream became a strangled sputtering, spraying her with deep red droplets.

His powerful arms closed around her like a vise.

Feila moaned as he squeezed the air out of her.

She brought the knife up, dragging bits of his throat out with it.

Did a monster like this have a heart?

She plunged the knife into his chest.

Yarrou's eyes went wild with the agony.

His arms fell to his side.

And, when Feila was sure that he was dead, she pulled herself off him. And she sat there, staring at the body, watching it redden the sheets and the mattress, until there was a pool of red surrounding her on the floor.

Chapter 5

The good food kept coming, every night. The prisoners even took to talking among themselves.

Most were simple peasants. Some had protested about their wives or daughters being forced into Yarrou's bed. Others had been caught pilfering a bit of food, or committing some other petty crime.

All of them expected to finish their days, however long they might be, in Yarrou's dungeon.

Then one night the food didn't come. And a deathly silence fell over the dungeon. Their good luck had ended, they moaned. Paralan heard a few fall to their knees, praying to the All-Mother.

Even Paralan grew worried. It had been frightening to watch his body fall apart, his sleek fur turning dull and haggard. If that were to happen again he knew he'd go mad.

On the night of the second day without food, he heard the door open. Everyone in the dungeon stirred. Paralan grabbed the bars.

But it wasn't the jailer. It was someone with a much lighter step, walking straight down the corridor to Paralan's cell.

Until Paralan could see who it was . . .

"Feila," he said quietly.

She was dressed in a gossamer-thin kilt, laced with tiny strands of gold and silver. Her fur was combed high and tinted a bright crimson. Her eyes were dark and old.

She was not the same mrem he had escorted to the castle so long ago.

He licked his lips, remembering for a moment just what he must look like. He scratched at the fur on top of his head. "I—"

"You're alive, Paralan. I had told the jailer to bring the food . . . but I thought he might be taking the gold pieces and lying to me. But you're alive." She looked back to the dungeon entrance. "Here," she said, digging keys out of a pouch in her kilt. "We must go fast."

Then his cell door was open. For a moment it seemed too strange to cross the threshold. But he stepped out, free but still feeling like a prisoner.

"Me!" "Let me out" "No, here . . ." The other prisoners began begging to be freed.

Feila looked at him.

Paralan nodded. He took the keys from her and tossed them into the nearest occupied cell. "Pass them along when you're out!" he yelled at the occupant.

"Come," Feila ordered. "Quickly."

"Yes," he said, staring at her even as she took his hand. She was so different, as if years had gone by. She pulled him up the stairs, leaving the clamor and smell of the cells behind.

"I may be in time to help Talwe," Paralan said. "There was a sending—Ar is—"

They were at the top of the stairs. And Feila froze, and turned on him. "You won't be going to Ar," she said quietly.

"Why, yes I will. Cwynid has returned; he has cast a spell over Talwe. Already he must control much of the city. I—"

Feila shook her head. "I did not free you to go to Ar. Soon the guards will discover Yarrou's body—"

"His body—"

"On top of his bed, hacked into pieces. The guards are used to his sleeping. But soon they won't be put off. And then, they will not stop until they find me."

"But we can—"

"No, they will find me, and kill me. They will do the same to you if you are with me." She opened the door, leading to a dark, drafty hallway. "But they won't find my kit . . . because he'll be with you."

Paralan looked down.

The kit was inside a satchel, resting in a small basket. The kit's head stuck out and its twin eyes glowed like tiny candles. Paralan stepped close to the satchel and peeled away a bit of material near the kit's throat. It licked Paralan's hand.

"He has his father's markings," he said quietly.

Feila crouched down next to Paralan. "And his father's temperament, too. It's all I can do to keep him in one place."

"I will take him to Ar," Paralan said, standing up. "Surely when Talwe sees—"

"No. In Ar he would be killed. Talwe must never know where his son is." She came close to Paralan. They both heard the sound of the prisoners, screaming and squealing with joy. "Take my kit to a small village. Find someone who will care for him. But don't tell them who he is."

Paralan turned away. "But I should be in Ar. I should—"

"Talwe asked you to see me to safety, to see his kit to safety. If you don't take him away from here, he will be killed."

There was a clatter from somewhere in the castle.

"I know a passage out of the city. And there's food inside the satchel, enough for four or five days of travel."

She reached up to Paralan and he felt her cool hands on his cheek. "You will do this?"

The kit made a small sound, as if eager to be away.

Paralan leaned forward and kissed Feila.

The door to the dungeon burst open, and the prisoners streamed out.

"Come with me, then," Paralan said. "I can just as easily bring you—"

"No. Whatever trail you leave would be followed—if they thought I was with you. No, I will try to get away by going south. But I will not endanger my kit."

She picked up the noisy little mrem, holding it up to Paralan. The satchel fit like a pack on Paralan's shoulders.

Prisoners, wild-eyed, grinning crazily, rushed past them, desperate to be free.

"There," she said, sure that the satchel was well fastened to his back. "Come, I will show you the way out. There can't be much time before there are soldiers everywhere in the castle."

And she led him through a twisted trail of corridors and

doorways, then out onto the streets of Pleir, past abandoned buildings and dark side streets, until they came to a small building near the northern wall of the city.

"There's a tunnel. It leads to a rocky outcrop just past the wall. Keep heading north and you'll come to an old trail used by herd tenders. Now go!"

He looked her one more time. She wouldn't look at the kit.

He kissed her, tasting her silent tears on his lips.

"Go!" she ordered.

And Paralan turned and fled the nightmare city of Pleir.

While every step he took brought him further and further away from Ar.

He didn't even stop at the first village.

The females were cowed as they scurried about, carrying heavy jugs of water to the small wooden huts. The males wore kilts fashioned of the rough pelts of Rar, and one of the mrem was wearing what had to be the tanned skin of a liskash.

They eyed Paralan as if eager to relieve him of any of his possessions. But Paralan had gained back much of his lost strength. He walked with strong, purposeful steps. And the mrem let him pass unmolested.

Still moving north, right to the foothills of the Great Northern Mountains, he came to another village. But the villagers wore their poverty like a sad badge, and a few of the older kits came up to beg from the stranger.

Still, Paralan pushed on, pausing to give the kit some arbunda milk from a gourd or a slice of dried and salted meat.

The sloppy noise of the kit's mouth, merrily chewing away in Paralan's ears, made him smile. The kit seemed so carefree and happy, untouched by the danger that surrounded him.

And then he came to another village. It was filled with neatly kept huts, rows of them, all with their small chimneys puffing out lines of grayish-white smoke. And beyond the village, filling the nearby hills, was a great herd of arbunda.

A herd that would be any village's treasure.

It was a prosperous village, wealthy.

Paralan unstrapped the satchel and swung the kit around.

A few of the mrem came up to him cautiously. An old mrem, with long reddish fur, spoke.

"Greetings, traveler. You look as if you and your . . . companion have come a long way."

Paralan smiled. "Yes, I have come a long way. And I've further to go." The village she-mrem came near, peering at the kit, then touching the twin points of its ears, smoothing the soft fur. "But I hope that this kit may have come to the end of its journey. . . ."

One of the she-mrem pulled Feila's kit out of the satchel, holding it up naked, in the cold clear light of the mountain morning. She held it up, and then brought it close, as it rooted around, smelling the milk of her teats.

And Paralan knew that at least the kit had found a home. A place to grow.

Perhaps one day to tend the great herd browsing on the mountain meadow.

And, Paralan thought, who knew what else?

Cwynid looked in Talwe's bedroom.

There is the king! he thought.

Curled up on his massive bed, wrapped in a sweaty tangle of silken sheets and young bodies.

It would be so easy to walk over and cut the mrem's throat. So easy . . .

And so unnecessary. The city and throne of Ar were ready to fall into his hands. Already he controlled the palace army and a spy network that extended to cities to the North and South. Talwe's trusted advisors were all gone, Paralan to the North, and Mithmid ordered to stay with Sruss at Cragsclaw.

I am almost king, in all but name. All trade requires my consent, my approval. Foreign dignitaries seek conferences with me, ignoring Talwe. Every day more control and more power are in my hands.

Cwynid shut Talwe's door quietly. He walked slowly to the reception hall. Already there were twenty or thirty petitioners lined up for an audience, each with their special plea, their special request.

Cwynid was growing tired of the charade.

Soon he'd move to have Talwe enforce by law what already existed in fact. *I will be named counselor!*

And then, Cwynid thought, a small smile playing across his lips, *it will be my son's chance.* The Eastern Lords had told Cwynid that they approved his decision. His own son could be king.

It would be years before they'd be ready to invade the Western kingdoms. When the time came, his son would be there.

He grabbed the heavy silver doorknobs leading to the reception hall.

At the click of the opening door, dozens of faces, eager and attentive, looked at him. Awaiting his attention . . . his decisions . . .

So *easy* . . . why should cities be fought over . . . when they could be seduced so easily?

It was a cave.

Filled with strange smells and small chittering sounds that echoed from the darkness within.

For all Feila knew, it might be hiding some Rar ready to rip her to pieces for lunch. But she had to stop, had to rest.

She sat down on the damp cave floor, staring at the brilliant glow of the cave's mouth.

Feila couldn't believe that she had gotten this far. She had expected that Yarrou's troops would make quick work of finding and killing her. They were hunters, murderers, trackers. . . .

By all rights she should be dead.

Then she worried that they had taken off after Paralan, after Paralan and her nameless kit.

She could see him now, his bright eyes, the brilliant color of his fur. The only thing she cared about was his safety.

Yet, with each day she started to grow hopeful. Maybe she'd live, she dared hope. Maybe she could wander to the South, lose herself in some great city, and wait . . . and wait . . .

Until it was safe to find Paralan, dear Paralan, and ask him—

Where is my kit?

She sat there, her breath slowly returning to normal. She

sat, unaware that she was crying. The tears dropped onto the dirt. The light became all blurry.

And then it darkened.

Somebody was there.

Voices!

They paused at the entrance, and she found herself struggling to breathe quietly.

It grew darker.

Her fingers dug into the hard dirt floor, grabbing at it. She heard the blades being pulled from their sheaths.

"Whore!" one of Yarrou's soldiers yelled, swinging his blade.

Feila closed her eyes. And thought of Paralan . . .

Paralan had entered Ar in the middle of the night. The first surprise was the difficulty he had in passing through the gates.

But he made up some story of a sick, dying sister, and the weary guards waved him in.

He kept his cape pulled tight, not wanting anyone to recognize him.

The city looked different. Soldiers marched through the streets with an angry clatter. On a warm night such as this, the streets of Ar should be filled with mrem walking around, enjoying the steamy heat, with a bottle of sweet wine in one hand and a grain-cake in the other.

But there was an almost funereal pall over the city.

He passed the courtyard, usually home to assorted dancing troupes. It was deserted except for a lone guard standing at the far end.

Paralan hurried to pass him.

"Halt!" the guard yelled.

Paralan stopped and turned, and light from the twin crescents of the moons outlined his face.

"Where are you going?" the guard demanded.

Paralan tried to keep his face down.

"My sister, she is very sick. I am visiting her for perhaps the last time."

The guard nodded.

"You should be off the streets. Curfew. Wydnic's order."

Paralan nodded. *Wydnic's order!*

"Yes," he said quietly. "I will be there very soon."

The guard grunted, and signaled to Paralan to move on.

Now he knew that it would be foolish to go directly to the palace. More than likely he'd be cut down before he got within sight of Talwe. No, he'd need help.

And he knew where to look for some.

He hurried across the courtyard, and then hurried up one of the nameless twisting alleyways that crisscrossed Ar. Perhaps, he wondered, it would be closed—or, even worse, gone!

But he saw the light, a warm yellow glow that spilled out onto the dank alley. The Inn of the Black Moon was open. Even a curfew couldn't keep it closed!

Paralan guessed that too many of Talwe's friends had asked for it to be spared.

If he was to find any allies, it would be in here.

He pushed open the heavy wood doors, and the raucous sound and smoke spilled out. Paralan pulled his cape tighter and entered.

Glancing left and right, he checked that no one was taking undue notice of his entrance. Then he walked up to the bar, squeezing beside two striped mrem, both with the distinctive markings of the clansmrem from the Southern islands. He ordered a dark ale, and retreated quietly to a corner bench.

Now, crouching down, he could search the inn for someone who might help him. At first all he saw was the usual bunch of drunken and rowdy citizens. It was too late to expect anyone from the palace to be here. No Jremm, no Arklier—where were they, all the nobles and friends?

Then, against the far wall, he saw Ondra.

Paralan took a sip of the ale and watched Ondra.

He had obviously had more than enough to drink. He was saying good-bye, clapping his compatriots on the back, turning this way and that.

Ondra! Young, impetuous, but there was no one more brave or loyal to Talwe.

He was leaving. Paralan watched him maneuver between the islands of tables, tipping this way and that, laughing good-naturedly . . . a ship without a rudder. Finally, he reached the door and walked out.

Paralan stood up quickly, and followed him. For the moment, he didn't worry whether anyone saw him rushing to leave the inn.

Paralan went out the door and panicked. Where was Ondra? A left or a right turn branched out into countless other alleyways, each capable of swallowing up a lone drunk in seconds.

Paralan froze. He heard something.

The sound of someone relieving himself, and then a voice singing, too loudly . . .

"There was a dancer with claws shaped like knives . . . and when she caressed you, it was like having three wives. . . ."

Ondra! Paralan ran in the direction of the sound and found Ondra careening down the alleyway, bumping into one wall, and then the next, refusing to allow it to interrupt his song.

"There was a vixen named Tam and—"

"Ondra . . ." Paralan said quietly.

Ondra stopped, shook his head as though he were hearing things, and then started in again. "And when she took her kilt off she—"

"Ondra!" Paralan said, louder this time. He walked behind the drunken mrem and touched his shoulder.

"Huh," Ondra said, turning. "What?"

Paralan knew that his face was in the shadows. "Ondra . . . it's me . . . Paralan."

"Excuse me, guard. I know about the curfew. I've just been trying to—"

Paralan grabbed Ondra roughly by the shoulders and shook him. "Ondra, it's me. It's Paralan. Listen to me!"

Ondra blinked, shook his head. "Para . . . Paralan . . ." he said quietly. "I didn't . . . I—"

Ondra collapsed against him, mumbling, "Paralan. I thought, we all thought that you were gone." He looked up, becoming more sober with every word he spoke. "Oh, Paralan, so much has happened here, so much evil—"

"That's why I'm here, Ondra. And we're going to fix it, you and I. But first, let's get you home and see if we can walk some of that ale and wine out of you. And then, you can tell me what happened. . . ."

Ondra poured Paralan and himself another cup of the now-tepid green tea. Paralan had forced the young mrem to duck his head into a pail of water, which he did only when Paralan pushed him down with his hand. That, and the cups of tea, made Ondra as clear-eyed as one might hope after a night at the Inn of the Black Moon.

"First he sent Sruss away," Ondra said between sips, "to supervise the completion of the reconstruction of Cragsclaw. He just seemed to sort of lose touch, get lost in himself. Next, Wydnic became his only advisor, his only confidant. Then, Talwe stopped showing up at official functions. Wydnic was acting as his counselor—with full power to act in Talwe's name."

Paralan shook his head. "But why did Talwe do that? Didn't any of you try talking to him?"

"Of course, but it did no good. No one was as close to him as you were. When he sent you away with Feila, a feeling of hopelessness fell on all of us."

Paralan stood up and walked to the small window near the door of Ondra's room. Already the sky was losing its inky black color. He turned back to Ondra.

"So you've done nothing?"

"No. We supported Sruss, stood by her when she tried to return. But Wydnic was always there, whispering in Talwe's ear, a squad of his best soldiers behind him. Talwe dismissed Sruss without blinking an eye. And Wydnic warned us. We could stay—but only if we vowed to follow any edict, whether from Talwe or his new 'counselor.'"

"And everyone took the oath?"

"No," Ondra said sadly. "Arklier left with Sruss. Reswen disappeared." He looked up at Paralan and smiled. "Me, I've staked out my claim to a corner table at the Inn of the Black Moon. I've been allowed to melt into the floorboards there."

Paralan brought his fist down on the table.

"I can't believe it. We fought for this city, mrem died for it, and this wizard has been able to come and steal it away—"

"Wizard? What do you mean, wizard?"

Paralan spit out the words. "This ambassador, this Wydnic, is a lackey of the Eastern Lords. He is Cwynid. And you let him take the city."

Ondra stood up, his face wide with horror. "But how do you know this—"

Paralan held up his hand, and Ondra slumped back in his

chair. He knew the truth of it, Paralan realized, the moment he had heard the words.

"But what could we do?" Ondra moaned. "There was nothing—"

Paralan grabbed Ondra and pulled him to his feet. "I'll tell you what we're *going* to do, my friend. We're going to rid this city of that lackey of the Eastern Lords. You and I."

Paralan walked over to the door. He opened it and a sweet morning breeze filled the room. "And," he said quietly, "we're going to do it today. . . ."

Chapter 6

▲──▲

                   Paralan let Ondra lead him to the palace.

"It's almost impossible to get to Talwe anymore. The last time I tried to see him I ended up herded with the rest of the good citizens, you know, the ones asking for favors and extensions on their taxes."

"Tell me about the guards Wydnic has with him. How many are there?"

"Usually about eight mrem, heavily armored, real tough customers."

"Veterans of Cragsclaw?"

Ondra shrugged. "I don't know. They could be a special squad from some kingdom already friendly to the Eastern Lords. But the regular soldiers don't waste time in following this Wydnic's orders—"

"Cwynid, Ondra, it's Cwynid."

"Cwynid, then. He pretty much runs the city."

Ondra led Paralan to a large gate at the rear of the palace. Carts were being unloaded, and mrem were carrying in crates of patter fowl, all clucking noisily, and cartons of the small greenish eggs.

"Here?" Paralan asked.

Ondra nodded. "The guard is one of the veterans of Cragsclaw. He lets me enter or leave whenever I wish. Just keep your face covered. He might get nervous if he sees you."

Paralan followed Ondra through the stream of foodstuffs. He stood behind the young soldier as he bantered a moment with the guard.

"Eh," the guard said, pointing at Paralan. "And who is this?"

"A friend," Ondra said. "Told him I'd give him a grand tour. He's only seen the reception hall."

Paralan saw the guard rub his chin. "I don't know."

Ondra clapped him on the shoulder. "Don't worry, old friend. We'll be in—and out—before this crew here is done with their delivery."

The guard stared at Paralan. "All right then, but be quick about it. You know Wydnic's rule."

"Sure . . . we'll be right back. . . ."

And Ondra moved quickly inside. Paralan followed.

There was no turning back now, he thought. The fate of Ar—perhaps the fate of the Western kingdoms—depended on the next few moments.

"We'll take this staircase," Ondra said, his voice sounding tired and nervous. "It's not as direct but there's less chance that we'll be seen."

Paralan gripped the handrail, the smooth metal cool to the touch. And he felt something then, as if he'd been here before, at this same place, walking up these very stairs, ready to kill someone.

Or was it something to come, some image from the future?

"Quickly!" Ondra hissed. "Get a move on, Paralan!"

Paralan hurried to catch up, letting the feeling fade.

Until the staircase emptied out into a large hall.

"There," Ondra said, pointing. "Talwe will be—"

But Paralan put up his hand. "I know. He's in his room. With Cwynid. With the soldiers. I know."

Now Paralan took the lead, walking quickly, then running up to the door. Two guards let their lances crisscross as they blocked the entrance.

"Stop!" they ordered.

Paralan nodded. Then he flung back his cape, letting it fall to the floor. And his blade was out. He swung up, catching the first guard in the throat, and then swung around to plunge his sword into the second guard. He kicked the bodies away, still quivering with the last spasms of life.

"Now," he said to Ondra.

He reached out, grabbed the door handle. He turned it gently, and then kicked it in. He entered the room.

Talwe was on his bed, lying between two females. A tray was in front of him, laden with crystals and powders. Talwe had a single claw embedded in one of the powders, bringing it up to his lips.

The king turned . . . and saw his friend.

"Paralan," he said, in a voice devoid of its strength and power.

"Kill him," Cwynid said to his personal guards, pointing to Paralan.

Talwe rose up with a start. "No. Stop."

Cwynid raised a hand and the guards paused.

Talwe struggled off the bed.

And, as Paralan watched, he wondered, *What has happened to you, oh my king? What has befuddled your mind, clouded your vision?*

Paralan turned to Cwynid. "This man is no ambassador, Talwe. He is—"

Cwynid laughed. "Please, my king, let me cut this traitor down. They obviously planned to assassinate you," Cwynid said.

"No, Wydnic. Paralan was once my most trusted—"

"Was?" Paralan said. "I leave, and you give away your kingdom to this beast-mage from the Eastern Lords. Have you seen your city, Talwe? Have you seen the fear—the soldiers marching?"

Paralan saw Ondra circling to the right, just behind Cwynid.

"And what of Sruss, and Arklier, and—"

Talwe's eyes seemed to cloud over, as if he were remembering something, images from the past. . . .

"Enough!" Cwynid said. Then, to his guards: "Remove him. He is disturbing the king."

The guards took a step.

Paralan raised his sword to Cwynid.

"Go ahead," he yelled. "Send your guards at me. Or better yet, use your powerful magic. Show Talwe just how he has come to this."

Cwynid smiled. If he did anything magical, Paralan knew, he'd risk Talwe's seeing it. The mage turned away.

"We can deal with you later," Cwynid said, sensing the trap, "when—"

Paralan nodded to Ondra. Ondra pulled out his sword and flung it towards Cwynid. The mage turned and caught it.

"This is how it will be settled," Paralan said, taking a step forward.

"Paralan!" Talwe yelled.

But Paralan had already taken the first step in the ritual of the Dance of Death. Even Talwe would not interfere.

Cwynid stood there.

He'll have to do it, Paralan thought. *Come on, take the first step.*

Cwynid seemed frozen, staring right at him. Then he moved, ever so slightly.

He made a signal to his left, and one of the guards drew his sword.

But then Ondra was there. Ondra took a swing at the guard, but the guard parried the blow, and then sent his blade into Ondra's gullet. Ondra collapsed to the stone floor.

Paralan took a step.

He raised his sword.

Cwynid raised his free hand, and then the sword.

Stay undecided, bastard.

By the All-Mother, stay undecided just long enough.

Paralan broke the dance.

With complete and unforgiveable suddenness, he plunged the sword into Cwynid's chest.

Talwe stood up. "Paralan!"

Paralan let his sword fall to the ground. It clattered on the stone floor, and sent a spray of blood into the air.

The guards grabbed him, pushing their swords roughly against his throat.

"He was Cwynid, Talwe. He was taking your city, taking everything we fought for—"

The guards looked at Talwe, waiting for a signal from Talwe to cut Paralan down.

But Talwe just shook his head. "Cwynid is dead, Paralan. That battle is over." Talwe gestured at Cwynid. "This was an ambassador, Paralan. And you have killed him." Talwe came right up to Paralan's face. "His king will ask for your death."

Talwe turned away, and walked over to the great windows that overlooked the palace gardens.

"You cannot stay here, even be imprisoned here."

Talwe turned sharply.

Already his eyes were clearer, Paralan saw.

But Talwe can't see that, Paralan thought. It's as if I'm telling him some mad tale. Of spells, of a transformed wizard.

"You are," Talwe said slowly, "banished. Your name will be struck from all records of Ar, from all records of my kingship, from even the records of Cragsclaw. From this day forward, you will no longer exist. You will live where no mrem live, near the desert, away from your own kind. Should you not obey me, you, and any who live with you, will be cut down."

Talwe gestured at the guards.

They began dragging Paralan back out of the palace.

Banished!

But even as they dragged him away, Paralan knew . . . he felt . . . that one day he'd return.

Yes.

For this, my king, is the place where I will die.

BOOK
TWO

CAT'S SHADOW

▲————————————————————————▲

1

Alone!

Was there anything worse?

Well, thought Falon, there was the cold. The way the wind came tearing off the mountain, it cut right through his reddish-brown fur.

Small gray clouds had gathered at the top of the mountain, making the dark rock look almost black.

He pulled his lined cape closer, until it was close against the thin fur at his throat. The herd-beasts, just below him, milling about in a flat, open piece of ground, didn't seem any happier. The lead uxan shifted back and forth, as though to stir too much would only make it colder.

Falon knew the feeling. If he moved, his cape let in tiny pockets of air. But to stay still was to feel as frozen as one of the grayish-green clumps of rock that dotted the mountainside.

How long had he been an outcast? He pulled thoughtfully at his whiskers. Once, it was important to him to keep track of the days as they crawled along. But time brought an inexorable message. *It doesn't matter, Falon. Not when you're fated to spend your days apart from the clan.* Except for the five or six times he brought the herd down to the village, he lived apart from his clan.

His clan lived far from the warm cities to the south, in a sprawling village hidden in the northern hills and mountains. They were highlanders, a proud race.

None, he thought glumly, more so than he.

He stepped behind a narrow parra tree, a scrubby, wind-beaten thing that offered the only shelter on the slope. He brought his hands out from under his cape, up to his mottled face.

I was an outcast long before I arrived here, he thought with a smile. No other mrem of his clan had the distinctive splotchy markings. The other highlanders seemed joined together by their mottled calico fur. His markings were like twisted hemp, swirls of red and brown. When he was just a kit, he was teased about it. Often he would reward his young tormentors with a good swipe to the ears. But as he matured other, more interesting problems developed.

The females were quite taken with his appearance. Despite the angry glances of his young fellow mrem, he encouraged the females . . . some of whom needed no encouragement. Of course, that led to his current situation.

It turned out that one tawny female had been claimed by one of the young leaders of the clan, a large, jowly fellow who, despite his nasty face, presented no real threat.

But there are other things that count in a duel besides speed and accuracy. Falon knew it was important to avoid the first blow, to let their cautious circling of each other go on until sundown if it had to. And, if he had just a touch of the scorned beast-magic, he might have been able to tell that his older opponent would try to trick him into making the first blow.

Which is exactly what he did.

It looked like the chunky mrem was going to pounce right on top of him. Falon, startled and stunned by the maneuver, brought his short, curved sword up.

His opponent's lips curled back in a triumphal sneer. He stopped short and pulled back, letting—actually letting—the blade cut into his rich underbelly just so . . . just enough to give Falon the disgrace of having made the first blow.

His departure was swift. It didn't help that the clan was in need of someone to tend the herd on the upper slopes of Mount Zaynir. And all of a sudden, the clansmrem had him banished from the community of his clan.

They had been just in doing so. It was the law.

Yet, on cold nights, staring at the stars, he held his anger close to him and nourished it . . . his lone companion.

Would he ever be allowed to reenter?

That was for the clan elders to decide.

But it wouldn't be soon. His whole body shook as the wind just seemed to pick up strength. It wouldn't be today. Gone forever were the oh-so-warm and inviting attentions of the many clan females. Just above him, among some large outcrops of grayish stone, there was a small cave that supplied the only warmth he'd be feeling for a long time.

He looked out at the herd-beasts. Some munched unenthusiastically on the tough clumps of grass that dotted the slope. Others just pressed together, rubbing their scratchy hides to share what warmth they could.

The lead buck stirred.

Falon had become attuned to this great beast. The herd-beast looked dull and slow-moving. But the uxan's eyes never rested. The herd-beast warned him of each change of the weather, and once it alerted him to a pair of poachers who attempted to make off with a young calf. The two thieves would both carry scars with them to their graves.

The buck moved away from the herd, lifted its great head, and gave out a loud snort.

Falon crouched down and, without thinking, his hand closed around his sword. The fit was sleek and comfortable, custom-designed for him before his days as an outcast.

He had a small bow and arrows, but they were at the cave. And the buck's bellowing signaled something approaching rapidly.

The herd-mrem scanned the hillside, searching for some sign of movement or color amidst the dull shading of the cold season. The intruder was easy to spot.

"No need for your magic, old fellow. Our visitor doesn't seem to be overly concerned about who knows he's coming."

Still, the big uxan bellowed, then stamped its three-pronged hooves, a command to the herd to move further up the slope. Crouching, Falon studied their guest as he trudged up the slope.

This was no clansmrem, that was for sure. The very threads of his many capes caught the dull light and positively sparkled. Falon didn't know if he'd ever seen such rich, sumptuous cloth. But that wasn't what made him blink his golden eyes in confusion.

The lavishly dressed mrem trudged closer and closer . . . and Falon saw the fur. The rich swirl of color around the maw, the streaks that trailed down from his shoulder, under the capes.

It looked just like him! After years of being a curiosity among the highlander clans, here was someone—someone wealthy—whose fur looked like Falon's.

The outcast stood up, keeping the sword discreetly at his side. He stepped out from behind the tree. The uxan's bellowing grew even louder.

"Quiet, Old One! Enough noise for the morning," he yelled.

The visitor smiled.

"An effective alarm," the richly dressed mrem called up the slope.

The buck's bellow changed into a low, disturbed moan. Falon took a few steps out towards the visitor.

"I watch out for them . . . and they watch out for me."

"I see, young Falon." He looked down at Falon's sword. "And I'm sure you do a fine job at it."

The intruder wore his own weapon, a large, heavy sword with a hilt that Falon knew must be the purest silver.

The lead herd-beast slowly quieted.

"And I'm glad to see that you are exactly where your clansmrem said you'd be."

Falon took another step towards the stranger. He was unable to keep from looking at the yellow-and-brown fur, the mrem's bright yellow eyes that seemed to not miss a thing. A strange sadness came over Falon.

He was so used to being alone . . . it almost hurt to be with one of his own kind.

"Then they surely told you that I am an outcast, my friend. I have lost my honor—if, indeed, I ever had it."

The stranger laughed, a full, hearty sound that filled the hills. The herd-beasts stirred. "And that, dear Falon, is why I am here in the first place, . . ."

They sat in Falon's small cave, huddled before a small fire that left smudgy blotches on the too-low ceiling.

"Sorry I can't offer you something a bit more comfortable." Falon gestured at the bare walls and dirt floor.

"No matter. It's warm and the herbs you have cooking smell very good indeed." The stranger looked up at him. "I've been on the road many days now."

The young mrem just couldn't stop looking at the stranger. His people usually disdained the rich city-dwellers. Nor were highlanders above raiding the occasional caravan that made its way through their steep hills.

But this stranger was the first city-dweller Falon had ever met, without trying to rob his uxan cart.

"Why would you travel so far to see me?"

Another smile, and Falon saw that his guest was enjoying all this curiosity.

The stranger undid the clasp of one of his capes, and let the plush material slide to the floor. "My name is Plano, once chief counselor to the House of Rhow, of the city of Tizare. I served the old lord for . . . well, too long, to be sure. After a successor was properly settled, I took my leave."

"You traveled from Tizare to see me?"

Again, Plano laughed. "No, my friend. The herbs are ready, I believe?"

"Sorry," Falon said, scurrying to remove the bubbling herbal concoction from the fire. "I'm just a bit confused . . . it's been a long time since—"

Plano held up one hand. "I understand. You have not spoken with anyone . . . for a long time."

"A few times a year I can enter the village. But no one speaks. No one dares look." He made a small grin. "I have lost my—"

Plano's golden eyes widened, the slit of the pupil flaring in the firelight. "You lost *nothing!* Do you understand? Nothing."

"But how can you say that? I struck first in the duel."

"I know that story, Falon. You were merely tricked by someone older and wiser. You were different . . . a challenge. The highlanders are sometimes foolish mrem, Falon."

Falon poured the tea. Tiny swirls of steam rose from each cup. He handed a cup to Plano. "How do you know so much?"

"It was my job to know. And even though I'm retired to

my country estate, I have not forgotten how one goes about collecting information."

Falon took a deep, warming sip of his tea while he studied Plano. "So you learned who I was, and you sought me out. Now that you are here, maybe you will tell me why you went to such great efforts."

Plano groomed the top of his head, as if ready to deliver some official pronouncement. "I have need of a messenger to go to Lord Rhow, in the great city of Tizare."

"Why not use the official messengers?"

"I'm afraid my lord and I don't place the same degree of trust in the messengers that you do. My message requires the highest discretion. It can not, *must* not fall into anyone's hand but Lord Rhow's."

"And so you come to me—an outcast—to help." Falon put his cup down. Already the tea was turning cold and tasteless. "I don't understand."

Plano gathered up his discarded cape and tossed it towards Falon. "Here, put this on. It will keep you warmer. As you see, I have plenty." Plano watched while Falon picked up the heavy material. It was a skin of some kind, but tanned to an almost incredible softness. "You are alone, Falon. Unloved and unwanted. The options for your loyalty must surely be open."

Falon pulled his new outergarment close. "Perhaps you're right," he said cautiously. "Still, Tizare is a long, difficult journey to the south—"

"More difficult than you imagine since you must, for security's sake, avoid the roads and travel near the abandoned city of Fahl."

"You're not exactly selling me on the proposal."

"I think," Plano said smiling, "that you'll do it." He opened a small flask and poured an amber liquid into the teacup. He tilted it towards Falon, offering him some.

But Falon shook his head. He had long ago decided that he'd surely go mad if he started taking solace in spirits. If he started that, then someday the clansmrem would come up the hill and find him half frozen, an empty bottle in his hand, and the herd-beasts vanished.

"You'll do it, perhaps, for the gold." He flung a small satchel to him. "With much more awaiting you when you reach Lord Rhow. Or you'll do it to escape this mountain." He leaned forward, close enough to the fire that Falon thought he smelled the stench of singed fur. "After all, how many cold seasons do you think you can last?"

Plano downed his cup, and then curled up close to the fire, apparently ready to sleep.

"Or," he said, his eyes shutting, "you'll do it for the honor, my friend. Your honor . . ."

Falon had trouble sleeping.

While his guest snored away, curled close to the fire, all he could do was stare at the dwindling flames and wonder about the older mrem's proposal.

Falon knew he could, of course, ignore it. He was a highlander, and the strange customs and perverse ways of the lowland cities were not for him. The ways of his people were more ancient than the latest rules promulgated by the King of Tizare.

He belonged here . . . on Mount Zaynir.

But his fingers kept going to the fine cloth that he now had draped over his shoulders. There was no denying the rich, luxuriant feel of the cloth, or the way its muted shades of gold and red complemented his own coloring.

And there was this Plano, this 'counselor' to Lord Rhow. The fact that this mrem looked like him affected Falon in deep, confusing ways. He had lived for so many years as one apart, accepting the virtues and difficulties of his differences. But now, to see another—well, it made him question so many things.

I am a highlander—or am I?

I belong to the mountains—or do I?

He kicked at the fire, encouraging it to spit into flame for a few minutes more.

He curled as close to the flame as possible, enjoying the heat on his face as it warmed the fine layer of fur and whiskers.

Chapter 2

▲————————————————————————————▲

"Come, come, your beasts are bellowing for you. The morning is already well advanced. And my bones do ache so."

Falon blinked awake. His head was almost resting in the black soot of the now-dead fire. The stale smell of the burned wood filled his nostrils.

"You're lucky you didn't singe your whiskers, young friend. Your coloring is distinctive enough without adding a few burned spots."

Plano laughed, and then coughed, clearing his throat. He spit off to the side.

Falon stood up. It was a cold morning and he was glad that he had the extra cape. "I didn't sleep well last night—"

"Last night? I'm surprised you can sleep here any night." Plano came close to him and gave his shoulders a great squeeze. "I haven't felt this horribly uncomfortable since I went with the old Lord Rhow on an excursion to the Eastern City of Kayne. Sandstorms all day, losing mrem and bunndor to the weevils. But at night, ah, there's nothing like sleeping on a freezing desert, the sand ripping right through your tent. Some of our troops went mad . . . just couldn't handle all the cold and racket. Still," he said grinning at Falon, "last night was none too pleasant."

"If you're hungry there's some fruit . . . off in the corner there." Falon indicated the spot where the old mrem had just expectorated.

"Oh," Plano said coyly. "Breakfast, eh? So sorry. . . ."

Falon walked over and dug out a bunch of orange gradle berries. "Not quite ripe," he said, offering the bunch to Plano. "But they should hold you until you get back to your estate."

He watched Plano take them eagerly, pulling off a dozen or more before returning them to him. "A tad bitter. By the All-Mother, I can't tell you how great this 'roughing it' is for me." He grinned, then clapped a hand on Falon's back. "Feels absolutely wonderful."

Falon munched on the berries, which, along with herd milk and the occasional unwary rodent, made up a good part of his diet.

"So you slept poorly, you say?"

He nodded.

"Been thinking about my proposition?"

"Yes."

"And you've decided . . ."

"I don't think I can do it. This is my home. Those beasts down there are my responsibility. My lot in life," Falon said with a smile, "may not be so wonderful. But things may not always be this way."

Plano shook his head. His eyes flashed and his ears seemed pointed right at Falon. "Don't be so foolish. What will you do? Languish the rest of your days on this horrible hill, listening to those dumb beasts conjuring their foul magic? I'm offering you a life, Falon. Danger, perhaps, but also a chance to see more wonders than you ever dreamed of."

"But what of my beasts?"

"I have already arranged everything. There's a peasant orphan who will live here and tend to their needs—be they as they may—until you return. If you don't return, the simple fool will be more than glad to warm his hide by the small fire of your cave in return for what little your clan may give him."

Falon turned away, looking out towards the opening. It was a gray morning, chilly and uncomfortable. On most days, about now, he'd lead the herd to a new spot on the slope where they could graze on some fresh grasses and shrubs, while their lowing filled the wind.

Plano came behind him, and rested his hand on his shoulder.

"It's something else, isn't it, Falon? You are worried about an even greater disgrace."

Falon nodded.

"I can only ask you to trust me . . . no matter what happens, no matter what you see. Trust me, and I will tell you this: Greater honor awaits you than any highland mrem has ever dreamed of. It is not too much to say that you will play an important role in the future of the mrem."

Then, as if in disagreement, the lead buck snorted.

"He's calling me to move the herd on."

Plano patted him. "Do so. Your replacement will be here by midday. I will stay with them until he arrives. Move your herd, and then carry my message to Lord Rhow."

Falon crawled out of the chilly cave, stood up, and looked at the herd.

"What do you say?"

The young mrem turned and looked at Plano. "I'll do it."

An enormous grin broke on the old mrem's face. He went to Falon and encircled him, crushing him with tremendous and surprisingly powerful hugs. "Wonderful. You'll not regret it, Falon. A great adventure awaits you, a fabulous adventure. I only wish that I could be with you to show you my old city."

Falon pulled away, and began gathering his belongings. His sword, bow, and quiver filled with arrows. A small pack, including a light kilt for the warmer climate that lay ahead. Lastly, he picked up the satchel of gold Plano had tossed to him the night before.

"Come," he said, starting toward the uxan. "I'll move the herd—and then I can be off."

Plano hurried to keep up with him.

Falon looked around, back up the hill. Plano looked entirely out of place, standing on a hill overlooking the herd-beasts. Plano waved, a final cheery good-bye.

And good-bye to the mountain, Falon thought with no regret.

Already it was warmer as he trudged down to the base of the hill. The winds were less fierce, and Plano had warned him that, before long, he'd have to remove his capes.

The herd-beasts seemed to sense that something was up. Instead of their normal lazy munching, their heads were

off the ground. A few scuffles broke out and the lead buck
had to jab at the combatants.

Plano had written out directions, using a deft mixture of
pictures and simple words written in the highland dialect.
Falon could read and write, but his command of the language was far from masterly. Already, the striped mrem
worried about meeting the hundreds of accents that were
sure to fill the city of Tizare. The message for Lord Rhow
was cleverly sewn between layers of the cape that Plano
had given him.

As he descended, the mountain ended abruptly, tumbling into a wide, bowl-shaped marsh area. To the left was
the main road that passed his village and continued on,
past other highlander strongholds, before leaving the
cooler steppes for the plains. Every day's journey along
that route would bring more and more travelers—merchants making the great yearly route to sell their wares in
each of the cities, disgruntled highlanders out to improve
their lot in life, soldiers, priests, dancers, and messengers.
That way would bring him much company. After the isola-
tion of the mountain, companions would be welcome.

But Plano had been very clear in his instructions. He was
to skirt East, passing quite close to the old city of Fahl, a
place some of the village elders said was not abandoned.
From there, he could cross the gentle hills to the west and
move to Tizare.

"How long will it take?" he had asked Plano.

"Beats me, Falon. Along the roads, given good weather,
it's a journey of a week or so. But you'll be traveling
through the Eastern woods, over narrow cart trails." He
grinned then, already enjoying Falon's 'wonderful adventure.' "Move quickly and don't dawdle."

At least his backpack was light. He wished he had been
able to get better sleep the night before.

The day stayed overcast, darkening even more. It was
hard to tell when night would fall and, with the forest just
ahead, he'd soon be making his way in a gloomy light.

No matter. Falon would be sure to use the last few minutes of light to build some kind of shelter. Tonight he'd
sleep.

Falon hummed as he neared the great forest. While it
was circled with hardy, squat parra trees, the forest was

filled mostly with great stands of scratch trees, so named for the nasty thorns that girded and protected the bark.

The mrem sang a song from his youth, one he had learned while helping his father turn the soil of their small farm. It was a song of the mountains, of people who live away from the cities, a song of the highlanders. But he found he had forgotten some of the words, repeated a verse, and finally was left humming the simple melody.

It was the only sound Falon heard as he entered the great forest.

It wasn't long before it was so dark that the blue-green leaves looked black, and the narrow trail disappeared before his eyes.

"Enough for today," the messenger said to himself. He looked around for something that would give him some shelter. There were the trees, but no loose limbs he could fashion into something to keep the dew off. To the right, though, he spied a great chunk of rock. Not much of a home, but he could build his fire near it and lean against the heated stone.

Falon snapped off some low-lying branches of the fresh wood, hoping it would burn. His belly rumbled, and he wished that he had brought more than the meager items in his pack. Tomorrow, as he hiked, he'd have to keep his eye open for some small game. Perhaps some tasty rodent to be grilled over his fire would hit the spot.

The highlander busied himself with lighting a small fire, then eating—with slow, deliberate bites—some of the gradle berries and chunks of tough cheese whose smell must surely rival his own.

A slug of water from his pouch washed down the meal.

Falon looked up. No stars could be seen through the roof of the trees. It was probably still overcast, he imagined.

The fire began to fade, but he was too tired to care. He groomed his face, then his ears, before laying one outstretched arm over his eyes and falling fast asleep.

That night Falon had the first nightmare.

At first, the mrem thought he had awakened in some unfamiliar place. It was a narrow corridor, with a ceiling much too low for a mrem, and walls that pressed in tight. *How did I get here*, he wondered.

And, more importantly, how do I get out?

Then, he heard the sound, coming down the darkened shaft. Strange, rustling sounds, accompanied by a slithering noise, growing louder.

I have to get out of here, he thought. But there was no way to turn around . . . all he could do was back up, slowly, tortuously as the sounds came closer and closer.

He knew it was a dream then. He knew he was someplace else, perhaps back on the hill snoring loudly near the herd-beasts. *Soon, I will wake up.*

It was near him now, and Falon's panic grew, his fur bristled, and his claws were ready. The slithering shape was almost upon him, almost in the small pool of light. He kept backing up, faster and faster.

Until he felt something grab him—from behind.

He howled in his dream, a horrible sound in the narrow tunnel.

Then he howled out loud, waking himself.

He had rolled away from the stone, his capes sprawled on the dusty ground. He shivered. He looked up.

The clouds were gone, and though it was still dark, a hint of rosy color to the east signaled that dawn was not long away. And there, just at the horizon, was a pale crescent moon.

He gathered up his capes, wrapped them around his cold body, and lay there, eyes shut but not sleeping, until the first rays of light lit the treetops.

After waking, Falon wasted no time getting back to the small trail. He was still upset by the nightmare and he checked the ground for footprints. He saw nothing that indicated that anyone else had been on the trail recently.

Though, as an outcast, he was used to being alone, it was still unpleasant to make his solitary way through these old woods. His only company was the shrill hoot of a trumpeter fowl. And that was a noxious noise he knew too well from chasing stray herd-beasts that wandered down into the valley.

He was lonely.

And then the mrem heard the screaming.

The sound cut through the woods with its shrill sound of

total panic. Falon's claws closed quickly around his short sword.

He ran at full speed. The sound was just ahead, right on the narrow trail. He heard the voice bellowing for help, barely intelligible with so much high-pitched squealing and wailing.

What could be causing so much commotion?

The highlander rounded a narrow curve in the trail, around a thick old tree that seemed to be guarding the path. The trail emptied out into an open space—a perfect site for a campground.

Then he saw it. An uncommon sight, to say the least.

It was a Rar, an animal that some city dwellers liked to believe was extinct. An ancestral enemy of the mrem. It was said that the beast traveled on two legs, like the mrem. But the highlander hunters who spotted the occasional Rar knew better. It ran, like any other beast, on four legs, rising on its hind quarters only to attack. Its claws were only for traction, but its long snout and canines were designed to quickly rip an opponent apart.

The opponent in this case hardly seemed a fitting match for the Rar. It was a chubby mrem, with dull, gray fur. He had added splotches of blue and yellow to his otherwise bland markings.

He was hanging, dangling really, from a tree limb, while the Rar reared up and growled out its intentions.

"Please, my friend, help me-e-e-e-e!" Despite the mrem's claws being completely dug into the flaking bark of the parra tree branch, it was obvious that gravity was going to dump the mrem at the feet of the Rar momentarily.

The creature turned, and seemed to sneer at Falon.

Back off, it seemed to say. *This juicy morsel is mine.*

One of the mrem's claws slipped, and his tail dangled close to the Rar's open maw.

The Rar, standing on its back legs, towered over Falon. And the mrem wished that his sword was longer. He took a step toward the growling creature.

"Oh, thank you . . . thank you. . . ." the mrem in the tree wheedled.

"Don't thank the All-Mother yet. . . ." Falon said.

The Rar went down to all fours, and then turned. It

advanced slowly, almost carefully, perhaps, Falon thought, not wanting to lose another lunch to a tree.

No fear of that, Falon thought.

I don't climb so well.

Falon brought the blade out in front. It looked so terribly small. The mrem in the tree slipped a bit more, and one hand came completely free. "Oh, no!" he yelled.

The Rar glanced around, tempted by the plump mrem.

Falon hissed, and the Rar spun around quickly, instinctively recognizing the warning sound.

Now if it just doesn't figure out that I might be in over my head.

The highlander could see that the Rar was getting ready to spring. If its teeth should close around his throat, the contest would be over. But if he tried to lunge, and missed the creature, he wouldn't get a second chance.

Falon backed up a bit.

"Help!" the fat mrem in the tree bellowed as he lost his grip and plunged down onto the leafy ground. The Rar started to turn.

"Over here!" Falon yelled at the Rar, as he kicked up the dirt at his feet.

Not much of a gesture, he admitted, but it brought the creature's attention back. With no warning, it leaped into the air.

And just as quickly, Falon rolled toward and under the Rar, neatly ducking under its powerful front legs. Falon sprung to his feet quickly—quick enough, he hoped, to get the jump on the Rar.

The young mrem spun around, and he saw the Rar looking left and right, as if his lunch had just vanished in thin air.

Falon wasted no time running to it and bringing his sword back for a great slashing blow.

Not too sporting, he admitted. But hey, these creatures were supposed to be extinct.

The Rar's head twisted and fixed on Falon, and then on his blade, with dark, soulless eyes. It tried to dart away.

But it just wasn't quick enough and Falon's blade chopped into its midsection. The dull, bloody sound of the blade chopping into the Rar's body seemed to hang in the small glade for a second.

It howled, then sprung back, alive and ready to attack.

"By the All-Mother, you've got it mad now, you have," the other mrem whined.

Falon ignored the complaining voice of the mrem he just saved.

The Rar wasted no time attacking. This time it galloped towards Falon, taking care that there'd be no more tricks.

Falon held his blade close to him, the bloody, pointed end aimed right at his attacker.

It stopped, snarling, while its blood cascaded down to the forest floor. It snarled, and then, with a final, almost wistful glance at the plump mrem, it darted away.

Falon lowered his blade.

"Lucky thing for you, I'd say. Real lucky. I thought for sure that the monster would make short work of you, before turning his unwanted attentions to me."

Falon looked carefully at this living wellspring of gratitude.

The smaller mrem was a sorry sight. His cape, what was left of it, was in tatters, and his kilt was in three pieces. Numerous small nicks and cuts marred his pelt. The odd dabs of color and makeup only made him look all the more disheveled.

He smiled and made a small bow towards Falon. "I do, of course, appreciate your help."

"That's good to hear." Falon was wiping his blade against the splintery bark of a parra tree. He sheathed the sword and started to walk away.

"In fact . . . I'd be glad to accompany you on your journey. I was, er, heading that way myself."

"And which way was that?"

The chubby mrem waved a hand in the general direction of the South. "Why, that way—you know, the way you're going."

"Yes." Falon laughed. "Well, I think I might travel a bit faster alone."

The mrem hurried to keep up with him. "Why, yes, but I can help you . . . in other ways."

Falon trudged on.

"And how, my friend, is that?"

"I am Caissir. I passed that way more than a few times. I was in the city of Fahl just shortly before it was abandoned. I am known to many nobles in the great cities. There are dangers ahead, my friend, and I can help you avoid them."

Falon looked at him, his golden eyes trying to see beyond the tattered and scarred mess struggling to keep up with him. His golden eyes narrowed. "I don't know—"

Caissir grabbed Falon's arm.

"And," he said breathlessly, "I am a wizard."

Chapter 3

▲————————————————————————————————▲

I$_t$ was perhaps a foolish move, Falon thought.

Letting this Caissir, this 'wizard,' come along might only make for trouble. But it was pleasant having someone to listen to, even if much of what he said was utter nonsense.

"I can see," said Caissir, "that you are having a bit of trouble believing me."

The highlander nodded. "Where I come from, Caissir, magic is for the herd-beasts."

"Of course," Caissir said good-naturedly. "Much of it is. I mean, it's nothing more than some simple danger sense among most beasts, that's all. But I offer a more sophisticated kind of magic."

Falon looked around. It was getting dark already. And it was hotter than the day before. According to the map Plano had given him, they were nearing the end of the great woods. Soon, they should come to farm country, villages, and a main road.

Before passing quite close to the city of Fahl.

"Why, if you had any magic ability whatsoever you could sense my own powers in that regard," the wizard rambled as they walked. "Suffice it to say, my power to predict what will pass, as well as move material through the air, well . . . it has to be seen to be believed." Caissir's hands fluttered and waved in the air, emphasizing each of his points.

"Tell me, Caissir . . ." Falon said, arching his eyebrows, "why didn't you use this fabled ability of yours to see that hungry Rar coming your way?"

"Good question, Falon. An excellent question." Caissir raised one finger in the air, then paused as if thinking of an answer. "You see, even *my* abilities are severely limited. That was an unfavorable spot for any magician. It's altogether too complicated to explain, but there was something 'wrong' with the woods. But even with that problem, I did foresee the event sufficiently to climb up a tree."

"His growls didn't help?"

Caissir shrugged, and looked to his left. "I see I shall never convince you, my friend. Until you need my help, that is."

When he turned away, the cape parted and Falon noticed something that hadn't caught his eye before.

Caissir's tail. It was a stub. Mrem tails aren't very long to begin with, but this looked as though something had happened to it. Not used to restraining any comments that might occur to him, Falon mentioned it.

Caissir's pout deepened. "That is an indignity suffered upon me by some more of your enlightened highlanders. Some village elders objected to my magic. This was their way of warning me away from their good and trusting females."

Falon smiled, his short whiskers catching the mottled, late afternoon light. He could imagine the domestic trouble that this 'wizard' might get into.

"And is that how you ended up on a little cart trail days away from the nearest village?"

Caissir nodded. "Yes, and if truth be told I'm quite eager to get back to the city and ply my trade. There are many city dwellers who pay well for useful magical information."

"I'm sure."

Caissir looked at him, his whiskers twitching in concern. "You'll let me accompany you, won't you? All the way to Tizare."

"Perhaps . . ."

"There are rumors, you know."

"Of what?"

The chubby mrem pressed close to Falon, as if there were anybody there to eavesdrop.

"Another city may have fallen to the Eastern Lords . . . a city on the ocean."

And for the first time, what Caissir said gave him pause.

The highlanders now considered themselves above the skirmishes and battles that riddled the city states of the mrem. They traded with the city merchants, tended their crops and herds, and, when the spirit moved them, were not above raiding the wealthy cities. It mattered not who ruled.

But the Eastern Lords were something that every mrem —no matter where he was born and who his mother was— feared. Once thought defeated after the great wars, it became clear that the Eastern Lords had simply been biding their time.

When the great invasion from the East began, even the highlanders knew they would have to come down to fight and save the world of the mrem. So the clanmrem had promised long before Falon had been born.

"That's not good. . . ." he said quietly.

He remembered his mother then, threatening him when he was young. *You'd better be good,* she said, *or the liskash will come and get you.*

His good friend Patje, a natural artist, would draw him pictures of the reptile armies of the Eastern Lords . . . pictures so clear and frightening they kept Falon awake at night.

"And worse, it is said that the city fell too easily."

"Collaborators?"

"Some say that there are mrem who take their orders, secret orders, from the East."

It had turned a shadowy dusk. Before long, travel would be difficult, perhaps dangerous. "We should stop for the night here," Falon said.

Caissir looked around. "I had hoped we could at least get out of the forest."

"I don't know how much further there is to go. Let's make the most comfortable camp that we can. You can start gathering some wood."

Caissir grumbled and mumbled, but, though easily twice Falon's fifteen years, he did as ordered.

He also went on talking, of the great cities, of the ships that traveled the Southern islands, and of his own adventures as a wizard . . . long after Falon had curled up close to their smoldering fire, ready to sleep.

Falon was awakened by some mud-encrusted foot pushing at his face.

"What are you—" he started to yell.

"Easy off the ground, my striped friend. I'd hate to shave those fine long whiskers of yours."

His claws moved, searching for the carefully formed holes of his sword hilt. It was, of course, gone.

"Nice and easy . . . no funny moves." The mrem towered over him. He was pointing a graceful rapier right at Falon's nose.

Bandits. Uncommon in the hill country. What, after all, was there to steal? But they were the plague of the unguarded roads between the cities. With all the cities looking after their own self-interest, the roads and highways were left to these ragtag squads of thieves.

These were decorated with odd bits of jewelry, hung strangely from their noses, their ears, even their tails. A few seemed to be wearing bones as an added decoration.

Falon slowly brought himself to a standing position.

"We have nothing worth stealing," he said quietly. "You can see the tattered condition of my friend there." He paused, and looked right at the greenish eyes of the leader. "Let us be."

The leader stood taller than Falon, unless it was merely the effect of the boots he wore. The raiding party consisted of five other mrem, all loaded down with a couple of blades each.

A nasty bunch to run into . . .

"Nothing worth stealing, eh?" the leader said, his unusually furry lips curling into a sneer. "Then what's this?" The leader dangled the small satchel of gold pieces before his eyes. "And that cape you're wearing?"

Falon touched the folds of his cape, feeling the message he carried.

"Off with it!" the leader barked.

Caissir started yelping. Falon turned and saw them poking at the chubby wizard with their blades. "No, stop!" the wizard screamed. He spun around, trying to avoid their giddy thrusts, while they laughed at him.

"Tell them to stop," said Falon.

"They're just having some sport."

"You've got what you want. Let us be."

The leader stepped close to Falon, and put his nose right

up to him. "You're in no position to give orders, high-lander. Just be glad that we don't leave you all cut up for the Rars." He held the eyeball-to-eyeball position and re-moved the cloak carefully. His eyes never left Falon's. Stepping back, the leader said, "Tie them up . . . let's be gone from here." He sounded pleased with the easy loot.

Falon saw one of the bandits lean close to another and mumble something. Then they came and tied him up, pulling the knots so tight that they dug painfully into his skin.

When they had Caissir tied up next to him, they van-ished into the woods, heading north.

"I thought for sure they'd kill us," Falon said.

Caissir shook his head. "Bandits are tolerated by the cities, Falon. Murderers are not. Though who knows what happens in the forest here. Well, so far I haven't seemed to bring you much luck."

The highlander struggled against the cheap frayed rope around his wrists. It was tied tightly, he noted, but with some effort it should snap pretty easily.

"Where . . . were . . . your fabled powers?" he asked as he twisted and squirmed on the ground.

"For the life of me, I can't tell you."

Some wizard! I'd do better if I had brought along the lead buck from the herd. At least he could tell when some kind of danger is arriving.

Falon crawled backwards, on his rear end, rubbing his stubby tail into the leaves and needles of the forest floor.

"Where are you going?"

He didn't answer Caissir, but just continued bumping and sliding his way towards a nearby parra tree. He stopped when he felt it against his back.

"Got an itch?" Caissir called to him.

Falon rubbed the rope against the scratchy bark of the tree, back and forth. He heard the strands snapping, first singly, then whole bunches. In a moment, he was able to shake off his binds.

"Hooray!" Caissir called out. "Now do me, quickly."

He walked over to the now ever-more-suspicious wiz-ard. "Do you still want to come with me?" Falon asked.

"Why certainly, I expect—"

He put a hand on Caissir's shoulder. "I won't be going to the City of Tizare . . . not directly."

Caissir gave him a cagy glance. His plump tongue snaked out and licked his puffy lips. "Please . . . untie me, Falon."

"You were near the mangy crooks. Did they say where they might be headed?"

"No . . . I mean I heard something, but—"

Falon gave his shoulder a gentle squeeze. "What did they say, Caissir?"

"They said something about Fahl, but I'm sure that was only—"

Falon stood up, a small grin crinkling his face. "Good. Now tell me about Fahl."

"Please, Falon . . . the ropes . . ."

"Soon." Falon smiled.

"It's a city, almost totally destroyed, just a lot of rubble, and caverns—"

"In other words, the perfect place for a band of thugs and looters to hide out."

"Well, yes—"

"Then that's where we'll go."

Caissir smiled. "No, I don't think I want to do that, Falon."

"Nor do I. But without that cape, I'm back tending the herd-beasts. Or worse."

"But I don't *want* to come."

"I'm afraid I may need your help." Falon took a step away.

"Wh-where are you going?"

"Will you help me recover my stolen property, my magical friend?"

Falon watched Caissir struggle against his bonds. But his layers of fat and too-thick fur made it unlikely he'd be able to free himself.

"Very well. I'll come. By the All-Mother, you'd probably get lost without me and wander into the desert."

Falon hurried back to Caissir, crouched down, and undid the many knots that held the wizard fast.

He watched him rub the matted fur.

"Take the lead, Caissir. And while we walk, tell me about Fahl. . . ."

Fahl! To hear Caissir tell it, the fall of this border city was one of the great tragedies in the history of the mrem. It was a small garrison city, a first line of defense against the Eastern Lords. But the invaders' true power, and their true plans, had not even been guessed at. When the walls were overrun, only a suicidal last stand saved the fleeing White Dancers, the villagers, and the beleaguered remnant of the army.

"But why didn't the Eastern Lords hold the city?" Falon asked.

Caissir trudged slowly now. He seemed to find all this hiking very difficult.

"Fahl was not the prize they sought. An obstacle, yes. But for them to try and defend it when they had no real use for it . . . well, it made no sense."

"And the cities chose to leave it abandoned?"

"It was left in ruins. To reestablish it as a garrison was beyond the resources—or desires—of the various nobles. Besides, when the Eastern Lords invade again it will surely not be through that city."

As they talked, the lush forest was changing. The tall parra trees gave way to scrubby shrubs and clumps of spindly trees. Their leaves were narrow, designed to catch whatever moisture fell. Falon had never seen them before. There were more bird sounds as well, sweet chirps and calls that made the late afternoon seem almost pleasant.

Falon couldn't get used to being without a weapon. Since the day he reached his maturity he'd always had some kind of blade strapped to his side. Rich capes and gold were foreign items to him. His sword, though, was his constant companion.

For a long time it had been his *only* companion.

"Much further?" he asked Caissir.

"We should come to a bridge to take us across the River Clawm. If we don't stop for dinner, we should get near the old city before nightfall."

"Good. Then we won't stop."

Caissir groaned. "I wish I knew what they took that was so all-important to you."

Falon laughed. "You'll learn everything—I promise."

If we live, he thought. *If we can find the bandits and get the cape back.*

They climbed a small rise, and as they climbed they heard the rush of water.

"The river . . ."

Falon nodded. The water made him uneasy. Even when he used to watch the herd-beasts wallow in the shallow streams of Mount Zaynir it made him uncomfortable. How could they enjoy all that splashing, all that wetness? It made him shudder just to watch them. Water was for drinking. And grooming was something best done under the moonlight, an attractive female arching her back up against him—just so!—while he let just the tips of his claws run through the downy fur.

It had been a while. . . .

The roaring sound of the water grew. And, as he reached the crest of the small hill, he almost didn't see what was wrong.

Caissir's moan snapped him out of his reverie, and brought his attention to the river.

"What is it?" he asked.

"The bridge, you dim-witted highlander. The bridge!"

"What bridge?" he asked.

Caissir fixed him with a withering glance. "Exactly. There is no bridge. Perhaps it washed away—"

"More likely, the bandits tore it down."

He looked at the water. It was rushing torrent, frothing and spitting as it traveled quickly below them. A few large boulders sent the rushing water into the air.

It didn't look appealing in the slightest.

"Well, I guess we have no choice," Caissir offered. "I can take us west and pick up the main road."

Yes, Falon thought. And Fahl would be days away by the time they got across the river and came back east.

"No . . ." he said softly. "We'll cross the river."

"What! Are you crazy? A highlander and a wizard are going to cross—that?" Caissir pointed at the river as though it were a living thing.

"Yes." He turned and looked at Caissir. Such an unlikely companion for such adventures. "There are mrem who travel the great Southern oceans. This is just . . . a little stream."

The wizard's hair seemed to stand on end. "Yes, there are madmen who sail the oceans. And I hope they're paid well. But how do you plan on crossing this?"

Falon smiled, actually amused by the absurdity of the thought.

"Why, we'll make a raft." He draped an arm around Caissir. "A nice big one, so that neither you nor I get wet."

Chapter 4

▲————————————————————————————————————▲

"There's no way you'll catch me traveling in that. Not in this life." Caissir turned away from the makeshift raft.

Falon examined the odd-looking fruit of his labors: the roughly lashed vines, brittle branches, and twisted tree limbs.

Even he had to admit to being less than enthusiastic about taking it across the river.

The highlander dragged it close to the water, as if girding himself for the great adventure to come. There, he thought. Now all that they needed to do was just sail it across.

"No, I'm not interested in continuing our relationship any further. . . ." Caissir's speech degenerated into grumbling and mumbling. Falon heard bits and pieces about how he had been "better off facing the Rar."

Could be true, friend, Falon thought. The more he looked at the water, the sicker he felt. Water! It was so horribly wet! The spooky tales the old village she-mrem told about the liskash even said that they would immerse their whole bodies into water . . . even lay their eggs in it.

And this river was very noisy, gurgling and sputtering so close by.

Falon walked over to the wizard, noticing how his fur seemed to be all on end. He draped an arm over his shoulder. "I won't say you *have* to come, Caissir. Though having dispatched a Rar, I could certainly bring some pressure to bear. And I won't even mention that you might this very moment be inside the belly of the Rar, if not for my timely arrival. Let me simply say this." He fixed him with his golden eyes, hoping that he could be more persuasive than the thundering roar of the river. "I need help. I lost something in that cape that was entrusted to me. And I want to get it back. With your help, I just may have a chance."

Caissir's eyes went all filmy, like Falon's herd-beasts' when he scolded them, prodding them along to their next piece of mountain.

Caissir hesitated. Then—"But look at that! Just look at that!" He pointed at the raft. "What kind of craft do you call that? It will fall apart with the first lurch."

Falon gave his shoulder a squeeze. "The river is a mere six spans across. A few minutes, and we're off."

Caissir stepped cautiously over to the raft. He gave it a rough shake, obviously hoping that all its bonds would fall apart. But after a few rough jiggles back and forth, it seemed to be all of a piece.

"There!" Falon said. "I may be a simple highlander, but when I build something it stays together."

Caissir shrugged. "Very well. If the All-Mother should decide that my allotted time is up, so be it." He sniffed. "Come, if we're to do it, let us begin."

"That's the spirit."

Falon pulled the raft closer to the water, edging it in. The trick here was to have it far enough in that a good shove would get it launched. But not *so* far that he'd have to step into the water.

He pushed it into the river until he felt it start to be caught by the current.

"Quickly! Step onto it!" he yelled at Caissir. Falon watched the raft sink into the river muck as Caissir crawled onto it. He gave it an added push, getting most of the raft floating. Then he turned and grabbed a long stick. It should, he figured, be enough to pole his way across.

"Here we go, wizard. Let me know if you sense any danger."

Caissir merely grumbled some more.

He gave the clunky raft a shove, and he felt it sliding across the sand. Then it was floating freely on the water, moving quickly out to the current.

"Do jump on!" Caissir yelled, afraid that he might be left alone on the raft.

Another hefty push, and Falon stepped into the water. The water was just as cold and uncomfortable as he could imagine.

He held his stick tightly as he jumped on.

For a second he thought he was going to go flying right over the raft, so strong was his leap. But instead he landed on top of Caissir.

"Ooph! You clumsy fool."

"Sorry, I—"

Falon felt water reach his claws. The whole raft was precariously tilted.

It was going to flip right over!

The highlander threw himself off Caissir. He rolled back over the rough surface of the raft and sat up.

I've still got my stick, he thought.

"We're moving downstream fast, Falon. Will you please do something!"

Falon stuck his makeshift punting pole into the river. And he felt no bottom. He thrust it down as far as he could. His claws touched the water, but the stick just dangled freely.

"Well," Caissir barked at him. "Give it a push!"

"Sure," said the young mrem.

What next? The raft was holding together just fine. A most seaworthy craft, all things considered. Except that he had absolutely no way of directing its course.

It started picking up speed.

"Come on, then, move us to shore."

Falon looked at Caissir. He withdrew the useless stick from the water. The water was bubbling and churning even more eagerly.

"I—I—" he started to explain.

They hit something. Some half-submerged rock or boulder banged into the fast-moving raft. The raft stopped suddenly, with a sickening jolt. Without thinking, Falon let his claws emerge and dig into the splintery wood of the raft.

Caissir's reflexes didn't serve him nearly as well.

One second he was there, bleating at him to get them out of the river.

Then Caissir was gone, knocked right into the water.

"No . . ." Falon said quietly. The raft was free now, spinning in crazy circles. He searched the surface for some sign of the wizard.

I should have let him leave, Falon thought. *He didn't want to come, and now he is about to drown.*

Caissir's ears popped to the surface, then the puffy face. He was gasping for air. The sound coming from him made Falon's insides go all funny. He was too far away from the raft, Falon thought. There was no way he could grab him, pull him closer. . . .

The ears sunk under the water.

Now, like most mrem, Falon did not know how to swim. The very idea of swimming was repulsive. The highlanders thought the stories about mrem sailors—mrem who actually spent their lives *on the water*—were just that: stories.

But, if nothing else, his being alone—on the hills, traveling through the valleys—had given him time to watch the wild creatures that were his only companions.

And Falon thought that he understood at least the idea of swimming.

The highlander searched the spot that Caissir had just been.

No ears or tufts of fur surfaced.

Falon took three breaths, cursing the stranger that called him off his mountain, and cursing himself for listening.

"Ya-a-a-owww!" he yelled, leaping into the water.

Then everything was silent. And wet. And cold.

He started scratching at the water, as if there was a way to claw out. He opened his eyes.

There's no way I'll find him, he thought, *if I just bob around blindly!*

It looked as bad as it felt. Murky, brown—worse than any early morning fog. He tried to force some pattern onto his wild kicking at the water. *Up . . . I've got to get up!*

He felt his ears break the surface. Soon his head was up and he gulped the air. Then down, once again, into the gloomy water.

Falon didn't see anything.

But he felt something. Big and lumpy.

He closed his claws around it. If it was Caissir he was acting pretty much like he was dead already.

He got to the surface. He looked around quickly, strug-

gling to hold onto Caissir as the current tugged on him.
The shore was mercifully nearby.

I can do this, he thought. *I can get him over there, and
get him and me out of the river.*

The roar of the water, just ahead, sounded different.
There was a shift in the sound . . . a new openness. As
if—

He choked the air down, sometimes taking in equal
amounts of water. The roar grew.

He felt the bottom.

Never have I felt such joy, he thought. *Nothing could
equal this moment.*

I'm alive.

He wasted no time getting completely out, even if Caissir's body grew increasingly leaden as he tugged it out.

He knelt down by the wizard's head. His eyelids were
shut and he didn't seem to be breathing. Falon shook the
body.

Come on. Come on. I saved you! You can't die on me now.
He brought his muzzle down to Caissir's. He breathed into
him, felt the swell of the puffy chest. He pushed down hard
on his chest. And again. And again—

Until he was rewarded with a spray of river water and
partly digested berries. Caissir curled up, coughing violently, grabbing at his throat.

Caissir was still hacking when Falon went down to the
water. He certainly wasn't eager to get back into it, but
anything would be better than the stench of Caissir's last
meal.

Falon was splashing at his face and chest when he finally
heard him.

"You mangy fool—you nearly killed me!"

Falon paused in his cleaning up. "Such gratitude . . .
Once again, I save your life, and this is how you talk to
me?"

"If I ever get back to—"

The striped mrem looked downstream. Standing there
at the water's edge, he saw now what had made the roar.

A white fog rose up from the water, a misty cloud that
whirled above a waterfall.

How close! Another few moments, and they would have
tumbled over the edge.

He looked at Caissir and raised his hand.

"We're both lucky to have survived, my friend. And now, if you're well enough, it's time we moved on."

Caissir shook his head, cleared his throat, and then stood up, so wet and uncomfortable looking it almost made Falon laugh.

The young kit crouched down and watched them carefully.

He had to be careful . . .

Ashre knew he was not as big as they were. Not yet . . . nor as old . . .

The concealed kit knew that, as he scurried through the abandoned streets of Fahl, his sleek gray fur glistening even in the gloom. His tiny satchel of precious items was strung close to him.

But without them, the loud ones who yelled and fought as they ate in the big old hall at the center of the city, he could not live. They brought in food, and water, and something more.

It was a game. Like those he remembered playing with his mother. Something fun, without danger and without fear. A game. Often he tried to see just how close he could get to them, while they counted their gold pieces.

They saw him, many times, scurrying along the stone balconies that overlooked the great hall. Some would even chase him, their eyes flashing angrily in the glow of the candlelight.

No matter. He'd howl, and dash away. Always swifter . . . always getting away just in time.

I am Ashre. Son of the Dancer, Kaarina.

I am fast and I am smart. So she had told him.

And something more. Something that kept the ugly thieves from ever catching him. His mother, so beautiful with her pale green eyes and so-thin coat of white fur, would rub his head with her hands . . . whispering to him to say nothing of the strange feelings he sometimes had.

He had remembered that. Remembered, and said nothing.

And when he saw his mother killed, cut down like the great fields of grain they used to walk through, he stood there. Waiting . . .

For them to come and get him.

But the soldiers rattled past him, as if he wasn't there. Ignoring his crying, his howling.

He went over to his mother, crept up to her body. Already it felt cold, unfriendly. Her bright eyes were pale and empty. He touched it once, before running away from it.

He watched the others leave, some sneaking away, some in chains, led out toward the great desert.

But he had no place to go . . . no one to take care of him.

So he stayed, stealing from them, watching them, learning all the tricks of the bandits who came to the deserted city.

Tonight, he took his normal route inside the great hall. Up the side of the building, using the heavy brick wall as if it were a staircase.

When he reached the highest window, he climbed in, sending the small mynts running away. Then he walked down a pitch-dark hall until he reached his special place. It was a stone platform, just big enough. From there he could see them, and not be seen.

And if he was seen?

He'd know it in plenty of time to back away and run back down the corridor, out to the dark side streets of Fahl that he knew so well.

For now, he could simply look, waiting for a chance to snatch some dinner as the robbers drank, and ate, and fought.

"There it is," Caissir said. "The city of Fahl." He turned and looked at Falon. "Never a great city, to be sure, and once it fell, it was abandoned. The Eastern Lords apparently shared that feeling. Once its main defensive wall was reduced to rubble, they abandoned it as well."

Falon looked out at the city. It was a dark hulk on the horizon. Almost on the edge of the desert, Fahl could only be reached by the neglected trail that they had just taken.

"I expected more lights."

He felt Caissir looking at him.

"Lights? This is not Ar, Falon. Even in its prime it was just an out-of-the-way rest stop. That's all."

Falon kept on staring at it.

"It's my first city."

Caissir shook his head. "More's the pity. Still, you'll see your share of wonders when you reach Tizare. That, my friend, is definitely a going concern."

"I've seen enough," Falon said. "Let's get going."

"What? Now? I really don't think that we want to enter a city of thieves, and worse, in the middle of the night."

Falon laughed. "When better? When the sun finds them all alert and angry? No, we'll go in now, catch them with their bellies full of gradle wine."

He stood up, and a cool breeze gently ruffled his fur.

"Come, Caissir. It's cold." He laughed. "And I want my sword and cape back."

Chapter 5

▲──▲

It was no problem finding where everyone was in the city. Except for a few small lights in scattered buildings, all the noise and bright lights came from one place.

"It used to be the palace. The lord fancied himself a king. But then, they all do. Everything in the city was made of the cheapest material, including his home. When it was overrun, entire buildings were burned. From the looks of things, only the Great Hall survived."

They were in the shadows, down one of a dozen narrow alleyways that spilled out into a large courtyard before the shell of a palace.

Falon studied the odd assortment of mrem standing outside. They had bottles in their hands and were laughing and talking loudly, but they also all wore heavy swords. Drunk or no, they could prove to be dangerous.

"Well, there's no way we can just walk in there," Caissir said.

Falon tried to think. There had to be some way to find the bandits who robbed them . . . *if* they were even here.

"Not for me, my friend." He turned and looked at his all-too-reluctant companion. "I'm just an angry highlander, better dead and quickly. You, though, are someone of interest."

Caissir started to sputter. "What do you mean?"

Falon edged closer to the light of the courtyard. "You can present yourself as a traveling magician . . . someone willing to trade a few prophecies for a mug of wine, and some sliced uxan."

He heard Caissir lick his lips.

"But if the bandits see me—"

Falon shook his head. "They'll remember nothing. We were just an unimportant stop on their way here. If you're worried, just keep smiling and moving."

"And what am I to do?"

"Why, look for the bandits, or my cape. I'll try to find some other way in. When you find them, raise your hand, scratch your head. Just don't do it unless you see them."

Caissir started to back away from the courtyard but Falon grabbed him firmly around his plump middle. "Just keep telling yourself you're here to entertain them. I'm sure you've done it in other cities."

"Why, yes, but—"

Then Falon gave him a push out into the light. Caissir froze for a second. A few of the drunken bandits looked over at him.

"Better get a move on." Falon spoke from the darkness. "They'll start to wonder why you're lurking so suspiciously by the shadows."

Caissir cleared his throat.

"This clears it, highlander. All debts paid."

"To be sure." And Falon watched Caissir walk towards the stone stairs leading up to the palace.

Now, Falon thought, what other way in can there be? He doubled back along the alley, then moved in a direction that he hoped would lead him to the back of the palace. After a few wrong turns that brought him right back to the courtyard—and, once, bumping into two mrem groping in a doorway—he found a side street that seemed to lead away from the light and noise.

In moments he was staring at the back of the palace.

There were two heavy doors, both yawning wide open.

After all . . . why lock the doors when the place is filled with thieves?

He scuttled up, looking left and right in case he should be seen by any bandits returning from some late-night frolic.

The smell . . . in the cool air . . . it was more than just roasting meat and wine. It was the smell of she-mrem. This was obviously more than just a way station for the bands of thieves who plagued the main roads.

He found himself stirring, responding to the pleasures he imagined could be found inside the doors.

He ran up the back steps quickly, then past the doors. It was totally dark inside, with only the sound of music and laughter to guide him. He moved ahead slowly—and fell over two grunting mrem tangled on the floor.

"Sorry," he said. "Didn't see you. . . ."

They took no notice of him. He went on, each step making the sound louder, the temptations of the party that much richer. He reached the kitchen, lit with a few scattered candles. There was no way anyone would question his being here. It was just too dark.

Then, just ahead, he saw another pair of doors. The servants had probably used them to bring out trays of food to the now-departed lord and his guests. He walked over to them and gently pushed one open.

It was a scene that he had only dreamed of, never imagining such things to be real. The walls, decorated with enormous murals of mrem in full armor, had been redecorated with slashes and marks. The new residents cared nothing for the glories of the old landlords.

But the hall itself was one great serving room, filled with row after row of tables. Open fires burned on the stone floor, sending a dark, smudgy smoke spiraling up to the vaulted ceiling. The bandits went over to the roasting meat and cut off great chunks of it—cooked or raw—drunk from the casks of wine that lined the walls.

And the females! No one that any mrem would want to claim as mother. But she-mrem, dozens of them moving from table to table, attacking the wine, the meat, and the bandits with equal abandon.

It was all almost too much for him.

Someone pushed into the open doors, unbuckling his kilt. He stepped off to the side of the half-lit kitchen, ignoring Falon and relieving himself with a great sigh. Then, with a satisfied grunt, he returned, once more, to the fray.

Where was Caissir, Falon wondered.

Then he saw him. He was making his way from table to table, a sick-looking grin on his face. He also wasn't above grabbing a piece of meat or two from an unattended table.

And he looked just disheveled enough to fit into the raucous crowd of thieves.

Falon watched him closely, waiting for some sign that he
had found the cape.

Then what? Ah, that would be interesting to see. Of
course, Falon had the advantage that he was sober. That,
and his youth, were considerable advantages. But in a
room filled with cutthroats and robbers, dozens of them,
his chances of getting away seemed slim indeed.

Caissir moved toward another table. A large group were
sitting on chairs, and on the table itself, toasting each
other. He saw Caissir try to be casual as he looked them
over.

He saw his eyes stop.

Caissir raised his right hand to his head and scratched.
He looked around, obviously searching for Falon. He
scratched his head some more, his eyes glowing with fear
even in the smoky light of the great hall.

It's now or never, Falon thought.

And he pushed open the door leading to the hall.

Ashre had been watching them for a while now. The fat
one . . . he was so funny, so scared. But then he saw the
other, over by the door that lead to the kitchen and the
back of the palace.

He was not one of them.

His fur, lined with swirling stripes of brown and gold,
was unlike any he had ever seen. And the way he stood at
the door, watching the fat one . . . No, these two did not
belong to this town.

Then he got the feeling.

And it always made him feel a bit sick. It was as if he
could see them just a few minutes later. Lying on the
ground, the both of them, torn open by the heavy blades of
the drunken robbers.

He could see it . . . and it made him feel sick.

He crept closer to the edge of the platform, looking
carefully now at the strangely colored mrem at the door.

For a moment Falon could do nothing. To do nothing
was safe. No danger. Just the loud noise of the partying, the

smell of the roasted meat, the very aroma of the rough rutting going on, some of it right on the tables as if it were just another item on the menu.

The outcast waited.

Until he knew he could wait no more.

Now! He went through the open door, and he saw poor Caissir, searching around, looking totally abandoned. The young mrem walked, slowly, but steadily, making as direct a line as possible to Caissir.

Caissir saw him now, and for a moment Falon was worried that he would start raising his arms, or give out some call, bringing attention to him.

But he stood there, a grim, glum look on his face, waiting for whatever might develop.

Falon was tempted to reach out and grab a chunk of meat. Perhaps he'd fit in better with a tasty morsel of roast uxan in his mouth. But he just moved forward in a daze, unable to do anything for fear that someone would take notice of him . . . and wonder . . . just who are you?

Someone bumped into his back, and he turned around. A drunken, smiling face, all greasy and wine-stained, bobbed in front of him.

"Hey," the weaving head said. "Wash where you're goin'. . . ."

Falon smiled and nodded. The drunken robber nodded back, and then tilted away, ready to career into someone else.

Caissir's table was just a few steps away.

Falon saw him lick his lips.

Caissir was eager to get out of there, Falon thought. Not without reason.

The highlander recognized the robbers. They were, indeed, the very same ones who had stopped them near the river. He moved close to Caissir.

And stood close to the bandit wearing the fine cape given to Falon by Plano.

"When I move," he hissed at Caissir, "start running towards the back, to the kitchen door. It's dark there, and it leads outside."

"If we get that far . . ." Caissir mumbled.

Falon moved from Caissir, smiling broadly, joining the party. He slid next to the bandit. The cape was draped loosely over the bandit's shoulders. He saw a few of the bandits give him quick glances . . . a moment's recognition, perhaps.

He brought his hand close to the bandit's shoulder. Then he swiped at the cape, catching it in his claws. Then he snatched the bandit's sword.

"Now!" he yelled at Caissir.

Who promptly slipped on some spilled wine. Falon reached down and jerked him to his feet.

The cape trailed behind him, a brilliant flag drawing the unwanted attention of whole tables of bandits.

Some of them started stumbling to their feet.

"Move, Caissir! Get your fat mrem tail moving."

The door was not far, but already Falon felt that they weren't going to make it. He should have had Caissir get out first. The lumbering oaf was slowing him up and—drunk or not—the bandits could probably make quick work of him.

And was he really sure that the meat they were all munching so gleefully was uxan? Maybe they had a taste for young mrem interlopers.

Caissir reached the door, and fidgeted—too long!—with the handle.

"C'mon, please, Cais—"

Falon looked over his shoulder.

A blade was flying at him, a long heavy blade thrown with the deadly expertise of a practiced brigand. No more than an arm's length away, and aimed perfectly at the center of his chest.

He tried to duck. But his reflexes, good as they were, were not fast enough to get his body out of the way.

He didn't see the quick-moving blur crashing into his legs.

"What the—"

One second he was standing, the next he was flat on the sticky floor. He heard the blade crash into the door with a tremendous thud that sent splinters flaking down upon him.

He had landed on the blur.

It was a young mrem, no more than a kit, but not by much. He crawled out from under Falon, looked at him and said, "You'd better get going."

"Right," Falon agreed, and he popped to his feet and followed the youngster out the door.

Where was Caissir? Falon wondered. Already out, on the dark streets of Fahl?

The bandits were just on his heels. But the young mrem was leaving a trail of tumbled pots and pans as they scrambled through the kitchen. Falon heard some of the bandits stumble over them as they followed them into the dark kitchen.

"Where's the door?" he asked, suddenly losing his bearings.

"There, follow me now . . ." the young mrem said, almost calmly.

Amazing! Falon thought. *Here we have half a dozen thugs chasing us, and this little one is as calm as can be.*

The door had become lost in the darkness.

"Falon . . . Falon! Are you here?"

It was Caissir.

"Yes, this way, my friend." Falon heard the door being opened, and then he saw the faint light from the night sky.

"Stay with me!" the young one said. "I can get us away from the others."

And, at that point, Falon didn't doubt it at all.

Their guide led them on a nightmarish journey, up and down the dark streets of Fahl. They passed burned buildings that looked like dead animals. The smell of the burnt wood was still strong. They crept through narrow alleyways where guards once had their apartments. Around and around the deserted city, until finally they came to a small building, all by itself. Beyond it there was nothing but darkness.

"We are safe here," the small one said.

Caissir was panting too heavily to say anything.

"Safe?"

The small one looked up at Falon. "It is my home, and it's much too close to the desert for the others to come out here." He grinned, then scuttled into the house. When Falon didn't immediately follow, the young mrem popped his head out.

"Come in . . . you're welcome to stay . . ."

Caissir touched Falon's arm. "I could use the rest."

"Let's enjoy his hospitality then."

They went inside the small house, almost like the huts that dotted the hillside of Falon's homeland. But once inside, he saw that it wasn't at all like the cheery homes that he and his friends grew up in. The floor was strewn with a strange assortment of clothes, bits of leathery armor, kilts, and scabbards. The wall was filled with weapons, most of them clearly much too heavy for the small mrem to wield. There was a foul, close smell that suggested that the young one didn't know too much about cleaning. Bits of food lay on top of the clothes, and small pairs of glowing eyes in the dark corners told him that their host didn't live alone.

"Ar-ggh! The smell, Falon, really."

"Be polite, my friend, I believe that both of us are in his debt."

Their host had dashed around the room, lighting more candles, which only made the room look stranger.

Falon could finally get a good look at the young mrem. He was small, looking no older than a kit of eight years. But the way he talked and acted spoke of a mrem with much experience.

He wore just a thin sash for a kilt, and he had a small blade strapped to his waist. His body was covered with the most delicate gray fur. It glistened sleekly in the soft light.

When every candle that could be lit was burning, he turned to his guests.

"I'm called Ashre."

"Well, Ashre, I'm Falon, and this is Caissir. And I want to thank you for saving us."

"That's all right." He smiled. "Because you're going to take me out of here."

Falon smiled back. "What about your father, your mother—who takes care of you now?"

"No one," Ashre said proudly. "I take care of myself, taking from the others what I need to live. But," he said, his face turning serious, "I can't stay here much longer. They know about me and I think that they want to find me. And when they do," he said with a grin, "ka-a-a-a-a!" He made a slitting motion across his throat.

So young, Falon thought. Yet he spoke like a seasoned warrior. Where were his toys, his playmates . . . ?

"Your parents?"

Ashre told him, so matter-of-factly, of the last day he saw

his mother alive. Quickly, with no apparent feeling. Except Falon saw him look away, to a small box beside his bed. And he could imagine what was there. A lock of her fur, some other cherished item that she gave Ashre when he was still suckling.

But there was probably nothing in that box as vivid as those last few moments before his mother was killed.

Caissir was grunting as he prowled the room. "No decent place to lie down," he muttered.

"You may take my bed," Ashre offered.

Caissir looked at it. It too was filled with bits and pieces scavenged from the abandoned city.

"No, thank you," Caissir said. "I'll move some of . . . this . . . on the floor."

Ashre shrugged.

"Tell me," Falon said, leaning close to Ashre. "Why did you help us? And how did you know we were in danger?"

Ashre turned away from him. "I go there, to the great hall, to spy, and watch for food and things I might steal. I saw you. . . ."

And more, Falon thought. He was holding something back. Ashre's eyes kept scanning the wall. "Yes, my friend here was certainly easy to spot. But tell me, how did you happen to be at the right spot, just in time to knock me down and save my life?"

"Disgusting!" Caissir moaned, finally lying down.

Ashre stood up. "I . . . I just knew, that's all." He jumped atop his bed. "I'm fast, and I—saw the blade coming."

No one was that fast. No. And suddenly Falon saw more in front of him than just a resourceful young orphan.

Ashre might not be able to tell him all his secrets yet, but, with trust, he *would* tell him.

And those secrets might prove helpful indeed when they got to the great city of Tizare.

For now, some rest would be welcome.

"Thank you, Ashre. I owe my life to you."

"Then you'll take me away with you . . . out of the city." It was said flatly, a statement, not a question.

Falon grinned. Already Caissir's loud snoring rattled the walls.

"We'll talk of that in the morning. For now," he said,

pulling the retrieved cape around him tightly, "I really must sleep. . . ."

He felt the young mrem watching. And then he was lost to his dreams.

Chapter 6

Ashre woke them before first light, a happy smile on his face.

"What's wrong?" Falon asked, wanting nothing more than to curl up on the floor and go back to sleep.

"We must leave before the others awake. It will be day very soon."

Falon had already decided to take the young mrem. However Ashre had kept himself alive so far, this was no way for him to grow up.

Though he certainly seemed able to take care of himself.

When they got to Tizare Falon would find someone to look after the kit.

And wouldn't they have their hands full! He smiled at *that* thought.

Ashre was beside Caissir, shaking him hard.

"Wake up, wake up!"

Caissir grunted and then, when Ashre kept up his shaking, he let fly a string of curses. When he finally blinked awake, a most foul look on his face, Falon was already standing and looking out the open door.

It was beautiful out there. The great desert was picking up just a hint of color and light from the brightening sky. The lesser stars had faded leaving only the very brightest sparkling in a deep blue sky.

"It's cold, Falon. Shut the door!" Caissir barked.

The highlander turned around. The wizard was still on the ground, pulling the smelly piles of material close to him. He didn't seem to mind their strong odor in this chilly air.

"Come, Caissir . . . Ashre says we should be off before daybreak."

Ashre was crouched by a small chest, picking through it . . . selecting the treasures that he'd bring . . . and those he'd leave behind. Caissir saw him staring.

"He's not coming, is he?"

Falon nodded. "He asked for our help, and he'll get it."

"By the All-Mother, now I know why the highlanders live in the hills. They're too stupid to come down to the cities."

Ashre shut his chest with a sharp snap and then popped up.

"I'm ready." Whatever he was bringing was packed in a small satchel slung over his shoulder. A long dagger was also strapped to his side.

Caissir was at least standing now, but still holding the warm rags close to him. "And what, no breakfast?"

"I know a place just outside of Fahl. We can find fruit there, and fresh water in the stream," Ashre said eagerly.

"I'm used to having breakfast on awakening."

Falon stepped outside, looking left and right, checking that they were indeed alone. But this small house—perhaps a cottage for guards—was off by itself, almost outside the city itself.

"Come, Ashre. Get us out of here."

He saw the young mrem run past him, grinning. The kit didn't look back.

By midday, Fahl was far behind them. And after a lunch of berries, not-yet-ripe boomu fruit, and icy water from the River Clawn (all of which Caissir grumbled about), they reached a main road.

Now they wouldn't be alone, thought Falon. He had already seen some solitary travelers making their way back from the city, and they passed a few farms getting ready for the harvest.

Ashre became oddly silent. Falon wondered what could be bothering him. When they met a caravan, he figured out what the problem was.

The caravan was not unlike the ones that occasionally

visited the mountains of his home. It was the only way his people could see, and trade for, the wondrous goods of the city. Much of what the caravans brought was just too beautiful and too unnecessary for the tough life on the hills. Still, the highlanders loved to come up and run their hands over the lustrous fabrics and handle the graceful cups and fine bows.

The caravan they ran into must have been returning from some such expedition.

Ashre, who had been acting very glum and quiet, hid behind Falon as soon as they came upon the caravan.

"Thank the Mother," Caissir said. "Now we can get a decent meal. Merchants like to travel on full bellies."

"With what?" Falon laughed. "We have no gold coins—" He felt Ashre pressing shyly against his side.

Is this the same tough little mrem who saved his life?

"I . . . I have some gold," Ashre said quietly.

Then Falon knew the reason. Fahl had been Ashre's city, his playground. Now, for the first time in his life, he was in a different world, a world where the strangers weren't thieves.

He's a bit like me, Falon thought. *Both of us leaving our homes behind.*

The merchants were squatting by the roadside, sipping some hot tea out of steaming mugs. Their wagons were heavily loaded with goods gathered from the small villages and distant cities. Rough tarps, tied down tight, kept the wagons covered, but Falon could see small chinks revealing a hint of silver, or some fine carved wood. Each of the three heavy wagons was pulled by a tired-looking uxan.

"Hello," Falon called out.

One of the merchants stood, his hand sliding close to his sword. Despite the heat, he wore layers of fine capes and sashes.

"Good day, friends." The merchant was cautious.

Ashre's hand dug into the rough material of Falon's kilt. Another merchant stood up, openly resting a hand on his sword.

"A bit jumpy . . ." The highlander said quietly.

"The trail's a dangerous place," Caissir said. "There are no kings, and no lords here. For these merchants to survive, they had best be prepared for anything."

The apparent leader of the merchants, a tall, dark-colored mrem with black eyes, came close to them. "You are heading to Tizare?"

"Yes," Falon answered.

Another merchant came beside the leader. "It's a closed city."

"Closed?" he looked at Caissir for explanation. His friend shrugged.

"Closed." The leader explained. "No one gets in unless they have official business. Only merchants licensed by the king are permitted inside. No wanderers permitted. It's much too dangerous."

Falon looked at Caissir. So, perhaps this had been his reason for sticking with the highlander. Without Falon's help, Caissir might be unable to get into Tizare.

"I—we are on official business. For Lord Rhow."

The leader looked at Falon and his party very carefully. "If that's the case, you'll have no problem. Things are getting very bad. There are rumors. More cities that may fall . . ."

Caissir stepped closer to the merchant. "Rumors? Of an invasion? Have any cities joined the Eastern Lords?"

The merchant shook his head. "No, not yet. But along the trails we hear stories of farms being raided, and border villages destroyed." He looked Falon right in the eyes. "Nobody knows how many agents have already secreted their way into the cities. The city of Ar itself might even be in danger."

There was a smell in the air, a delicate, sweet smell of fresh meat. Falon couldn't help but let his nostrils flare.

The leader couldn't help but notice. "You're hungry?"

"Most definitely," Caissir said.

"You're welcome to join us . . . and travel on to Tizare."

"Thank you." Falon smiled.

Caissir was already hurrying over to the fire and the crackling trumpeter fowl roasting above it.

Ashre had felt it—just at first, when they came upon the caravan. Something that scared him.

But when he went and stood next to Falon it faded. His

fear went away, and all he could think of was getting a piece of the fowl.

But it had been there. Like a breeze blowing off the desert, sending tiny grains of sand scratching against his house.

There was danger. Maybe not here. Maybe not now.

A new danger . . . stronger than bandits, stronger than those who chased him down the dark alleyways of Fahl.

But right now, all he wanted to do was eat.

"Tell me, what is your business in Tizare?" The caravan-master, called Krirr, poured himself another cup of tea.

Falon took a long sip of his tea, and thought of his answer. "I'm to help Lord Rhow with his herd-beasts. He's lost many to poachers, and more to disease. He thinks that the ways of the highlanders might help his stock."

Krirr arched an eyebrow. "I didn't know the lord kept animals. Where do his herds graze?"

Falon smiled good-naturedly, trying to keep any recognition of his blunder off his face. "I really don't know . . . I was just asked to come."

Krirr nodded. "And those two?" he said, indicating Ashre and Caissir, both still picking at the remains of the roasted fowl.

"The young one is an orphan. I hope to find someplace for him to stay. The other . . . well, he is my traveling companion."

Krirr looked right at Falon and lowered his voice. "Let me warn you, highlander. These are dangerous times. Just as I don't know you, I won't trust you. And I suggest that if you don't know those two you had best be careful." He dumped out his tea. "It grows late and we won't get to Tizare until tomorrow. That means a camp on the main road."

Krirr stood up and signaled his companions to begin leaving. Falon walked over to Caissir and Ashre.

"We're leaving."

"Well," laughed Caissir, "I've had my fill. They," he pointed at the merchants, "must be pretty nervous being on the road to just invite us along."

"Yes, wizard, I imagine they must be."

Caissir's expression changed. He stepped close to Falon.

"Look, Falon, I'd much appreciate it if you would not call me 'wizard'—at least until we are in the city. Merchants can be amazingly provincial about such things."

"Yes, Caissir." Falon grinned. "Your magic secrets are safe with me."

Falon looked down. Ashre's face was a greasy mess, the gray hair all dark and matted. Falon took a corner of his own kilt and gave the young mrem's face a swipe. "There! At least you look a bit less like some half-starved mynt."

The uxen were being pulled out onto the road, grunting their displeasure at being moved. The carts rattled noisily, and their axles creaked. Krirr took the lead uxan and pulled it hard, setting a brisk pace on the trail.

Caissir dallied behind, fiddling with his sash.

"Probably too full to fit anymore!" Falon called back at him.

And Ashre laughed.

A small, almost tentative giggle.

It was the *first time* Falon had heard Ashre laugh. And when was the last time the kit had had any cause to laugh out loud?

Falon put an arm around him.

The evening camp was no small thing. Once Krirr decided that enough ground had been covered, and before it grew too dark, he selected a flat, grassy spot just off the road. His fellow merchants, who were obviously old hands at this, brought the wagons around to form a wall. A fire— much bigger than the lunchtime blaze—was built.

One of the wagons held the food stores, and an amazing array of fruits, vegetables, small wheels of cheese, and strips of what looked like dried uxan. When great flagons of wine were brought out—three different varieties, at least —it was a meal Falon looked forward to.

But while they were eating a steady stream of travelers passed their cozy camp.

"Busy road," he said to Krirr, helping him arrange the platters for the meal.

"We're close to Tizare. Those mrem will march on, getting there before midnight. I don't like to push the beasts, though. They have journeyed long and hard."

Caissir had been pressed into hauling armfuls of wood to

the campsite, and he looked his usual discomforted self. Ashre was nowhere to be seen.

"Caissir . . . have you seen—"

"He's around the side . . . with the uxen," Caissir said, rolling his eyes.

Falon finished laying out the trays for the food, and then walked around the wagons to where the uxen were tied up.

Ashre was standing next to the lead beast, his head pressed close to its huge nostrils. Almost as if . . .

"Ashre . . . are you all right?"

Ashre nodded.

Falon waited for him to say something. What *was* he doing here with the animals?

But he just kept rubbing the beast's great head, his own small nostrils pressing against the uxan's dark hide.

"Come on then, let's get something to eat. Tomorrow we'll be at Tizare . . . and we'll find you some kind of home."

Falon walked back to the fire. The merchants were already eating, as was Caissir, and talking excitedly of the next day. He heard them mention the various wonders they were bringing to sell . . . and the prices they hoped to realize. After a while, Ashre wandered over, grabbed a plate, and ate.

But none too heartily.

Falon wished he knew more about young mrem. He was the only offspring of his parents. They had probably taken one look at his markings and said, "Enough."

But whenever he asked his mother why he never had any brothers or sisters, she always turned funny, busying herself with something in the house. At other times she'd say . . . *maybe if your father hadn't died* . . .

A father he never knew. There were pictures, drawn by the old female who collected gold pieces for her drawings. And the pictures looked nothing like him.

His friends—the ones that didn't join in teasing him about his swirled markings—sometimes had young kits for brothers and sisters. He saw how they liked to play, how the older ones made such a great fuss over them.

But Ashre was no young village mrem. He had taken care of himself for a long time. He had scavenged his own food and avoided the thieves who would have liked to catch him.

Perhaps he had even killed.

And now? Does he think of himself as mine? I just brought him out of Fahl to help him.

Not to adopt him.

He watched Ashre finish his small plate of food and then wander off.

"Stay near," Falon called quietly to the kit.

After the sumptuous dinner, he and Caissir helped clean the trays and prepare the site for the night.

"We'll post a guard," Krirr said. "It's too tempting for thieves, this close to the city."

Falon volunteered for a watch but Krirr smiled, and shook his head.

Don't trust strangers, Krirr had warned. And he followed his own advice.

Later, before going to sleep, Falon found Ashre curled up, sleeping near the uxen. He bent down, scooped him up, and carried him back to the warmth of the fire.

Chapter 7

▲──▲

Falon's first glimpse of Tizare was a great winding line, leading from what he imagined to be the gates of the great city up to surrounding hills.

"And what do we do now?" he asked Krirr.

"You get on line with the rest of us and wait. It moves quickly."

He seemed to be speaking the truth. Krirr was continually urging his uxen to pull the wagons a few steps forward. As they reached the crest of a small hill, Falon got his first glimpse of the walls of the city.

It was a fortress, nothing less than an immense walled city. Guards prowled the parapet, protected by shiny metal armor that caught the early morning sun. And just as many travelers were streaming out through the gates—moving much more quickly, though.

"It doesn't look particularly inviting."

"Security," Krirr snorted. "Actually the old king ordered the walls built. The city, for those that get in, is a friendlier place."

"I hope so. . . ."

The line moved briskly and, when Ashre asked if he could run up and down its length, studying the merchants and Tizarians on line, Falon gave his permission.

Amazing! One day the kit was throwing daggers at thieves, and the next he was asking permission to play.

I'm not your father, he wanted to say. But Ashre would learn that soon enough.

To hear Krirr describe it, Tizare was one of the lesser

cities. Lesser, but with wealth and resources that could only be guessed at. It was rumored among the nobles at court, Krirr said, that the Eastern Lords would surely attack Tizare before making a large-scale invasion on Ar.

The wall kept that fear in check, he had explained. Most of the city-dwellers were united behind a strong defense—meaning a strong army—for the city.

But Tizare was too lucrative to be left free from internal power struggles. The king played one faction against the other, always seeking to consolidate his hold over the independent nobles. When all else failed, he had his army.

And so did the nobles.

That was the part that really amazed Falon. Each noble maintained his own personal army. As long as he contributed soldiers and gold to the city's forces, a noble was free to organize whatever personal protection he or she wanted.

Falon had attempted to probe Krirr about Lord Rhow.

The nobles, Krirr informed him, kept their affairs secret. Whatever Falon would learn about Rhow, it would have to be firsthand.

The line meandered closer to the gates, and now he could see the purple-cloaked officials looking at papers and documents presented by the weary travelers.

Would they let him in? he wondered. Would the message in his cape get him past the wall of guards? He fingered it then, feeling the outline of the message sewn between the layers of material.

Caissir had been terribly quiet during the slow approach to the city's walls. Now, he slid next to Falon.

He was nervous, Falon thought . . . fidgeting, craning his neck to see how far they had left to go. Then he heard Caissir clear his throat.

"You'll take me in with you? I mean," he said, trying very hard to smile, "I had hoped that you'd help me. . . ."

"Don't worry." Falon smiled warmly. "You've earned your free passage. Just stick close and I'll say you're with me."

Caissir gave out a great sigh. "Thank you, Falon. I knew I could rely on you."

Ashre came running back. The entry gate was only a few steps away.

He looked worried.

"There are soldiers there!" he said breathlessly.

"Of course," Falon answered. "And there'll be more inside. Come now . . . stay close to us."

His explanation did nothing to change Ashre's expression. He looked nervously at the gate, and then back at Falon.

"We should wait . . . until later."

"I'm not waiting. It hasn't been easy getting here, Ash." He reached over and rubbed the kit's small pointy ears. "Just relax, and stay here."

Krirr's caravan was at the gate, and Falon watched the merchant present a thick stack of papers to the officials. Then he had to remove the tarps from the tops of the wagons. The guards came around, lifting up Krirr's treasures, poking around in the pile.

Caissir stood right beside him.

"You haven't been in any trouble here, have you, Caissir?"

"Trouble . . . me? Whatever gave you that idea?"

"Best to tell me now, Caissir. Before we try to get in."

Caissir licked his full lips. "All right . . . once, I was forced to leave. A small misunderstanding—I prophesied many offspring for a rich, young noble. Turned out that he didn't consort with females."

Falon laughed. "Can't imagine why he doubted your powers."

"Had me thrown right out of the city."

"Well," Falon said quietly, "if I'm your 'pass' in, Caissir, I want perfect behavior . . . at least till we're inside."

Krirr and his fellow merchants were cleared to enter, and the guards signaled Falon to approach. He looked at the grim-faced guards.

Though not armored, the guards wore flat dark blue uniforms and headgear that made their puffy, dull faces anything but inviting.

"Papers!" One of them barked.

Falon smiled, even as Ashre clutched his hand tight.

"I bring a message for Lord Rhow, sent from the North by Plano, once counselor to the lord. These two are traveling with me." He gestured at Caissir and Ashre.

The guard looked at him, then signaled to another, standing by a small wooden table. This new guard ambled over, a big fellow, Falon thought. He towered over all the other guards.

"You have . . . a message . . . for Lord Rhow?"

Falon nodded. He could hear Caissir's labored breathing.

"And just where is this message?"

Ashre gave a tug on his hand . . . urging him to pull away.

"In this cape, given to me by—"

But he never had a chance to finish his sentence. The oversize guard backed up and then, from just inside the massive wall, four soldiers dressed in a black material, with gleaming swords held in front of them, came out to Falon. They took his cape and expertly stripped them of their weapons.

"These personal soldiers of Lord Rhow will conduct you to his estate," the large guard announced.

But the swords were pointed directly at Falon's back, and at Ashre and Caissir.

Not the welcome Falon had expected at all. What happened to the swift trip to the lord's castle, maybe a sumptuous dinner . . . the rest of his gold, and then a chance for a new life at Tizare?

All of a sudden he felt trapped.

"I tried to tell you," Ashre said quietly.

Sure you did, kit . . . sure. . . .

He gave Ashre's hand a squeeze.

"Move," one of Rhow's soldiers growled. "To the left."

"Perhaps you'd like to leave the group, eh, Caissir?"

"No talking," another soldier ordered. Then he stuck the tip of his sword at the base of Falon's back, just above the tail.

Normally such rudeness called for a challenge—a duel—

And you'd do so well with them, eh, Falon? . . . You just have a bit of trouble keeping from striking first. Just a bit too eager to lash out without thinking. . . .

"I'm moving," he answered dully.

He squeezed Ashre's hand tight.

And together they marveled at the streets of Tizare as they were marched, at sword-point, to Lord Rhow.

Except that they weren't taken directly to Lord Rhow.

No, they made their way through the narrow side streets of the city, past merchants and shops offering things of which Falon didn't even know the purpose, let alone the names.

But even more than the shops, Falon was struck dumb by some of the more unusual 'services' offered. One alley-way offered a gallery of females on one side, and males on the other—all offering variations on the very act that Falon used to enjoy so much when he lived in the village.

Lately he had been subsisting on mere memories.

In fact, he had to admit, if he wasn't engaged in a forced march he might have been tempted to linger along this exotic row.

It was Caissir who told him that a fee was required for any such pleasuring.

"No!" he said. "You are fooling me!"

It was Caissir's turn to smile. "Maybe such sport is free where you come from, Falon, but here it's merely one more item of merchandise to be bought or sold."

Falon couldn't believe it.

"But how do those females restrain themselves . . . I mean, from their natural inclinations?"

Caissir laughed. "The power of the gold piece, my friend. It can move—"

"Quiet," one of the guards ordered. He gave Falon another jab at the base of his spine, and Falon turned and looked at the guard.

The guard wore heavy throat armor, and his peaked helmet covered much of his face.

But he saw enough. And he held his glance a second, letting him know that he'd remember.

The highlanders had an expression: Till another time.

If there was another time.

They left the provocative alleyway, and crossed a court-yard lined with noisy inns and restaurants. Some offered tables just outside, and Falon found that he and his companions were providing a show for the patrons.

"I could leave," Ashre said quietly.

Falon looked down at him. While still walking, they could talk. The hubbub was much too loud for them to be heard. "I could run—get away—" Ashre went on.

It might not be a bad idea, Falon thought. After all, he didn't know what kind of mess he had gotten the kit into. Considering his diverse skills and prowess, Ashre would probably do just fine in the great city of Tizare.

"No," he said. "Let's see what's in store for us. I've done the task assigned me, and I expect that this will all turn out all right."

"And I hope to the All-Mother that you're right," Caissir said, leaning close to him.

They left the courtyard, and went down a street of stark, gray-stone buildings. There were heavy metal gates at the doorways, and the only sound was their march-like steps. The street widened, before ending at a plaza. A few trees girded by strings of flowering plants blocked a clear view of what was ahead. But Falon saw enough to know that they had reached their destination.

The guards walked them around the small park, and right up to the impressive entrance to Lord Rhow's home.

It was a fortress. And it was a city within the city. It had its own wall, its own gate, its own army—who looked even more impressive than the soldiers of Tizare—and an absolutely beautiful castle. There were dozens of spires, one rising from another, higher and higher until Falon knew that it must be the highest structure in Tizare.

It all looked very festive, as if a great party was in progress.

But the guards escorted them through the entrance, with perfunctory nod to the soldiers who opened the heavy metal gate. And, just as quickly, they took them around to the back of the castle.

Fewer lights . . . less inviting.

The gates clanged shut behind them.

"Sorry, Ashre . . . I may have been wrong."

"Me, too. I should have let that Rar chew my tail up."

Another jab brought silence to Falon and his company. Not good, he thought. Though the mountains were cold and lonely, they offered a sense of security and routine. This adventure was beginning to look like a bad decision.

It grew even darker before he could see a small grid of light. There was a door, of sorts. Someone opened it up, with great creaking and squealing, at the sound of the guards' approach.

The smell that greeted him was incredible.

Like herd-beast offal, or the carcass of a dead mynt that had been lying in the sun too long.

"I think that you have the wrong idea," Falon said, attempting to stop the party on the first of what he imagined were many steps down. He turned to the guards. "Fact is, I have a very important message for your lord. So important that he will be most distressed to discover your rude treatment of us."

He thought he heard one of the guards snicker. That was before one of them kicked him just above the kneecap and he went tumbling down the first four steps.

"They're all yours," the guards said, laughing.

Falon looked up to see his new keeper.

He looked like a new species of mrem. About twice as big, with a head like the biggest grabble from the fall harvest. Even in the murky light the ugly fellow's teeth gleamed, and they looked as though they had been neatly filed.

"Get up!" the monster barked, giving Falon a solid kick to the head.

Another one for my list, Falon thought feebly. *Though maybe this brute should be left till I have my own army.*

Ashre had rushed to him, quickly raising his head off the damp stone.

"Get up," the keeper barked again. "Or this time I'll smash the kit."

Falon got to his knees, then stood up . . . dwarfed by the creature.

"Welcome to Lord Rhow's dungeon!" His laugh echoed, down, down, who knew, Falon thought, how far down.

"What is this?" he asked.

Caissir snorted. "It's called a cell."

"I know, but why have they locked us up?"

It was dismal here, worse even than the mountains during the cold season. A hole in the corner, a tray of water . . . on the ground! Other prisoners were moaning out of boredom or agony, or just from habit.

"Ashre . . . are you all right?"

They had put the kit in his own cell. Falon had expected

the kit to complain, to fight to keep them together. But he
went along rather complacently.

"Sure," he answered. "I'm just hungry."

"I'll second that," Caissir said.

Falon went to the bars. They were chunky, heavy things
that didn't even allow him to fit his hand through them.

He could see through them, and the keys to the cells
were hanging from a big spike, dozens of keys on a big,
black ring.

"So close . . ." he said quietly. It was, he figured, time to
stop relying on the good intentions of Lord Rhow.

He turned to face Caissir. The fat wizard, who so far had
been miserly in his display of his magical abilities, was
squatting in the corner, grooming himself.

"It occurs to me," Falon said, "that you keep hoping that
hooking up with me will help you. And it hasn't quite
turned out that way."

"Tell me about it, Falon." Caissir looked up at him, his
full face seeming angry for the first time in their friend-
ship. "You've been used, friend. Maybe you were sent as a
threat to Rhow—some clever, 'inside' message. Whatever
it was, you are expendable."

Falon nodded.

Then, he heard something. A rattle. The slight shift of
metal scraping against stone.

"What the—" Caissir started to stay.

Falon raised a hand.

More rattling and scraping, and then a great crash.

"The keys," he hissed to Caissir.

Was the guard back so quickly . . . perhaps with a nice
tray of warm food?

Or, more likely, had the lord decided how he wanted to
dispose of the interlopers?

But there were no footsteps! Just the eerie sound of the
ring . . . sliding across the floor.

He looked out of the cell.

And sure enough the key ring was inching its way across
the floor, almost like some wounded rodent dragging a
dozen legs behind it. Moving, sleepily, right towards
Ashre's cell.

He knew right away what was going on. Maybe, he
thought, he even had suspected it. Back at the gate, when

Ashre seemed to know, really know, that something wasn't quite right.

Poor kit, he thought. Probably didn't know what to think about himself. A secret that he shared only with the herd-beasts.

The keys were almost at his cell.

"Ashre . . ." he said quietly, looking for the word to reassure the kit that his secret was safe with him. "I—"

Now he heard footsteps.

Caissir stood up, and came over beside him. "Who is it?" he asked. "Someone's coming."

"No fooling." He watched the keys stop. "No more, Ashre. Wait till—"

The heavy wood door opened, and someone entered still hidden by the shadows and the thick bars. The newcomer stopped. Falon could see the boots. Someone bent down . . . and a delicate hand picked up the key ring—

So close to Ashre's cell!

Whoever it was kept the keys and walked over to Falon's cell.

She was young, this late-night visitor to the dungeon. Young, with a light golden fur that glistened even in this dank place. Her nostrils were delicate, but her lips were full, sensuous.

She was the most beautiful mrem he had ever seen.

"You are Falon," she said. He nodded. "And these two . . . are your companions?"

"Only in my travels," he offered.

She dangled the keys in front of the cell. "You are a magic user?"

He shook his head. Let the wizard take the blame for this one.

But she didn't pursue the question. "I am Taline, and I've been sent to bring you to Lord Rhow."

He heard Caissir let out his breath.

"We apologize for these . . . measures. But treachery is everywhere. We choose to make no mistakes. Now that we have checked out the papers you have brought from Plano, Lord Rhow is ready to greet you."

She found a key on the ring and opened the cell door. Then she let Ashre out. The young mrem ran to Falon's side.

"My companions will come with me," Falon said.

"Whatever . . ." Taline said distractedly. "But we must hurry. Lord Rhow is not used to waiting."

And I, Falon thought, am not used to dungeons.

But he said nothing, as he followed Taline out the door and up the massive stone steps.

Chapter 8

▲————————————————————————————▲

She moved with the sleekness of a hunter around curving stone steps, then down dark halls that seemed to lead nowhere, until she led them to a small staircase that took them to the chambers of Lord Rhow himself.

All of a sudden the air smelled clean, with a hint of rich food and perfume. They were in a small anteroom, softly lit by candles on the wall. The two guards at the finely carved doors stood perfectly still, almost relaxed.

Taline stopped and turned to him.

"These two will have to wait here. At least until the lord is done questioning you."

Falon turned back to Caissir and Ashre. "Go ahead," Caissir said, waving his hand. He looked relieved to be out of the belly of Rhow's dungeon. "I'll keep Ashre occupied. This isn't the first castle I've been invited to."

"Very well," Falon said. Taline's eyes glistened in the soft yellow light. If she was a hunter, he wished that he could be her prey.

She opened the double doors, and led the way in. He followed, and a matching set of guards closed the door behind him.

The room was overwhelming in its beauty. The walls were a pure white, with a delicate pattern of filigree etched in gold. Paintings, all of them depicting great battles, lined the walls. There was a chair—more of a throne— and sitting upon it had to be Lord Rhow himself.

But it was a table to the side that caught his attention.

It was filled with the most incredible array of food: great slices of pink meat, a fowl bulging with a steamy stuffing that smelled irresistible, and piles of fruit, some unknown to him. Creamy cakes filled any open space left on the table.

Falon couldn't help but inhale deeply.

"Hungry? Don't worry. All of that," Rhow indicated with a casual wave of his hand, "is for you."

"My companions—"

"Yes, they will be able to eat their fill too." He looked up, studying Falon for the first time. "After we've talked."

Lord Rhow was something different from what he had imagined. He had expected some overstuffed noble, someone who enjoyed the fruits of his wealth without stirring too far from his own chambers, leading the wonderfully indolent life of the rich and the lazy.

The lord looked anything but indolent. Despite being well advanced in age, his body had the suppleness of a young mrem. His eyes radiated an alertness that unsettled Falon. He felt exposed and defensive standing before this powerful figure.

"You found the message . . . from Plano."

Rhow laughed, and stood up, chuckling. He walked over to the table and poured two glasses of a purplish wine. He was still laughing gently when he brought the wine over to Falon.

"Yes, the message." Rhow handed him a goblet, and clinked them together. "Here's to the message."

Falon took a sip. It was strong, almost bitter—not at all like the sweet wines made from the gradle berries. It made his tongue tingle.

Taline had moved next to Rhow's chair.

Rhow came close to Falon, looked him in the eye. "There was no message. We had to, er, detain you below until I could make sure you were who you said you were. All that you carried, actually, was a description of yourself. It didn't, by the way, make any mention of traveling companions."

"I met them on—"

Rhow raised a hand. "I'm sure they're fine. Once I knew you were the same highlander sent by Plano, I had Taline bring you up quickly."

He saw the lord glance at Taline. Were they lovers? She

was certainly beautiful enough to be a noble's consort. But her face revealed nothing.

"There was no message, Falon, because *you* were the message." He made his way back to his chair.

"I don't understand. . . ."

"This is the beginning of the end—for the cities, for the highlanders, for all mrem. The way of life on our small planet is about to change forever. Either the Eastern Lords will succeed in their plans for conquest or we will slowly—and finally—wipe them out."

"Excuse me, but I don't understand. What you are saying may be true, but what does it have to do with me?"

"Heh, your highlander cousins ask much the same thing. The barbaric fools don't see that the cities protect them, keep their families safe."

Falon didn't like the way Lord Rhow sneered at the mention of the highlanders. But then, the highlanders sneered at the dandies that lived in the clutter and filth of the cities. It all balanced out.

"Trust is a rare commodity in Tizare, Falon. Outside of Taline, there are none I'd really trust in my whole court."

"Your army is surely loyal—"

"As long as they receive a paycheck. No, real trust is much too scarce. Which is why I had Plano search out someone from the hills . . . someone unknown and uncorrupted."

"How do you know I'm uncorrupted, or incorruptible?"

Rhow smiled. "Point well taken. But you aren't likely to have other allegiances. And I hope my offer will be sufficiently inspiring to win your loyalty—for a time."

"What do you want me to do?"

"I thought you'd never ask." Rhow moved from his chair and stepped to one of the great battle paintings. He touched the corner of the painting and a great map fell, covering the artistic mayhem.

"Our world . . ." the lord said, gesturing to the map ". . . the civilized parts, at least. We don't really know what's on the other side of the great desert to the east. Old tales and rumors are for the young. Here," he said, touching the map at various marked points, "are the major cities."

Falon was intrigued to see that he included Tizare.

"Here the lesser cities. And here, in the middle of the southeast desert, are the ruins of the holy city of Gfaar."

Falon stepped closer to the detailed map. It was the world, his world, rendered as he never saw it before. The cities, the great southern seas, even the immense desert—all unknown to him.

"Holy? Holy to whom?"

"A forgotten cult . . . before this 'one true faith' of the All-Mother," he said, not attempting to hide the sarcasm in his voice. "They openly practiced herd magic, even encouraged it. And it is said that they learned many secrets before being destroyed."

"By the Eastern Lords?"

Rhow walked away from the map. "That isn't clear. The city was destroyed, the cult's magic users killed, ending the cult. . . ."

Now Falon was right on top of the map, fingering it, as if trying to feel the presence of the names . . . Ar . . . Kazerclawm . . . Marirr. . . .

Rhow came up to him, and put a hand on his shoulder. "There's a book that's been hidden in the ruins for years. Hidden, that is, if it hasn't been discovered by the renegade mrem using it as an outpost. Perhaps the Eastern Lords have found the uxanhide book . . . perhaps not." Rhow turned him so that they were face to face, no more than inches away. "It's called *The Song of the Three Moons,* and I want you to get it for me. It may be vital to the future of the mrem."

Almost without thinking, Falon shook his head.

It hadn't been easy getting here, a journey through 'civilized' lands. What would it be like facing the desert, the unknown? Renegade mrem and liskash could be the least of his problems. There were the terrible storms, and the sand weevils . . . and who knew what else?

No, it didn't take him long at all.

"I don't think I'm interested. I think I'd rather take the gold I'm entitled to and—"

"Then I'll go alone." Taline moved for the first time, away from the chair.

"No!" Rhow said quickly. "It's much too dangerous—"

She stepped forward. "Are there others that you trust? If not, then there's only me."

She looked at Falon then, a long lingering stare that

made his skin prickle. Her whole body was tense, like a bow pulled taut.

Falon didn't doubt her ability to take care of herself.

"Let me," she continued, walking past Falon as if he wasn't there, "have the weapons I need, perhaps an uxan and a cart. I'll bring Anarra."

Rhow stormed over to Falon. "You see!" he bellowed. "My own daughter is willing to risk her life. You—you're just another stupid highlander."

His daughter! thought Falon. He had read *that* scenario wrong.

Rhow raised his fist to Falon, who wondered what exactly he had done wrong this time. "I could throw you in my dungeon and forget the key. You, and your companions. No one would care."

Quite possibly true, Falon thought. And he found something else stirring in his breast. A not exactly unfamiliar sensation.

He felt shamed.

Admittedly he had only bargained for a quick run off the mountain, maybe an extended stay in Tizare. Anything would be better than the smell of the herd-beasts on a warm, humid night, or the cold winds.

Now, there was this. A quest, noble but obviously quite dangerous. And if he should pass on it, the daughter, no timid flower, seemed more than eager to carry on. Perhaps Lord Rhow would even make good on his threat to lock them up again.

And he thought of the keys, sliding on the stone floor . . . towards young Ashre.

"I'll go," he said quietly.

Rhow grinned. "Splendid. I'll have you outfitted with the best—"

Taline stepped between them. "There's no need, father. He is just another spineless one, more afraid of your dungeon than the desert."

"No," Falon said quietly, this time giving Taline the benefit of his no-nonsense eyes. "It is foolish to send you into the desert alone."

She turned from Falon, and walked close to her father. "He'll probably run away just as soon as we're well away from the city."

"Perhaps . . ." Rhow said thoughtfully.

Falon had to admit it didn't sound like a bad idea.

"And perhaps not. I trust Plano's judgment in selecting him. He made his way through some rough country." He stepped close to Falon. "If you bring the book back you can have any place in my . . . household . . . that you desire."

Was he imagining things or did the noble lord's voice catch on the word 'household'? And what other word almost tumbled out?

"If you insist," Taline said.

"I do. We will get you outfitted and you can leave tomorrow."

So much for his sampling the delights of Tizare. He remembered, then, his two companions just outside the heavy double doors.

"What of my friends?"

Lord Rhow had replenished his cup, and was back on his chair. "Tell me about them."

"The chubby one presents himself as a wizard—"

"A magic user?" Rhow said, looking over his cup.

Falon smiled. "I said he presents himself as one. His real abilities lie in more earthly pursuits."

"Do you wish him to accompany you?"

Good question, Falon thought. But at least he felt he could trust the timid Caissir. "I do. But I don't think he'll want to come."

Rhow laughed. "Don't worry about that. I'll make the option unusually attractive . . . and the alternative remarkably painful. What of the kit?"

"He's an orphan. His mother was killed in the last battle for the garrison town of Fahl."

Rhow slurped the wine, draining his goblet.

He was not particularly moved, Falon saw.

"I had hoped that there would be some agency in Tizare, some place for the homeless. . . ."

The lord went back to the table, pulled at some reluctant meat, and then sloppily refilled his goblet. "Yes, we have workshops and factories where the young can earn their keep and, if they're lucky, learn a trade."

Falon cleared his throat. "That's, er, not exactly what I had in mind. I wanted to find someone to take care of him, a family—"

Taline snorted, and walked over to the map.

Rhow, his mouth full, just shook his head. "We have nothing like that. Best to turn him over to one of Tizare's factories. They employ many bastard mrem."

"He's not a bastard!" Falon said, a bit more loudly than he intended.

"Are you sure that he's not a mother in disguise?" Taline laughed.

What a bunch of sweethearts, Falon thought. In his village, an orphan would be loved and cared for by many families, perhaps even more than their own kits. Why should he risk his life for them, or their precious book, or this city of Tizare?

The noble sensed his confusion. "Forget this kit. Perform this service for all mrem." Rhow eyed him carefully. "Take your destiny into your hands."

And then, Falon thought of the answer. Foolish, in some respects, and certainly dangerous. But he could use all the allies he could get.

Especially, yes, especially one so powerful.

"I'll take him with me then."

"What!" Taline shouted, turning sharply on her heels. "What nonsense is this?"

Now it was Falon's turn to raise his hand, silencing her. "Ashre has survived among bands of thieves since his mother was killed. Running, stealing, perhaps even killing. There's no one else I'd prefer at my side in a fight. And there's this: If he cannot come with me, then I will not go."

Taline walked over to her father, her whispers hissing loudly.

"So be it." Rhow said, waving his daughter away. "You travel at dawn. Taline, Anarra, you . . . and your two companions. May the All-Mother protect such a motley party. Now let us call your friends in and begin planning your journey."

They were in Falon's sleeping quarters: a large bedroom that featured a massive fireplace (already scenting the air with burning parra wood), a bed that could have accommodated the three of them and twice as many more, and a huge couch covered with the most incredibly shiny material, a deep turquoise and laced with gold threads.

Ashre was thrilled at the turn of events. Besides bouncing on the massive bed, he kept talking of the wondrous adventures that lay ahead. He seemed ecstatic at the possibility of danger.

Caissir, as Falon had expected, was another story. At first he had tried politely declining. And even when Lord Rhow kept upping the amount of gold pieces that would fall to him, Caissir kept smiling and saying no. Finally Rhow, with a smile as warm as the fat wizard's, told him that there were, unfortunately, rather strict regulations regarding the licensing of magic users. A stay, of undetermined length, in the dungeons would be the only recourse. At least until the necessary paperwork was taken care of.

And who knew how long that would be?

Falon had to hide his face. He just loved the way Caissir's fur bristled when he was angry. Later, he commiserated with the wizard, while all the time deftly admiring Rhow's straightforward skill in pulling the party together.

Taline had retired, rather quickly Falon thought. She was off to check the armor, weapons, and pack wagon. But more likely, she seemed to have had enough of Falon. She was totally loyal to her father . . . and she simply didn't trust Falon at all.

With good reason, Falon thought, stepping to the great glass windows of his room.

The windows were opened just a bit, and he gave them a push, letting the cool night air fill the room. The largest moon of Mrow, in its first quarter, was just beginning to rise above the city. This air was not the clean mountain air he was used to.

"Do tell him to stop, Falon. He'll break the bed and Lord Rhow will deduct it from our share of the gold."

"Let him play," Falon said quietly.

Play . . . Is that something the gray mrem even knows? Daggers, thievery, rutting (of every kind) . . . yes, these he knew. But play?

Unlikely. And sooner or later Falon would have to talk to him.

They had a magic user in the group.

But it was not Caissir.

And that secret of Ashre's might prove valuable in the hard days to come. He felt a bit selfish at the speculation. Still, he was somehow glad he would see more of the kit.

He turned back to his two friends.

Chapter 9

Morning came too soon.

Though it was nice waking up in a soft bed, with the heavy blankets pulled tight, it was still dark when some barrel-chested soldier came by, kicked the bed, and announced to Falon that it was time to leave.

He also deposited a tray of fruit that was apparently designed to substitute for breakfast.

Ashre came into the room, munching purple berries.

"Is Caissir up?" Falon asked groggily.

"I don't know."

Then Caissir strolled in, looking even more out of sorts than Falon felt.

"You *didn't* tell me we were traveling at night. Why, I could easily sleep till midday."

"I'm sure you could."

Their wake-up guard reentered the room. "The lord's daughter is expecting you immediately at the stables."

"Oh, she is? Well, you tell her—" Caissir began.

"That we'll be right there," Falon finished. The guard left. "Let's try to start this trip on as good a footing as possible."

Caissir came by, and spoke softly, for Falon's ears only. "If you ask me, we're already off to a bumpy start."

Then he turned and went to his own room to get dressed.

In minutes, Falon was leading them through the labyrinthine halls of the castle, pausing now and then to ask some equally sleepy guard just what the quickest route to the stables might be.

After a few wrong turns that led them through the main kitchen, and past the main banquet hall, Falon finally found the wooden staircase that led to Rhow's stables.

Taline barely turned at their arrival.

"Can we help?" Falon asked pleasantly.

"Just pick up your bundles of gear from the back of the stable."

She was fixing a harness to a mammoth uxan, assisted by an almost equally mammoth she-mrem. There was a maze of straps and belts that crisscrossed the beast's great midsection. The cart was just behind them, its rigging poles ready to be attached to the harness.

Falon shrugged and walked to the back of the storeroom. The three bundles were large and, he discovered, incredibly heavy.

"What in the world is in these?" Caissir blustered.

"Armor. Swords. Ropes. Medicine. Food." It was Taline, standing at the opening to the storeroom. The sky had picked up pinkish highlights, and first light couldn't be long in coming.

"I can't move it," Ashre said. Falon ran a hand through the young mrem's fur.

"No problem, Ash. I doubt you'll need all that—"

"Anarra and I have packed enough material so that any one of us could survive alone."

Caissir stepped close to Falon and whispered. "Sorry to be complaining so much, but that big old bag isn't going with us, is she?"

As if in answer, Anarra—who looked like she could hoist both Falon and Caissir with one arm—appeared in the doorway. She was incredibly furry, and Falon wondered why she didn't trim her hair like the females in his village.

But he had a vague idea that she didn't do a lot of things that the females in his village did.

"Anarra is in charge of the cart and the uxan. She also will have responsibility to see that you know how to use what's in your packs. Now, load up and we'll start."

"Best not to get off on the wrong foot, eh?" Caissir muttered. "I want you to know, Falon, that I haven't felt this— this—discomfited since I was a schoolboy in Marirr."

Falon grinned, and picked up Ashre's pack. The young

mrem seemed undisturbed by the trip ahead, or the company. Already he was at the uxan . . . setting Falon's mind to wondering just what strange talents Ashre possessed.

He threw the packs in the back of the cart. Anarra had the cart hitched up, and she patted the bulbous head of the uxan.

"Probably whispering sweet nothings in its ear . . ." Caissir said, hurling his pack on top.

"Ready?" Taline asked.

Falon nodded. And, as Taline turned sharply and led the way ahead, he found himself admiring her shape.

None too friendly, but she was one taut little mrem.

Their first stop of the day nearly proved to be their most disastrous.

The lumbering party reached the crest of a hill long after Ashre had run back and told them that the road ahead was impassable.

Anarra chuckled, amused that Falon would even listen to the young mrem.

But as soon as they reached the crest it was obvious that they did, indeed, have a problem. Some recent landslide had covered the meandering road with rocks and rubble of every size. It would take hours to travel the road with the uxen—if it was possible at all.

There were, Falon thought, only two good options. Taline and Anarra were having their own private conversation about the predicament, and he waited until they came to him.

"Well, that does it, eh, Falon?" Caissir said. "Let's pack it in and get on with the rest of our lives."

But Ashre—always hovering by, excited—gave Falon's hand a tug. "No, we *can* do it, Falon. There *must* be some way."

Taline walked over to Falon. "Anarra says we can lift the cart over the worst parts, and make our way down the road."

"Oh, is that what she says? And is she planning on doing all the lifting herself?"

The uxan gave out a great low groan. Maybe he knew what was up, Falon thought.

"No," Taline said, a bit less confidently now, Falon observed. "We'll all help. It shouldn't be too bad—"

"No," Falon laughed. "Not if you want to spend the night and a good part of tomorrow making your way down the mountain."

Anarra stormed over. "What's the problem? We have to get moving."

Taline's eyes seemed to radiate less of her usual arrogance. "He says it will be too difficult."

Anarra shrugged. "There is no other choice."

Falon stepped closer to Anarra . . . and actually had to look up at her. Best to let her know now that he wasn't going to spend their entire journey being pushed around —no matter how big she was.

"There are other options—two that I can think of. And I haven't even asked my friends here for their ideas."

He waited. Let her ask, he thought.

"And?" Taline said petulantly.

"We could follow the slope down the valley. It should eventually level out enough for us to get the cart across."

"Too much time," Anarra barked.

"Possibly," Falon agreed, pasting a good-natured smile on his face.

"The second choice?" Taline finally asked.

"The slope is steep, but fairly straight. A few boulders, perhaps, some loose rock. But it isn't nearly as obstructed as the road . . ."

He ran his fingers through his whiskers.

"What are you proposing?" Anarra said, growing angry with his game.

"One of us leads the uxan straight down the slope, running it as fast as it can go. And, if it doesn't lose its footing— and the cart holds together—we can have all the packs down to the valley in a matter of minutes. The rest of us can take a more leisurely pace."

"You're crazy!" Anarra said, bringing her brown furry face right up to him. She licked her lips as though she wanted to take a big bite of him. "Who'd be crazy enough to do that?"

"I would." He almost surprised himself in his eagerness. Taline said nothing.

Anarra exploded. "Just another highlander fool! Why, the—"

"You'd do it?" Taline said quietly.

"Rather than spend two days working it down? Sure, of course I would. I've run whole herds down mountainsides just for fun."

Taline was studying him carefully. With a new appreciation, he hoped. Perhaps, he thought, they need not be such mortal enemies on this adventure.

"It won't work," Anarra announced. "The beast will trip on its legs, the cart will smash into it. We'll lose every-thing—"

"Perhaps." He grinned. "Perhaps not."

Taline turned away, another glance down the hill, then at the road.

"Do it, highlander. Let's see if you're as crazy as you sound."

Now Falon looked at the slope more carefully. Had he been a bit too confident? Could the cart stand up to all that bouncing around?

Would the poor uxan's heart burst as it galloped down the hill?

Questions soon to be resolved, thought Falon.

"Help me tie everything down as tightly as possible."

Anarra didn't move, but Taline came over and tugged at the lines, making the web of ropes hold the assorted packs as tightly as possible.

"Good," he said, favoring Taline with a smile. "Let's check the undercarriage of the cart."

They both crept down, and peered under the wooden cart.

They were close to each other, their fur almost touching as he pulled at the bolts and heavy metal pins that kept the wheels in place on the axle. He breathed deeply, and smelled a rich, musky odor.

He looked at Taline, but she turned away . . . embar-rassed by the telltale signs of her unplanned excitement.

The body doesn't lie, he thought. And he purposely let himself press against her firm body.

"Oh, excuse me. Narrow working space and all that."

She turned to him, her eyes glowing, almost feverish. "It . . . it looks fine," she said, the tip of her tongue touching her lips.

"Yes, it does," he said, grinning, not talking about the cart at all. "I'd better get started."

He slid out from under the cart and walked over to the large Anarra, who was pouting off to the side.

"Is there anything I should know about the uxan?"

She looked at him, an ugly glance that let him know that while he might be making a new friend with Taline, he already had one good enemy.

"Yes," she spit. "Her name is Daynia, and she hates to run. And if you kill her, I'll kill you."

"Thanks for the help," he said.

Caissir was grooming himself near the back, well away from the ledge. Ashre, though, stood right on the precipice, jumping up and down, unable to contain himself.

"Are you ready?" Ashre called out. "Are you going to do it now?"

"Yes," Falon said. "Stay up here near the others until I'm all the way down—if I get down."

Finally he walked over to Daynia, whose strong odor belied such a dainty name. "Okay, honey, it's you and me now. Just don't decide to stop on the hill." He patted the rough head of the beast. "All set?"

The uxan raised its head, and shook it.

Too bad, Falon thought.

He grabbed a strap of the harness.

He pulled the uxan forward, and it snorted and whipped its head left and right, snorting out its protest. Falon tugged harder.

"She's no fool, highlander," Anarra called out.

"Come on!" he yelled at it. Then, more soothingly. "Come on, Daynia, let's get down the hill. That first step is the roughest. . . ."

But the beast actually backed up, digging its heavy hooves into the sandy soil.

Falon dug his own feet into the sand, and threw his whole body weight into a massive tug over the precipice. But the only thing that gave way was his hands, as they started to slip along the sweat-coated strap.

Ashre came trotting over, and stood just behind Falon.

"Get—away—Ash—This thing may start to move any—"

"No, it won't," Ashre said, almost chucking. "She's not going anywhere." Then, more quietly, "Unless I help."

Falon looked down at the small kit. The tufts of gray fur

above his eyes seemed to wrinkle and twitch. The uxan reared around and looked down at Ashre. It roared.

"She doesn't want to do it," Ashre said.

"Tell me something that I don't know."

The puffy milky eyes of the beast rolled around, even as the beast went from looking at Ashre, then the slope, then Ashre again.

"Get ready," Ashre said. "I think she's ready to try it."

But without warning the uxan grunted and pulled forward. And suddenly Falon was holding onto the harness strap and being pulled down the hill. He lost his footing on the loose sand and stone, but quickly scrambled to his feet. The cart reached the edge and tumbled down, after the uxan.

Not bad, Daynia, keep this up and we'll be down the hill in no time.

Falon had to run to keep up with the uxan. Its short, stubby legs seemed surprisingly surefooted on the slope, and it charged down the hill as if that were the most natural thing in the world.

Just what, he wondered, had Ashre told it?

Then the first bit of trouble began. The slope was covered with a fine, almost silty dirt that slid away from him as soon as he stepped onto it. The animal was leaping down the hill, galloping almost, when its two front legs collapsed on it. The uxan crashed to its knees, pulling Falon down.

He tumbled right next to the great black belly of the beast.

But the creature just kept sliding.

Falon was sliding down now too, the rocks and sand digging through his kilt, shaving off his back fur. He was too stunned to notice the pain. The cart seemed okay, bouncing merrily down the hill, up into the air, and then plopping down onto the sand.

The uxan was sliding down, and Falon knew that its underside was being ripped up too. He twisted around, and kicked madly to get to his feet.

"Get up," he screamed at the uxan. He ran alongside it, hearing it scream out its terror. "Get up, you stupid animal!"

Then, as if it realized that to continue grinding down the slope would kill it, the uxan pushed up with its front legs. The first time it just collapsed again. But then it got up on its front legs, then its back legs, and ran wildly, bellowing, all the way to the bottom.

Falon let go of the harness as soon as the ground leveled out. He rolled onto his stomach.

Daynia kept running, as if unsure that the hill had indeed ended.

Falon lay there alone, his nostrils pressed close to some pungent krarl grass. It felt rough and scratchy—even the herd-beasts wouldn't eat it. But he didn't move, and just lay there waiting for everyone else to come down the mountain.

Anarra was first down the hill and walked past Falon without saying a word. She went directly over to Daynia, and began washing the animal's wounds.

But then Taline was down.

"Ashre is helping Caissir down. Are you badly hurt?"

She knelt down and put her fingers to his open cuts and tears.

"Oww. I'd rather you didn't touch me . . . there."

"I'll get some ointment," she said.

He looked up the hill. Caissir was having a worse time getting down the slope than the uxan. Every few feet, one of the wizard's legs would buckle and he'd go tumbling down into the sand. Ashre was right beside him, though, pulling Caissir up after every fall.

Taline returned, a metal tin in her hands. She unscrewed the lid.

"This will clean out the wounds, and help them heal."

She scooped out a gob of the orange gel and brought it to his back. "Does it sting now?"

He turned his head slightly and grinned at her.

"Not at all. I didn't expect that you were the nurse on our trip—"

"I'm not. Anarra is trained, but she is attending the uxan."

He looked right in her golden eyes. "I'd rather have you anyway."

That seemed to make her feel uncomfortable. She quickly coated the rest of his wounds, and then sealed the tin. "Keep them open to the air. I'll have Anarra take a look at them, when we camp tonight."

She hurried away.

Ashre came over to him, and crouched down very close. "Did you get badly hurt?"

Falon stood up, his legs wobbly. "Not as badly as I could have been if that monster had fallen on me." He ruffled the kit's fur. "Nothing to worry about, Ash. Tell me . . . what on earth did you tell the uxan to get it moving?"

An impish grin bloomed on the kit's face. "You know I spoke to her?"

"I've been around herd-beasts for a long time."

"Well, I just said that we were going to cut her up for dinner if she didn't go down the hill." Ashre laughed and then looked off into the distance. "They're signaling us, Falon. I think they're ready to move on."

"Yes, I suppose they are." He took a step, and he felt the cuts on his back stretch painfully. "Stay with me, Ashre. I may need a hand staying on my feet."

He walked slowly, and listened to the kit describe how wonderful it had been to watch his great and wild run down the mountain slope.

Chapter 10

▲————————————————————————————————————▲

Taline called a stop to the day's journey just as the sky turned a deep blue and the first stars made an early appearance.

Caissir helped Falon gather some firewood, as instructed by Anarra.

"I thought they were going to keep us at it till the twin moons rose," he complained to Falon.

"The more miles we travel each day, the sooner we'll get back," Falon said.

Caissir came close to him.

"I have news for you, Falon. I'm leaving our little group tomorrow. Right after lunch."

Falon looked over at Ashre. Taline, while not overtly friendly to any of them, seemed to be taking an interest in the gray kit. She had him slicing up chunks of vegetable and meat for a soup. Anarra was, as usual, tending to her beloved Daynia.

"Don't do it, Caissir. I need you with us."

"Aye, that you do, Falon. But I have other places to spend my allotment of lives. I hate to say this, my friend, but I was better off before I met you."

Falon laughed. "You're probably right there. Though I imagine Rhow will reward us handsomely when we return with the book."

"*If*, Falon, and I don't want to be around to see whether you make good on that 'if.' "

Falon reached out and patted the wizard's shoulder. "I'll miss you, Caissir. Do what you must."

Caissir grinned at him, obviously pleased to be relieved of his burden.

"Thank you. Now, why don't you . . ." The wizard's voice trailed off.

Why don't I leave too? thought Falon. *A good question. Except that my life doesn't particularly have anything better to offer. If I leave I can add being an outcast from Tizare to my résumé. I agreed to this task. If my word becomes worthless then my honor will truly be gone.*

Besides, he thought with a smile, *I'm curious. Whatever happens, it can't help but be more intriguing than watching the herd-beasts chew their cud.*

And there's Taline . . . perhaps a not totally hopeless situation.

"Don't you have enough wood by now?" Taline shouted at them.

"Come, Caissir, it's time to get dinner started."

Taline prepared a delicious soup that had everyone huddled close to the fire long before it was ready. She tasted it, and she let Ashre take an experimental slurp, but everyone else had to wait until the moment she declared it ready.

Then, under a brilliant field of stars and the just-rising twin moons, she served the rich soup to a chorus of grateful lip-smacking sounds.

"This is," Caissir proclaimed, "the best soup that I've ever had, anywhere."

Taline laughed—the first time he'd seen that, thought Falon. "That's just the hunger of marching on the trail. Anything would taste good now."

Anarra, finally done with ministering to her beast, squatted right next to Falon. She dug out a loaf of brown bread from her pack, tore off a large chunk, and passed it to Falon.

Without so much as a look or a nod.

Ashre was curled against Falon, every day growing more like the sleepy-eyed kits he'd see at village meetings, all cozy and warm against their mothers.

Taline attacked her soup as eagerly as any of the rest. But she looked *very* beautiful, Falon noticed, as the yellow and blue of the fire caught fine highlights in her fur. When the peace and quiet of well-fed stomachs settled over the group, she said quietly, "We'll leave tomorrow, early. We should reach the border of the desert by night-fall. And," she said, standing up, "if we're lucky we'll reach the ruins by the afternoon of the next day."

"If the weevils don't get you . . ." Caissir muttered.

"If the weevils come, we'll be ready for them." She stretched, reaching for the sky, her lean body becoming one long golden line pointing to the zenith. "Falon—Ashre —you're on cleanup."

While everyone retired to their private grooming, Falon and Ashre cleaned the bowls and plates with water brought by Anarra.

"You've been quiet today, Ash. Missing Fahl?"

The gray kit was sloshing water onto the soup bowls. "Miss Fahl? Not at all. This . . ." he looked around at the fire, the wagon, the other travelers, "is like being in a family. Not that I know what *that's* really like. But this is something like it, isn't it?"

Falon laughed. "Something. Sure it is." Then he turned serious again. "Ash, there's something I need to talk with you about."

Ashre continued his sloshing and rubbing, but his body was rigid, alert.

"Yesterday, when we were in the dungeon, the keys moved—"

Ashre turned to him, a terrible fear filling his face. "You won't tell the others, will you? I thought we should escape —I was trying—"

Falon went to him. "There's nothing wrong with it, Ash. It's a good thing, it's—"

"No! I've heard the others, the thieves at Fahl talk about magic. It's something only for the animals."

Falon shook his head. "No. You are proof enough that that's not true. Whatever powers you have are good. They are yours, and you are supposed to have them. But you're right—for now—to keep them secret."

He let Ashre think about his words a moment. Then he added, "I want you to trust me, Ash. Trust, and tell me. No one else will know, unless you want them to."

Ashre put down his bowls, letting them tumble into the big pot of water. "My mother talked to me about it . . . but I was young. . . ."

And what was he now? Falon thought. An old mrem?

"When she was gone, I just used it when I had to."

Falon patted him. He looked around the camp, checking that they were, indeed, away from anyone's hearing. "Tell me, Ash . . . what can you do?"

The kit bit his lip. "I can move things . . . sometimes . . . small things. But it hurts to do it. And I know what the animals are thinking"—he giggled—"when they think anything. And I can tell when something bad is going to happen—"

"That's how you saved me at Fahl, when that dagger was coming right at me."

Ashre smiled shyly. "Yes, I knew that was going to happen. Usually, I just get a feeling that something might happen. It's like a tightening in my stomach."

Ashre stopped, and reached into the now-cool water, digging out some more bowls to be scrubbed.

"That's it?" Falon asked.

"As far as I know." Ashre looked up at Falon. "Now, it's our secret, right?"

"Right. Except, if you get any of those feelings, you'll be sure to tell me."

Ashre nodded.

Ashre watched Falon walk away.

He scuttled close to the fire, all alone, with just the stars and Daynia for company. A few large nightwigs flew near the fire, only to be quickly snatched from the air by a big-eyed kolow perched on a tree, finding its hunting made easy by the glow of the fire.

He hadn't told Falon everything.

That would have been *too* hard.

He didn't tell him that there was danger ahead.

No. That wouldn't have been possible . . . not with it coming from so *many* different places.

What could he say? That there were bad things ahead?

He knows that, Ashre told himself. *And when the time comes, he'll do what he has to do.*

And I'll do what I must to save him.

Falon found Taline on top of a smooth boulder that rose above the grassy plain. It was bright out now, the twin moons just above the horizon, casting their yellowish glow on her.

"It's beautiful out here," he said, startling her.

She turned, her hand paused at her face, smoothing her fur there, thinking. . . .

"Yes," she said flatly.

"Do you mind some company?" he said, strolling over to her boulder.

"Suit yourself."

Not exactly an invitation, he recognized. Still, she hadn't exactly told him to leave.

"I'm sorry," he said quietly, "that you don't want me helping. Your father must think he needs help—"

"My father doesn't have faith in me." She turned, her eyes glowing. "Not that he trusts you . . . a stranger . . . a highlander. But it was Plano's idea, and my father went along with it."

Falon risked sitting down on a corner of the boulder. "And why isn't Plano in the city to help the lord?"

She turned away. "There was a problem. Plano . . . disagreed with some of my father's proposals in the Tizarian Senate. Rather than stay and oppose my father, Plano accepted his retirement."

"Sounds like he's been exiled."

"What would you know of such things? He is a loyal and trusted counselor to the family."

"And how did you get to be your father's right-hand mrem?"

She stood up and jumped off the boulder. "Because I'm his new counselor. His personal army takes its orders from me, second only to my father."

She started to walk away.

He couldn't help but admire the way she looked sauntering away under the bright light of the twin moons.

"And do you ever disagree with your father?"

She stopped, turned, and looked.

"Never," she hissed. She spun, and then kept walking away.

True to her word, Taline had the party moving while it was still dark, a misty cool morning.

The low scrubby grass grew more lush as they reached

the Arrian River basin. And it grew hot, a moist, prickly heat that had them all stripped down to the smallest of kilts. Even Ashre seemed enervated by the glaring sunlight.

The land they moved through, though, was beautiful. The lush parra trees were unlike anything that Falon had ever seen in the mountains of his homeland. The leaves were immense, rendering the nearby woods a dark, almost sinister shadowy green.

But they stayed on the overgrown trail, the uxan struggling to move the cart through the tall grass which wrapped around the wheels. It snorted and a huge ball of foam gathered at its mouth.

Anarra saw that it was constantly supplied with water, and soaked its back.

"I hope she's not so free with water when we hit the desert."

"She knows what she's doing." Taline said.

The stop for lunch was barely a stop at all. Taline dug out some stale, crusty bread to be eaten with sliced cheese that was a poor substitute for the stouter stuff Falon used to make for himself. After a few gulps of water, Taline gave the order to start moving.

Falon looked at Caissir.

Besides his continual lingering at the back, he gave no indication that he was about to leave. Ashre was with the wizard. The kit enjoyed listening to him carry on about this great city, or that great king, or the wonders of the southern seas.

Then Ashre trotted up to Falon.

"What's wrong, Ash?"

Ashre shrugged. "Caissir said talking to me was tiring him out. Sent me up to be with you."

It's now, Falon thought. *He must have made a small pack for himself, secreted somewhere inside the folds of his kilt.*

They came to a bend in the road.

"I have to—er, you know . . . relieve myself," Caissir called out. Ashre giggled.

Taline, at the lead of the party, right beside the uxan, turned and yelled, "Should we stop and wait?"

"Oh, no," Caissir yelled back. "I'll attend to my affairs and catch up. No problem . . . you just go on ahead."

Ashre grabbed Falon's wrist, and looked up at him.

His eyes registered alarm, concern. . . .

Falon shook his head.

"Don't worry, Ash." He winked. "He'll be fine." Falon leaned close to the kit. "He just won't be with us," he whispered. "That's all."

The kit looked sad, and Falon gave him his best cheer-up smile. "Everything will be fine."

They reached a small hill, no challenge for the uxan or even their tired bodies.

Taline brought the cart to a halt.

"Where's your friend . . . where's this Caissir?"

Falon looked behind them. The grassy trail stretched to the horizon, and there was no one following.

"He's probably run off, the scared old fool," Anarra grumbled.

Taline, her eyes afire, ran up to Falon. "Is that true? Has he left?"

"Probably."

"Probably? Probably! Tell me what you know."

Falon stroked his whiskers, enjoying Taline's consternation. "I know he didn't want to go into the desert and explore some ruins for your Lord Rhow."

"Dishonorable renegade!" Anarra said. "Should I go get him back?"

"No," Taline said. "It would take too long, too much time." She looked right at Falon. "You knew about this, didn't you?"

But Falon just shrugged, as if he didn't know what she was talking about.

He walked up to Anarra, who started the uxan up the small hill.

He could feel Taline's eyes boring into the back of his head.

They reached the edge of the desert near sunset. And they found a farmhouse.

It was a small, ramshackle building with a grassy thatched roof and two small windows. Surrounding it was a wide field filled with dark strands of the grass used to make the brown bread found everywhere in the region. There was a small shed at the back, holding perhaps an animal or

two, and a small enclosed garden where Falon was sure
he'd find a few rows of vegetables.

This all was watered by the small stream that snaked its
way past the farm.

And, just as obviously, it was about as close to the end of
the world as one could hope for.

The farmer, standing stock-still in the center of his field,
had seen them long before they noticed him.

"What do you think?" Falon said to Taline.

He saw her look beyond the farm, to the beginning
hummocks of sand, the great Eastern desert.

"I didn't expect to find a farm here . . . or anyone. . . ."

There was a narrow bridge that crossed the stream, and
it led to the farm.

And still, the farmer didn't move, leaning against his
hoe, ready to work until all the light was gone.

Ashre was on the ground, ready to fall asleep wherever
he dropped.

"Maybe we should greet the farmer, perhaps spend the
night."

Taline looked over to Anarra. She was sponging the back
of the uxan, using their water liberally. "It wouldn't hurt to
talk," she said.

"And it wouldn't hurt to rest," Ashre added.

"We'll go," Taline said. "But say nothing about what we
are doing."

"That," Falon said, "should be interesting. He'll ask what
we're doing, and we'll say what? Just taking a walk. C'mon
Ash," he said, scooping him up from the ground, "I'll carry
you the rest of the way."

The kit was almost asleep. Even while being jiggled
around, as Falon walked down the hill, Ashre's breathing
grew slow, rhythmic, accompanied by the faint stirring of
a relaxed rumble from deep inside.

Falon questioned, then, the wisdom of bringing him
along. Would the kit have been better left off at the city?
Could the workhouses have been so bad?

It may have been too hasty a decision.

*Too hasty . . . like other decisions. Too hasty . . . like
drawing a sword and striking, without thinking.*

Falon moved over the narrow bridge, the farmer still not
moving, or waving.

So far, he didn't seem like the friendly type.

"Stay here," Taline said to Anarra as they reached the fields. "You'll come with me?" she asked Falon.

"Certainly." He placed Ashre atop the cart.

They walked through the tall grass, nearly ready to be harvested. The farmer stirred, no more than a subtle movement of his feet, as if growing more uncomfortable the closer they got.

"Hello," Taline finally called.

The farmer nodded. Was he a mute? Falon wondered.

"We've been traveling all day," Falon said, by way of explanation.

"And where might you be going?" the farmer said. His voice was low, a rough and scratchy-sounding thing.

Falon gestured at the desert. "Out there. Tomorrow."

"We were hoping that we might rest with you tonight. We can pay."

The farmer looked beyond them, out to the edge of the field, to Anarra standing with Ashre and Daynia.

His eyes narrowed.

"This isn't an inn. My wife has two kits, still suckling."

"Perhaps we should just move along—" Falon argued, turning toward Taline. But she shook her head. "Our animal could use some fresh grass to graze on, and we have a young one with us as well. It will only be for one night."

Falon sighed. He studied the farmer.

Then he saw it.

The hand that held the hoe, closed so tight around it. Gripping it as though his life depended on it, tight enough for the claws to peak out and dig into the rough wood.

But there were no claws. *No claws,* because he didn't have any.

And there was only one type of mrem that went about without claws.

Convicted murderers. It was the ultimate disgrace.

"Taline," he said, trying not to rush, "I think—"

The farmer smiled, a half-sad grimace. "Very well, you may stay, and eat, and refresh your animal. As long as you leave tomorrow morning."

He returned to cutting down the fresh blades of grass.

"What was it you were going to say?" Taline asked.

The farmer looked up.

"Oh, nothing," Falon said. There would be time later to point out his unfortunate news to Taline.

At least, he hoped there would be.

Chapter 11

▲————————————————————————▲

There were a couple of things Falon didn't like about their shelter for that night.

It had nothing to do with the hut itself, though it was as sparsely furnished an abode as he had ever seen. Whatever this farming couple had, they had built with their own hands. The chairs were simple wood slat things, strong, sturdy, designed for plenty of rough use. The table, the centerpiece of the small three-room cottage, was twin slabs of dark changa wood, polished to a high sheen from daily use and the oil of simple meals.

A kitchen, two small bedrooms, and that was it.

But the smell from the kitchen was more than pleasant. It was a stew filled with all the farm's own vegetables and another musky flavor. The few furs inside the cottage told Falon that the farmer also knew how to shoot an arrow or set a trap.

And so far, the farmer—a murderer, if that's what he was—hadn't given any sign of malicious intent. He just restocked the fire, lit a pipe, and settled quietly into what must be his place: a chair at the head of the table.

Whoever he was, this mrem was not yet old, but he moved slowly, as if tired of his life. His eyes glowed almost too brightly, not about to miss a trick.

His mate was heavy with the teats that a twin birth brings. Their two kits were frolicking on the dirt floor, rolling over each other and mewling for milk at what seemed the most inopportune time. The farmer intro-

duced his wife as Lonirr, and she nodded shyly before
bustling about the small kitchen area.

The farmer didn't introduce himself at all.

His markings seemed to be a mix of dark swirls of color,
the fur rough and unkempt, mixed with the rich dirt from
his fields. He said little, unconcerned with the niceties of
playing host.

But none of that bothered Falon. At least, not much.

Not as much as seeing Taline's reaction.

It was as if she had been bottling up her normal feelings.
All of a sudden she seemed like any other female Falon had
ever known. Despite the presence of the farmer's wife,
Taline was sending out signals, and more, that Falon could
read loud and strong.

The farmer chose to ignore her. Her looks, the lowering
of the eyes, the slight arch to her sleek, smooth back when
she leaned down to loosen her boots.

The farmer's eyes moved not a bit.

Falon, on the other hand, at once felt amazed by Taline's
sudden aggressive display—amazed, and annoyed that it
wasn't on him that she was dispensing all this wonderful
attention.

It excited him tremendously.

And still, despite the swirl of thoughts and fear that
swept around him, there was something else.

He missed Caissir, though he wasn't sure why. Caissir
wouldn't be much in a fight, and his constant complaining
could be incredibly grating. But after years with the beasts
on Mount Zaynir, he had found Caissir wonderfully re-
freshing.

Lonirr brought a great tureen of the soup to the table.
Without a word, she sat down near her husband and, with a
nod to Falon, Anarra, Ashre, and Taline, invited their
guests to join them.

Falon had no problem squelching his concerns when the
very full bowl of soup was placed under his nostrils.

After everyone had their first hearty spoonfuls, the
farmer finally gave his name: Sirrom. Then, he asked a
question. "Where are you headed?" he said, in a tired,
scratchy voice.

Falon glanced at Taline, trying to indicate that she
should watch her words. But she was too fast for him.

"We are going to the ruins at Gfaar," she said.

Falon looked over at Anarra, trying to rouse some help in his campaign to silence Taline. But she was up to her whiskers in soup.

The farmer laughed, an unpleasant, cruel sound. And Falon kept trying not to stare at his hands, to not let him see that he knew.

"I hope you enjoy being eaten," he said, punctuating his comment with a loud slurp of the soup.

This made even Anarra pause in her dining. Ashre held his spoon in front of him, eyes wide open.

"What do you mean?" Taline asked.

Another long slurp. He was enjoying himself, the bastard son of some street bitch. . . .

"What do you know about the liskash?"

"What? The liskash? Rumors, old tales . . . you can't know anything about what you don't see."

"I don't think—" Lonirr started to say, but the farmer fired her a look that could have melted stone. He looked at Taline, then Anarra, finally right at Falon.

"The liskash grow more bold. They grow stronger. Some renegades . . . and some criminals work with them. I am safe—for the moment. But if you go out there, there's no telling what you'll find." He laughed again. "Though it's doubtful that you'll find Gfaar."

"And why is that?" Falon asked.

"How many years old is it? And buried under so much sand. It storms constantly there. . . . I know, I've seen it. No, you'll not find it."

He picked up his soup bowl and drank from it as if from a goblet.

Then Ashre did the same. He saw the kit look at the great, burly farmer. And Falon wondered what Ashre could see behind the farmer's smoky black eyes.

Taline leaned across the table and touched Sirrom's arm.

"But you could find it for us, couldn't you? You would be well rewarded."

What kind of reward, Falon wondered, forgetting for a moment that Taline had just invited a murderer to join them.

"I have my harvest . . . my wife . . . my kits. . . ."

The two kits rolled around his feet, scratching with their soft baby claws at his tough boots. Sirrom let a hand dangle

and he wriggled his fingers, causing the kits to leap fero-
ciously on him. "I cannot go."

A good decision, Falon thought.

"No," Taline said coldly, regaining some of her former
demeanor. "There's more involved here than a trip to the
ruins. The future of the cities—"

Sirrom laughed.

"There's a book," she said, "and it must be found."

"For the cities?" Sirrom asked.

"Yes, the cities," she continued. "Without you we may
not succeed as easily, but we *will* succeed. But if you help
us, I can help you."

She took Sirrom's hands in her own.

She looked right at his hands, at the tips . . . where the
claws should have been.

And Falon knew the strange truth.

She knew he was a murderer. A disgraced outcast. Possibly dangerous. And it didn't bother her in the slightest.

"You won't have to live here . . . on the edge of world,
away from—"

"We like it here," he said.

But Taline said nothing, letting the hollowness of his
claim fill the smoky air of the cottage.

Sirrom stood up and went over to the fire. He poked at
it, teasing it, sending sparks onto the floor. He gently
nudged his kits away from the spit of sparks and glowing
embers.

"It is growing dangerous here."

It was his wife, talking to him now, standing at his elbow,
her hands nervously fidgeting with her scratchy quilt.
They were the only words that she had spoken, and they
made him turn to her, and finally look down at his kits.

"If it grows more dangerous," Taline said slowly, "how
long can you stay here?"

He looked up to his wife, then over at Taline, one hand
stroking his grizzly cheek, the other holding a makeshift
poker, a heavy gnarled stick.

"I'll take you to the ruins. We'll make the journey in one
day, and return the next. If you do not find what you need
after that, it is no affair of mine. And," he said, "I expect
you to keep to your agreement."

"You should have no fear of that," Taline said, her voice

rich with a delicious promise that nearly drove Falon crazy.

Instead, he got up and quickly walked outside.

Ashre sensed that Falon wasn't happy.

For the first time he felt, once again, the aloneness that had been his constant companion in Fahl.

The others were still eating, talking . . . all of them enjoying the warmth of the fire and the good hot food. But Falon had left.

Ashre slipped off his chair, and made his way to the front door. The farmer's wife heard him move. She gave him a quick glance. He smiled, and kept on walking.

It was cold out! A chilly wind blew from the east, wiping away the warmth of the day. Falon had walked away from the small house and was standing by a small fence, looking out at the desert.

Don't leave, Ashre thought. Because that's exactly what he feared his brave new friend might do. Just vanish into the night air.

He ran over to him.

"I—I didn't know where you were." He smiled up at him.

Falon turned, a funny kind of expression on his face.

"Well, I've been here, Ash. Standing here, shivering, thinking . . ."

Ashre climbed the fence and turned, putting himself between the vastness of the desert and Falon's eyes.

"What were you thinking about?"

Falon lowered his eyes. "Sirrom . . . Tell me, do you get . . . I mean do you think that there's anything we should be worried about? Not that there's—"

Ashre shook his head. He understood why Falon was concerned. Sirrom wasn't the first murderer he'd seen. But there was no danger coming from him. In fact, just the opposite.

"No." Ashre said.

Falon smiled. "And are you ever wrong?"

Ashre grinned back. "All the time."

"Then I'll just go on looking out at the desert and worrying."

Ashre came close to him. The wind was growing fierce,

and he felt tiny specks of sand flying through the air, cutting into his skin.

"I miss Caissir," he said.

"So do I, Ash. So do I."

"Why did he leave?"

The highlander laughed and threw an arm around the kit, pulling him close, shielding him from the wind. "He left because he was smart. Now, let's you and I get back for some rest."

The wind roared and snapped at their backs as they went back inside the cottage.

Falon didn't sleep well.

It seemed to take forever for him to make himself comfortable, curling and uncurling on the dirt floor. The sounds of all the others, the heavy snores of Sirrom, the hungry mewlings of the kits, Anarra's strange wheezing, and even Ashre's gentle calling out in his sleep, all put Falon on edge.

But most of all it was Taline.

She was giving off an aroma that could have had him tossing and turning all night. Eventually he covered his head tightly with his kilt, wrapping it around and around, blocking out the sounds, and everything.

It was well into the night before he fell asleep.

And he dreamed.

He was surrounded by mrem, of every color and class, some dressed in full battle armor, others in simple kilts armed only with a simple stick, sharpened to a point.

But none of them moved. They stood on some ghostly black plain, their eyes all fiery and golden, like the glowing embers in a fire. They stood, and watched him walk ahead. Into the dark.

Then it was there. Twice as big as he was.

Looming over him, looking down.

He saw its forked tongue come out, tasting the air, savoring the moment. Falon tightened his grip around his sword —*so* heavy that his muscles were clenched just holding it erect in the air.

As he came closer to his opponent, its grayish-green skin glistened even in the blackness. Its eyes were dull, though, big limpid pools that were of another world.

But that was just it. They weren't of *another* world. They were of *this* world.

And the battle to come was a battle for this world.

He raised his sword.

The liskash stirred. It looked more like a demon. But it didn't reach for its weapon, some great clunky thing strapped to its side. Instead, it simply moved, swishing its tail around, and Falon was knocked off his feet.

The others started to back away . . . until he was all alone.

It came closer, leaned over him. He smelled its breath, suffocating from its foulness. He moaned, fumbled for his weapon. The liskash opened its mouth.

He called out. Over and over again.

Until he made a sound out loud. And another. A helpless, inchoate moan.

The last time he made the sound his eyes were open. And Sirrom was standing over him, looking down.

"Are you all right?" he asked.

"Wha—"

The army, the liskash . . . where were they?

"Yes . . . I . . . I just had a dream."

Sirrom nodded. "And well you might. Get your rest now."

Falon nodded, and turned over.

When he again opened his eyes, the skies showed their first hint of morning light.

True to his word, Sirrom had them moving early. Falon watched him take his two kits, and hold them close. Then, he gave his wife a quick nuzzle—a gesture that seemed to embarrass her.

The whole venture threatened to collapse when he told Anarra that Daynia would have to be left at the farm. The desert, Sirrom patiently explained, is no place for uxen. They have no footing and they have to struggle just to move. The wheels of the cart would just sink into the fine sand.

All perfectly sensible, but Anarra stormed around the small cottage, asking Taline whether she was going to listen to a simple farmer.

And Taline said she was.

Abruptly, Anarra unpacked the cart, divided up the weapons, food stores, and other gear, and even prepared a small pack for Ashre, who couldn't have been more pleased.

But as they left the farmland and with it the last green ground before the desert, Falon kept wondering if maybe Caissir didn't have the right idea. With Sirrom now in charge, and Anarra fuming, there seemed to be little need for an ambitious highlander eager for a new life.

No, and Taline didn't seem to care if he was there or not. Openly, almost brazenly, considering that Lonirr was watching, she walked beside Sirrom from the very start.

Only an all-consuming curiosity and the lack of any future elsewhere kept him from turning around.

The desert soon gave him other things to think about.

It was a hot yellow sea, its waves and troughs frozen into position. Every step was an effort, and the simple act of walking became an act of grim determination. The pack, which hadn't felt so bad when they were on hard ground, now felt like a dead weight around his neck, ready to pull Falon down.

Even Ashre, who had been enjoying everything so far, started complaining.

"Can you take my pack?" he asked, after they had been climbing their first sandy hill.

The kit's pack was light—just his own dagger, some food and water. But any weight was too much.

"Hold onto it a bit, Ash. When you're really beat, I'll give you a hand."

The highlander watched Sirrom. He was clearly experienced in the ways of the desert. His steps seemed more surefooted, and he had a pace and rhythm that suggested he knew how to work with the sand rather than against it.

But as badly as Falon felt he was doing, Anarra was worse. Still pouting over her lost Daynia, she lingered near the back, grumbling, gasping at the hot air. She was a big she-mrem, and her weight, though layered in muscle, made it difficult to move on the shifting sand.

It was getting near time for a meal break when he saw his first sand bird.

Nobody had warned him about it, so the sight of the large ungainly bird soaring overhead was disconcerting.

"What is that?" Falon asked Sirrom.

As soon as he asked the question, another bird flew overhead, then another appeared, until there were six of them making large circles in the brilliant sky.

"Sand birds," Sirrom explained, without a pause in his marching.

The birds had bodies shaped like twin wine bladders. The wings were large. The heavy bird could fly, but just barely. But it was the neck that was most peculiar.

It stuck out of the bird like the branch of a tree, ending in a head shaped like an oversize dewberry.

Falon ran up to Sirrom. "What are they doing here?"

"Feeding."

Falon smiled, thinking it some grim joke.

"Feeding! On what?"

Sirrom gestured to the left, where the birds were soaring, now lower to the ground.

"On sand weevil larvae. That's why they're circling over there. They can check the sand for signs of any movement."

Sand weevils. There was a lot Falon didn't know about the creatures that lived in the desert. But sand weevils figured in many of the strange legends and tales told by the old mrem of his village. Usually they were stories of treasure, or the magical power to be found in skin of a mature weevil. One tale told of a highlander who made his way into the desert, and fought a weevil.

He was granted three wishes.

At this point, Falon had only one wish . . . to get out of there.

"Aren't we in danger here?" Falon looked at Sirrom, then at Ashre. "I mean, where there's weevil larvae, aren't there weevils?"

Sirrom nodded. He walked confidently alongside Taline. Falon couldn't see very well, but he wouldn't have been surprised to see their hands entwined.

"Yes, you're absolutely right. Over there," Sirrom pointed, "is a weevil field. I saw it well before we got here —and I avoided it. As long as we stay away, there should be no problem. . . ."

Falon watched, fascinated, as the birds went lower and lower, until finally they landed, sending up a shower of fine sand. Then they matter-of-factly plunged their necks into the sand.

"Amazing," Falon said.

"I can't see it . . . could you lift me up?" Ashre asked.

Falon hoisted Ashre onto his shoulders as Anarra passed them.

All of the birds had their necks buried in the sand. Their bodies were wriggling this way and that, as if struggling with something.

"Aren't they worried about the weevils?" Ashre asked.

"I should think so," Falon laughed. "Unless they know—"

Just then one of the birds pulled its long neck from the hole, brandishing a pinkish white thing that wriggled wildly.

"Got one!" Ashre yelled.

Then another successful burrower popped up, and another, until all of the birds were standing on the sand. One by one they took flight. Falon could see them gobbling on their prizes even as they tried to get their chunky bodies up in the air.

No easy task that, he thought, amused.

The last bird left on the sand bent its legs, ready to leap into the air.

But then the great mountain of sand heaved, rising like a real wave now, knocking the bird down, burying it, until the sand poured off the sides of some great blackish thing rising underneath it.

"What's—" Ashre began.

Alarmed, Falon looked for Sirrom. He and Taline were far ahead now, almost out of earshot.

"We'd better get—" Falon began to say.

Another mountain started to grow . . . this time, right beside them. Falon felt the sand shifting around his feet, the deep, low rumble of something under the ground.

"Hold on!" he said to Ashre.

But already he had lost his balance and was tumbling back, falling onto the hot sand. . . .

As a giant sand weevil seemed to sprout from nowhere.

Chapter 12

◆————————————————————————————◆

Falon thought he yelled.

But later he wasn't sure.

He did remember to get to his feet, pick up Ashre, and toss him as far as he could, away from the weevil.

He was turning around when the ground shifted again, like water settling into a sloshing pan.

The weevil was about the biggest living thing that he had ever seen . . . about half the size of Sirrom's cottage. It had two elegantly curved pincers that immediately caught Falon's attention. They were a shiny black, almost polished to a glossy glow. The sand cascaded off the creature's back, not sticking to it at all.

The pincers separated and something like a mouth, with fuzzy hairs where teeth should be, went all wet, opening and shutting all too eagerly.

It wasn't me, he wanted to say. *I didn't touch your babies. It was those stupid birds.*

And though his faith was a flimsy thing at best, he found himself muttering the name of the All-Mother, hoping she'd listen to one of her less dutiful supplicants.

Even as he struggled to stand again, with the sand still sloshing around, the weevil scuttled close and made its first attempt to trap him.

It missed easily.

No eyes, noted Falon gratefully. The thing was blind.

But blind or not it made another clean swipe, and this time one pincer jabbed into his elbow, breaking his furry skin. He jerked away just in time to avoid the opposing pincer.

It couldn't see, but the weevil sure could smell or sense *something*. With its aim improving so dramatically, he knew that the next attempt might be fatal.

He got to his knees.

A sword landed at his feet. A heavy weapon, a piece of metal designed to do major damage.

"Get up!" Sirrom hissed. "Before we have more of them to deal with."

Sirrom's words inspired Falon to scramble to his feet, dragging the weapon with him. The pincers made another grab at him—and this time he smelled the weevil, a smell of wet sand and sea eels.

Sirrom was beside him.

"Aim for above the mouth—and a hard blow. It's sensitive there."

There was one problem with Sirrom's instructions. To hit the sensitive spot, Falon would have to get awfully close to the pincers.

Sirrom wasted no time. He leaped toward the weevil just after its last attack. Then he smashed his blade down, producing a great clacking noise. The weevil screeched, the sound of a knife blade scraping across a smooth stone.

Then, there was another sword cutting the air. And Taline was beside him, her blade cartwheeling around. Her aim was perfect and the weevil screeched even louder.

Now it was his turn, but he wasn't used to so heavy a blade. And his timing was off. He brought his blow down just as the weevil readied itself to snap at him. Only Sirrom's tough yank backwards saved him from being skewered like a roasted mynt on a spit.

But Falon was nothing if not a fast learner. He brought his blade around quickly, gracefully, as if dancing a duel with the creature. Except that this time it was perfectly all right to land the first blow.

His heavy blade smacked the shell, and a thin crack appeared. A sickly yellow froth bubbled out. The creature scuttled backwards.

"Well landed!" Sirrom cheered, with a grin.

"Behind us!" Taline's scream shattered Falon's brief moment of victory.

Three more of the creatures were moving across the hummocks of sand. Gliding, sliding effortlessly towards them.

"Come on!" Sirrom yelled. "We can't face all of them."

Sirrom grabbed Taline's hand, and Falon followed them. He was wondering what would stop the weevils from catching up to them when he turned, and saw the weevils coming to an abrupt halt.

"Why are they stopping?" he shouted to Sirrom.

"They won't leave their nest and burrows."

Right, thought Falon. His mouth was open, panting, and his tongue was exposed to the hot air.

It makes perfect sense.

Except for one thing.

Hadn't Sirrom known the nest was there? So why hadn't he warned him?

Sirrom did come and try to save him. . . .

After three attacks. And even then, Falon knew he himself had landed the blow that made the weevil scurry away.

They caught up to Anarra. Ashre stood beside her, but so stiffly it was clear that he wasn't *with* her.

"Now stay with me," Sirrom ordered, barely glancing at Falon.

And to be sure, Falon would do that. And watch him too.

Ashre came beside him.

"Sorry about the toss, Ash. Didn't want you inside that thing's belly." He looked down at the gray kit's face. But instead of seeing it all calm, the danger past, Ashre's eyes were squinted and confused. He tapped Falon's arm.

"It shouldn't have happened," Ashre said quietly.

"I know. We should have stayed away from—"

"No! I should have had a . . . feeling, I don't know, some warning!" He tugged at his whiskers. "But there was nothing, nothing until the weevil was there."

"Don't worry about it, Ash. Maybe it only works with some people or some situations."

"It always works . . ." he said slowly, a determined look on his face. "*Always.*" He looked up at Falon. "It didn't work then because something made it not work."

Falon looked at him. *He's scared*, he thought. *Perhaps for the first time. Really scared.*

"Something," Ashre repeated. "Or someone."

The ruins appeared on the desert like some camouflaged animal.

Falon had expected a city, a town . . . something recognizable. A place where mrem had once lived and worked and played. Instead, he saw something that could have grown from the sand itself.

He would have missed it easily, if Sirrom hadn't pointed it out when it was still in the distance.

At first, Falon saw nothing but some irregular bumps, nothing that would catch his attention even in the vast yellow sea of sand. But as they got closer, the shapes became more distinct, even if they still seemed more natural than man-made.

There was only one location higher than any other, and it just barely protruded above the jagged outline of the ruins. They were walking into the sun now, with about an hour of light left, so that even later as they came quite close the whole area seemed indistinct.

The nearness of their destination inspired Ashre to trot ahead. Sirrom quickly called him back.

"Stay with us," he gently ordered. "I don't know what we're likely to face there."

Falon assumed that Ashre would be the first to know of any danger. On the other hand, he hadn't been doing so well with his magic lately. Maybe his village elders were right; it was all just undependable herd magic.

Falon walked over to Sirrom. Slowly, he was coming to trust him, even if he knew that he was a convicted murderer. There was a sense of calm assurance. Nothing was ruffling his fur.

"What is it we're likely to find there?" he asked him.

Sirrom pulled at his whiskers. "Most likely nothing. It has occasionally been used as a base to stage raids on the neighboring small villages and cities. But most of the time it's just an abandoned spot in the desert."

"My father," Taline interrupted, "says that the book was buried with the last Holy One of the cult, someone named Charissar."

"Charissar? Wouldn't grave robbers have made off with the book, and anything else of value?" Falon asked.

Sirrom shook his head. "I doubt it. The mrem are a

superstitious breed. Even a dead cult would make them
nervous. As for the Eastern Lords, they reportedly have
more gods than there are stars in the sky. I don't think any
simpleminded soldier would disturb the grave." He
turned to Falon, and grinned. "Of course, I could be
wrong."

Anarra was still behind them, Falon saw. Eyes down,
taking the measure of every step, struggling to get through
the sand. Even Taline seemed distant from her now, and
Falon almost felt sorry for the struggling female.

Almost, but not quite.

The ruins, he thought, looking ahead. Should be easy
now. Get the book, return to Tizare. Claim the reward,
maybe some position in the court of Lord Rhow, who certainly looked like a noble on the move.

The ruins . . . just ahead. And there didn't seem to be
anything that could go wrong.

Sirrom gathered everyone into a circle, taking full command now—a command that no one challenged. As shadows cut great swaths of brown-black into the alleyways and
squat buildings, the buildings lost some of their stolid sun-
niness.

"Anarra has torches for everyone," Sirrom instructed.
"Use them. I don't know if there are any traps and holes to
be avoided. I will help you search only because I want to be
sure of getting out of here on time. But successful or not,
we leave at dawn to return to my farmhouse. If you have
time to sleep, do so. If anyone finds the burial site, signal by
yelling and calling out. If no one hears you, recover the
book and return here. We can all check back here during
the night until someone finds the book."

Here, Falon saw, was a grim little courtyard surrounded
by squat buildings with stairs leading down. If anything,
the buildings seemed to submerge below the sand. Some
of the entrances were completely blocked by huge boulders. Others looked open for business.

"And weapons?" Taline asked.

"Take everything that you brought. Everything. There
doesn't seem to be anyone here now. If they are here,
they're hiding. But we don't know for sure. Be alert. And,
except for me, you'd best stay in pairs."

Falon looked at Ashre, who nodded eagerly.

The last bit of light vanished from the top of the buildings.

Falon gathered his weapons, a heavy, double-edged sword that had seen much use and a shorter, rapierlike sword, a weapon that seemed more appropriate to an assassin. For the first time in his life, he wore throat armor and shields that covered his forearms. His pack was loaded down with three torches, flints, rope, and a chunk of metal rod.

"For opening the coffin," Anarra explained.

"Oh . . ." he replied. How silly of him not to know.

"I'll take the eastern edge," Sirrom said.

Fine with me, Falon thought.

"South," Taline said.

"North," Falon added.

"Whoever finishes first can return to look in the west. Good luck to everyone."

Then Falon and Ashre were alone.

"Well, Ash, if you get any bright ideas along the way be sure to let me know." The kit grinned. "And I don't want to be chasing you through these buildings. Stay with me. Understood?"

"Understood. Falon?"

"Yes."

"Have you ever been here before?"

"Me? Here?" He laughed. "I doubt it."

Ashre's face seemed confused. He bit his lip. "You're sure?"

"As sure as I can be of anything. I've never been off the highlands before. Why?"

"I don't know. Just a funny feeling I had. Like you've seen this before."

"Not as far as I know, Ash. Let's get going."

The young highlander led the way toward the northern section of the ruins.

For a while it wasn't necessary to use the torches. There was enough light to see the buildings. And Falon could make out the strange carvings that he found on every entrance.

They were not in any written language he recognized.

But once they were inside, in the total blackness, they quickly lit their torches. Falon heard Ashre's breathing pick up an irregular rhythm. He found himself taking great gulps of the stale, dry air.

It wasn't exactly a bad smell. But it certainly was a dead smell.

The interiors were, for the most part, deserted. The searchers found nothing of interest except the bones and scraps of some visitors who came, ate, and left their garbage as a marker. There weren't even the furtive darting and glowing eyes of any small occupants.

Not surprising, since there wasn't any game for them to eat.

Gradually Falon and Ashre made their way to the tallest structure, a temple perhaps. Close up it loomed over the other buildings. It seemed to have an extra floor, and then some kind of open area.

Falon could easily imagine it as the setting for some strange ceremonies.

Then it hit him.

Slowly, starting as an undefinable feeling, uncomfortable, then growing into a chilly, disturbing unease. His fur seemed to stand on end . . . his lips pulled back from his teeth. Anyone looking would have seen his fangs protruding and wondered what in the world was wrong with him.

He turned left, pulling ahead of Ashre, down an alleyway . . . that he knew would be there.

"Wait!" Ashre called.

But now Falon moved quickly, breathing hard, turning left and right, knowing what each turn would bring. He ran on, not caring that Ashre lost sight of him.

This is madness, he thought. *How can I know this? What kind of sick sorcery has come over me?*

There was only one sorcerer there, he realized.

Right behind him.

Young . . . innocent . . . and loaded to the tips of his ears with powerful magic.

"Magic is from the beasts!" the elders preached, over and over. "There is no room for magic in the world of the mrem!"

Falon leaned against the wall. It was a temple, the highlander knew now, a place for ceremonies, dark and mysterious.

He closed his eyes; and he saw inside the temple.
He saw the great tomb, right inside the temple walls.

As soon as Falon had run away, Ashre felt it: the sudden
fear, the terrible confusion.

"Falon!" he called to the disappearing figure, but it
didn't stop. So the kit ran as hard as he could, following the
waving trail of Falon's torch as he weaved his way through
the deserted alleys.

The kit came to an open area. Beyond it was the big
building they had seen from the distance, looming over
everything else in Gfaar. Across the square Falon staggered against the wall, leaning as if he would fall down if it
wasn't there.

And then Ashre sensed the danger.

So strong, he couldn't imagine how he hadn't felt it all
along.

They weren't alone.

Ashre turned left and right, trying to see where the
feeling was coming from, his heart beating loudly.

"Falon," he said quietly. "We're not—"

He was looking left, then right. . . .

Then straight up. To the top of the strange building. The
top was ringed with heavy carved statues, massive shapes
that looked like nothing—and something evil at the same
time. One of them was quivering, shaking, rocking back
and forth—right over Falon.

"Falon!" he yelled.

Falon turned, so slowly, looking at Ashre.

The block of stone, now an animal, now a spiraling
curve, tottered back and forth and finally tumbled forward.

Ashre saw a hand just behind it. A glimpse, no more.

Still Falon stood against the wall, shaking, his tongue
darting in and out, in and out.

The block was tumbling down, right on Falon.

Ashre ran, screaming, crying.

You're all I have, he thought. *What is there left for me if
you're gone?*

Down.

The kit saw Falon turn and look at him. His eyes showed
that he understood nothing.

No matter, Ashre thought. *I'm quick. And strong.*

He sent his body flying into Falon, smashing into him, and Falon staggered backwards, while Ashre stopped dead.

He fell to the ground, where Falon had been leaning moments earlier.

The stone—massive, blocking out a whole section of the sky—came down.

Falling down upon him . . . as he looked up.

"Falon!" he screamed.

Then everything was quiet.

Chapter 13

———————————————————————▲

For a second, Falon didn't know what was happening. He was lost to his dreams, to the haunted feelings this place made him feel. And the undeniable knowledge that somehow, he seemed to know where he was.

Then, from far away, he heard Ashre calling out to him. It was a faint sound, barely audible amidst the rumble of his crazed thoughts.

Ashre . . . calling him, then knocking him down. The blow sent Falon tumbling onto the sandy ground, rolling over and over.

He heard him call again. A strangled sound now, not a warning cry but a plea for help. He heard that and, as he scrambled to his feet, he saw the great stone block land on top of Ashre.

Covering him completely.

"No!" Falon screamed. He ran to the block, now as still as if it had always been there. Unmoving . . . now unmoveable.

"No!" he yelled again, banging his hands against it, over and over and over until they were both bloody. He collapsed against it. His hands still touched the cold stone, as if he could feel the kit's heartbeat through the block.

His torch sputtered behind him, lying on the ground. Then it went out. He looked up, and he saw where the block had once rested. Other blocks—each one different—circled the temple.

He stood up and looked around.

Perhaps the danger wasn't over.

But it was still, quiet. No sound except the gentle desert breeze making high-pitched melodies as the wind traveled through the twisting streets and around the flat buildings.

"Ashre . . ." Falon said quietly.

He turned away. He started crying, rubbing at the tears, trying to clear his eyes, over and over, until the world was one terribly, terribly sad blur.

How long he stood there crying, Falon didn't know. Even when his eyes went dry, he still heaved.

His mind wouldn't let him stop seeing the final picture. Again and again, the last moment of Ashre's life was played out before him in cruel detail.

And only when he thought he'd go mad if he thought of it one more time, only then did he pick up his torch, rekindle it, and walk into the temple.

His first step away from the fallen statue was the longest he ever took.

The entrance to the temple was clear, but there were signs that it had been used by others before him. His torch picked up the remains of small fires. He held the torch up and swung it around.

The wall was covered with some of the same shapes found on the statues that sat on the roof. Here, inside the gloom, they took on the shape of animals, or worse. Here was a creature with eyes all over its chest. There was some animal with legs emerging from its chest.

He'd blink, and then they were just odd shapes, nothing more.

The great room was empty. Just past it, though, he saw a hallway.

He rested a hand on his sword . . . not that he'd be able to wield it too quickly. The sheer weight and size of it would mean it would take him a while to get it out and ready.

Still, it felt better having his hand on it.

Now that he was without Ashre—to give him warning, to laugh at his fears.

Had someone pushed that block? And were they in here, waiting for another chance to kill him? Some robber . . . some renegade mrem . . . some liskash?

If they're here, he thought, *I will kill them.*
Or die trying.

He moved down the hallway. It was cool, the air almost
:y. His torch blackened the ceiling, and his nostrils sniffed
t the pungent odor.

There were rooms on both sides of him as he walked.
Chambers for priests, perhaps. Or private meeting rooms.
Or for whatever strange activities the cult practiced.

All of them empty and deserted.

Finally he came to a room with a gate. He pushed
.gainst the gate, and it fell from the crumbly walls, clat-
ering noisily to the ground. Whatever secrets the temple
ried to protect must have been discovered long ago.

He stepped into the room and swirled the torch around.
There were names written on the wall. The letters were
:laborate and ornate, decorated with all sorts of flourishes
.nd filigree. There were five names.

And one of them was Charissar.

"Charissar . . ." he said quietly, and the sound of it in
:he small chamber startled him. He looked around the tiny
·oom, and at the names on the wall. He stepped outside
.gain.

Falon checked to see how close the next room was.

But he didn't even see another room. Just a wall, and the
end of the corridor. He started back to the small room.

He thought he heard a sound, from above him, or maybe
from outside . . . he couldn't be sure. The sound of steps
or rock moving. His claws went into the heavy hilt of the
sword, holding it tight. He turned and listened carefully,
sniffing at the air.

But there was nothing more. He turned slowly, back into
the room, pausing every few seconds to crane his neck and
listen.

Charissar! Could this be his tomb? he wondered.

There was, unfortunately, only one way to find out.

He found a place to lodge the torch, and then took out
his heavy sword. It felt good to have it in his hand, even if
he was about to use it to dig.

Anarra had neglected to include shovels in their handy
packs.

Falon started scratching at the wall, but his blade only
cut furrows into the porous stone. He tried following a

pattern, scratching at the surface of the wall, trying to find someplace where it felt different.

Then he realized he'd have to work his blade in deeper. He leaned against the hilt, jabbing his sword into the wall. If it all felt the same after a few inches, he pulled it out and tried another location, each time wondering if there even was a coffin.

Then, by the All-Mother, he felt something. His blade seemed to go crunching inward with a sudden ease.

He had found something.

Falon worked quickly now, clawing at the stone, trying to expose whatever was inside the wall.

And slowly the outline of a coffin appeared. The sword was ungainly in his hand, but it cut through the sandstone easily. It crumbled to the floor, and the crystal pile gathered at his feet.

Then he could see it. A coffin, much more ornate than the simple boxes his villagers went to the ground in. A handle stuck out and he grabbed at it.

He pulled, but nothing happened.

He put down his sword and grabbed the handle with his two hands. The torch was burning faintly. He pulled. And suddenly he heard someone step *over the fallen metal gate.*

"No!" Falon yelled. He spun around, groping down to the floor for his sword, his wild swipe missing the weapon.

If this was who was responsible for Ashre's death, they were going to die, he swore. He fumbled some more on the ground for the sword.

"If I were a liskash, you'd be in my belly by now," the voice laughed.

Finally he had his sword—"Taline—I thought—"

She shook her head. "Anarra and I heard voices, screaming. We hurried here and I heard digging sounds inside."

Falon lowered his sword. "Ashre . . . he's dead. Crushed . . ." He felt his control slipping. It was so cold in here. Cold and dark.

"No . . . by the All-Mother! How did it happen?"

"He saved me . . . he *saved* me!" Falon wailed. "Pushed me away from a falling statue. The stone crushed him."

She came to him, resting her hand on his arm. "I'm sorry. He loved you so much. What a horrible accident."

He looked at her. *What am I looking for?* he thought. *Some flash of insincerity, some sign that she knew about it? She seemed to have no interest in my being alive. Ashre's death could have been an accident . . . the twisted result of her attempt to kill me.*

Or was it our resident murderer, Sirrom, just trying to keep his hand practiced?

Or was it some other, some half-crazed renegade who haunted the streets of Gfaar waiting to kill some wandering pilgrim?

All he knew was that it wasn't an accident.

But Taline's eyes held only sorrow. "Yes," he whispered. He pointed at the exposed tomb. "And I've found the tomb. I just want to get the book now, and leave," he said with disgust.

Taline put down her sword. "I'll help."

Now they both locked their hands around the handle and started tugging. At first, their grunting efforts were useless. Even when he braced his feet against the wall, the coffin stayed encased in the wall. Taline licked her lips and he saw her arm muscles clench tightly.

Then it moved! The slightest of movements, but it now jutted out of the wall.

"Come on, Taline. It's moving."

"I'm pulling as hard as I can," she grunted. Then she too placed her feet on the wall, and they both reared back.

"Perhaps you'd better—" she started to say.

But the box suddenly slid out, almost as if it had been released. It slid back, sending them tumbling, and Falon saw that it was going to come flying out on top of them.

"Move!" he yelled, and he rolled to the side, hoping that Taline was doing the same.

The heavy box crashed to the ground and sent the torch and the swords clattering onto the floor. Falon popped up quickly and looked over the dark coffin.

"Are you all right? Taline?"

She sat up, snatching the torch off the ground. The dull yellow light made her golden fur glow brilliantly.

"I'm fine." And then she extended the torch over the coffin.

It was cracked right down the center, neatly split in two. The wood was old and brittle, and the dark swirls of the grain were covered with scratches from the sand.

Falon reached out and grabbed at the top, just where the wood was cracked.

Taline brought the torch closer.

"Try not to singe my hairs," Falon said.

"Sorry." She brought the torch up a bit.

He peeled back one part of the coffin.

It split in two, sending up a spray of dust and musty smells. Taline started coughing. The dust swirled in the air for a moment, then it cleared. Falon leaned forward.

He wasn't prepared for what he saw. He had seen dead bodies before. Death, in a small village, is no secret. Some of the older ones still asked that their remains be burned on top of Mount Zaynir, a ceremony Falon had seen more than once. Most were buried in coffins. The very poor were just placed in a hole in the ground. And he had seen bodies after they were dug up, bits of flesh still clinging tenaciously to tiny nooks and crannies of the skeleton.

But he had never seen anything like this. He gasped, and literally rocked back on his heels.

Perhaps it was because it was so dry here. Without moisture, there could be little real decay. There didn't seem to be any insects or rodents or other creatures that would feed upon the dead. A body would just slowly dry up until it resembled a shrunken version of a living mrem.

"Charissar," he said softly.

Taline came closer. "He looks as if he's sleeping. His fur looks perfect." She reached out to touch it—and then seemed to think better of it.

Falon took the torch from Taline, and checked the body from its feet to its head.

"I don't see anything, no book, no—"

Taline pointed.

And the gesture so startled him that Falon thought old Charissar had opened his eyes, ready to welcome them to the land of the dead.

Ashre would have loved it. *Just another street mrem,* Falon tried to tell himself. *Like hundreds . . . thousands in any city. Nothing special.*

"There," Taline said.

And she was right. Just below the body, its corners visible, sticking out.

It was a book.

"Yes," he said unenthusiastically. "Well, then, give me a hand here."

He reached down, and felt the leathery skin yield to the pressure of his fingers. "Go on," he said. "Grab it on the other side."

Taline didn't rush to pick the body up, but she did finally dig her hands under the dead mrem's buttocks. Falon worked his hands under a bit more. His fingers hit the stubby tail, all rigid now, and he recoiled.

"All right, all right," he said, speaking, he knew, to himself. "We're all ready now. On three. One . . ."

He tightened his arm muscles. "Two."

Taline took a deep breath.

"Three!"

They lifted together, but the body rose up only slightly, like a plank of wood.

He let one hand touch the corner of the book. "Almost— just got—to—"

His claws dug into the old book.

And he felt cold. His skin prickled. His fur stood on end. It was like before, when he was running through the streets of Gfaar. Something that connected him to this book . . . and this place.

He pulled the book out, grunting with the effort of his one-arm hold. "Got it!" he yelled, and they both released the body.

It clattered down into the coffin.

Charissar's jaw flung open with the jolt.

And, by the All-Mother, if he didn't seem to be smiling!

Falon stumbled out of the temple. He had let Taline take the old manuscript, its pages all crinkly inside dark covers.

We got it, he wanted to say.

At what cost . . .

Now, let's get out of this bone-dry town.

But Anarra was there, just outside the temple waiting for them. "What was all the noise in there?" she snorted.

Taline brandished the book in front of her eyes. *"The Song of the Three Moons,"* she said. "Falon found it."

"More likely that little runt he dragged along with him. . . ."

He thought he saw her sneer. He couldn't be sure—it *was* dark. He took a step toward Anarra.

Taline tried to place herself between them. "The kit is dead, Anarra, crushed by a fallen statue."

"Pushed . . ." Falon whispered, his eyes locking on Anarra's.

Undaunted, she took a step towards him, brushing Taline aside by her sheer bulk. "And what foolishness did you push on him, what highlander stupidity did you suggest that cost him his life?"

Falon went rigid.

A familiar feeling crept up his spine. The slow and, for him, inevitable loss of control.

His claws came out.

"Don't . . ." he said. "Don't say a word about Ashre . . . just keep your furry big lips shut." Now it was his turn to take a step closer to the burly female. "Because if you don't, I will shut them for you."

She smiled. She was enjoying this, that much was obvious. But just when he hoped that it would pass, that she'd let him lick at the wound of his grief, she spoke again.

"That," she said, "is something I'd like to see." Anarra turned to Taline. "Just what do you suppose this buffoon is hiding, Taline?"

"Anarra, please. Stop this now."

Anarra looked back at Falon. "What dirty little secrets is he hiding, secrets about him and his little street runt from Fahl?"

"Anarra. I order you—"

Anarra wanted this. Falon knew that, yet he was helpless to prevent it from going further.

Anarra came close to him, her breath and spittle falling on his nostrils. "Why don't you tell us what you did to kill him?"

He raised a hand and he screamed, the sound echoing weirdly in the deserted courtyard.

His claws shone in the light.

"Falon!" Taline called, but he ignored her yell. There was only one thing that he wanted to do.

He wanted to claw Anarra to pieces, no matter what the code of the mrem demanded.

She seemed to have expected his claws. Her sword was out, ready to slice at him. "Come on, my highlander misfit.

Come, and let me teach you how we butcher the uxen in Tizare."

He leaped at her, jumping, not really caring whether she was fast enough to get her sword out in front of her.

She wasn't. His frenzy so startled her that he was on her too fast, knocking her down, cradling her big head in his hands, the claws digging into her dark fur, cutting, tearing. . . .

"Is this how they do it?" he asked. And then he dragged his claws down her face some more.

Her sword was now useless, but he felt her hands fumble at his back, and then the pain of her strong claws digging into his skin.

No matter. He pulled at her face, imagining—hoping— that she was the one.

Let it be Anarra. Let her be the one. And let this be Ashre's revenge.

But she rolled over, and leaped backwards.

"He's mad!" she bellowed, blood tracing matted lines down her face. Her eyes, glowing with pleasure only moments before, now gave off the even brighter fire of fear.

Falon was off the ground, slowly stepping towards her. Without thinking, he made the first tentative steps of the Dance of Death.

Anarra had no use for such protocol. She gathered up her sword and took a great swipe at Falon. He leaped to the side, easily avoiding the blow.

"Another step, and I'll cut you down!"

"Falon! Stop! This won't bring Ashre back."

He took another step.

"No, it won't!" Another voice bellowed out from the darkness.

Falon knew it was Sirrom, but he paid the voice no heed.

"It took me to do that!" Sirrom yelled again, closer now.

And then Falon, still in the ceremonial crouch, heard another voice. . . .

Chapter 14

▲──▲

It was Ashre.

"Ashre!" Falon yelled. He looked at the two figures coming out of the gloom and there was Ashre, walking beside Sirrom.

"Found him over in my area. Gave me a good scare, he did," Sirrom laughed, rubbing the kit's pointy ears.

But how? Falon wondered. He had seen the kit crushed under the enormous stone. There had been no time for him to dodge away. And if he had, Falon certainly would have seen him.

He walked over to Ashre.

"The kit probably thought better of staying with you, highlander," Anarra sneered.

But he ignored her. Instead, he just went to Ashre, crouched low, and grabbed his shoulder.

"Ash—How? I—I—"

The kit grinned, a big wide-open smile that displayed his teeth, fangs and all. "I'll tell you later," Ashre said.

Taline came beside him. "What's going on?" she asked Falon. Then, looking up at Sirrom, "Falon said that the kit had been killed."

"Aye, it's a strange place, Gfaar. There are mrem who wouldn't even look at this town, let alone step in it," Sirrom offered.

"We have the book," Anarra growled, waving it in the air.

Sirrom took it from her hands. "I hope your lord finds it

worth all our efforts." He looked right at Taline. "And I hope he knows how to keep a bargain."

"You have my word as his daughter." She looked at Ashre. "What happened, Ash? How did you end up with Sirrom?"

He grinned again. "I don't know. Maybe I got scared, lost . . . wandered around. I'm not really sure."

"No matter," Sirrom announced. "But you have your book and we are leaving at dawn. We may as well make camp here, get some sleep. We'll be back out on the desert before long."

They all began unrolling their sleeping mats. And Falon saw everyone was taking care to get keep a weapon close by.

Then he watched Taline go over to Sirrom. Close.

She stood there beside him for a moment. Sirrom nodded.

"What's wrong?" Ashre said.

"Oh, nothing," Falon answered, trying not to watch. Taline went over to her pack and brought her mat back to where Sirrom was.

Not a surprise, Falon thought. Still, it was disappointing. Anarra cleaned her face—he swore he could hear her spitting in his direction—then found a spot to sleep well away from the others.

He unrolled his mat and lay it near Ashre's. Ash was already on his side, ready to go to sleep.

Falon sat on his mat.

The twin moons were almost behind the temple. Soon it would be very dark here.

"Tired?"

Ashre nodded.

Falon crouched down and spoke, now, in a whisper.

"Can you tell me what happened?"

Ashre's eyes blinked open. "Yes," he whispered. "At least what I know." He gulped.

The kit was scared, Falon could see.

"I saw the stone coming down . . . as if it was taking forever. I wanted to move. But there was no time. But still, I wanted to get away. . . ."

"And?"

Ashre gulped again.

"I started to feel this tingle, not like anything I've felt

before. And the next thing I knew I was standing next to Sirrom."

Falon nodded.

Well, then . . . it couldn't have been Sirrom who pushed the statue over. And it sounded as though Ashre had added a new wrinkle to his bag of magic tricks.

"I'd keep quiet about this," Falon said gently. "It's a neat trick, but let's keep it our little secret—for now." Ashre nodded.

Falon lay back, and he watched the stars grow even more lustrous as the moons were eclipsed by the temple. So many stars, much more than he ever could see even on the cloudy mountain top. The air here was so clear.

And cold. He pulled his sleeping mat around him like a blanket, but it did little to keep the chill off. Ashre was all curled up, falling fast asleep, his chest rising and falling evenly.

He'd sleep soundly until awakened.

Then Falon heard something faint. Whispered voices, the movement of fur against fur.

Then Taline's laugh. Gentle and sweet, and Sirrom's, muffled.

And oh, the images that began to dance in Falon's head.

He checked that Ashre was asleep. And he listened.

They tried to be quiet about their lovemaking. But whatever passion Taline was bringing to Sirrom's sleeping mat was just too strong.

She made a low growl, and then Falon—feeling a bit guilty—stared into the darkness. He saw her rise above Sirrom. Her sleek silhouette was barely visible. But still he could see her move, and he heard Sirrom's low grunts of pleasure.

Falon pulled his sleeping mat tight around his head, trying to block the sound.

But it was hopeless.

And even after they were done, he was left, wide awake, wondering why the good Lord Rhow's daughter would chose a murderer, with a wife and kits, rather than an ambitious highlander.

It didn't do much for his sense of confidence.

Ashre woke up, feeling the strange, uncomfortable tingle running through his body like never before.

Something bad was coming, real bad, right towards them from the east. The feeling was so strong it nearly had him scampering to find some dark corner in the town, some dismal hole he could hide in. He was practised at finding such hiding spots.

Only this time he knew that he wasn't alone. He was with others. Others that could help him . . . or trap him.

The feeling grew worse than ever before, and it was almost too hard to resist the temptation to just run, dash away.

Let the others face the danger alone.

Instead, he ran over to Falon and shook him once, then again. Back and forth, until he blinked awake, licking at his whiskers.

"Wha—It can't be time—"

"Falon," Ashre said, "Get up. Please."

Then he ran over to Sirrom, his massive body entangled with the fair-furred Taline. He hesitated a moment, then touched Sirrom's shoulder. Sirrom was alert instantly.

"Yes, what is it?" he asked. Taline stretched next to him.

"Visitors," Ashre said, and he pointed east. "Coming fast."

Sirrom was already on his feet. "A mrem of many talents, Ashre. Tell me, how many of them?"

"I . . . I'm not sure. There's more of them than us. And—"

"What else?"

Ashre shook his head. "They're not just mrem. There's something else . . . something, I don't know."

Sirrom patted Ashre's inky gray head. "That's okay, Ash. I think I have a good idea."

"What's up?" Falon said, stumbling over sleepily.

"Company," Sirrom said.

Falon grinned at Ashre. "Good work. Can we start getting out of here?"

Then Anarra was there, standing next to Taline, listening to Sirrom.

As though he was some kind of general, thought Ash. So calm, so at ease.

"I'll take a look from the top of the temple. Meanwhile, you start gathering our gear together."

Then, he was off, inside the temple. And Ashre followed him, eager to stay near him.

"Coming?" Sirrom asked, calling over his shoulder.

Ashre trotted next to him as they reached the stairs.

"Stay close, then."

The stairs twisted around to the left to the second floor of the temple. "Sure wish I'd brought a torch. I can't make out any way to go up."

"I'll run back and—"

"No," Sirrom ordered. "Stay close."

He waited a second, and Ashre felt his eyes begin to make out shapes in the gloom.

"There, a ladder just ahead." Sirrom grabbed Ashre's hand. "Quickly, now."

Sirrom went up first, but he kept glancing back at Ashre, making sure that he was following. Ashre heard him push at something, and suddenly he felt the cool air, just above.

"Quick, my hand!" Sirrom leaned down and pulled Ashre up with one effortless jerk.

And Ashre felt that something was missing. No claws.

It could only mean one thing.

Yet Ashre knew that it couldn't be true.

Sirrom couldn't be a murderer.

He flew onto the roof. "There . . ." Sirrom mumbled, somberly.

Ashre went to the edge of the temple's roof. He could see them, just barely outlined against the horizon.

"No time." Sirrom said. He looked right at Ashre, and gave him a big grin. "There's no time to get away, is there, Ash? So," he hoisted the kit on his shoulders, "we'll get a chance for a little fun, eh?"

Ashre nodded, but he wasn't so sure. If fun was coming then he shouldn't have the strange, sick feeling he had.

"Best for us to get back and give everyone the good news," Sirrom said.

And he seemed almost happy leading Ashre back to the others.

Falon had his pack all wrapped up, with just his own short sword out, strapped to his side.

He looked at Taline, fussing with her pack while Anarra hovered nearby.

He found it hard to say anything to her. Other images kept popping up in his mind.

Sirrom came back quickly.

"I'm afraid it's no good," he said.

"No good. For what?" Falon asked.

"For a getaway, friend. They'll be here too quickly. I suggest we start making some plans."

Taline came over. "Even if we leave right away—"

Sirrom shook his head. "They'd catch us in the open desert. Here, at least, we have a chance." He turned to Falon.

"Falon, you take a spot on top of the temple and lie low. Ashre will protect the stairs. Go after them when they pass you. Anarra will stay with Taline. If necessary, we'll fall back by the west wall of the town." He made a small laugh. "But let's hope they're a distant memory by then."

Taline came over to Falon. "You're not a fighter, so don't take any unnecessary risks."

"And you?"

"I've seen my share of battles. My father believed in a complete education."

"It looks like Sirrom's been around too," Falon said, gesturing at their self-appointed general. "I hope he knows what he's doing—"

"I think he does," Taline said with a smile. She knelt down close to Ashre. "And you, don't do anything crazy. Stay on the stairs. Watch out for Falon." She grabbed his shoulders. "And by tomorrow, what tales we'll have to tell."

"Come, we must get into place," Sirrom hissed.

Falon watched them leave, vanish down the gloomy sidewalks. Who knows, he thought, maybe never to be seen again.

It was still night, though there seemed to be the slightest glow beginning to bloom in the west. But the light wouldn't come quickly enough to help them.

"Shouldn't we move, Falon?" Ashre asked.

"Yes," he said, absently. Something bothered him about the setup . . . something simple. It stuck in his mind like a tiny thorn, irritating him.

Why was this small band arriving in the night? If it hadn't been for Ash, they would have been slain, pure and simple, the book removed.

It was as if, yes, as if the band knew they would be here. They arrived on schedule, with only one incalculable flaw. And something more . . . an idea that only now became clear. Could someone on their little jaunt be in league with them? Anarra . . . Sirrom . . . Taline. Was that impossible?

He was in over his head here, fighting bands from the East and an assassin from the West. Perhaps tending the herd-beasts wasn't such a bad life after all.

"Please . . . Falon . . . it grows late."

He nodded. The little one had more confidence than he'd ever have. And maybe more bravery too.

"Come then. Let's to our places. And I hope we miss it all."

Ashre led the way inside the temple, and then on up the stairs to the upper floor. After a moment's hesitation, he took Falon's hand and brought him to the ladder leading up.

"Stay here," Falon ordered. "Promise?"

Ashre nodded. And Falon climbed up the ladder.

Once on top of the temple, he ran to the edge and peered out over the desert.

The band was close, nearly to the edge of the town. Moving in a group like a single creature. Jumbling and bouncing along, moving very quickly towards the ruins.

Falon took out his short sword. He wished he felt comfortable with the heavy sword that Anarra had brought for him. It would do wonderful damage. But its weight made it too awkward, at least until he had had some practice with it.

He kept his eyes on the invaders. Then, their movements were masked by the eastern edge of the ruins and they were gone.

I'm blind now. No way to tell where they are . . . where they might be.

Then, he picked up a sound. Some horrible yell that traveled the desert air like the song of a moon swallow. Only this was a screeching, wrenching sound.

His grip tightened on his sword.

Then, more sounds, metal against metal, the clatter of swords. Distant . . . disturbing.

The clatter stopped, then started again, closer. More

screeching, then the howl of a mrem, a sound that made him shiver.

Behind him, the sky started to lighten, the dark black fading to a lush blue.

I'll be neatly outlined here, he thought.

The light would work to the advantage of the attackers.

He slid lower to the floor of the roof, and moved a bit back from the edge.

He bumped into someone.

"What!" he screamed, turning around like a mountain snake about to be skewered. He started to cut the air with his sword.

"It's me!" Ashre whispered.

He pulled his blow back, just in time. "I nearly cut you in two. You shouldn't have come up here. You should be—"

"I sensed a change, something—"

"A change? What do you mean?"

"They're not just . . . out there," he said, pointing east. "They're all around. I thought you should—"

And as if in confirmation of Ashre's warning, they heard something from the opening. A slithering sound . . . something large, dragging something, pushing the sands on the floor aside as it moved.

Falon gulped, and he quickly signaled Ashre to be quiet.

As if they knew he was here!

It was coming up the ladder.

He grabbed Ashre, and pulled him behind him, almost to the edge of the roof.

Then he crawled forward, not wanting to have his head too far off the ground.

Let me see them first.

He waited, his lips and whiskers sucking the air close to the sandy roof. Breathing quietly, waiting until something popped out of the roof.

At least I've got the light in front of me. They'll stand out while Ashre and I should be nearly invisible.

He waited, and waited, struggling to control his breathing.

And it started to come out of the hole.

A head, shiny-slick, with two bulbous eyes so alien Falon thought he moaned. It kept on climbing out of the hole, but he forced himself to stay still. He heard other sounds, close now, fighting.

He hoped that his friends were doing well.

Because he had absolutely no confidence in himself.

It brought a hand out and grabbed at the roof, making a strange guttural grunting sound. Then another hand, the spiky, clawlike fingers clearly outlined against the deep blue sky.

And Ashre struck!

Ashre leaped over Falon, landing right in front of the liskash. Its tongue lolled around, and then it reached down for its own weapon.

But it was too late, as Ashre plunged his dagger right into a spot just above the bulbous eye sockets. It screamed out, spitting gobs of slime into the air. Then Falon watched, amazed, as it slid down the ladder.

"Move away," Ashre said, helping Falon up. "There's bound to be more."

"You've done this before?"

Ashre tugged at him, urging him away. "Once or twice —they came to Fahl . . . recruiting. Usually the bands of mrem cut them into pieces."

"Good for them."

"And it always started with a quick jab to the head." Falon stood up and walked with Ashre. "I'm impressed." Then they both froze, as more sounds reached them.

"They're coming," Ashre said. "Lots of them."

Falon held his sword tight. "What do you suggest?"

Ashre looked left and right. "We could jump down to the street. Maybe get away. But we might be trapped there." Then he looked back to the hole. Another liskash was climbing out, this time with its weapon held up. It lumbered up slowly. There'd be no surprise attack this time. "Or we could make a stand here."

With incredible speed, the liskash seemed to flip itself through the hole and onto the roof . . . then another appeared, and flipped itself onto a different spot.

"Their tails . . ." Ashre whispered. "They're using their tails—I've never seen that."

Then another, and another, until there were four of them, standing before the rising sun, ready to kill.

Chapter 15

▲————————————————————————▲

Falon let the liskash make the first move.

Except they moved together, closing in on him and Ashre, their tails swirling ominously back and forth.

"I've had better mornings, Ashre. But I'm glad this isn't bothering you."

But the kit seemed to have lost some of his incredible strength. He leaned against Falon, shaking.

"Only four of them, Ash . . . no problem."

The liskash kept coming, cautious, almost uncomfortable.

And Falon flashed on the reason why.

It was getting light out. These monsters were thought to dislike daylight. If he could hold out, he might be able to use that.

Then the one to his left made a charging jab at him. The blow was easily dodged, and the liskash almost tipped over the edge.

Falon checked that the others were holding their positions, and then he swung around, digging his blade into the broad back of their first attacker. It bellowed and screamed, reaching behind it to pull out the blade.

But Falon removed it suddenly, knowing that this would cause the others to move.

They seemed to skip closer, their blades crisscrossing the air, their tongues looking ready to taste him.

"Move left!" he told Ashre. And he jabbed his small sword at two of the liskash's weapons.

Too small! he thought. He needed a bigger weapon against them, something with reach and weight.

One of them tried to skip up quickly and take a swing at Ashre, but Falon jerked the kit to the side, and then jabbed at the liskash, cutting it right in its glistening broad midsection.

Another one dared jump closer, and Falon barely brought his blade around in time to slash upward, as hard as he could, to stop it.

Then all three of them crowded closer.

And Falon knew, as he dodged their blows, that it was all over.

"If you can—" Falon said between blows to his left and right, "get yourself—out of—here—do it!"

Then one of the liskash's blades slipped down, alongside Falon's sword, and then in, cutting Falon's leg. He moaned, feeling his blood begin to splatter onto the roof.

"Get out, Ash!" he screamed.

And he didn't know whether it was because the kit couldn't leave, or wouldn't, but Ashre's response was to make a quick poke at the liskash as it pulled its blade from Falon's leg.

Then they stood there, back against back, chopping at the unequal blades of the liskash, trying to keep the creatures away, as they inexorably came closer and closer.

Not a bad way to die, Falon thought. If only he knew what was in that book that made it so valuable.

His arm grew tired, as it smashed two blows away at a time. Not long now, he thought.

And then—someone else was there.

"Anarra!" he called out. She held her heavy sword in her hand like a great warrior. "Thank the All-Mother. Here, quickly—help—"

The words froze in his throat. She stood there, just stood there.

Another blow hit him, this time in his chest. A surface cut—painful, but not deadly. Ashre called out, a whimper that snapped him out of his horror-struck reverie.

"Ash . . . careful . . ."

One liskash came so close that Falon smelled its breath, a rich and sour smell. He brought his sword up right to the soft scaly skin under its large jaw. It opened its mouth and spit at him, a filmy mixture of blood and spit.

She stood there! Her sword by her side. Stood, and watched.

It was Anarra. She had to be the assassin!

She was the renegade in league with the Eastern Lords.

He thought he saw her smile.

Ashre tumbled backwards, slipping on the pool of blood that formed near them.

"Get up, Ash, get up!"

But why should he . . . to let them hack at them some more? No. Better to let him end it, quickly . . . with no more struggle.

Then someone was there, next to Anarra, pushing past her, hacking with his blade, left, right, left, right, until the liskash could do nothing but turn around to meet this new enemy.

And Falon took advantage of the target they gave him, slicing down on their backs, digging into their scaly humps over and over, cursing to himself, begging to have the strength to last to see them dead. Even Ashre was on his feet again, stabbing at the liskash.

It was Sirrom, and now the battle came to a quick end. The liskash were quickly outflanked and killed, gone all clumsy now that they were the ones surrounded.

"Anarra!" Falon yelled, watching Anarra attack Sirrom as the farmer lowered his sword.

"I'm ahead of you," Sirrom whispered, smoothly swinging his sword around like a great scythe. He sliced Anarra like a stalk of krarl grass.

Her face caught the first bit of morning light. Her eyes nearly popped out of her head.

It was a sight that made Falon feel very happy indeed, before he collapsed onto all the dead liskash.

His wounds bandaged, his pack now being carried by Sirrom, Falon trudged to keep up with the besieged party.

It was Taline who said that they had to get out, leave Gfaar, and fast.

"The last thing we want to do is cross the desert at night."

Sirrom agreed, though he seemed more concerned with reinforcements from the East.

Nobody said anything about Anarra, and Falon figured that Taline assumed she fell in the battle.

Every step was painful, trying to dig into the sand, pulling at his wounds. All the time, thinking, not with any joy, it could have been worse.

Apparently he and Ashre had fought all the liskash. Somehow, the renegade mrem tied up Taline and Sirrom, while Anarra led the liskash right to him. And once again, he was left with that burning question: Why me?

The pace slowed not a bit, as the sun burned down on them. They certainly weren't overly concerned about him. Ashre, though, was being given a grand ride atop Sirrom's shoulders. Despite his small wound, he seemed chipper.

Finally, when Gfaar was lost to the hazy yellow sun behind them, Falon felt he had to rest.

"I . . . need to stop," he called out. Taline turned first, looking none too pleased. Then Sirrom, holding Ashre aloft and looking like a monster with two bodies. He too frowned, but then came back to Falon.

"Pain?"

"You could say that. I just need a bit of rest. . . ."

Sirrom reached up and slid Ashre off his broad shoulders and down to the sand. "Rest then, and I'll walk alongside you."

Yes, Falon thought, *I could use a good arm right about now.*

"And I'll walk a bit. I'm not really hurt at all!" Ashre said. As if to prove the point, he ran across the sand, making curves and circles, laughing, wonderfully, before sliding, panting into the sand.

Falon sat down, and took a few blessed gulps of water, letting it trickle over his lips, down his chin, wetting his furry chest. "Okay," he said. "I'm ready."

Sirrom reached down and gently pulled him up. He locked arms with him, easily, naturally, and Falon felt like he was leaning against a stone wall. Taline had started moving again, a rejuvenated Ashre walking happily by her side.

"Better?" Sirrom asked.

"Much. I think if it were up to Taline she'd leave me here for the weevils."

Sirrom arched his thick eyebrows. "Don't mind her. She's just concerned. She's afraid for Tizare, and for her father. She's just afraid that last night's raid is the start of a major campaign."

"I don't think it's her father who's in danger."

They were climbing down an enormous dune, almost the equal of the rolling mountains of Falon's homeland. Except that his every step produced horrible pain. But, with Sirrom's help, at least he wasn't slipping.

"I think you're right there, Falon."

"You do?" Falon said, turning to him. "What do you mean?"

Sirrom looked ahead, as if checking to see if Taline could hear. Then he turned his dark eyes on Falon.

"They came for you . . . and almost got you."

"Right, exactly—but why?"

Sirrom laughed, causing Ashre to turn around, a puzzled look on his face. "Damned to the demons if I know, Falon. I thought you were just another stupid highlander. Guess I was wrong."

The mountain of sand leveled out, and now they entered the enormous sandy plain that ran back to the edge of the woods, and Sirrom's farm.

"And what of you?" Falon dared ask.

He felt Sirrom clench his muscles, as if bracing himself. "Better to be quiet now, Falon. Enough talking."

But Falon pressed on. He was feeling trust and respect for Sirrom. Being a murderer didn't fit.

"No," Falon said, "Why do you live out in the wasteland, what happened to you? If there's anything I know, it's that you're not a murderer."

Sirrom grinned. "Oh, you saw that, did you? Well, perhaps you'll tell the King of Ar. Perhaps you can win me back my claws, my life. . . ." He spit into the sand.

"I just meant—" Falon stammered.

They seemed to be walking more quickly now, trying to keep up with Taline.

"Fact is, Falon, I *am* a murderer. You're wrong."

"But how?"

"I was King Talwe's personal counselor, Paralan."

Paralan! Falon took a step back. Paralan had murdered an ambassador . . . and been banished. It had signaled the beginning of King Talwe's decline.

"I murdered the ambassador," Paralan snorted, "who was actually a powerful magic user working for the Eastern Lords. Of course, I had no evidence . . . just my own dumb instinct. . . ."

Or perhaps, Falon wondered, beast magic.

"I'm surprised you weren't killed."

"Oh," he laughed again, "I would have been—rather quickly too. Talwe never forgot our battles together. But he never forgave my act. He decreed banishment. My life was spared, but I was disgraced, declawed, and sent away, forbidden to enter any city again."

"Until now."

"Heh?"

"Part of this deal," Falon said, grinning despite the pain. "You'll be a hero in Tizare."

"Perhaps . . ." Paralan said. "I admit that I have not been disinterested in the affairs of the city states, or Talwe. I listened to every story passed on by every merchant, cherishing each bit of news as if it were a treasure. Even here, in this wilderness, I would become angered upon hearing of some suspected treachery against one of the kings, or their own foolishness . . ."

As Falon listened to Paralan, he heard the voice of the former king's minister appear, as if the simple farmer was transforming before his very eyes.

"And I have especially cherished the news of Ar, even when I suspected that it might be simply rumors."

"Good news?"

"Good news? That remains to be seen. Last week an old caravan-master stopped. And he proposed a toast. He said that the breach between old Talwe and his beloved Sruss is to come to an end. Within two moons she is to be brought out of exile, returning to rule at Talwe's side."

"Then that *is* good news. Perhaps you may be restored to the great city state, freed from your own banishment."

"Perhaps. And perhaps not. Living here, I have learned two things. Time moves too slowly or too fast, never what you need or desire. It is the real ruler of our lives. And I've learned not to depend on anything . . . or anyone, except myself."

Falon nodded.

The sun was in his eyes, hot, blistering, and only the hope of resting when they reached the farmhouse kept him moving at all.

The journey was almost over, the first trees had appeared at the horizon, and every step brought dreams of a warm supper and cool well water that much closer.

They were together now, Ashre and Taline side by side with them. But nobody talked—it took too much effort. The only sound was the swishing of their feet digging into the sand, step after step, one after the other, closer and closer until Falon thought he could almost smell the wonderful aroma of roast uxan and fresh gradle berries, with cups of wine filled to the very top.

They all hurried now, Falon moving quickly, urging Paralan on. Soon he could rest, close his eyes, and pray never to see a grain of sand again.

Then Ashre pulled back, as if not wanting to go on.

"Come on, Ash," Falon said, hobbling forward. "We're almost there."

"Yes, and my Lonirr will have something wonderful for us to eat."

But it did no good, and Ashre started whimpering, crying. . . .

"What is it?" Taline said, crouching down close to him.

"No," he said, shaking his head. "I . . . I don't want to see it."

"Eh, see what?" Paralan said. And he looked up, his great proud head staring into the distance. "What are you afraid of—"

Paralan froze, and let go of Falon at the same instant.

"What is it?" Falon said. "What's—"

It was a whisper. Icy, chilling all of them, even in the late afternoon light.

"Lonirr . . . the kits . . ."

Paralan stumbled forward, slowly at first, then running full out. His hands grabbed at the air, pulling at it.

"Ash," Falon said quietly. "What is wrong? Tell us."

But Ashre just stood there, whimpering, repeating, "No."

There was the farmhouse just ahead. A place they had dreamt about all day.

There it was.

The heat made hazy waves rise from the fields.

The farmhouse. And tiny plumes of smoke streamed up from it, almost invisible.

"Oh, by the All-Mother. No!" Falon screamed. "No . . ."

And he ran as fast as he could, ignoring the pain.

"What is it?" Taline screamed, but Falon didn't turn around.

Ashre would tell her. When the horrible pictures faded.

The tiny plumes rose almost straight up to the darkening sky. The house, though, still appeared normal in all respects —save one.

It was clearly black . . . a dark, smoldering hulk.

Falon imagined Paralan's horror, the immense feelings that must be rushing through him, touching his every nerve, filling his mind with picture after horrible picture.

He had to hurry. He didn't want him to get there—stand there—all alone.

He slipped in the sand, already starting to cool now that the intense light of day was gone. He struggled up.

Paralan had stopped running. He stood there, next to the hulk.

And the most terrible sound reached Falon's ears . . . the sound of Paralan screaming, wailing up at the darkening sky.

As Falon kept on hobbling forward . . .

Chapter 16

▲━━━━━━━━━━━━━━━━━━━━━━━━━━━━━━━━▲

Paralan was already walking inside the smoldering ruins by the time Falon got there. The smell of burnt wood, grass . . . and something else made his nostrils twitch.

"Paralan . . ." Falon said gently, reaching out and touching the blackened walls. The dense parra wood felt puffy and porous.

He looked over his shoulder, wishing that Taline and Ash would hurry up and get there.

What do I say, he wondered? *What can I do to help him?*

The wild moaning had stopped, replaced by the steady crunch as Paralan strode through his small farmhouse . . . looking . . . searching.

Please, Falon thought. *Don't let him find anything. Let the house be empty, deserted.*

Suddenly it was quiet inside. A gentle wind whistled eerily through the open house.

Falon went to the doorway and stepped in.

It was still warm inside. Not so hot that he couldn't walk, but uncomfortable. Everything seemed normal inside, the rough wooden table, the chairs, the fireplace.

Except that it was all black.

Paralan was kneeling by the corner. It was dark in here now. He could barely make Paralan out, just kneeling there. He took another awkward step closer.

"Paralan . . ."

But Paralan made no sound—nothing.

Another step, and Falon stood just behind him, looking over his shoulder, looking down, at the bodies.

Lonirr was curled on the floor, her two kits held tightly on either side.

So peaceful they could have been sleeping.

Falon tried to say something.

His mouth opened, but nothing came out.

The bodies! So black it made him want to scrub them, clean off the soot.

Paralan stood up slowly, and turned. His face seemed locked into position as he stared through, and past Falon.

"Paralan . . ." he said again, almost a whisper.

Paralan turned, and walked out of the burnt farmhouse, out to the yard. Then he knelt in the yard and he started digging in the dirt, using first his sword, then his hands, clawing at the dirt.

And now Falon heard his cry, terrible, an almost babylike sound as this giant mrem knelt on the ground and dug at the dirt. Then Falon came beside him, knelt down, and also started digging at the dirt, sharing the grief of his friend in the ancient way of their race.

Each handful of dirt, much more difficult for Sirrom, made the hole grow slowly, as if it were alive. Taline and Ashre arrived, and without a word, they joined in.

Falon looked over at Ashre. He sniffled, his beautiful smoky eyes all watery, but kept pace with the others.

Finally, Paralan spoke.

"I will find who did this. Find them . . . and kill them. And I'll kill any who help them, or have anything to do with them. I—"

His voice broke, and he collapsed into the dirt.

Taline touched his arm, rubbed his fur, and spoke sweet, gentle words of comfort. Over and over.

"It was a band from the East . . . like the other . . ." Ashre blurted out. Falon shot him a quick warning glance to be quiet. But Paralan rose up quickly.

"Where are they now?"

"I don't know . . . but they are moving west . . . not east."

"West," Paralan said. "Towards Tizare. Then that's where I will go."

He stood up, and went back inside his farmhouse.

And when he came out, he had two small bodies cradled in his arms.

They camped a short hike away from the farmhouse, just far away enough so that the stench of the wood didn't reach them. And they rose early that next morning, eager to be off to Tizare.

The road to Tizare is one filled with rolling hills and fertile valleys that make travel an eye-filling, if tiring, experience. But they had their own reasons for simply wanting to get to the city as quickly as possible. Despite beautiful weather, with a clear blue sky that painted the woods and grass in dark, bright colors, they marched, heads down, hurrying to the smoke and din of the city.

Falon hadn't given much thought to the rest of his life once he returned to Tizare. Would he find some secure position with the noble Lord Rhow's house, or would he be faced with a vagrant's life in the great city?

Time would tell.

If that was the case, he would, no doubt, prefer to return to his mountains. The air was fresh there, and the duties demanding enough to keep his mind off other matters.

But whatever happened, Falon felt that they were all changed, each of them in a different way.

Paralan had become their leader, and then lost everything he cared about. Taline seemed more confused and insecure the closer they came to Tizare.

Ashre said little, awaiting his next flash of unwanted knowledge.

And Falon realized why that was happening to Ashre so frequently now. Before he was alone, but now he was part of a group. All those connections brought unwanted images . . . unwanted fears.

As for himself, he felt his untroubled state of mind had been replaced with questions that wouldn't vanish. Why did Anarra try to kill him, for it surely had to have been she. And why was she helping the Eastern Lords? Why was this book so important?

And why, he smiled to himself, had Plano asked him in the first place?

And here his fur flared out . . . there was more to that than he was told, he was sure of it.

He thought of these things, his wound gradually re-sponding to the herbs gingerly applied by Taline. With Paralan so preoccupied, she seemed to be showing more concern for, if not interest in, Falon.

Despite everything, he knew that he was definitely in-terested in her . . . excited by her.

By the late afternoon, they started to run into small groups leaving Tizare. Most were hearty merchant bands, well armed, and about to make the relatively safe journey to Ar or one of the other cities. Others were headed for the distant ports to the south, perhaps to try their luck on the open seas, a prospect which made Falon shudder. He re-called all too vividly the time Caissir and he had tried to cross the stream.

That was more water than he ever wanted to see.

Most of the travelers hurried past them, eager to be on their way. Falon would have liked to tell them about invad-ers from the East . . . give them a friendly warning.

But their scowls and the ready hands on their swords persuaded him to mind his own business.

And that was another change. Up till now, Paralan had been their leader. That was no longer true, and Taline, without the barrel-chested Anarra by her side, didn't seem interested in the role. She pulled the sleepy-eyed Daynia along, the uxan sensing that—with Anarra gone—Taline was her new mistress.

That left Falon, who had called for the rest stops and selected the site for their midday meal of berries and dried uxan.

Now that they were almost at the city gates he waited for Taline to take charge. But outside of tending to his wounds and talking quietly with Ashre (and *glad* he was of that), she seemed disinterested in their quest.

The book, Falon thought . . . *I want to look at it. Before Rhow sees it. To see what makes it so valuable.*

Somehow, before they reached the noble's palace, he'd take a look . . . hoping that his simple village-school les-sons would serve him well enough.

And he was lost to these thoughts when they passed a small group of White Dancers.

Who hid a surprise.

At first, Falon simply saw the Dancers, resting by the side of the road, passing around a large gourd of water.

With their brilliant white fur they could hardly be over-looked. But then he saw a mrem, well off the trail, lying down like a female about to give birth to a dozen kits—and he grinned at that moment—

Caissir!

"Caissir! Caissir," he called, still way down the trail.

Caissir scrambled up to a sitting position quickly, his eyes wide with the guilty look of someone about to be arrested and thrown into the dungeon.

The White Dancers turned, smoothly, graceful even in their alarm.

The Dancers regarded Falon's approach cautiously.

I must look more than a bit bedraggled, he thought. *My fur is matted with blood, there are bandages hanging off my body, and I must have the wild-eyed look of someone back from the dead.*

But Caissir was already grinning, walking over, his arms extended. The Dancers, with a subtle, sleek movement, relaxed.

"Falon! I thought I'd never see you again!"

"There were moments when I shared that thought, Caissir."

"Here," Caissir said, running over to one of the Dancers and rudely snapping the drinking gourd away, "have a drink. You look," he smiled, "a bit dry around the whiskers."

Falon drank, and nodded. "That's for sure," he said.

Taline, Paralan, and Ashre came up to them.

"I see you still have your merry companions with you. Where's that monster and her uxan? What was her name?"

Falon brought a finger up to his lips, shushing Caissir. "Anarra. She's dead. And who knows what happened to the uxan. . . ."

Caissir came closer. "Dead, eh. Well, I knew that I'd do better to strike off on my own. Never did like the desert." He grinned.

"So what are you doing with . . . them? Didn't know you had any interest in the communication arts."

"What? Oh, you mean the White Dancers. I met them on the road south. They said that raiders from the East were attacking small villages and outposts. They carry some great message for the king and the people of Tizare. I'm not privy to that, I'm afraid. But they agreed to take me with them rather than letting me be cut up for the bellies of the liskash—"

"They don't eat dead mrem." It was Ashre, standing stock-still next to Falon.

"Say, he's in a cheerful mood. Why so glum, Ash?"

Falon raised a hand, trying to indicate that Caissir should back away and not press the kit.

But Caissir took no notice.

"Everyone knows the liskash aren't above a quick nibble on a mrem from time to time."

"If you're alive," Ashre said, his eyes glowing. Then, with a cruel smile playing on his young face, he added, "But don't worry. You'll have time to get a close-up look really soon."

Falon gave Ashre's shoulder a squeeze.

"What does *that* mean? What are you talking about, Ashre?" Caissir looked positively terrified.

"Don't mind him," Taline said. She walked up close to Caissir, smiling. She didn't seem to hold any grudge against Caissir for his departure.

"Oh, Taline, I'm sorry that I—"

She laughed, the first time Falon heard that sound in days. "Don't worry, Caissir. Falon explained that, whatever else you may be, you're not an adventurer."

"Quite right." Caissir puffed himself up. "In fact, I'm a wizard. Why, once—"

The Chief Dancer of the White Dancers walked over to them. Her fur was pure white, whether naturally or from the special dye used by the cult. Her eyes were a gentle, luminescent green.

"We are about to start moving again. You and your friends," she said to Caissir, "are welcome to travel with us. It will be safer for all of you." Her eyes seemed to flare and she glanced down quickly, meaningfully at Ashre.

Paralan was off by himself, running a stone back and forth on both sides of his blade. He seemed lost to them now, lost to his own world of revenge.

"Thank you," Falon said, "we'd like that."

The Dancer smiled, and returned to her troupe.

"I'll be glad," Caissir said, "to be back inside the city walls."

So will I, thought Falon. *Except why doesn't it feel like I'm moving to safety?*

He shrugged, and grabbed his heavy pack off the ground.

The gates to Tizare were, if anything, even more crowded this time than last. It was night, and enormous torches dotted the city wall, sending a flickering light down on the great crowds of mrem who waited to enter the city.

Obviously word was getting around about the disturbing raids in the countryside.

Many of them were being turned away. Groups trudged past Falon, grumbling, cursing in the many strange dialects found in the countryside.

What city now? some yelled at each other. A few talked about making their way to the south, to the great sea. Perhaps passage could be booked to some island sanctuary. Others talked with growing enthusiasm about seeking refuge in the north, and for the first time Falon wondered whether his own clansmrem were in danger.

Everyone who passed had the same word on their lips. Invasion!

"I hope we get inside without a problem," Falon joked to Taline.

She didn't laugh. The scene at the gates disturbed her. "This is not good," was all she said, quietly.

They neared the winding line of hopefuls seeking entry. The Dancers went to the end of the line.

"No," Taline said, her voice sounding strong. "I will move us through more quickly."

And she strode down the line, leading the way quickly to the platoon of blue-armored soldiers guarding the gate.

It was, Falon knew, now or never.

"Taline, I'd like to see the book . . . before we—"

Her hand went to her sword. The suddenness of the movement startled Falon.

"No one sees the book. No one! Save my father."

It occurred to Falon that he hadn't seen Taline in action, using her sword. And he didn't want to now.

"Fine," he smiled. "I was just asking. Just curious." He held his hand open. "A family trait."

She relaxed.

They were almost to the guards when Paralan stopped. "I'll stay out here," he said quietly.

Taline gestured for the Dancers to stop. "What do you mean, you'll stay here?"

"There are no raiding bands within those city walls. Those I seek," he gestured out, across the rolling hills that surrounded Tizare, "roam free, out here."

She walked up to him. "Yes, they roam free. But they are coming here, coming to Tizare, Paralan. And you can be here, ready to help fight them, ready to defend the city."

He seemed to think this over, shifting a bit uneasily.

"Yes," Falon added. "Come with us. It would seem to be a time of great danger for the cities. Together, we may help."

As if to seal the issue, Ashre scampered over. "I will help you," he said to Paralan meaningfully. "Together we will find them." The kit grabbed at Paralan's massive hand.

"Very well, then. But I'll not loll around the castle and courtyards waiting for something to happen."

It was a prediction, Falon later reflected, that would come only too true. . . .

Taline made quick work of the guards, navigating past the gates and into the crowded city. The head of the White Dancers thanked her, and invited them to come to the main square the next night for an important performance.

Taline then led the party through the streets of Tizare, quickly, down narrow alleyways, through arcades and tunnels, taking a route that she knew would be less cluttered.

The city was filled with mrem. An air of carnival prevailed, with much drinking, laughing, selling, and buying going on. Once again Falon was overwhelmed with the richness of the city. There were stalls filled with bolts of shimmering cloth, a luxurious material that begged to have hands glide across it. There were foodstuffs of unrecognizable origins such as sea creatures with many eyes. Falon nearly ejected his last meal when he saw a merchant dig out one eye and offer it as a sample to a potential customer. And once again there were the females, filling the warm night air with the delicious aroma of promised pleasures.

At times, Ashre had to give him a gentle shove to get him moving.

But all too soon, Taline had them at the side gate to her father's castle, striding matter-of-factly past the bowing guards, who kept their eyes down as she hurried past. She wasted no time moving the group to the upper floors of the palace, to a grand suite of rooms that Falon assumed must belong to her.

She stripped off her filthy kilt and throat armor.

A servant stood at attention awaiting her order.

"Bring food, wine, and nurses to attend to our wounds," she snapped.

She stood naked, in front of them, unabashedly beautiful.

Will I ever get used to city ways, Falon thought?

She hurried into another room, and Falon heard water.

"What's that for?" Falon asked nervously.

"Showers," Taline said. "To wash off the stink of desert and liskash."

Ashre hid behind Falon, while Caissir busied himself examining, with a practiced hand, the furnishings. Paralan studied the immense murals that filled the walls.

"You first, Ash. Then the rest of us."

"N-No," he stammered. "Water is for fish and fools."

She walked over to him, her fine fur glistening beautifully in the candlelight. "And it's for you, Ash. Because you'll not stay in my house smelling like a street kit."

She looked at Falon, giving him a warning glance should he also decide to protest.

Taline reached out and caressed the small ears of Ashre. "Besides, how will we ever know what wonders you have stored in these"—she ruffled the kit's ears—"unless we clean them out?" She smiled at him, and led him to the room filled with the ominous whoosh of water.

The yells and screams of Ashre turned Falon's blood cold.

He gave a quick glance at the door.

But before he could weigh the merits of leaving versus a shower, Taline was there. "Now, we'll clean you up, and my personal nurses will tend to your wounds." She pulled at one of his bandages, and bits of Falon's fur stuck to the dried mixture of cloth and clotted blood.

"Ouch!" he yelped. He looked down at his chest wound.

Nasty, but it was nothing a good night's sleep wouldn't help repair. Taline reached out and pressed her fingertips against it.

"Does it hurt?" she asked, biting at her lower lip.

Only when you touch it, he wanted to say. But he was so thrilled just to have her pressing close against him that he kept his mouth shut.

She looked up at him.

"I'll shower with you," she said, a small smile playing on her lips, "to make sure that the wounds are properly washed out."

"But—"

Suddenly, the room was filled with a small squad of maids and nurses, some bearing trays of fruit and flasks of wine, while others carried bundles of bandages and containers of what Falon imagined to be ointment.

Taline ordered one of them to remove Ashre from the shower and dress him in clean clothes.

"And now, it is our turn," she said to Falon lightly. She gave him a gentle push in the direction of the shower room.

She leaned up to his ear.

"And when you're good and clean, we'll take the book to my father."

As he entered the doorway, Ashre plopped out, his fur wet against his body. But he wore a strange sort of grin, half surprised, half stunned.

"It's not so bad . . ." he said, laughing.

Chapter 17

▲————————————————————————————————————▲

Her fingers traced lazy circles over his aching body, gently working the soap into his wounds.

He yelped a few times, responding to the sting of the water and soap. And he hated the feeling of the water cascading down upon him, pressing his hair flat against his body, darkening the swirls of color. It was a perfectly miserable feeling.

But Taline's hands . . . they were wonders, kneading his muscles, creating balls of lather on his pelt, then rinsing them away with a cloth and the torrent of water.

And he knew that if it wasn't such an uncomfortable, perverse feeling, this being *wet*, he would surely be aroused.

Taline seemed to be enjoying it, humming low to herself, pressing against him, moving her small tight body against his.

Her intentions were clear, even to an inexperienced fool like himself.

But then a gaggle of her maids burst into the steamy room. "Lord Rhow wants you and the highlander to come to his private chambers now."

Taline backed away, heaving a small sigh. "Yes," she said. "As soon as we're dry, and dressed." She grinned at Falon. "We'll be right along."

She pushed away from Falon, and turned off the water.

"We must," she said, a big smile on her face, licking at her wet lips, "do this again sometime."

And she walked out of the stall, wrapping herself in an enormous fuzzy cloth.

Taline left instructions for Caissir, Ashre, and Paralan to be attended to, and led Falon, book in hand, to the private chambers of her father, Lord Rhow.

It was a dimly lit, great expanse of a room, dominated by an enormous bed. Taline fell to her knees upon entering. Such an unlikely gesture, Falon thought—but he followed suit.

Lord Rhow sat up on his bed, supported by a raft of pillows, a silver goblet in his hand.

"Please rise," he said gently to his daughter.

She approached the bed, *The Song of the Three Moons* held tightly in her hands. She passed it to Lord Rhow almost reverently.

"You've done well." He fondled the book, running a hand along its rich hide cover. Then he looked up, and arched his eyebrows. "I'm sorry, of course, about Anarra." Now he fixed his gaze on Falon. "And I thank you, highlander. Your help . . . your trust has been invaluable."

Falon nodded.

Rhow put down his goblet. "Now, let us see what we have here."

They stood there, he and Taline, while the lord flipped the crinkly pages of the book, muttering, "Yes," and "Aha," as if the contents of the manuscript were not quite unknown to him.

And Falon wondered if he was now going to learn what was in the book. He shifted uneasily on his feet. He still wanted nothing more than to rest.

Finally, after what seemed like a tremendous time, Lord Rhow snapped the book shut and laid it down beside him.

He refilled his own goblet with a purplish wine that poured thickly from the flask. "Would you care for some wine?" he asked.

Falon shook his head.

"But you *would* like to know," Rhow smiled, "What's in this book?" He looked at Taline, then back to Falon.

Falon nodded.

Rhow swung his legs off the bed, standing up, his flowing

robe glistening in the flickering light. "Oh, I know that you must both be very tired. But I want you to understand what's in this book. Especially," he said, striding right up to Falon, "yes, especially you, highlander."

He turned away from them and looked up at the battle scenes that surrounded his room. "Old King Talwe had a consort, Sruss, beautiful but headstrong." Rhow turned, giving a knowing glance at Taline. "But when he sent her to supervise the reconstruction of Cragsclaw, he took Feila, young, beautiful . . . fertile. Feila was infatuated with the cult of Gfaar, but that was of no consequence to Talwe.

"But when she became with kit, Talwe banished Feila to a barbaric kingdom to the North. This book tells her story, of Talwe, and the proud but jealous Sruss. Of Feila's slaying of the barbaric king of the North, and her own bloody death."

Rhow paused, looking right at Falon. "And, preserved by the cultists of Gfaar, it tells the story of King Talwe's kit . . . and the sad story of Mineir of Tizare, the usurper of that city's throne."

"Usurper?"

Rhow nodded. "Mineir has always been a lackey of the Eastern Lords." The lord spit out his words.

Rhow was at the wall, his hand touching one of the massive paintings, feeling the ancient, thickly encrusted paint.

"This," he said, gesturing at the central figure of the painting, decked out in splendid blue armor, dotted with ribbons and medals, "is a painting of the proud, foolish King of Tizare . . . just before he dies mysteriously and turns his throne over to the Eastern Lords." Rhow took another sip of the wine.

Despite his terrible fatigue, Falon found himself totally absorbed by Lord Rhow's story. It was as if parts of it he knew, somehow, perhaps spoken of by the village she-mrem.

"But Talwe's kit is alive, a strong, mottled mrem whose fur bears the obvious swirls of someone descended from royalty." The lord looked right at Falon, the beginning of a smile creasing his lips.

"That book documents the strange story. It doesn't tell the rest, though. No, there's nothing there about the kit growing up, so different, among villagers who knew nothing about who or what he was. It says nothing about his high-strung nature, his fast temper, and his prodigious appetite for females. . . ."

Falon's whiskers twitched.

"It doesn't tell how the young mrem happened to dally with one of the females of a clan chief, how he fell into the taunting trap of the chief, how he struck first in the duel. . . ." Rhow walked up to Falon, and rested a hand on his shoulder.

"But then, you know that part of the story, don't you, Falon?" And here Lord Rhow laughed, a great booming sound that echoed through the room.

"I . . . I don't understand," Falon said, even as he had the unpleasant feeling that he actually did understand.

Impossible! he thought. *I have a mother, a father. I'm not—*

"It is this mrem who, prophecy tells us," Rhow said, "will save the throne of Tizare—even as his father saved Ar."

"But a king already rules—"

Another laugh from Rhow, snide. "Not a king, Falon. Mineir is merely someone who manipulated the court to take control after the old king of Tizare's death."

"But he has been ruling for years. Surely no one now has the right to depose him?"

Rhow threw down his goblet. "Right? Did you say right?" He walked back and forth angrily, like a caged Rar in a zoo. "No, perhaps not," he said, shaking a fist in the air. "Not to overthrow a good and loyal king. But this 'king' "— Rhow spat—"is no such thing. He is merely the latest step in the plans of the Eastern Lords. Their raiding bands already litter the countryside."

Falon felt that he had to sit down. He looked over to Taline. She was studying him with those blue-green eyes of hers. "May I?" he asked gesturing at a chair off to the side.

Rhow nodded. "This king is nothing more than an agent of the Eastern Lords. The big move against the city will be in two, maybe three days. You," he said, pointing at Falon, "shall stop it."

Now it was Rhow who stood before the resting Falon.

"Bring me the head of the king, and I will give you your birthright—your throne. Together, we will rule Tizare

. . . make it a fortress against any incursions by the Eastern Lords."

"But how?" Falon said, shaking his head. *It's too much,* he thought, *too insane.*

"We have," Rhow said, grinning, "a plan."

And he gestured at Taline.

Had she known all the time, Falon wondered?

She went to a hidden cabinet, sunken into the intricately carved woodwork of the wall, and removed an armful of heavy scrolls.

"It's Taline's plan, actually, and with your help I've no doubt we'll succeed."

She spread the scrolls out on a chest at the foot of her father's bed, and stood there, waiting for Falon to walk over.

Which, after a moment's hesitation, he did.

"The plan," Taline said with sudden authority, "is really quite simple. You will have ten confederates—some of our best soldiers—plus myself, Paralan, Caissir, if he's interested, and Elezar."

Falon was still trying to comprehend this improbable turn of events. The amazing thing is that it did, in fact, explain many things. He had always been treated as an outsider in his village. His markings had set him apart— nobody in the hills looked the way he did—but there had been other things that told him that he just didn't belong.

Now he was supposed to believe, and act on, the fact that he was the heir to the throne of Tizare.

"Elezar . . ." he said absently. "Who is Elezar?"

"My most trusted general," Rhow said, smiling. "Absolutely ruthless in his loyalty to me. And, when I so order, he'll be equally loyal to you. He also has the uncommon military advantage of being quite smart. Just one small suggestion, though." Rhow's grin broadened. "Don't make any comments about his rather large tail. He's a bit self-conscious about it."

"The ladies like it," Taline added.

Falon looked down at the charts on the table. "What are these?" he said, fingering through the layers of heavy parchment.

"These are the plans for the king's palace—your palace. We will attempt to enter in three different places." She jabbed at four locations on the map. "At each entrance

we'll create a diversion, something to confuse the guards
. . . just enough to get us inside the palace. From there, it
will be a quick romp to the bedchambers of the king."

"Quick? Romp?"

"I don't imagine that we'll face more than one, maybe
two hundred of his best guards."

"With only fifteen of us?"

She laughed. "Fifteen of us will *try* to get in. But I would
imagine that at most five or six of us will actually get inside."

For a moment Falon thought that Taline was telling
jokes. It sounded like a perfect way to get slaughtered. He
turned to Lord Rhow. "Why not send your best legions
against the palace?"

Rhow chuckled. "My army is wonderful. But it's a puny
thing compared to the might of the forces of Tizare.
They'd be cut down, I'd be imprisoned—" he arched his
eyebrows. "And I'd hate to imagine what would happen to
you."

"And afterwards . . . after we capture the king—"

"The false king . . . the usurper, Falon," Rhow reminded him. "Why, you'll kill him immediately. You. It is
your right. I'll produce this book, and you will assume your
rightful position, with my counsel."

Right, thought Falon. Except that it sounded all wrong.
There were more things wrong with this plan than merely
the odds.

And something else nagged at him. *Is this the way,* he
wondered, *that I'm to regain my honor? Going from a
disgraced herd-mrem to an assassin?*

Taline sensed his concern and came to him, linking an
arm through his. "Perhaps we had better start studying the
charts . . . just a bit, before you go asleep. . . ." He was
disappointed to note no promise in her voice. "And we
have to plan out the diversions. They should be subtle, but
effective."

"Now?" Falon moaned.

"Now," Lord Rhow said. "After all, you must do this
tomorrow night. The invasion by the Eastern Lords is only
two, perhaps three days away."

Falon looked down at the thick pile of charts.

"I'll get you a chair," Taline said, grinning.

Ashre strolled around the enormous room, munching on a great dripping bunch of dewberries. Caissir was curled up on the massive bed, snoring loudly.

And Paralan? He had ducked out, slipping into the hall, gesturing to Ashre to remain perfectly quiet.

Which he did . . .

Except that, as tired as he felt, he didn't feel ready to sleep. There was a puzzle to be solved here, a strange puzzle.

At first, when they entered the palace and were swamped with food, clothes, and showers, he felt it was a dream come true. No more sneaking food off others' plates while they tried to spear your rear end with their hunting knives. No more sleeping, utterly cold, in a cottage while the icy winds cut through the shack.

But then, just when he came out of the shower and the nurses were fussing with him, he felt something. Like the faint smell of something rotten, hidden off in some dark corner somewhere. It was a danger, a threat, the feeling almost unnoticeable amidst all the wonders of this castle.

But then, as he tried to concentrate on it, to try to find out where it came from, it ended. It was like following a piece of taut string, following it, hand over hand, and then finding it had been cut.

·Now there was nothing, just the warmth of the fire, the wonderful taste of the berries (and the sweet juice running down his chin onto the shiny wood floor) and the enormous bed.

Where had the feeling gone?

He walked around the room, trying to pick up the feeling again, as if trying to remember something.

What had caused the feeling, he wondered?

And, the question that made him really scared—

What had ended it?

Lord Rhow rolled up the stack of charts and carried them back to his hidden compartment in the wall.

"Enough for tonight. Tomorrow, after breakfast, you can study some more, plan how you'll use your forces. Now you can get some rest. . . ."

He watched Falon blink, as if slow to understand what he had just said.

King, Rhow thought, looking at the lanky mrem. It was hard to believe.

He gestured at his daughter to usher Falon out.

"Get the highlander some rest," Rhow told her, and she nodded and went over to Falon, pulling him out of his chair.

"Sorry," Falon said, snapping out of his daze. "I think," he said, with a small grin, "I could fall asleep right here."

Taline led him out the massive door, past the stocky guards.

"Till tomorrow, Falon," Rhow said. And he stood there, waiting for the heavy double doors to close.

Rhow stood, and listened to their footsteps echoing down the cavernous hall. Then he looked to the side.

"You can come out now," he said tiredly.

The curtains parted.

"Well, he seems eager enough. Though I must admit I had a time of it convincing him to leave Mount Zaynir to start this whole charade."

Rhow looked up. "Yes, Plano. Your plan seems to have had its merits."

Rhow, tired himself, watched Plano walk over to the bed and pick up *The Song of the Three Moons.*

Plano leafed through the pages. "Ah, it is as I had hoped. Page after page, my lord. The spells of the cult, all recorded in perfect detail."

"Yes, but are *you* capable of using them?"

Plano smiled. "By tomorrow night, there will be no one more powerful in Tizare, my lord . . . save you, of course. It all will be exactly as we planned."

Rhow nodded. "Very well, then, take the book away for study."

Plano nodded, and walked out toward the side exit.

He's hiding something, Rhow thought. *Magic user or not, he can't mask everything from me. Something has disturbed him . . . upset his plans.*

No matter. It was all in motion, exactly as it should be.

Nothing would be allowed to interfere.

Nothing—and no one.

Chapter 18

▲————————————————————————————▲

"Total nonsense," Caissir stammered, even as he forked yet another piece of the delicately flavored fish that was their breakfast. "You know," he said, gesturing at Falon with the forkful of food, "I thought that perhaps your sojourn in the desert had taught you some common sense. Now I see you're the same stupid, risk-taking fool."

Caissir gulped his morsel down.

"Paralan?" Falon said, turning to the thoughtful farmer. Sometime, in the middle of the night, Paralan had returned to their chambers. But so far, Paralan had said nothing about the proposed plan. And if there was anyone Falon knew he wanted with him, it was the big, brooding ex-general.

"As far as plans go, it's not bad. A small army would be guaranteed to fail. But a group of assassins, trained and equipped with detailed maps of the palace . . . well, there'd be a chance."

Falon wrinkled his face on the word 'assassin.' He hoped to find some loftier name for the coming night's activity.

"If you go ahead with it, I'll join you . . . especially if it brings the chance of meeting some of those slimy liskash."

"Not to worry about that," Falon said. "Lord Rhow says that a major battle is due any day now. I just hope we're in time to stop the king from opening the doors to the invasion."

"We should do it." It was Ashre, enjoying his fill of the

rich pastries and cakes served with the fish. "The king is bad," he said flatly.

Falon smiled. He'd like to take Ashre, he really would. The kit had saved his life twice already—and he could do it again. But the kit was too young. The desert had been risky enough.

"Thanks for the vote of confidence, Ash . . . but you will have to stay here."

He hadn't, of course, told them anything about the story in *The Song of the Three Moons*. No, he wasn't entirely sure of what to make of it himself. King . . . the idea was almost laughable. Better that they go in knowing only that they were removing a traitor, a lackey of the Eastern Lords. Besides, Lord Rhow could certainly rule Tizare effectively. A largely unschooled highlander was not an outstanding candidate to run a great city.

He felt the allure of power not one bit.

Caissir went on, "I still say—"

But Taline bustled into the sunny dining room that adjoined their sleeping quarters.

"Good morning! I trust everyone had a fine night's sleep?"

"I was just telling this, this—"

Falon stood up, offering a chair to Taline. He saw her glance at Paralan, checking to see whether he took any interest in her arrival.

But whatever they had felt for each other had obviously been consumed by the hate and guilt from that small farmhouse.

She turned, and smiled at Falon, who was not thrilled at being second choice.

"Elezar has arranged a selection of soldiers for you to look over." She looked at the tremendous display of food on the table. "Just as soon as you've had your fill."

"Paralan here has agreed to join us, and I think I'll be able to convince our friend Caissir here to come along. I have great plans for him in the distraction department."

"Yes," Taline smiled, "do help, Caissir. Your magical abilities would be most welcome."

"Magic, you say? But I want nothing to do with going inside—"

"You won't have to," Falon said. "But, as Taline says, we can use you."

"I'll think about it." And the wizard stuffed a creamy roll into his mouth.

"I want to come!" Ashre said.

Taline tilted her head, and once again reached out and ruffled the ears of the kit. "I bet you do, Ash. And we could use you. For a lot of reasons. But this isn't like our jaunt in the desert. Many soldiers will die. We can't go into the palace and have to worry about you."

Ashre's face sagged. "But I could *help*."

Falon shook his head. "It would be no help to us if we have to turn around and check to see if you're all right. After it's all over, we'll need your help. You understand?"

Ashre slipped off the plush red chair and walked over to the tall windows that looked down on the courtyard.

Why, I do believe he's pouting, Falon thought. *He's come a long way from the street kit we found in Fahl.*

"Well, I'm done," Falon said. "Let's go look at the soldiers." Paralan stood up.

Caissir was still sampling delicacies from Lord Rhow's kitchen.

He noticed everyone looking down at him, waiting.

"All right, I'm coming, I'm coming. . . . Can't even finish breakfast," he muttered, wiping his face and joining them.

Falon walked to the door and stopped.

"Ash . . . coming down with us?"

The kit stood stock-still for a moment, then slowly turned at the window and ambled over to Falon.

Falon fought hard to keep a grin off his face.

It was just like going to market, Falon thought.

The courtyard was filled with the best of Lord Rhow's legions, standing at attention, waiting for something to happen. Falon didn't have the faintest idea how to proceed, so it was fortunate that Paralan snapped out of his lethargy to begin interviewing the soldiers.

One soldier was already committed to the adventure: Elezar, the captain of Rhow's personal guard. He walked side by side with Paralan as he interviewed the soldiers.

Before long, Paralan had dismissed more than half the soldiers to their normal duties, while he went back and

requestioned the rest. Finally, he presented Falon with a
group of twenty, from which he was to select a mere ten.

And so Falon came to rely on that most unscientific
method of evaluation—the look in a mrem's eyes. If they
met his gaze, held it, and seemed to radiate strength without any braggadocio, he gave them the nod.

By midmorning, the group was ready and rehearsals
began. It was like the spectacle that his village had staged
when he was just a kit. Some local warlord was to visit
Falon's village and it was decided to do some reenactment
of great moments from highlander history.

He didn't remember much of what had been presented,
but he still remembered the moves: the raising of arms, the
brandishing of wooden claw-swords, so exciting to hold.
But after many rehearsals, though, it had gotten boring,
and he and the other kits had had to be sharply watched.

This group, though, needed no such controls. They went
over the plans for the night to come again and again, practicing their lines, many created by Caissir. They looked at
the charts of King Mineir's palace, selecting possible locations to meet, once they were all inside.

If, Falon thought. *If* any of us actually make it inside.

Then, the guards began to practice their battle movements, sleekly performing the dance steps that led to attack. Soon the hissing in the courtyard grew genuinely
frightening, and Falon indicated to Caissir that it might be
a good idea to get Ashre inside.

But the young kit pulled away from Caissir's grasp, eager
to stay and watch these elite soldiers practice their deadly
moves.

Paralan joined in their rehearsals, and Falon saw them
take note of his hands, a few even muttering to one another, the dark shadows on their faces slowly clearing once
Paralan was among them, joining in their steps, wielding
his great long sword as if it were a stick.

By late afternoon, Elezar called a halt, and he ordered
the guards to rest and eat.

At the same time, Taline indicated that everyone else
should also rest up.

Falon was too tense to enjoy the platters of food, luscious
bunches of dewberries, dried chunks of uxan, and juicy
trumpeter fowl, all crisp and brown.

No wine was served, but then they'd all need their wits about them tonight.

Especially me, Falon thought.

All day long he had been nagged by the growing feeling that there was more happening here than he realized, or Taline, or even Ashre.

When he tried asking Ash if he had any, er, feelings . . . any *bad* feelings, Ash just shrugged, smiled, and went on avidly watching the soldiers.

No feelings . . . no danger . . . except that Falon felt all tingly throughout the day, as if someone were going to take an ax to his tail.

Just nerves, he thought. Just never killed a king before.

And that was it, wasn't it? Despite all these heavily armed guards and the clever charades for the night, he would be an assassin fighting to regain his birthright.

It didn't fit, and he longed for the simplicity of tending the herd-beasts.

Now, with the sun just about to slip below the far walls of Rhow's palace, all he could think of was the coming night.

Let it hurry, he thought. Enough waiting. By morning he'd either be king, or be dead.

Except that, once again, he was wrong.

"Welcome, my citizens of Tizare . . . come closer now, don't be shy. Yes, that's it, press close, and you shall see wonders that you've never dreamed of. . . ."

Caissir was dressed in so many shimmering layers of cloth he didn't know whether he was a wizard or a garment salesman.

Such opulence! This was what having a bottomless chest of copper pieces could do for a mrem! He had trimmed his face hairs and whiskers, an uncomfortable procedure, but Taline had told him that anyone hoping to interest the passersby had better look important.

And that was, after all, why he was here. He had had enough adventures of derring-do to last him a few of his lifetimes. But to be wealthy! Ah, there was a dream that he warmed to, enough that he could overlook the outlandish risks posed by their plan.

He just knew that he would take every precaution to avoid getting involved.

"Yes!" he called out. "Wonders that you've only dreamed about . . ."

Some of the local mrem were already pressing close, looking curious and impatient, eager for his show to begin. The night air, warm but with a gentle breeze, was filled with the sound of other mrem hoping to snare a few coppers. There were fortune tellers and mystics, as well as those mrem offering exotic food from distant parts of the world. A puppet theater, just across the way from Caissir's small table, had a whole group laughing with its rendition of the myth of Krzarr, the mrem that became a liskash.

Still, Caissir was nothing if not a showman.

He dug under the tablecloth, a move completely unnoticed by his wide-eyed audience, and produced an enormous flower from the changa tree. The crowd smiled.

"Oh, that's nothing," he said, still directing his pitch to the others loitering at rival booths or just rambling around. "Perhaps this will impress you. . . ."

He waved a hand in front of the bloom, letting it fall into the folds of his gown, and replaced it with a jet black olna. It began to sing its bittersweet night song on cue.

The crowd clapped.

Easily pleased, he thought. He took a look at them. Some were definitely from the South. Odd shapes and pictures were cut into their fur, and they had the mottled, nasty look of seafaring mrem.

The bird trick brought him some more customers, even luring a few from watching the puppet show.

"Well, let us," he said, winking conspiratorially at the crowd, "have some real magic now. . . ."

He bent down close to the table.

The guards at the palace gate were stretching, trying to get a look at him.

Good, he thought. *Keep watching.*

And Elezar stood near the back. Big, mean, and dressed now not in his captain's uniform, but the brownish kilt of a common trader.

He too had his eyes peeled.

Good.

Still, it was really too bad, Caissir thought, that he wouldn't get through very much of his show. . . .

Elezar would see to that.

Paralan had insisted that Taline have four of the guards with her, even though he himself would be at her side.

"No matter," he had argued implacably over dinner. "Our entry will be the hardest, and we'll need all the protection we can get."

And everyone, including Taline, knew that he was concerned for her. She doubted that he had any room for a thought for himself.

He didn't talk about revenge, but Taline didn't doubt that it was his only goal. And he wore his guilt like a badge. She was sure he blamed himself for what had happened to Lonirr and the kits. He was a haunted mrem. Right now, he even scared her a bit.

Still, there was no one else she'd rather have beside her in the hours to come.

The plan . . . It had all sounded so possible when looking over the papers in her father's chambers. But now, the odds seemed overwhelming. How could their three small bands succeed where an army would fail?

She scolded herself then, walking beside Paralan, the others trailing at what she hoped was a natural distance. If she started questioning everything they were sure to fail.

Part of the difficulty was her physical discomfort. Instead of her simple kilt and her sword, she wore the flowing robes of a courtesan, eager to convert the warm night into a healthy cache of coppers.

Already randy-eyed young mrem were following her—discreetly, of course—but definitely eager to see where she was going.

They'd have a ways to go, she thought with a smile. But she was glad to see that her appearance, enhanced by a few streaks of color in her otherwise golden fur, was working the proper spell.

If she could just keep them at bay until the twin moons made their appearance.

Then, just when they reached the northern entrance to the palace grounds, she'd begin the small charade that would, the All-Mother willing, lead them into the palace itself.

She looked behind as her crowd of admirers grew and grew.

The fabled White Dancers! Though Falon had heard about them, usually mentioned in hush tones of respect, still it was an amazing sight to see them take their positions in the gardens just outside the palace.

A crowd, quiet and well-behaved, had formed, talking quietly among themselves, waiting respectfully for the performance.

Except that even Falon, highland bumpkin that he was, knew that what the troupe would do went beyond mere 'performance.'

They told the tales of history, sang the song of the mrem, made the lessons of the past live once again, and brought the warnings of the future so close the audience could feel it.

He wasn't sure he could keep his mind focused on his objective. The three guards he had selected mingled in the crowd quite effectively, disappearing almost. Falon just hoped that they would be there when he needed them.

He had argued for including the White Dancers in their plans. Who better than they to help expose the fraudulent king and establish Falon's rightful, if improbable, claim? But Rhow had grown silent, concerned, shaking his head as he moved onto other topics.

Falon kept off to the side, watching the Dancers take their places. He thought that the head of the troupe looked over, recognizing Falon even though he quickly turned away.

But no matter. They started moving through the garden, taking broad steps, landing gently on the pads of their shoeless feet. The audience grew hushed.

"This is the time," the chief Dancer said in a surprisingly gentle voice that nonetheless carried in the open space as clearly as if it had been a yell.

Immediately behind her, four of the Dancers came together, twisting their bodies into terrible shapes. "This is the time," the chief Dancer repeated, spinning, her sheer white kilt creating a smooth blur with her brilliant white fur.

Falon, totally and immediately absorbed, came closer, as did his accomplices. It didn't worry him—they had plenty of time.

The group of contorted Dancers joined hands and legs, and became one.

It was an ugly shape, and the audience muttered, confused by the unexpected action. But then a slow rumbling started to build up as first one, then many people began to repeat a word.

"*Liskash* . . ."

Yes, thought Falon. Of course. He couldn't see it before because he just saw the individual Dancers. But now, it was so clear. The Dancers had made a liskash, lumbering on its legs, toward the chief Dancer.

"The time—here—" she said spinning.

The liskash came up to her, and she seemed to slow, then waver, and it reached out for her.

The audience gasped—and it startled Falon. *It's just a dance,* he thought.

But no. It was more than a dance. The White Dancers did more than carry messages and tales. And they were surely doing more than that now.

It was a warning. And some of the Tizarians were visibly disturbed. Falon checked for his confederates. They stood, much like the others, open-mouthed, watching this strange dance.

The message was so clear! *Liskash are coming. . . .*

But the thing that scared Falon was the sheer ferocity of their dance. And more—the size and power of the White Dancers' creation of a liskash.

Falon didn't even realize that he had begun fingering his sword during the performance.

He looked up, checking for the first faint glow as the twin moons broke the horizon.

Hurry, he once again prayed. *Let this night begin* . . .

So that it might end.

Chapter 19

▲————————————————————————————▲

The crowd was nice and large now, Caissir observed, but he couldn't put them off too long with such pithy displays of magic. This *was* Tizare, after all, one of the great cities. Even the bedraggled group in front of him would expect better.

He looked over his shoulder. The sky was still dark, he noted with disappointment. But there, yes, he thought with a smile, just at the edge of the palace itself. The tiniest sliver of a glow. In minutes the tiny crescent of the first moon would break through.

Caissir looked back at his audience, searching for Elezar.

Caissir gave Elezar a quick wink—the prearranged signal—before resuming his patter.

"Yes, and now I'll begin one of the most incredible, mystifying displays of—" he grinned at the audience "—you-know-what, that anyone has seen." The crowd laughed at his political joke, chuckling to themselves, even as they looked over their shoulders for any sign of the king's secret police.

No such worry, Caissir knew. Tizare was, if anything, loose. Magic, even real magic, was tolerated.

"Yes, but I'm afraid that I will need an assistant, someone . . ." He was looking through a thicket of hands. "Yes, you," he said picking one of Rhow's guards out of the crowd. "Now, just step behind this curtain," Caissir said, parting a creamy black piece of material that acted as his backdrop.

A bit of fiddling with the curtain, just for effect, and then some earnest distracting by grabbing at some items on the table. "By the most powerful wizardry, I declare you . . . gone!"

Caissir quickly snapped the curtain down, and the crowd gasped and clapped to see nothing there but the palace walls.

Well, thought Caissir, they might live in a great city but even the village bumpkins usually saw through that bit of business. Perhaps his act was better than he thought.

His confederate, meanwhile, had rolled completely away from the booth and had surfaced in plenty of time to watch his own vanishing.

Caissir grinned. The moon broke the crisp line of the palace walls, bathing the rich indigo sky with a gentle, diffused light. He licked his lips.

Alas, he thought. Much too brief a show.

"And now—" he said, bringing a series of goblets out on top of the table.

"Yes, now we'll put an end to this!" the voice screamed out. And the crowd, just a moment ago all grinning and expectation, howled out in alarm.

Caissir stepped back, his eyes wide with fright.

It was almost dark down here. The northern wall of Mineir's palace was well away from the attractions of the marketplace and the festive courtyard at the palace gates.

Still, Taline was pleased to see that she had done well for herself. A healthy contingent of mrem, eager to spend some delicious moments with such a beauty, trailed behind her. A few were even bold enough to come right up to her elbow, making enticing proposals that mostly involved dumping the rest of the group.

"Soon," she smiled, teasing, excited despite the terrible danger to come. She saw the small entrance to the palace up ahead, marked by a lonely outpost manned by a trio of guards. From the rutted tracks carved into the dirt she walked on, it looked to be the main delivery entrance.

She saw that she had plenty of company here.

Other Tizarians were using this quiet stretch of songomore trees that ran parallel to the wall as a quiet, secluded rendezvous. The night was filled with the sounds of vigorous rutting, the soft mewling as lovers nibbled at each other.

A few of her potential customers dropped away, perhaps to pursue easier sport, or perhaps daunted by the gloomy darkness of this part of Tizare.

She stopped and turned.

For a moment she didn't see Paralan, and she almost panicked. Then she picked him out, lurking near the back like any other randy soul.

She looked away.

The crescent moon brought a pale glow to the darkness here.

She turned back, licking her lips, moving her body slowly, issuing a promise to any and all who watched.

"So now," she said with a smile, "Who shall be first?"

No one at Lord Rhow's knew anything about watching kits. That much was obvious to Ashre.

As soon as the guards had delivered his dinner and guided him to his room, he was left all alone.

Which suited him just fine.

He waited a bit, strolling anxiously around the massive bedroom, before opening the heavy wood door and peering down the long hallway. He heard voices—laughter, and the low rumble of talking—but they came from far away. The hallway was empty, and if he was going to get going, he had to get a move on.

He stepped out, smiling to himself, then started down the hallway very slowly, almost casually. It was best not to arouse any guard's suspicions should they see him.

Just need to pee, I could tell them. *Oh, there is? Right in my room? So sorry. . . .*

Or he could pretend he was hungry, or lonely, or whatever. Anything, just as long as he got off this main corridor.

Because he had done more that day than simply watch the others checking the guards and devising their plans (and he was sure surprised at Caissir—his ideas were wonderful). No, he had done one other thing.

He had made sure he knew the layout of King Mineir's palace. Maybe he knew it even better than they did. After all, he had spent most of his life dodging down corridors, through rooms, and out open windows.

The hallway was still deserted. It probably helped that some of the guards were off with Falon. He started to relax, but then he heard steps coming towards him, heavy steps.

He looked around for someplace to hide. There was nothing. The footsteps were closer, climbing up a few steps to the hallway. There was a door, just to his left—and he ducked in.

At first the room seemed empty. A pair of candles cast some light in the room, but it was dark and shadowy. He put an ear up to the door, and heard the steps jangle past. They were wearing full armor.

An odd touch, thought Ashre. He waited till they were well past.

And he heard voices behind him. A she-mrem . . . and then a mrem. Talking quietly, laughing to each other.

More sounds that Ashre knew all too well.

Then . . . a few words, quite clear. Mineir . . . battle . . . surprise. Then the mrem said Falon's name, and he laughed, a cruel sound that made Ashre's fur stand on end.

The mrem stood up, and Ashre heard him say something about more wine.

Quickly, Ashre grabbed the door handle and sneaked out.

He stood outside the doorway, his heart beating like a drum, more confused than ever. He wished he could have heard more. Whatever it was, it didn't sound good for his friends.

He hurried down the hallway, taking the curved steps at its end two and three at a time, convinced that he had to do this, had to disobey Falon.

He never *was* any good at following rules.

The stairs led to a small waiting area. Ashre looked around, before seeing the small door off to the side. He ran to it, hoping that it would be open. He pulled on the metal bar, but it didn't budge.

"Come on," he hissed, biting at his lip, tugging on the heavy metal handle. Then, "Please!"

As if in answer, the bar budged, sliding just a bit . . . enough of a movement to let him know that he'd be able to open it.

More voices! And the same clanky footsteps . . .

Coming right towards him, from a corridor just over his shoulder.

He pulled on the bar with all his strength. It popped up, rudely, making a loud clanking sound.

He wasted no time sliding into the dank staircase, and shutting the door behind him.

Close now, he thought. If only Falon would believe his story.

He went down these stairs cautiously, watching it grow lighter as he reached the bottom.

The stairs opened up suddenly, and he was looking at a great room. Here were rows of swords of every size and shape. There were claw swords of all lengths attached to the wall. And a whole rack of lances, all of them bearing the same intricate designs. To the back, Ashre could see machines whose purpose he could only guess at. They were dark, hulking shapes, with enormous cups that could catapult boulders through space.

And the oil, barrels and barrels of it, lined up against the wall, filling the room with a smell that made his nostrils twitch.

The weapons room! With such an armory, Rhow could conquer half the great cities.

And maybe, thought Ashre, that was exactly his plan.

There were a few guards down here, milling about, watching over this great stockpile. Ash began to walk casually around, whistling, letting them know he was here.

"Ho, there," one burly guard called out. "And just what do you think you're doing down here?"

Ash flashed what he hoped was a winning smile.

"I couldn't sleep . . . and Lord Rhow suggested that I might like seeing—"

At the mention of Rhow, the guard seemed to straighten up, sucking in his ample belly.

"Why, sure, young kit. Explore all that you want. And if there's anything I could help you with, just let me know. . . ."

The guard backed up, and Ashre walked by him, strolling past a line of crossbows, and then racks of armor.

Ashre sniffed. It was as if they still smelled of battle, of blood. He reached out and touched one suit. . . .

And quickly snapped his hand back. There was death here. Not all mrem get to return their armor themselves, he thought. And suddenly, this exciting room became, for a moment, a place of terrible sadness.

He began to paw through the armor, watching the guard relax, and finally return to his duties.

Throat armor. A claw sword. And yes, maybe a dagger. That's what he needed.

None of it too heavy. All of it familiar to him.

If only it was enough. . . .

And if only he was in time.

He whistled, as he gathered his weapons.

The crowd around the White Dancers was immense, so large that Falon lost sight of Rhow's guards completely.

He'd have to just hope that they'd be there when he made his move.

But even he was held fast by the terrible tale told by the Dancers.

It had started out as a warning, a very clear warning to the people of Tizare, of the invasion to come from the East. But they made it an immediate danger, something almost upon them.

Some of the weaker souls in the audience actually turned away, horrified by the images of the carnage to come.

But then it got worse. The Dancers, acting as messengers, brought tales from the surrounding villages, tales filled with a horrible beauty as they spun around and portrayed the last moments of whole villages before the eastern invaders arrived.

Not a sound was heard in the audience.

Nothing, save the occasional tear.

But oh, the moment they told the story of the small farmhouse, the lone wife, the young kits . . . Falon thanked the All-Mother that Paralan wasn't with him.

His own tears fell freely, silently. The dance seemed to go on forever, lingering with excruciating beauty on each detail of the life of the small farm. The chilly mornings, the noises of the beasts eager to be fed, the kits rolling around on the dusty ground, playing, laughing. . . .

Waiting. For their daddy to return from the desert.

Falon turned away, and he could hear the audience sobbing, all of them trying desperately to muffle their tears.

He took one step toward the gate, then another, trying

to ignore the words of the lead Dancers, blocking the vivid images their subtle movements created.

His hand closed around a curved dagger.

Please, be here, he prayed, hoping that the Dancers hadn't so devastated Rhow's mrem that they would forget their role.

But then he saw one, then another of the guards and he knew he wouldn't be alone.

The guards at the gate took no notice of his approach. They were, like everyone, completely absorbed by the spectacle.

It would have to be fast, he knew. Any prolonged confrontation would only bring the attention of other guards out mingling with the crowd.

He eased himself right against the wall, and started digging around in a small sack, as if looking for official papers.

And Falon took a quick glance to see how many guards there were.

Four, at least that many milling about the opening. Perhaps a few more inside.

Not too many, he hoped.

He stopped rummaging around, and looked up, giving Rhow's mrem the prearranged signal.

The gate guards saw nothing.

Falon slid out the elegant curved dagger.

Assassin! his mind suggested, once again.

"Yes," he whispered.

And he moved, quickly, smoothly, not giving his chosen target a moment to respond. The blade slid into the gap between the guard's chest armor and kilt, smoothly piercing the fur and skin. When it was in deep, Falon ripped up, pulling, tearing, killing. . . .

He saw the guard give him a horrified, questioning look.

Though his mouth was twisted in a snarl, Falon tried to say something with his eyes.

It had to be, friend . . . had to be. . . .

His confederates had all found their own targets, but one of them had been caught in midstrike. He was fighting with a bullish guard, and losing.

The palace guard opened his mouth to scream for help.

"Get him," Falon hissed. "Shut him up!"

Behind him the White Dancers were singing, frantically

pleading to the All-Mother for the souls of the dead already
lost to the invasion.

One of Rhow's men literally leaped into the air, claws
extended, and clapped a hand over the mouth of the still-
active guard.

Then Falon, the nearest, moved, his blade still dripping
the blood of his first victim. . . .

Assassin!

He stuck the blade in, clumsily, missing the exposed
spot, and sliding down, almost tumbling onto the ground.
The guard threw off Rhow's mrem.

And Falon leaped up, watching the giant go for his own
sword. And this time his blade found its home.

The guard gasped, and his fingers froze on the handle.

Once again Falon drew the blade upward.

The guard fell to his knees, his hand abandoning his
weapon, reaching, instead, for his wound.

The gate was clear.

No one looked at them.

And no one came running from inside to help the
guards.

"Let's go," Falon ordered. "And quickly!"

He ran past the palace gates.

Above him, the twin moons were still low in the sky . . .
still tinged red.

"Enough of this beast magic—you'll stop now, or we'll
hang your carcass on the city walls for the olna birds to
peck at."

Caissir fought to keep a smile off his face. Elezar was
playing his role perfectly, brandishing his sword like a
madmrem.

The crowd, quite naturally, parted to let him come close.

"I've seen the evil that magic brings, and we'll have
none of it here, my fat friend. . . ."

That wasn't in the script, that part about being fat, Caissir noted. Still, Elezar was doing a fine job with his lines.

"Now sir, perhaps you aren't enjoying my small presen-
tation, but I'm sure that there are others who are more
than—"

On cue, one of Rhow's mrem, disguised as a drunken
rowdy, stepped up, drawing his sword out.

"Yes," he slurred, "I like thiss. So why don' you just get your furry little tail out of here . . ." and he hiccoughed, drawing a titter from the crowd, "before I cut it off."

"That," Elezar said, "I'd like to see."

And he was joined by another of Rhow's mrem, as was the 'drunk.'

Caissir quickly looked over to the two guards at the gate. *C'mon, you lazy louts. Do your duty.*

For a moment they seemed all too willing to let the exchange proceed in whatever direction it was heading.

But then a young female went to them and Caissir could imagine her pleading for their intercession.

And the young guards ambled over, not yet drawing their swords.

All right, Caissir thought, *let's get this performance rolling.*

"Now, sirs," he yelled, "if you will just let me—"

And then they started to go at it, swords clashing, the audience screaming, backing away. As expected, a few of the more rowdy Tizarians decided to join in the fun, until it was a full-fledged battle, with Rhow's mrem trying to avoid the sloppy, amateurish blows of those who just wanted to join in.

The gate, though, was clear and unguarded.

The guards were pleading for order, drawing their own weapons.

It was time.

Caissir slipped away, unnoticed in the mayhem.

It was a nerve-wracking moment moving inside the gate. He stood in the shadows, breathing heavily. Then Elezar was there, beside him, then two of Rhow's mrem. The plan called for the third to remain behind to keep the battle raging.

"Well," said Caissir. "It looks like we're all here."

"Yes," Elezar answered. "You'll come with us, won't you?"

"I was afraid you'd say that."

And the amazing and mystical wizard started to creep toward the castle of King Mineir.

"Me, please let me," shouted one.

Others joined in the chorus, some of them digging into heir kilts and withdrawing great fistfuls of coins.

Soon the group of randy mrem split into factions, all arguing as to who'd be the first to taste the wonders of this delicious beauty.

It might, she thought, *even be fun to stick around and watch just what will happen.*

But that wasn't on the agenda.

"None shall possess this female except me," Paralan bellowed, drawing his sword.

His announcement brought howls of displeasure from the excited group. At first one, then others went for their swords.

It was dark, the moons were up, and they were not to be denied, Taline thought wickedly.

Except that everyone, including her, would in fact be disappointed.

The guards at the gate came over, and she went running up to them.

She gave them her best soul-stirring stare, letting her hands touch their shoulders, pleading, promising. . . .

"Please stop this . . . They've all gone crazy, completely out of hand."

The guards smiled. "We'll do our best," one said.

"And I'll be ever so grateful," Taline purred.

The guards marched into the wildly arguing crowd.

Poor fools, she thought.

She gave Paralan a wink, and then dashed away, into the delivery entrance of the palace. She looked behind her. The guards were engaged in sword-brandishing arguments.

Much too busy to notice her, or Paralan, or their four confederates enter the small doorway to Mineir's palace.

Out the window.

It was the only way, Ashre knew. All the regular entrances and exits were sure to be watched.

But this window led down to a dark garden where he was sure he could get out.

The weapons weighed him down, though. And he won-

dered whether he could hold onto the rope, easing himself
down.

He stepped out onto the ledge. The light from the
moons caught his gray fur, and he hoped that no one was
looking up in this direction.

He tested the rope, tugging hard on the knot.

It seemed secure.

The claw sword dangled awkwardly from his side, while
the throat armor jabbed at his neck.

It was too uncomfortable . . . he could hardly breathe.

He thought a moment, then reached up and unsnapped
the protective armor.

I'll just have to be extra careful.

And with that last caution to himself, he grabbed the
rope, stepped off the ledge, and began to climb down. . . .

Chapter 20

▲————————————————————————▲

Taline found herself in the kitchen, the many pot scrubbers still hard at work cleaning up from that evening's meal. They barely looked up at her.

But there was also a cook, at the far end, supervising the tedious oiling and cleaning of the huge stove. He turned and arched his furry eyebrows.

"What—" he said, pointing at Taline and her entourage. "What is this? Are you delivering something?"

Taline didn't know what to say. She felt for her weapon, buried under so many layers of material. But Paralan pushed past her.

"A delivery of sorts." He winked. "For the king himself."

The cook seemed to study Taline carefully. "Oh, then," he said, clearing a path to the door leading to the main staircase of the palace. He waved in the direction of the door. "Then carry on. . . ."

Taline smiled at the cook, and walked past Paralan.

If it's this easy, she thought, *we'll get to the king's chamber without any problem.*

She opened the door, and led the group up the stairs.

The king's private chambers were at the very top of the palace, overlooking Tizare.

And, in between, two positions marked on the map as guard posts.

Just how well guarded Taline was about to discover.

As soon as Falon entered the palace he ran right into a small army of King Mineir's guards.

Apparently their entry hadn't been carried out as quietly as he imagined.

As soon as the guards saw Falon and his three fellow invaders, they stopped, fell into position, and drew swords.

"Lay down your weapons," a captain yelled.

There were eight of them, standing shoulder to shoulder, a wall of trained soldiery.

The one advantage Falon had was that his own small squad were also soldiers, the best Rhow could muster.

"Yes," Falon said, letting his voice go shallow. "It was foolish of us to—"

He moved quickly, drawing his full-size double-edged sword. It was heavy, without being impossible to carry. Rhow's mrem also moved quickly, falling into established defensive positions, pulling swords out with a speed that startled the other guards.

Not a fair fight, Falon thought. But bound to be an interesting one.

And the battle began.

There was no room for Mineir's guards to spread out in the narrow hallway, so they were bunched up, two deep. Falon acted cautiously, waiting to see their skill before risking his first blow.

Rhow's mrem were not so timid. They made noises as they smoothly slid into position, poising on one foot, while raising their swords over their heads. Falon saw the alarmed expression on some of their opponents' faces.

Then Rhow's mrem struck, carefully, with an incredible accuracy. Their blades hit the front rank, ignoring their attempts to parry and duck. In a flash, three of Mineir's guards were on the floor. Then, as the others stepped over the bodies to take their place, Rhow's mrem struck again. This time, a few of the blows missed. But Falon made his first moves.

And while he nearly lost an ear to a wide-swinging blow over his head, he got in a deadly jab that brought down one of the guards.

Soon, the odds were uneven in the other direction, and Mineir's guards were steadily backing away.

"Don't let them escape," Falon whispered.

A general alarm of the Tizarian army would doom them.

But Rhow's mrem needed no encouragement. They creamed as they charged after them, scaring even Falon himself.

He looked away, as the guards were cut down, almost effortlessly.

Now on, Falon thought, *and quickly too, before the palace gets filled with the blue-armored soldiers, loyal to Mineir.*

Mineir. A traitor.

Or so I'm told, Falon thought. *So I'm told. . . .*

Caissir couldn't believe his good fortune . . . nor the incredibly bad timing.

For in this chamber, off the main entrance hall, was none other than King Mineir's personal staff of concubines.

And what a staff! Most lounged around wearing gossamer kilts with more slits than material. Others wore nothing at all, as they lazily strolled around sipping wine and eating from trays filled with luscious dewberries.

And they looked luscious indeed. They showed no sign of alarm at his arrival, probably used to the king's guests stepping down to make a personal selection for that evening.

A few of them even smiled at him, languidly stretching, showing off their glistening pelts (touched up, no doubt, by some clever makeup artist).

The enticing smell in the room was overpowering.

"Steady, lads," Caissir said to Elezar and the pair of Rhow's men that followed him. "No one said our job was going to be easy."

Caissir smiled as he moved through the room, navigating the fluffy pillows, the trays of fruit, and the beautiful she-mrem.

With a sigh of disappointment, they reached the door at the back of the room. Behind here, Caissir knew, was a staircase leading directly to the king's quarters.

And most assuredly, the very best of King Mineir's guards.

"Okay, you can take the lead now," Caissir said to Elezar gesturing at the doorway. Elezar grumbled as he went past Caissir. He then began a slow trot up the stairs with his soldiers, leaving Caissir behind huffing and puffing.

"Wait, please, I can't—"

Then, from the stairwell, he heard the sound of fighting. The clash of swords. He backed down a step.

Perhaps I could secrete myself somewhere downstairs . . . perhaps among all those pillows?

One of Rhow's men tumbled past him, crashing into the wall, spitting up blood as he tumbled down the steps. Finally he just rolled awkwardly down the stairs.

"Oh, dear," Caissir said, reluctantly withdrawing his sword.

He went down another step.

Then he heard the voices coming from below.

And they weren't the sweet voices of the king's concubines.

More soldiers, and coming up fast.

"Trapped . . ." Caissir said, as the other of Rhow's mrem went tumbling down, horribly cut all over his body.

"I—I give up," Caissir stammered. Then, sadly, whimpering, "Please . . ."

The guards arrived quickly, their dark blue armor almost black in the shadows of the stairwell. Caissir saw Elezar and the others in the back, their weapons gone.

One of the guards came right up to Caissir, snatched off his throat armor, and placed his blade right on his throat.

Thinking it an appropriate thing to do, Caissir fell to his knees. . . .

Taline and Paralan, along with three of Rhow's best, reached the first guard post.

And once again Taline couldn't believe how easy this was.

The two guards made some show of resistance, but soon realized that they were clearly outmatched.

"Have them tied up," she told Paralan. And Taline studied the walls of the waiting room. The brickwork was of a quality she'd never seen before. All the corners were perfect, and the edges straight. Likewise, the fitting of the blocks was perfectly even.

It was beautiful work.

But that wasn't what caught her attention.

She had never seen work like this—not in Tizare, not in her father's castle, not in any of the great cities.

None of the great Western cities.

It reflected a skill with stonework beyond the capabilities of the mrem.

So it's true, she thought with a shiver. Hidden here, in the king's personal chambers, was the evidence . . . of an alien presence.

She sniffed the air, as if she could pick up some trace of the smell.

"They're all tied, Taline," Paralan whispered.

"Come then," she hissed. "Let's capture the traitor . . ."

She walked right up to the heavy double doors.

King Mineir had been at play when word first reached him. Two beauties, whose pleasure he hadn't yet tasted, were rolling around on his oversize bed, playfully clawing at him, nipping his too-fat belly (the cook really had to go . . . he was just *too* good), and giving him a wonderful romp.

He hadn't felt this full of youthful randiness in a long time.

Unfortunately, the reports of an unauthorized entry from two locations—two!—reached him and he had to act quickly. Following established procedures, the captain of the guard set the proper traps, all designed to interrupt the normal flow of life in the palace as little as possible.

Of course, thought Mineir, he'd have to deal with the invaders himself.

He got up off the bed, provoking whines of displeasure from the young beauties.

"Later," he said, patting each one's rump.

He picked up his robe off a nearby chair.

There was someone else to be notified too, he knew.

And he shivered, even though the room was quite warm from the blazing fire.

Taline pushed open the doors.

The room was dark, and she signaled the others to stay back.

She took another step, and Paralan came beside her.

"It's empty," she said. "There's no—"

And then the room came to life. Lanterns were opened, bathing the small band of invaders in a pale yellow light. Then she saw the soldiers. Dozens of them, all charging, their swords held high.

"Back!" she yelled. "Quickly!"

They turned to go out the doors, but the doors shut from behind.

Two of Rhow's mrem leaped past Taline and Paralan ready to meet the guards. Despite a few well-aimed blows, they were quickly cut to pieces.

Paralan raised his weapon.

"No!" Taline yelled.

He paused, and just as the guards were about to reach him, he lowered his sword.

"Lay down your weapons!" one of Mineir's soldiers snarled.

Taline let her sword clatter to the stone floor.

So easy, Taline thought.

So easy for fools to be captured.

The way was clear, thought Falon. After eliminating the squad of guards, there didn't seem to be anyone in their way.

"Run!" he ordered, and he broke into a trot, eager to make good use of the deserted corridors.

He climbed up one set of stairs, and then ran down a long hallway, before coming to the doors that led to the king's bedroom.

"Ready?" he asked Rhow's mrem, before pushing the heavy doors open.

Still panting, they nodded.

"Here we go then—"

And he pulled out his claw sword, a nasty weapon if there ever was one, and threw open the doors.

He ran in, fast as he could, spinning around, ready to kill whoever got in his way—

Then he froze.

"Welcome. We hadn't planned on your arrival. Poor security. Still, you're more than welcome to join your friends. . . ."

For a moment all Falon could do was look around this enormous waiting room, looking at Caissir, Paralan,

Taline, and just a couple of Rhow's mrem. They were kneeling on the ground, with their throats held up high, exposed. . . .

The traditional position of total surrender.

The king stood up.

He was a plump thing, whose bushy fur had lost whatever luster it once had. The king was chewing on a meat bone as if this were a party.

"You can drop your weapon, friend," the king said between chews. "And best be fast about it. My soldiers aren't pleased about the damage you've done to their compatriots."

Mineir turned away, and Falon looked at Taline. She was just barely able to see him, so high was her throat held. But she made a small nod.

There was no way Falon could take on this small army that Mineir had in the room.

He let his sword fall to the ground, feeling disgraced. Then the others followed suit.

The king signaled to a few of his guards and they hurried over, scooping up the weapons.

The king sat down, and smiled at Falon. He extended one long finger, and pointed down.

"If you don't mind . . ."

Falon felt a blade jab rudely at the base of his tail— another insult—and he knelt on the stone floor.

"Good. Now we can get on with our business." The king called over a functionary of his court and whispered some instructions. The functionary hurried away.

"I've invited someone to join us. But first—" He made a signal to one of his captains. The captain barked out some orders and the bulk of the small army left, leaving behind a handful of guards, their swords out, ready to jab at the invaders.

The last of the soldiers filed out, and Falon watched one of the guards go over and bolt the doors behind them.

Mineir doesn't want his army to see who's coming. These guards, the ones left behind, must be special . . . trusted.

A heavy curtain rustled, off to the side, and finally parted. A door opened.

At first Falon saw nothing.

But then he heard the sound—the strange swishing of

something dragging on the stone—and became aware of a ripe, pungent smell unlike any he had ever sniffed.

Then it was there, lumbering through the doorway, blinking in the bright candlelight of the room.

He heard one of Rhow's mrem moan.

Paralan lowered his neck, his eyes blazing. Taline reached out, touching him, warning him. One of the guards poked her in the back and she yelped.

Falon kept looking at it.

So the old tales are true! This liskash was like something created by the old tale tellers in his village. Its skin was a shimmering, almost greenish hue, with clear scaly plates all over its body. With every step it stuck its tongue out as if tasting the air.

Its sick-looking yellow eyes scanned the group of prisoners.

Then it spoke.

"K'laagh, senei fraal, speite, Mineir."

The king laughed.

"Our friend is curious, and I am too, as to who sent you charming folk." Mineir scanned the group. "Who'd like to be first?"

"I'd rather give my throat to the jaws of a Rar," Paralan hissed.

The king arched his eyebrows. One of his guards gave Paralan a jab.

From the sound of the yell Falon knew that it did more than poke the brave mrem.

"Now, I hope we don't have any more outbursts. Time is, as they say, wasting . . ."

"Milaash, k'laagh mitei."

The king shook his head doubtfully, but a small smile on his lips told Falon that he was enjoying this whole scene.

"Oh, I don't know, my Eastern friend," Mineir said, looking at the liskash. "I had hoped that they would be more cooperative than that." He returned his gaze to the group. "Surely one of you will have the sense to talk . . . before it's too late."

Falon felt one of Rhow's guards stir behind him.

"If you say a word—one word—I will personally kill you," he whispered.

The king stood up, and went to the liskash. The creature rested a hand on the king's shoulder.

How could he stand it? Falon wondered. It made him want to throw up.

"Well," said Mineir, turning to them, a big smile on his face. "My friend and I have, in the interest of speed, come up with a little inducement to encourage you to talk with us . . . tell us who the madmrem is that sent you. Was it the King of Ar, perhaps, or some merchant?" He looked at Taline. "Or is it someone important in Tizare?"

Everyone remained quiet.

How long . . . how long before we're dead? And how will we die? Falon wondered.

And what is it like to die?

Falon licked his lips, almost ready to say the name himself.

The king shook his head. "Very well, then." Mineir nodded to the liskash. The creature turned around, its tail leaving a slimy trail on the floor. It pulled back the curtain again, and opened the doors. Then Falon heard it working some kind of crank, or pulley. The sound of heavy machinery filled the chamber.

"My friend has brought his own . . . entourage with him. Just a few, well-hidden soldiers from the great army that comes tomorrow, ready to claim this city, Tizare, the first jewel in the Eastern Lords' crown."

Paralan spat on the floor, and the king shot him an angry glance. But he recovered his composure quickly.

"Yes, just a small band to keep my friend here company." He turned slowly. "Unfortunately . . . they require an unusual diet. . . ."

Mineir snapped his fingers and one of the guards jabbed at the back of one of Rhow's mrem.

"What?" he stammered.

"Up," the guard hissed.

"That's right, this way," the king said, indicating the doorway. "You see, there's a pit there . . . nice and dark and cool, their preferred environment. One by one," he said lightheartedly, "you'll be pushed into it. One. By. One. Until one of you tells me who sent you," he snarled. He waved his hand.

"No," Rhow's mrem said. "No, I—I—" Falon saw him look down at him. "I—"

"Talk and I'll kill you!" Paralan yelled, and once again the guard drew blood from him.

The king waited a moment, standing next to the liskash, dwarfed by it. He waited to see if he'd speak.

Then he shook his head. "Very well, then," he said with disgust, and he signaled the liskash to throw the mrem into the pit.

"No," the mrem blubbered, clawing at the walls while the liskash took firm hold of him and pulled him along. "No!"

Then, in a flash, the mrem disappeared, into the darkness, his scream echoing strangely as he fell down.

Everyone was silent then, for a moment. And they heard other sounds . . . the biting, the crunching, the terrible sounds of eating.

Caissir was blubbering, crying out loud. Elezar stood close to him, his fists clenched, his face grim.

"Come, come," the king said. "There's no need for us to go through this anymore. No need at all." He walked over and patted Caissir's head, which only made the mrem howl that much louder.

The king looked at Falon.

"Yes . . . you shall be next. Perhaps if you were gone, everyone might lose some of their . . . stubbornness."

The guard behind Falon poked at him, signaling him to get up.

Falon got to his feet and marched dully over to the liskash.

"There's still time," the king suggested.

"No, there isn't," Falon answered.

Another poke, and he took a step closer to the liskash.

He could smell the pit now, the foul, almost sewerlike odor.

And the eager sound of swishing, scaly bodies. So eager for the next course.

So this is how I regain my honor. . . .

Falon had to smile at that.

It was an expensive way to regain status in the community of his fellow mrem.

One word would save him.

Rhow.

He shook his head.

The liskash grabbed him.

Taline called out to him. "Falon!"

Caissir's gentle crying never ended.

"Take him," the king said, waving his hand in the direction of the pit.

The liskash dragged him roughly into the darkness. . . .

Chapter 21

▲————————————————————————————————▲

The creature's clawlike hand felt slimy, squeezing his shoulder.

It could rip me in two in a moment, Falon thought.

The pit was just ahead, and now the sounds and smells of it were nearly overpowering. Such a stench, it made him gag as he dully shuffled, following the liskash's lead.

"There's still time," Mineir said. "Just one name . . ."

Falon turned, and shook his head, disgusted with the bogus king, and disgusted with himself for getting into such a spot.

What did it feel like to be eaten, he wondered. . . .

Some forlorn creature from down below cried out, eagerly, a guttural, hungry sound.

The liskash gave him a push.

Falon started to turn back to the pit.

And in midturn, he saw something very interesting.

Two small eyes, staring down at him from the farthest corner of the massive room. The eyes stared, then winked.

By the All-Mother, he thought. It was Ash! Neatly wedged into a corner of the room, hidden in the shadows. How he was holding on, with just the thick wall molding for support, was incredible.

"Perhaps," Falon said quickly, "I should reconsider my stubbornness." He took a step back to Mineir. A small smile of victory began to bloom on the king's face. "Yes, what are these mrem, or even this city to me. I'm a highlander and—" another step "—you know how independent we can be."

Taline's face registered total shock, as she shook her head slowly, left and right.

"I'll tell you who sent us. What do I care?"

The liskash lumbered behind Falon, puffing hard to keep up with him.

"Yes . . . then tell us—Who?—Who?".

"None other than—"

Falon looked back up to Ash.

All right, my little orphan. Make your move now. If you have one. . . .

And Ashre responded to his unspoken order.

The liskash was the first to see Falon looking up. He turned his great green head, his tongue flapping curiously, and stared up at the corner. He cried out something in his own language.

Then Ash's dagger flew through the air. So fast, Falon couldn't tell who the intended target was, not until it plunged into the liskash, smoothly into its shoulder.

It screamed out, and Mineir's guards all looked about for the attacker.

"Falon!" Ash called out, and then he threw a claw sword down to him, a throw of perfect precision and arc. Falon caught it handily, and faced the wounded liskash.

And as he turned, he saw something that had Mineir and his guards frozen, terrified. The cache of weapons taken from the invaders started sliding noisily across the stone floor, each sword coming to a stop before one of them.

"Now!" Paralan screamed, standing, scooping up his weapon.

The liskash opened its mouth and started towards Falon.

"Not now, you slimy bastard!" Falon said, and he took his strongest swing with his claw sword. The creature saw it coming and tried to duck. But it was too slow, too tired, perhaps, and Falon screamed even louder as the claw-shaped blade dug into the tough scaly flesh.

And the creature stopped.

He pulled it out for another agonizing blow while the liskash flailed, ineffectually, with its claws.

Mineir's guards formed a wall to protect him. But the odds were almost equal now, and with Paralan and Elezar fighting, the king didn't have a chance.

The liskash reached out and hooked Falon around the throat. It squeezed, quickly and with tremendous power.

Falon's arm went limp. All air was cut off and it felt like the liskash was going to squeeze his throat through his fingers like so much dough.

And then Ash was there, his short sword poking the great creature, quickly sliding in, drawing blood.

Still the liskash held on, and Falon gave one last look around, searching for help.

"No," Ashre cried with each jab.

Falon felt himself beginning to black out. Still so tight! The claw just kept squeezing, squeezing. . . .

He saw Paralan.

Hacking his way past a pair of Mineir's guards, leaping across the stone floor of the great room, coming right up to the liskash.

And the hate that burned in his eyes made Paralan look almost as terrifying as the liskash.

"For my wife, my kits!" he screamed as he brought his great blade back. Then he struck home.

The blade sliced through the creature's neck easily. For a moment the head rested there, looking only confused, the filmy yellow eyes blinking, the tongue still wagging out.

Then it toppled over, landing with a dull thud on the stones.

Slowly, the creature's claw released Falon, and he sputtered, trying to breathe in the wonderful air.

"Thank . . . you . . ." Falon coughed.

"Paralan!" Ash screamed.

"Eh?" Paralan said, turning.

It was the king himself, a curved delicate dagger held high.

Ashre ran toward him.

Too late.

The king brought his blade down hard, right into Paralan's chest. The once-disgraced officer, the farmer, their brave friend reached up to the blade, as if feeling the wound. Then he fell to his knees.

The king's guards were dead, scattered on the floor by Taline, Caissir, and the others like so many unwanted carcasses.

"Traitor . . ." Falon hissed, leaping at Mineir with his claw sword, and he cut the king down.

"It's over," Taline said, walking over to him. She knelt

down beside Paralan. "Over . . ." she said quietly, resting
Paralan's head in her lap. Ashre came beside her, knelt
down, and leaned against her.

"He saved my life . . ." Falon said.

"The way he fought he saved *all* our lives," Caissir said.

Falon looked over at the wizard. He too was covered
with enormous splotches of blood. *You have come a long
way,* Falon thought. He walked over to Ashre and Taline.

"And I thought I told you to stay in Lord Rhow's castle,"
Falon said, letting his hand rest on Ashre's head.

"I couldn't," the kit said, quietly. "I . . . I knew that
you would need me."

Falon gave him a gentle smile.

"And that we did, Ash. That we did. . . ."

Then Falon walked over to the head of the liskash, posed
at some strange angle. "Except Taline's wrong, I'm afraid.
It's not over. This," he said, giving the head a kick, "can
only mean that it's just begun."

He bent over and picked up the heavy head.

None of them knew what to expect once they opened
the doors and attempted to leave Mineir's palace.

Falon went first, the head held none too steadily in his
arms. Behind him, Taline walked with Ash, her arm
draped over the kit's shoulder. He heard her talking to
him, soothingly, of Paralan and his great bravery.

The first guards drew their swords.

Falon held the head before them. "The false king is
dead," he said, with an authority that surprised him. "And
his friend from the East is also dead." He held the head up
high. "I suggest you make sure any other such guests are
killed. Then, you'd best begin preparing for a siege."

They hesitated for a few moments, looking at Falon,
then the head, then Falon again. Slowly, they lowered
their swords.

They hurried past Falon's party, into the royal chambers.

"You'll find a whole pit of the monsters!" Caissir called
out to them as they passed. "Just use your noses—you
won't be able to miss it."

Falon led them on. When he spoke, his voice had a
rough, raspy sound, as if the liskash had damaged his vocal

cords. His fur still carried the matted-down imprint of the creature's claw.

More guards appeared.

Some even tried to force Falon to stand his ground.

But the bloody head, eyes still open, spoke volumes.

It tapped into a deep, almost primeval fear in all mrem.

The liskash are coming to get you, the old nayas would sing out to the overly playful kits in the village nursery. *They're coming to get you. . . .*

And here, Falon had proof that it was all true. They were coming . . . to this city. And soon.

But such problems he'd be able to turn over to Lord Rhow. He would surely have plans for resisting the invasion.

Elezar, who had been staying towards the rear, keeping watch, came strutting up to Falon. His blood-splattered fur made him look like a ghastly painter.

"What are your plans, Falon, once we get outside?"

Falon knew exactly what he was going to do.

Tizare was a city of pleasure and wealth. If the citizens were to be ready to repel a full-scale attack from the East, they needed to be shocked.

"This head will be placed on the highest flagpole in the central courtyard."

"But Falon, the kits—"

"Everyone must see it, Elezar. *Everyone.* It's not some old tale, some superstition that we're talking about now. Unless the normal life of this city is stopped, and preparations begun, we will all end up inside the bellies of the Eastern Lords . . . or as slaves in their new Western empire."

"But Lord Rhow—"

"I'm sure Lord Rhow will agree. At any rate, he's not here now."

Elezar scowled, then withdrew.

King. That's going to be a hard one to sell to all these . . . my subjects.

Perhaps it was best to let Rhow rule. *So what,* he thought, *if my father was from the royal line of Tizare? I've lived my entire life as a hot-tempered highlander.*

And there was something more, wasn't there? His clansmrem had a saying . . . "Dishonor is the stain that lasts forever." And Falon believed it . . .

They came to the main entrance hall of the palace.

By now it was filled not only with Mineir's guards, but also the staff of the palace, the cooks and chambermaids, the court flunkies and the king's concubines—the only group that seemed undisturbed by the hour.

The noise of their excited chatter filled the cavernous room.

But they all grew silent when they saw the head. Like the ripples in a pond, the silence moved through the crowd, as each palace resident got a good look at just whom their king had been hobnobbing with.

A few of the more fragile onlookers began coughing and spitting up on the floor.

Falon, though, was inured to his burden.

Let them see it, he thought. *Look at it, study the creature closely, get scared, and then make ready to fight for the life of your city.*

He strode out the massive twin doors and out into the cold night air. Morning was close and it felt wonderful to leave the sweaty world of the palace for this clean air.

"Take that flag down," he ordered one of Rhow's guards.

It was Mineir's personal flag. The guard brought it down. Falon undid the ropes holding it, and then lashed the rope to the liskash's head.

It dangled at an odd angle, pathetic and eerie at the same time.

Just as well, he thought. *Let them walk around it, stroll around, studying it, as its eyes remain open and it drains itself of blood.*

He started pulling the rope up. The head lifted, swung free, a pendulum now as Falon quickly hoisted it up, high, higher than even the palace itself.

There, he thought. It would catch the first rays of light in the morning . . . and the last glow at night.

Taline came beside him, linking her arm with his.

"It's terrible-looking," she said. "Like a nightmare. . . ."

"Yes . . . let's hope it scares these mrem before it's too late." He pulled her close, enjoying her warmth, her soft fur, so reassuring after holding the scaly head. "Now let's go tell your father that Tizare needs a new king."

"Incredible, absolutely incredible. In a pit, you say?"
Rhow poured another goblet of wine. He gestured at
Taline and Falon, asking if they wanted any. They both
shook their heads.

"You didn't, I hope, tell anyone of your claim to the
throne?" he asked, arching his eyebrows. "I mean, it
wouldn't do to confuse the citizens . . . not yet . . . not
till—"

"After the invasion," Falon added.

"Precisely. Let's defend the city. Then," he stood up and
came over to Falon, "we can tell them the wonderful
news."

Lord Rhow patted Falon's shoulder and then quickly
walked over to a large mural on a side wall. He pressed into
the wood, and the mural swung around revealing a map.

"This," he said, "is Tizare. I'll have to assume that
Mineir's troops will cooperate in the city's defense—"

"I'm sure they will," Taline added. "Judging by the look
on their faces when they saw the head, they should
rally. . . ."

Rhow stroked his whiskers. "Yes, of course. Still, we will
lose some who choose to flee the city, make for neighboring villages or the woods, and wait until the battle is over.
After he's rested, I will send Elezar over with a contingent
of my best soldiers. He will be able to keep them in line."

"What can we do?" Falon asked.

Rhow pointed at two spots at the back of the map.

"The city has two weak points . . . here and here. The
walls are not as high as they are near the main gate, fewer
good positions for archers, and almost no protection for
battle catapults, fire machinery, anything heavy to protect
us from a siege.

"I expect that they will attack tonight. And they will, for
the benefit of the liskash, have to succeed by dawn, or wait
until the next night."

Falon walked over to the map. "You want me to take a
position back here?"

Lord Rhow nodded. "Yes—and hold it. I'll give you a
small but experienced group of soldiers. Once the main
attack eases, I can send support . . . to help you hold your

position. It won't be easy, especially before the Eastern
Lords make their intentions known." He reached out and
touched Taline, gently caressing her cheek. "My daughter
will stay with me as my first lieutenant. She will keep us in
contact. Should I fall in battle, she will take over. You can
keep Caissir with you—"

"And Ashre."

"The kit? Are you sure you want him with you?"

Falon laughed. "I'd like to see us try and keep him out of
this. No, he's proven his worth. A kit in size and age, certainly, but he's a clever fighter by your side. . . ."

And *more*, Falon thought, but he didn't say anything
about the weapons moving across King Mineir's bedroom
floor. And, he was glad to see, neither did Taline.

"Very well. Now, I suggest you get some rest—till midday, at least—before you start assembling your troops. I'll
start warning the city dwellers, get the able-bodied to
help, and the rest of Tizare off the streets and into their
homes."

Lord Rhow came and led Falon back toward the doors,
leaving Taline behind. "If you don't mind, Falon, I'd like a
private word with my daughter. Get your rest . . . you
have served Tizare with bravery, with honor . . . but
there are greater challenges to come."

Falon looked at Taline. He had hoped that perhaps—but
no, not now, not so soon . . . after Paralan. He smiled at
her and walked out of the room, his weariness finally washing over him as he made his way to his quarters.

Rhow shut the door behind his daughter, his smile fading on his face.

So close! Yet a hundred things could go wrong. Everything must go perfectly, so perfectly, or his years of planning could lead to defeat and worse.

"Pensive, my lord?"

"Eh," Rhow said, turning quickly. "Oh, Plano . . . you
shouldn't creep up on me so."

Plano sat down in Rhow's chair, draping one leg casually
over an elegantly carved arm. He dug a fistful of berries
out of a nearby bowl. "We won't have long to wait, my lord.
Just one more day—assuming you can repel the invasion."

Rhow glared at Plano. "And you think I'll fail?"

Plano held his palms out. "Not at all. The invaders should be completely surprised that the gates aren't wide open for them." He took some more berries. "On the other hand, I'm not sure that Mineir's army will be as, er, intact as you'd like. Already my scouts report that some of the younger captains have fled the city for the Tulingara Forest."

Rhow cursed, then spat on the floor. He ran over to the main door to his bedroom.

"Temper—my lord—"

Rhow opened the door, startling the guard on duty.

"An order," he snapped, "for all of the king's captains on watch. Anyone found leaving his post is to be tracked down, killed, and displayed in the public square."

"And by whose authority should I say—" the guard started.

"By the authority of Lord Rhow, Acting Regent. And send over a dozen soldiers armed to their ears."

He slammed the door.

"They'll wonder," Plano said, "what gives you the right—"

Rhow shook his head. "Thanks to Falon, they saw that head. If they're not running away, they'll rally behind whoever promised to help them. Besides . . . my guards can be very persuasive."

Plano tipped his goblet in salute. "And the rest of the plan?"

A small frown crossed Rhow's face. "That, my friend, is a bit trickier. Trickier, and more dangerous. But then, much of that will be your department."

Plano stood up and came over to Rhow. Once again, Lord Rhow was reminded of the wizard's great size. Plano was old, and filled with secrets that he shared with no one. Despite his age, he was a fearsome-looking mrem, capable of sudden shifts of mood, from an almost fatherly benevolence, to something dark and terrifying.

Rhow wanted him gone—now.

And perhaps later he'd have to do something about his minister. Permanently . . .

After it was all over.

After he was king.

He gestured at the door, and after a moment's pause,

Plano put down his goblet, made a slight bow, and walked out.

So proud . . . so confident of himself. And powerful.

When it was over, Rhow told himself . . . yes, when it was over, Plano too must die.

Chapter 22

▲————————————————————————————————————▲

The dream started out so beautiful, so sweet!

Falon was with Taline, in a peaceful glen. They lay together, curled close together on great patches of powder moss, luxuriating in the wonderfully soft feel of it and the hot rays of the sun slicing through the leafy roof.

And for a while, that's all it was, that peace, that tremendous sense of just being with another, and feeling so wonderful.

But then she started nudging him, pressing against him, running her hand along his sleek back down to his stublike tail.

Persistently, and with a trained expertise, she worked on him, touching, caressing, now letting her claws press ever so gently into his fur. Laughing, smiling, until all he could do was turn over, mewling like a newborn while she mounted him.

A dream . . . he knew that's all it was . . . but it was wonderful.

She blocked the sun, her beautiful eyes in the shadow, barely visible. He reached up for her . . . began to caress her breasts.

She froze.

Her body went rigid, and in his dream he was still laughing, so slow to catch on. He asked her what was wrong. She put a finger to his lips and craned her head left and right, listening, listening . . .

Until he heard it too.

They were coming! Liskash, dozens of them, all converging on his sweet spot in the woods.

Taline shot up, ran for her sword, ran as hard as she could.

He sat up, reacting slowly to the threat.

Then the first ones came lumbering out of the woods.

One grabbed Taline before she could reach her sword.

"No—" he cried out.

"No . . ." he moaned in his hot bedroom, the bedsheets all twisted around his naked body.

It picked up Taline and ripped her in two as though she were some kit's cloth doll.

Then they came for him. Slowly, so slowly that it should have been easy to get away.

Except that his own movements were even slower. He tried to kneel, then stand . . . but he just couldn't get up fast enough.

And then they were there. They surrounded him, each of the liskash looking more eager than the next. He started to scream and yell, as they brought their foul-smelling mouths closer and closer. . . .

He woke up in the dark, his fur matted with sweat.

He touched himself. *I'm here. I'm alive. It was a dream. It didn't all happen.*

He got up and went to the window. He pulled back the heavy shade.

There was Tizare below him. He heard the rumble of carts and wagons on the street. And then, in the distance, a line of soldiers marched toward the main gate.

It had turned nasty and hot.

Enough sleep, Falon told himself. There would be plenty of time for sleep later.

He dressed in battle kilt and armor, as he listened to the sounds of Tizare making ready for a siege from the East.

Surprisingly enough, panic didn't break out through the entire city. Rhow's guards showed up at Mineir's castle with his detailed orders. And the king's soldiers, quite used to taking orders, fell into line. A few of the more inexperienced captains had already left, heading west under cover of night. But the rest seemed impressed with Rhow's order that anyone running away would be killed.

The able-bodied mrem, and she-mrem without kits, set about building barricades in the crucial street of Tizare, while others less able, or less inclined, sought the refuge and peace of The Flying Copper Inn.

Soldiers, from both Rhow's service and Mineir's, took up positions on the walls of Tizare. The heavy war machines, most of them never before used in actual fighting, were wheeled out, tested, and made ready for the great battle to come.

By midday Lord Rhow began visiting the different fortified positions, and he was more than pleased to see Mineir's captains come to him to present their reports.

Everyone checked the sky as they worked. As the sun went down they worked with redoubled speed, constructing more barricades, running more tests on the battle machinery, always watching the sky.

Then, just as the light took on the late-afternoon glow, scouts from the eastern hills brought the report all were waiting for:

The invaders were moving.

Falon hurried through the halls of Rhow's palace.

"But surely we have some time for a bite, perhaps some Southern fish. It's a delicacy that I never—"

Falon's answer was to pick up his pace.

Ashre was already ahead of him, skipping ahead, totally excited.

Let him enjoy this, Falon thought. *These last few moments of expectation. Before the truth becomes clear.*

But who am I kidding? he thought. *What do I know of war?* A few border skirmishes with other highlander clans, and that was about it. And no one had died during those frays.

This would be much worse.

"At least," Caissir wheedled, "let me run down to the cook and pick up a small parcel of food. It's going to be a very long night," he said in all seriousness.

Falon grinned. "Very well, then. But hurry, and meet us in Rhow's weapons room."

Caissir trotted away, in the other direction.

Ashre came running back to Falon.

"Falon, can I arm myself too? You know how handy I can be."

"I wouldn't let you go out there without weapons, Ash. Just don't weigh yourself down with too much metal. Your speed and size are great advantages." He paused, studying the small kit. "Ash, do you think if you were in great danger—like the last time—that you would just, you know, vanish?"

The kit's face made a grimace, as he thought about the question.

"I . . . I don't know." Then, with a wide grin, "I sure hope so."

"Me, too." Falon laughed. He reached the spiral steps leading down to the weapons room, and Falon hurried. He was eager to get to the wall, while it was still light. "Tell me," Falon said, on the way down, "do you have any feelings about the siege?"

"No," Ash said quickly. "And that's funny. I mean, with all that's going to happen I should have lots of feelings, little warnings of dangers to come." Falon reached the bottom and turned to face Ashre. "But there's nothing now." The kit tilted his head. "Maybe I don't have that power anymore."

"Or maybe we're not in any danger. Wouldn't that be a nice idea?"

But Ashre's face told him that the kit didn't think that was a likely prospect.

There was plenty of danger headed their way—but something was stopping Ashre from sensing any of it.

It was an advantage that Falon would rather not do without.

"Help yourself," Falon said to the kit, gesturing at the room filled with weapons.

Ashre ran over and picked up a gracefully curved short sword, one of a kind, hanging alone on the wall.

"This," he said, giving it a few test swings in the air.

Falon walked over and looked at the blade. It was not one of Rhow's weapons. It matched none of the other swords. He noticed some inscriptions on it—a strange language, unlike anything he'd ever seen.

"I'd say what you have here is a captured weapon, Ash. Perhaps from some liskash."

"Good. Then I'll use it to kill as many as I can."

Falon looked at the barrels filled with swords, lances, and pikes. "Here," he said, selecting a good-size sword. It had a sharp gleaming edge to it and, though it was heavy, Falon felt he could manage to wield it effectively.

I want all the cutting power I can get, he thought.

"And throat armor," he said, turning to Ash.

"But it's uncomfortable."

"And it can save your furry head. Over there, and take the thickest you can find."

Then Falon strapped a short sword and a pair of small daggers to his side. He too put on throat armor, annoyed at the way it pressed into his pelt. Still, it could save his life should any liskash try the throat-squeezing trick again.

Ashre selected another small dagger.

"Ready?" Falon asked.

Ashre nodded.

"Then let's—"

"Wait . . . I've got us some food," Caissir called out, waddling down the spiral stone staircase.

"You had just better select some weapons—and quickly," Falon urged.

"Weapons . . ." Caissir said, surveying the room with disgust.

Falon and Ashre watched with great amusement as Caissir clumsily tried first this blade, than that one.

"Stay toward the back, Caissir," Falon laughed. "And, if you get in a really tight spot, just do a magic trick."

And he led them out of Rhow's castle.

Falon climbed the steps of the western wall.

Rhow wasn't joking. The wall was barely half the height of the eastern wall, with only a few fortified positions in which to place a line of archers. And, of course, there was no way that the fancy battle machines could be used. They would stick up higher than the wall, an easy target for fire arrows.

The soldiers, though, seemed to be as good as Rhow had promised.

They accepted Falon's leadership with an eagerness that alarmed him. He just hoped such trust wasn't ill-founded.

As soon as he was on the ramparts, the two captains

under him came for orders on how he'd like the soldiers placed, and where to station the reserves.

There was no point, Falon saw, in lining the wall with soldiers—they'd just make easy targets. Better to keep two small groups to the side, well behind the stone turrets. Then, when the invaders were about to breach the wall, the Tizarian soldiers could spread out along the wall and cut down the enemy.

Falon looked up to see what the captains thought of his plan. They nodded, and he felt that they must have had a similar idea themselves.

"And where should I go?" Ashre asked.

"With the reserves," Falon said. "And now . . . I don't want anyone on this wall until it's filled with invaders."

"I'll guard the provisions," Caissir offered.

Falon shook his head. "You stay with Ashre. Keep him covered, and off this wall until I say it's safe."

"Certainly," Caissir said. "I was just—"

Falon nodded, preoccupied with his plans.

I wish Taline were here, he thought. *To give us her opinion, maybe to stay and fight alongside us.*

Instead, they would live through this night with a city between them, not knowing each other's fate until morning.

The sun touched the hills in the west, melting into the green ridges, as the shadows of the valley grew and spread, racing toward the city itself.

It can't be long now.

Ashre grabbed Falon's hand.

"Can I stay here with you . . . until it begins?"

Falon smiled, then looked at Caissir. "No, Ash. Stay below, with the others . . . help Caissir eat some of his food. And don't worry—you'll see plenty before this night is out."

Caissir gently led Ashre down the steps, off the ramparts. While Falon stayed there, watching the night arrive.

All was ready, thought Rhow. And it would begin at any moment.

How many, he wondered? They would expect no resistance, or a token battle—that was all. Not a completely armed and alerted city.

But was it strong enough?

He looked down to the area just inside the wall. Elezar was once again reviewing the instruction to the operators of the battle machines. If they were to fire too early, the damage they could do would be wasted. Too late, and the battle would already have progressed to bloody hand-to-hand fighting.

And he looked over at the rows of archers lined up on the wall. Taline was guiding them, making sure that no one fired until their targets were in range.

In range . . . and in sight. The twin moons would not rise until the siege had been going on for a long time. Perhaps the fate of the city would have been decided by then. Perhaps it would be over.

Elezar would use one of the catapults to set fire to piles of brush placed outside the city walls. Rhow hoped the fire would provide enough light to see the enemy.

He turned back, once again, to look at the city. He saw Plano standing there, waiting.

Soon, my eager minister. Soon, you'll get your chance. And Rhow felt disgust at his counselor's taste for pain.

Soon it will be your turn. Soon I'll be rid of you.

"They're here—on the hills! I can see them!" the soldier screamed out the warning that everyone was waiting for. He clambered down from his perch on the small tower on top of the gate.

"They're forming ranks now, along the slope of the hill . . . all spread out."

Rhow looked east, at first seeing nothing. Then, through the smoky haze of dusk, he saw them, like small dots, lining themselves up.

How many? he asked himself. *Are we strong enough?*

He rubbed his hands together, annoyed at his growing fear.

The dots kept lining up.

By the All-Mother, let them stop, Rhow prayed. Taline came running up to him.

"Father, they're still forming."

"Yes," he said. "There are more than I . . . imagined. Still, we're ready, right, Taline?" He looked down at his daughter, so brave, so faithful.

And what will she think? he wondered. *Will she stand by me, ever loyal? Or will she turn away . . . in disgust?*

"They're moving!" the lookout screamed.

Now the line of dots started its slow march to the walls of Tizare.

Rhow reached out and touched Taline's cheek.

"Best to get to your position," he said softly.

She threw her arms around him and hugged him tightly. Then she ran back to the rows of crouching archers.

"Elezar!" he shouted down to his captain. "The invaders have begun to move. Prepare your machines."

Elezar raised a hand, and the teams began turning the massive winches, pulling back the catapults and fire machines.

Then, almost sadly, Lord Rhow let himself look at Plano. He nodded.

And Plano, a terrible grin on his face, turned and headed west. . . .

"Perhaps they'll not come at all," Caissir said, chewing on some crusty bread from Lord Rhow's kitchen. He held the loaf towards Ashre, who just shook his head. "You have to eat, Ash—keep your strength up. No, I think that the invasion will just fade away. Especially when they get a look at the way the city is defended. Why, then you and I and Falon can enjoy ourselves—" he leaned close to the kit "—and our connection with friends in high places."

He watched Ashre get up, all fidgety, pacing back and forth.

"Settle down, Ash. There's nothing you can do now. Why—"

"Falon's in danger," Ashre said, almost whispering. "I felt it . . . just then . . . like a message that's been trying to come through all day."

"Well, of course he's in danger. We're all in danger," Caissir said, between chews on the bread.

"No," Ashre said, violently shaking his head, and pacing faster and faster. "No—something else. Not a danger from out there. Something . . . I don't know. It all ended. Just as I felt it."

"Well, don't worry," Caissir said, smiling, but also a bit scared by the kit's vehemence. "You and I are here to protect him."

Ash nodded.

Then they heard the steps of someone running towards them from out of the gloomy back streets of Tizare. A half dozen soldiers stood up, weapons ready.

It was a messenger dressed in the uniform of Lord Rhow's personal army.

"Yes, what is it?" one of Falon's soldiers asked him.

"There is a need for the one called Ashre. I am to stay here—" he said breathlessly. "To assist Falon. Lord Rhow said—"

Falon stepped down from the wall and walked over to the messenger.

"Lord Rhow says what?" Falon snapped.

He was edgy, Caissir thought. Maybe he was in over his head. He might be a brave highlander, but who knew what his abilities as a soldier might be?

"Lord Rhow said that there was a need for Ashre . . . that Taline had something to ask him. He's to go to the main gate."

Falon looked at Ashre. "I don't know. I'd rather he stay here with—"

"But if Taline needs me for something," Ashre said, "Then that's where I should be."

Falon looked around.

"Has the attack begun?" he asked the messenger.

The messenger nodded. "Just now—a line of the invaders is moving against the main gate. You had best keep careful watch."

"Very well. Ashre may go, but I want Caissir here to take him."

Caissir looked up, startled, telltale crumbs sticking to his whiskers. "But hadn't I—"

"I was told to ask only for Ashre," the messenger said.

"Caissir takes him, and," he said, coming close to the now well-fed magician, "and Caissir, you will bring him back."

"Falon!" a soldier yelled from the wall. "There's movement out there—coming towards us!"

Falon came to Caissir and rested a hand on his shoulder.

"Be careful, my friend." And then he returned to his post on the wall.

"And you too . . ." whispered Caissir, to the night air. "You too. . . ."

Chapter 23

"Mrem," Rhow said to Elezar.

Elezar spit over the wall, onto the ground. "Renegades. We'll give them a special welcome."

Rhow grabbed at the edge of the wall, steadying himself. "There are more than I imagined. I don't think—"

"We'll do fine. If Falon holds the west, we'll have no problem here."

The invaders came faster now, not exactly running, but the soldiers tried to keep pace with the chariots that now passed them. They were of a design that Rhow had never seen before. They moved quickly, and it even looked as though there were mrem riding on them.

"Best get to your position," he said to Elezar.

Elezar made a slight bow and left.

Now they were clearly visible, even though it was night. Their armor caught the starlight and the glow of the torches on top of the twin towers that flanked the gate.

Rhow looked at Taline, crouched low next to her archers, ready to give the order, and then back to Elezar, who would await his signal.

The rest of the soldiers crouched on the ramparts, ready to leap up and throw the invaders off the wall.

And then, as Rhow watched them draw close, another, new line of attackers began forming on the distant hills.

Rhow tried not to let any of the soldiers see him standing there, shaking. . . .

"Pretty quiet, eh, Ashre?"

The streets seemed ghostly to Caissir. A haunted city. "I guess everyone's taking no chances."

He looked over at Ashre, who said nothing.

"What's the problem, Ash?"

The kit shrugged. "This isn't right," he said grimly. "We shouldn't be leaving Falon."

"But if Taline needs you . . . I'm sure there must be a reason. . . ."

They turned a corner, and now passed The Flying Copper Inn. The windows were all lit up, and the sound of music and laughter spilled out onto the street.

"At least some good souls are taking advantage of all the excitement," Caissir said. "You don't suppose that we could stop a moment and—"

Ashre shook his head, walking on, away from the friendly glow of lights.

"Oh, well," Caissir grumbled, hurrying to catch up.

They took more turns, down the twisted streets of the city, getting closer to the center of the city.

They came to a narrow alleyway, wet with the shiny stream of an open sewer. It was the type of place you'd expect a mynt to be foraging for scraps of food, Caissir thought. But there was nothing, nothing except—

A figure in the shadows. Moving, slowly, steadily out into the open.

"Ashre . . . I've been waiting for you."

Caissir put an arm around the kit, pulling him back. "Careful, Ash . . . stay beside me."

"Now, don't pull him away," the stranger said. "please don't do that—"

Caissir heard something behind him. He turned, and there was a creature with two heads, each of them giddily rolling back and forth as it chewed at the air. It was a twisted thing, part liskash, part mrem.

"Oh, no," Caissir gasped.

His hand released Ashre, as he whimpered and fell against the wall.

The stranger grabbed at Ashre. "Don't be alarmed . . . Ashre." His voice was low. "It's just something to keep your meddlesome friend away . . . while we talk about important matters." He started to lead Ashre down the alleyway, leaving behind the moaning and crying Caissir.

"You see, my name is Plano, and I too am a very great magic user. . . . But that you shall see for yourself."

There were only four or five of them, Falon figured, running around out near the thick stand of parra trees.

"What do you think?" he asked the captain standing beside him.

"They're looking us over, I'd say. Trying to see how well the wall is defended."

"Keep your men down, then," Falon said. "I don't want them sending any larger force against us than they feel they have to."

The captain nodded, and walked down the stone steps to the assembled soldiers.

I wish Ash were here, Falon thought. *It's like being blind, this waiting, and watching, not knowing what's coming . . . and when it will come.*

More invaders appeared, only now they stood their ground, out in the open, looking at the wall.

At least one of them was a liskash, Falon saw. It towered over the other invaders. They stood there, also waiting, perhaps for the Tizarians to make a show of force on the wall.

Sorry, Falon thought. *If you want to see the cards I hold you'll have to raise the stakes.*

Then, around the opening that led into the woods, more of the invaders began to gather, not forming any position, but slowly coming together, ten, then twenty, then more, until it was beginning to look like an army.

This was it. They were probably sneaking away from the main attack force, regrouping in the woods, and getting ready to attack.

"Everyone ready!" Falon called out, and the soldiers, most of them lolling around talking, quickly sat up and stood near the wall.

The army, a shadowy horde, started to move.

Falon readied his sword.

The small fires on the wall cast a dim glow on the army moving against the main gate.

So many! Rhow thought. It was a much larger army than he had imagined.

Perhaps they didn't expect to enter the city unopposed.

They were close enough for him to hear the rhythmic clatter of their armor as they marched together, and the squeaking wheels of the chariots upon which, yes, mrem and liskash actually rode side by side.

It was cold now, and Rhow pulled his kilt tighter.

Plano should be back by now—how long could it take him to tie the kit up, keeping him away from Falon? Not long at all. . . . Where was he?

"Ready, my Lord!" Taline called.

"Ready, Lord Rhow!" Elezar yelled from down below.

Ready . . . yes, but am I ready?

He pulled out his sword.

"On my downstroke!" he called out.

He raised his sword in the air.

The two-headed thing came closer, sniffing and snorting at Caissir, opening its foul mouth, breathing right on Caissir's face, seemingly taking its own sweet time to eat him.

As well it might, thought Caissir, his face no longer registering terror.

He stood up slowly, passing close to the monster, so close, then right through it.

Like a heavy morning mist, it dispersed through the alleyway, joining the fog.

A very clever illusion, Caissir thought, with a funny sort of admiration.

He started walking in the direction he saw Plano take Ashre.

"You see, young kit, I was to have tied you up and stuck you right over there, near those bales of sporass for the herd-beasts. That is, in fact, what Lord Rhow expects. . . ."

Ashre looked around the large, cold storeroom, searching for some way to run from this stranger. . . .

"Oh, don't trouble yourself looking for a way out. You're quite my prisoner . . . for so long as I will it."

Ashre shook his head.

"Oh, yes—you see, I'm the reason your danger sense hasn't been working very well. You couldn't even tell that Falon is going to be killed by Rhow. And all of your other magic will, I'm afraid, be rather ineffective. . . ."

Ashre watched him slip a long silvery blade from under his tunic.

"You're much too dangerous to our plans to be left alive. You're young now, Ashre, but in the future, who knows? Rhow will be disappointed . . . he had hoped to use you. But after the Eastern Lords take the city—as they most certainly will—he will have . . . other things to be concerned about." He gave a sick little laugh.

Ashre tried to move, just to take a small step, toward the back, away from Plano.

Plano shook his head. "No, I'm afraid that won't help you, my small friend."

The blade caught the light of the two large torches hanging off the side of the warehouse.

"There will be only one magic user in Tizare, Ashre, and that is me. With the spells from *The Song of the Three Moons* my power will be complete, and I will be able to help the Eastern Lords become the new rulers of Ar. . . ."

He took some more steps towards Ashre, and the kit struggled to say something, to call out—anything to break this incredibly powerful spell. Plano raised the blade in the air.

A door opened at the back of the warehouse.

"You're not the only magic user. . . ."

It was Caissir, fat, foolish Caissir. Ashre felt almost sorry for him.

"Oh." Plano laughed. "Well, you've got me there. I guess a bogus wizard certainly counts. I thought I took care of you. Too bad . . . I would have liked to keep you around to entertain the liskash. If nothing else they could feed you to their slaves."

Plano moved quickly to Caissir, ready to make fast work of the fat old mrem.

"I don't know how you escaped my illusion. Still—"

Caissir raised his hand.

"Mara, t'leir, terrem sookir mara!"

"Wha—what?" Plano said, stopping.

The words were strange to Ashre, meaningless, but they filled him with an indescribable sense of wonder—and power.

He could move.

"You fool!" Plano spat. "Don't try to match magics with me—"

Caissir made a move through the air, and Plano's blade flew out of his hand. Ashre took a step. . . .

Caissir's face was grim, determined, a look Ashre had never seen him wear before.

Now it was Plano's move, and he pointed at the floor and walls of the warehouse. Tiny plumes of smoke began to rise up from the dark wood. Then, with a snap, they burst into flame. Soon the fire started traveling, right toward Caissir.

Caissir gathered his flowing kilt close to him, pulling it tight. Then he stretched out a hand, and the flowing river of fire split in two, turned around, and started heading back.

"No—no!" Plano screamed, and he started to run away, out toward the open door of the warehouse.

And Ashre stood there, right in front of him.

The fear coming from Plano filled the room, and Ashre knew that whatever powers the old wizard had were lost to his wild-eyed panic.

Ashre stood there in Plano's path, and the old wizard stopped, staring at the kit, and then at the door, frozen . . . unable to move. . . .

Now it was Ashre who wouldn't let him move.

The stream of fire picked up speed and rushed to Plano.

He stood still, and then, all of a sudden, he was engulfed in the flames, burning, a horrible stench filling the warehouse.

His flesh crisped and peeled away, leaving the grisly exposed body still standing there, its bubbling eye sockets still looking right at Ashre.

"Come . . ." Caissir said gently, putting an arm around the kit. "It's getting a bit warm in here. . . ."

Ashre took one more look at Plano, watching him finally collapse into a puddle on the floor, and then let himself be guided out.

Caissir's arm was tight around him, holding him close.

The night air barely took the smell of the burning warehouse out of his nostrils.

"There's a lot I have to explain to you, Ashre. Too much," the wizard laughed. "But let's just walk a bit first, eh? That tired me out even more than I thought it would."

Ashre nodded, thinking of other things. . . .

It was the first time I ever used my magic to kill, he thought. *The first time . . .*

And he knew it wouldn't be the last.

Rhow's blade wavered slightly in the torchlight.

Everyone's eyes were on it. The soldiers, Taline and her archers, Elezar and his teams working the battle machines. All waiting for his judgment.

He licked his lips.

Not too soon, he thought. Not too . . .

The invaders' chariots picked up speed, the great bulls charging ahead, prodded by long hooked poles. They were close enough that their fiery eyes were visible.

Then, behind them, the ranks of soldiers, the renegades beginning a fast trot while the liskash lumbered along as fast as they could.

They were slow, but Rhow knew that they could produce some incredibly fast movements, flipping themselves up and around with their powerful tails.

The sword wavered . . . then Rhow screamed—

"Now!" And he brought the blade down, a silvery blur against the dark sky.

Taline stood up and gave her own signal to the archers. The first volley of arrows went sailing through the air. Rhow watched their flight, noting how many missed. The second rank of archers came up to the wall and, on Taline's signal, let go their arrows.

Again, so many more misses than hits.

"Come on," Rhow hissed. "By the All-Mother, start aiming. . . ."

The first rank returned for their second volley and now they started to find their marks, hitting an equal number of invading mrem and liskash.

Except, Rhow saw, the liskash seemed to take their hits with little or no effect. All those scales, that tough hide.

. . . The mrem were quickly cut down, but the liskash seemed little bothered by the arrows.

Then, from down below, Rhow heard Elezar scream out the order to release the catapults. Enormous chunks of stone and boulders went flying over Rhow's head.

And it became clear that he had waited too long to give the order. Already the first line of invaders was at the wall, and the second rank lingered towards the back, waiting to see how the breaching of the wall went.

Then Elezar gave the order for the fire machines to eject their flaming balls. Most of these also missed the attackers, but they landed close enough to give good light to Taline's archers, who were increasingly finding their marks.

Then the chariots reached the wall, and Rhow watched the passengers raise ladders from each chariot. Renegades started scurrying up the ladders wearing nothing save swords strapped to their sides. Their dark markings spoke of distant lands, a race of mrem who knew no loyalty to the great cities.

Rhow signaled his captains, and the soldiers filled the wall, ready to repel the attackers.

Then, from behind the second wave of the attack, Rhow saw battle vehicles being wheeled forward—strange machines, some like enormous bows, others rolling towers filled with heavily armed liskash.

"No," he said, shaking there in the shadows.

It was all too much.

His soldiers crouched along the wall, waiting for the first contact between the two armies.

They came so slowly, Falon thought.

But then, he always did have a problem waiting.

Now, every moment of his patience was crucial.

He risked sticking his head up again to look at the small army advancing against the western wall of Tizare.

Not long now, he noted. They had their weapons out, and some were holding ropes, and small ladders.

He looked down at the soldiers. Grim-faced, eyes flashing in the torchlight.

Then he looked back toward the alleyways of Tizare. Where was Caissir . . . Ashre? Had something happened at the main gate? Was the battle already lost, and this fight useless?

And what of Taline? Was she already a prisoner of the invaders—or worse?

Then a great cry came from the west. A rallying sound. Falon heard the invaders marching toward his position.

Steady, he told himself. *Wait until they're almost on the wall.*

He heard them run to the wall, then heard their crazed sounds just below him.

And he recognized one of the sounds, the strange, clipped guttural sounds of the liskash. *Yes,* he told himself. *This battle will be for Paralan, his kits. . . .*

Then he heard the sound of the ladders being placed against the wall, some of them tall enough that they protruded above it. Ropes were thrown over, and these too Falon ignored.

He heard the Tizarian soldiers below him stir, impatient.

Still Falon crouched, waiting for the attackers to reach the top of the wall. Off to the side, he saw the two small groups of archers secreted behind the ramparts.

He looked above his head. A gray, scaly hand closed around the wall edge. Then another.

Falon stood up, almost casually, calmly.

He waved his sword in the air, and then, looking right into the eyes of the surprised liskash, he took a swing, strong and powerful.

To his great relief, the blade neatly chopped the thing in two. And in a moment he was shoulder to shoulder with the soldiers who scurried to their positions. The screams of the invaders filled the night air, as the soldiers easily hacked at them and the archers took their easy shots at the ones on the ground.

And in that first giddy moment Falon thought, with a big grin filling his blood-splattered face, *Paralan would have loved this. . . .*

Chapter 24

▲━━━▲

"You see, Ashre," Caissir
went on casually, as if the sounds of a great battle didn't fill
the city, "I knew that Plano's treachery would lead not
only to Falon's death at Rhow's hand, but also the death of
the ambitious lord himself . . . and the loss of the city to
the Eastern Lords."

"But why didn't you tell Falon?"

"Because," Caissir patiently went on, "if I told him, or
you, then Plano or his agents would have learned who I
really was. I could control my own thoughts—sometimes I
even forgot why I was here—but I couldn't guard against
anyone probing you or Falon. Also, I wasn't sure what they
had planned for you—"

"So you knew, all along, what was going to happen?"

Caissir laughed. "No, not at all. But I knew Falon was the
heir, and what Plano and Rhow had planned for him."

Ashre looked up at Caissir, feeling more confused than
ever. "Then why did you leave us?"

"I knew that you could protect Falon from Anarra. Your
power was great enough. I needed to find the White Dancers and learn news of the invasion, to see if Rhow and
Falon could stop it."

"Rhow is a loyal mrem?"

"Yes. Loyal, that is, to the city of Tizare. He had no
knowledge of Plano's treachery. That was another reason I
wanted to be near the city, should Falon have been de-
layed in the desert."

Caissir looked down at the kit. "He still plans on killing

Falon, and making himself king. That I've known for a long time, and we must tell Falon, warn him. Just don't tell him about me . . . not yet."

Ashre nodded, then bit his lip, almost not wanting to ask the next question.

"And Taline . . . is she . . . does she—"

Caissir shrugged. "I don't know, Ash. Is she helping her father? I don't know. In fact," Caissir said, looking right at him, "you'll be able to tell that better than I . . . when you see her again."

They turned down an alleyway, the sound of the fighting to the west now louder than ever.

"If we see her again . . ." he said.

And Caissir picked up his pace, rushing now to rejoin Falon.

The wall was filled with battling liskash, taking two or three blows without slowing while slicing down Rhow's soldiers with one great arc of their strange swords.

It was not going well, thought Rhow.

Then the first monstrous crossbow fired, sending an enormous arrow thundering into the city gate. Rhow heard it smash into, then through the gate.

Another blow like that and the doors would go flying off their heavy hinges like a door on some peasant's larder.

Taline had her archers firing at redoubled speed, now taking aim at the advancing siege machines.

But it was no good. The rolling towers were almost at the walls, offering an easy way for the hordes of invaders to climb onto the walls.

Elezar's catapults had reached the limit of their usefulness—all of their targets were in too close range. Rhow signaled down for Elezar to abandon them and join the fight on the wall.

Then Rhow saw the liskash, having made quick work of some soldiers, quickly hop toward the battery of archers.

Toward Taline.

"Help her!" he screamed to some of his nearby soldiers, but they had their hands full just keeping the enemy's swords away from themselves.

Where was Plano? He could conjure up some illusion to terrify the renegades while the walls were cleared.

But it grew more hopeless every moment.

The liskash reached Taline, and she swung, not missing a beat in her orders to the archers, jabbing at the great monsters, keeping them away, until Rhow saw one liskash leap towards her and send his blade smashing into her shoulder.

She tumbled back, off the wall, down onto the ground. Elezar was there, and he picked her up.

The enemy was everywhere.

"Retreat!" he screamed, searching for his captains. They could get their mrem to their fallback positions.

The wall shook as another shaft plunged into the gate. A moment later Rhow heard a groaning sound, and he knew that the city was now open.

The walls were breached . . . the gate destroyed. Tizare lay exposed to the invaders from the East.

Falon turned again, and he saw Caissir leading Ashre towards the wall.

Good, he thought, *now I can get back to killing these foul creatures.*

The surprise had worked wonderfully. The first group to climb the walls were quickly cut down by Falon and Rhow's crack soldiers. The invaders kept coming, but they were no match for these soldiers.

They had expected little or no resistance here. Instead, they walked into the best blades in all of Tizare.

Still they came, hoping to fight their way onto a perch on the wall. Falon's kilt was soaked with the oddly mixed blood of both renegades and liskash. His hands were slippery on his weapons, and he had to dig his claws in hard just to keep his grip firm.

But soon he saw the reward of every victor in a battle: the slow, agonizingly painful realization of an opponent that it was, indeed, lost.

First a few of the renegades pulled back, throwing their weapons to the ground, running off into the woods. Then the liskash, their normally expressionless eyes wide with horror, started stumbling away.

"Shall we chase them?" one of the guards asked, excited.

"No," Falon said. "We'll leave a small force here in case

they decide to try again. But I think we had better see how things are at the city gates."

Ashre came running up the stone steps.

"Well, what did our good Lord Rhow have such an urgent need of you for?" Falon asked.

Ashre hugged him hard.

"Hey, was it that bad?"

Then Caissir was there, standing behind Ashre.

And there was something different about him, thought Falon. A subtle change in the way he looked—and stood.

"I'm afraid," Caissir said, "that we never made it to Lord Rhow." Caissir paused, and looked Falon in the eye. "And I very much doubt we should continue calling him 'good' Lord Rhow."

"Falon!" Ashre screamed. The kit's eyes looked right over Falon's shoulder.

"Eh?" Falon said, turning around. It was one of Rhow's captains coming towards Falon, a slim dagger poised to strike.

Falon brought his arm around, catching the full force of the blow on his forearm. He howled out in pain as the captain brought his weapon back for another blow.

Why? Falon wondered. What was making this good soldier attack him?

But then he knew . . . as if it were something he should have realized all along.

The crown . . . the city.

Orders from Lord Rhow.

The blade was coming at him again, aimed for his now-unprotected throat.

Caissir took a step forward and raised his hand, and the captain dropped the weapon uselessly to the stone floor.

The captain looked at his empty hands, and ran away.

Falon looked over at Caissir, totally confused.

"Well," he said, "I *did* tell you I was a wizard, didn't I? Now let's get that nasty wound bandaged. . . ."

Rhow's soldiers jumped and leaped off the wall, many breaking their legs and falling onto their own weapons. His captains tried to scream above the din—to form some fallback position behind the barricades.

But it seemed hopeless.

Rhow stood there, shaking in the courtyard, while the chaos spilled round him.

With the gate open, the invaders could stream into the city, even as the liskash on the wall followed Rhow's mrem down the stairs.

He saw Elezar kneeling behind the barricades, Taline's head cradled in his bloodstained lap.

He hurried to her, thinking, *these may be the last moments I spend with her.*

"Go, Elezar, try to get the soldiers to hold some position. I'll stay with my daughter."

Elezar nodded, and then, as Rhow knelt next to his daughter, the soldier gently slid her bloody body onto the lord's lap.

"I'm here, Taline, everything's fine. . . ."

"Was . . . was I brave, father?" she said, sounding so weak that it made him want to howl at the sky.

"Very, Taline. The bravest of my warriors. With ten such as you I could have saved the city."

Her eyes went wide. "You haven't given up . . . not yet."

He smiled sadly at her. "No, Elezar will try to hold them a bit longer . . . but it's only a matter of time."

"And what of Falon?"

Falon, he thought. Perhaps he too was facing death.

Better that way, than what Rhow had planned for him. If they had won, Falon would have been found among the corpses. That had been prearranged.

And Rhow would have claimed the throne in his memory.

Now, there would be no throne, just death at the hands of the liskash.

Let me hope it will be a quick one.

Taline closed her eyes. She was losing blood quickly, and only if he could get her to one of the old she-mrem with their special herbs and bandages would her life be spared.

"Oh, my daughter," he said, pressing his face against her cheek, the clatter of swords deafening.

"There!" Falon called out, seeing the barricades near the city gates.

He hurried now, running ahead of his soldiers, leaving Caissir and Ashre behind.

It looked all but lost. A good number of Rhow's army were either dead or dispersed through the city, while the remaining soldiers were fighting great hordes of liskash storming over the barricades.

Then Falon saw Rhow.

Off in a corner, crouched low in the dirt.

Lord Rhow! And there, resting in his lap, Taline.

Falon raised his sword high, not feeling its heaviness at all. And he screamed to the soldiers behind him to hurry.

He rushed to Rhow's side, only for a moment considering ending the noble's life right there.

But he looked at Taline. Her eyes lolled open and she didn't seem to know where she was.

"How is—" Falon started.

Rhow looked up, showing no surprise at seeing him.

"She's . . . she's lost a lot of blood. We have to get help."

Falon turned as his soldiers arrived. He pointed at two. "Go with Lord Rhow and take his daughter to the palace. Bring an herb healer."

Rhow stood up, shaking, licking his lips. His fur was covered with dried blood. Whatever he was, Falon saw, Rhow had been in the thick of the battle. "The battle is lost . . ." Rhow said slowly.

Falon looked over the wave of invaders streaming over the barricades, hacking through the defenders.

"Yes—if we go on like this. Quick, take your daughter away. These soldiers with me are fresh." Falon looked up at the sky. The twin moons were overhead, adding a ghostly glow to the battle scene. How long before dawn . . . before the liskash must withdraw?

"Leave," he said, looking at Rhow, his eyes cold and gray.

And in that instant Falon realized that Rhow understood that he knew. Rhow's lips moved, as if he was about to say something.

"Go," Falon ordered.

The two soldiers picked up Taline carefully, and started to carry her away. "If I survive, I'll meet with you at the palace . . . later."

Rhow nodded, then hurried away to follow his daughter.

And then Falon's small army was there awaiting directions. He wondered if there were any more assassins hiding amongst them.

"We're not going to fortify the barricades," he ordered. "Instead, we'll split into four, maybe five groups, and scatter on the streets between here and Mineir's palace. Let us fight and run, ducking into houses, climbing from rooftop to rooftop, fighting for every dark alleyway. Stay in the shadows, hit your enemy, and then move on."

"But Falon . . . they'll reach the palace sooner or later," one of the captains argued.

"With that kind of fighting, it will be later. And then, when the twin moons are behind the western hills, we'll attack them in the courtyard, together, and push them out of the city. By then, the liskash will be checking the sky for signs of dawn. We'll hurt them, delay them, and then when they're preoccupied, we'll run them out of the city."

Falon looked around and made a quick assignment of captains, allotting an equal number of soldiers to each group.

He looked at the barricades, now all but covered by the invaders.

"You two can stay with me," he said, grinning at Caissir and Ashre.

"Gladly, Falon," Caissir said, lowering his voice. "I'm not too sure how much I trust those others, eh, Ash?"

Falon raised his sword in the air. "To your places!" he shouted, and he watched the street empty of soldiers.

He led his own group through a meandering trail of streets and alleyways before bringing them to rest near some quiet buildings, in what must have been the wealthy part of the city. He gestured to the soldiers to hide themselves in the shadows. A few actually entered buildings and took positions near windows overlooking the street.

"Tell me," Caissir whispered, crouched low beside Falon, "where did you get your great training as a strategist?"

The moonlight picked up Falon's smile. "When I was younger my people were still raiding the caravans. I used to go with them . . ." he looked at Ashre ". . . when I was no bigger than our friend here. A few times, the caravans repaid the favor. They attacked the village. The street fighting could be something to see. The village would look

empty, but every home, every street held death for anyone seeking the highlanders." Falon looked around at the
apparently deserted, quiet street. "That's all this is—the
same trick."

"Well, I hope it works as well—"

"They're coming!" Ashre said, his small claws digging
into Falon's arm.

"All right, Ash . . . easy on my pelt. I don't hear anything. Are you s—"

But then he heard the sounds clearly enough. A great
jangling line of soldiers, making their way toward them.

"Good work," he said to the kit. He made a few broad
waves with his sword . . . the prearranged signal.

"Get your weapons out, Caissir," Falon said, seeing him
just sitting there.

"Oh, yes," Caissir said, distractedly. "Just not very good
with it, that's all."

Falon saw him look at Ashre, a secret look. *There's something they're not telling me.* In his straightforward highlander way, he decided to ask them what was going on—
but then the invaders showed up.

"Ready . . ." Falon hissed.

Closer, their scaly bodies were clearly visible in the
moonlight. They were all liskash, talking to each other,
feeling that the battle for Tizare was over.

They tolerated the renegades fighting alongside them
all right, Falon saw. But after it was all over, they quickly
became a closed society. He could only imagine the fate of
the renegades should the Eastern Lords come to rule over
the mrem.

Closer . . . Their guttural voices echoed weirdly off the
bumpy brick facades of the buildings. Then, that unmistak-
able stench. A smell Falon felt he'd never get out of his
nostrils.

And closer . . . If one of the liskash soldiers were to
glance at their doorway he might wonder what all those
lumpy things were. A few more steps.

One of the soldiers turned and blinked its milky yellow
eyelids—looking right at Falon.

Falon sprung out of the shadows like a demon. The
soldiers with him all quickly appeared from equally improbable locations, some leaping from roofs, others crawl-

ing from nearby windows, a few just jumping out of an alleyway.

And nobody wasted any time in striking at the enemy. *Slash!*

Falon's blade felled one, then another of the weary, overconfident creatures. All around him the other mrem fought with a crazed passion born from the knowledge that if they lost this battle, the city, and their lives, would be gone.

"Stay back!" he ordered Ashre, but the kit ignored him, artfully dodging the lumbering blows of the liskash, jabbing at them with his oddly curved sword.

He was using one of their own weapons, Falon realized.

Ashre so distracted the liskash that the soldiers found it easy to cut them down as the kit weaved his way in and out.

Even Caissir made a few good blows, though he stayed well out of the range of most of the liskash.

A few of Falon's soldiers were also quickly cut in two, screaming horribly. But his small band fought with undiminished fervor.

Then the only sound on the street was the incredibly breathy panting of Falon and his band, and the hollow, watery moans of the dying, scattered on the stone road like so much garbage.

His soldiers gave out a victorious howl.

"Good mrem . . . but there is much more to do. Take a breath, and then follow me."

And Falon led them down more streets, past another alley where another band had ambushed some of the liskash. He brought them to a street that led directly to the palace.

Once again they hid, waiting for the sounds, slowly catching their breath. A few cleaned their swords by rubbing them against the soft porous brick that most of Tizare was made of.

And again, Ashre grabbed Falon's arm, giving him a warning.

This time, though, the surprise was less than total. One of the invaders spotted some movement on a rooftop and the invaders tried to find some cover. Falon gave the order to attack, knowing that more of his mrem would be killed.

Still they fought with incredible bravery, stepping over

their own dead comrades as they fell, ignoring the size and ferocity of the liskash. The few renegades with the group fled at the first sign of attack.

Falon felt a blade open his old chest wound, and he staggered back, sure that the enemy would drive his blade home.

But when he looked up, there was Caissir, standing between him and the liskash. The liskash stumbled backward, slipping on the gooey mess made by the dead bodies.

Caissir turned to Falon, his expression serious . . . concerned.

"Are you all right, Falon?"

Falon nodded. He pulled his kilt tighter, pressing it against the open wound.

When he looked up, the street skirmish was over.

"Quick," he said, for the first time his fatigue starting to show. "To the courtyard . . . outside the palace."

My palace, he thought.

Though Lord Rhow might differ with me on that.

"Come," he said tiredly. "Let's end this invasion." He looked up at the sky.

Just a hint of light, to the east. The slightest pale shade of blue.

If we can hold on . . . just a bit more . . . then we'll have won.

He led his band towards the great open plaza outside the royal palace of Tizare.

Lord Rhow stood at his bedroom window, staring out at the great plaza. From four different directions the invaders streamed toward the palace gates.

But not so many of them, he thought.

Whatever Falon had done, he had cut their army down. Now as they marched toward the heavy metal gates of the palace, Falon's small bands appeared from nowhere, and surprised the liskash from all sides.

He's doing it, Rhow thought. *Falon is saving the city.*

And every moment that the battle went on brought dawn that much closer.

Was it true, he wondered, about the liskash and daylight? Would they begin sneaking away to their hillside camp, eager to shield themselves from the hot, drying light?

Some of the renegades made a wild break for the gates, but Rhow saw Falon spot them. A few of his soldiers went after them and cut them down as their claws closed around the heavy black metal bars.

Still the sky grew lighter.

Rhow saw Elezar . . . somehow he had survived the battle at the barricades.

My most loyal captain, he thought. *What would he think of my deceptions . . . my treachery?*

Rhow turned and looked at his daughter.

She lay on his bed, resting on top of the too-bright crimson sheets, her fur still matted down with blood and grime. The nurse was forcing oddly colored liquids into her mouth.

He walked over to her slowly, not really wanting to be so near . . . to see her eyes closed so tightly . . . to hear the shallowness of her breathing.

"How . . . how is she?" he asked the old she-mrem, hoarsely.

"It's too early . . . she has lost much blood. But her heart is strong. We must wait. . . ."

Rhow nodded, turning back to the window.

Outside the battle finally turned. First one group, then another of the invaders started moving back, away from the palace, returning to the small side streets. And the army of Tizare, some in the royal blue uniform of Mineir, and others dressed in his own black uniform, fell into giddy pursuit.

Despite the closed windows Rhow could hear the horrified screams of the liskash.

And of what were they most terrified? he wondered. The wild-eyed soldiers . . . or the dawn, just about to break?

And what of you? he asked himself. *What are you most afraid of?*

Losing your daughter while you stand helplessly beside her?

Or facing Falon, as you know you must?

In answer, he knelt down beside his daughter's bed, holding her hand tightly.

Chapter 25

▲————————————————————————▲

Caissir grabbed Ashre and held him back, away from the jubilant soldiers crowding around Falon, all of them screaming at him.

"I must talk with you, Ashre—before we go back to the palace."

The kit looked up, a great big smile on his face. He was confused, and didn't understand why Caissir held him there.

"I want to be with Falon," Ashre said. "He's won . . . he's defeated the Eastern Lords. . . . Don't you understand that?"

Caissir shook his head.

"No, my young friend. He's defeated one army, one invasion—this time. There are more difficult and dangerous days ahead . . . days when he'll need your help."

"Yes!" Ashre said, agreeing. "That's why I want to go now—help him—"

The crowd of rejoicing Tizarians poured out of the once-deserted streets, everyone smiling, offering the soldiers great goblets of wine and fat loaves of rich Tizarian bread. The she-mrem jumped onto the soldiers, seemingly eager to make love with each and every one.

Still, Caissir held Ashre back.

"There is someplace else you belong, Ashre . . . someplace where there are others like you . . . like me. It is a place where you can learn the secrets of your power, grow even stronger, and return to help Falon rule."

Ashre's face was solemn, disappointed. "I don't understand. . . . What is it?" he asked quietly. "This place . . ."

Caissir started walking now, trailing behind the raucous crowd that led Falon to the temple.

"It's not so much a place, Ashre. It is a group of very special mrem . . . called The Three. If you come with me, you will be part of the group in the great city of Ar."

At the name of this most wonderful city, Ashre's eyes went wide. "I've heard so much about that city . . . its different buildings . . . goods from all over the planet . . ."

Caissir smiled, gently. "And about one half of it is true, Ash. I will be personally involved in your training, but others, more adept than I, will work with you. Until the day you're ready—"

"Ready? Ready for what?"

Caissir gave the kit's shoulder a gentle squeeze. "To help Falon rule. He won't always just be king of this small city. His future, like yours, holds larger things."

Ashre nodded. "And if I refuse to go?"

Now it was Caissir's turn to let his face look sad and disappointed. "The future is a funny thing. We can't really say what will happen, not for certain. But I know this much. Falon, his crown, his city, perhaps other cities, will need your help. You're a good little magician," he said, ruffling the kit's ears. "But he'll need more help than that."

Ashre looked around. The noise of the jubilant celebration was further away, as they moved towards the palace.

The kit stared up at Caissir. "Is this something I have to do, Caissir?"

He nodded.

"Then, I'll do it, I'll tell Falon and—"

But Caissir was shaking his head, his eyes starting to go all watery.

I promised myself I wouldn't do this, he scolded himself. *No crying, no silly blubbering, old mrem. Not now, not when this is all so important.*

"No, Ashre. That's the other thing. Falon can't know where you've gone . . . he must not know about The Three—the group you'll be with. It would put him in too much danger from our enemies."

"What! I can't tell him I've gone, that I'll be back?"

Caissir said firmly, "Do you want him to be in danger?"

Ashre shook his head, and Caissir knew that the kit understood the truth of what he said.

"What must I do?"

Caissir sighed. "Leave with me, right now. We'll take the western trails to the city of Ar. Falon must know nothing, but I will leave word that we are safe and alive. But Falon will never be far from us . . . that I promise you. And," Caissir smiled, "he will need us again. That is all I can tell you."

Ashre looked around, at the distant crowd, at the blue sky spotted with only a few puffy clouds.

"Are you ready?" Caissir asked, giving Ashre a few more moments to think.

The kit nodded.

Caissir forced a smile onto his face. "Then, let's be off!"

This is what it's like, thought Falon. *To conquer an army and have a city at your feet.* The noise of the crowd carrying him and his soldiers along was almost deafening, with everyone forcing handfuls of food on him, smiling, kissing his bloodstained hands, his weapons.

They brought him closer to the palace gates . . . and Lord Rhow. *And which one of us do they expect to rule them?* Falon wondered.

Part of him wanted just to bow before Lord Rhow and say, "Here is the city I won for you."

But it's my city, my throne! He thought of the mother he never knew, fleeing to the rugged mountains, carrying him.

Part of it would be for her.

He looked around at the crowd, at the delirious soldiers, all happy and drunk with excitement. And there, off to the side, he saw Elezar, looking right at him.

Falon smiled at him.

Does Elezar know . . . has he always known?

The gates were just ahead, and the palace guards stood at their post, looking nervous as the wild throng approached.

"Put me down!" Falon yelled, and he finally found himself on the ground again. "Caissir! Ashre!" he called, looking for them. But he did not see them anywhere among the happy crowd.

And there, on the steps of the palace, stood Lord Rhow. Waiting. Knowing.

Falon walked up to the guards at the gate.

They didn't hesitate to let him in. Falon turned around, seeing Elezar hurry over to join him.

They squeezed through the crowd, and past the gates, which the guards clanged quickly shut.

Falon said nothing to Elezar but walked as quickly as his aching body allowed him right up to Rhow. He saw the lord glance up at the palace windows.

Taline, thought Falon. *She must be in there.*

Perhaps she stands there, watching.

Falon reached the bottom step. "The enemy has been defeated, my lord," he said.

Rhow took one step down. "You have saved the city, Falon—"

"But there is still an enemy of the crown here, Lord Rhow."

The old lord's face fell, his eyes looking down. "You have no more enemies here, Falon. The crown is yours—"

Falon walked up the steps slowly, carefully, his eyes locked on Rhow's. "No . . ." he said softly. "It can't be that easy." Another step, and Rhow was just above him. "If it weren't for the kit I'd be dead now . . . at your hand. . . ."

"Falon," the Lord said, pleading, "I—"

Falon pulled out his sword. He heard Elezar stir behind him, and a gasp went up from the crowd.

He threw his sword down at the feet of Rhow.

The noisy crowd grew quiet. Elezar had his own weapon out.

The challenge had been made.

There was nothing for Rhow to do. Slowly, almost painfully, Falon watched him slide his own bejeweled weapon out of its rich sheath.

He let it fall carelessly on top of Falon's weapon.

Falon turned to address the now perfectly still crowd.

"I, Falon, heir to the throne of Tizare, challenge Lord Rhow to the Dance of Death!"

The crowd moaned, some shocked to see their hero turn into an heir, others just disappointed to see their wonderful festive mood replaced by this dark turn of events.

Elezar came up the steps, hurrying two and three at a time.

"Are you mad, Falon? Why are you claiming such a—"

But Lord Rhow raised his hand, quieting him. "It is as he says, Elezar." Then, looking at his brave captain. "Would you help us?"

Elezar scowled at Falon, his eyes flashing in the morning light. "Please," Rhow said.

Elezar grabbed the two swords and held them up for the crowd at the gates.

Then he carried them down the steps to the courtyard of the palace. While Rhow and Falon watched, standing together, Elezar arranged the swords, side by side, one facing north, the other south. Then he stepped back and, with the heel of his boot, carved a large circle around them.

Satisfied with the arrangement, Elezar stepped back and awaited Falon and Rhow.

"Are you ready?" Falon said, his voice cruel, cold.

Rhow nodded.

And together they walked down to the weapons.

Taline opened her eyes.

"What . . ." she said. "Where am I? What's—"

The old she-mrem patted her hand. "There . . . rest easy. . . ." Then the strange she-mrem began chanting some grim dirge while running her gnarled fingers through Taline's facial fur.

"No . . ." Taline said weakly. "What happened?"

Then she heard the noise of the crowd outside the palace. She struggled to slide herself off the bed. The old nurse tried to stop her, but Taline pushed her aside.

"No . . ." She took a step, her wounds tearing at her with each step she took. With a terrible grimace on her face, she struggled to the open window overlooking the courtyard. She grabbed at the red curtain, her claws digging into it tightly.

"What . . . what is this?" she said, staring down at the courtyard.

There was her father, moving in a slow circle, and facing him, Falon. Between them lay their weapons.

"No . . ." she whispered again.

Once before she'd seen the Dance of Death. It had gone

on for nearly the whole day, the circling, the feints, the posing, all so crazily ritualized, until those final moments where one duelist went for his sword.

She turned away and started shuffling to the door.

I must get out, get down there. Stop them. Why are they dueling? she asked herself. *Falon saved the city . . . my father is restoring him to his throne. What could be happening?*

The nurse pulled at her now, screaming some strange mumbo jumbo. But Taline was strong enough to pull away, shrugging off the she-mrem's attempts to restrain her. "Let me be," she hissed.

Even here, in the great hall of the palace, she heard the cheers and yells of the crowd echoing, reverberating off the bare stone walls.

Must hurry, she told herself. *And stop them.*

The stairs were enormous, and she moaned when she saw them.

Each step was agony. To walk down the staircase would be torture.

She gritted her teeth and took the first step.

She felt her wounds begin to flow again, moistening her bandage.

One. Two. She counted each broad step.

And all the time the cheers and screams of the crowd grew louder and louder.

Please, she prayed to the All-Mother.

Please, let me be in time. . . .

How many times had they circled, wondered Falon, each time drawing closer to their weapons?

And all the time Rhow kept his eyes on Falon.

But Rhow wasn't responding to anything Falon did, he realized.

Both of them were following the ritual steps, but Rhow seemed disinterested in the actual contest.

The crowd, at first shocked, even repulsed, now watched with all the boisterous yelling they could muster.

Elezar stood on the side, and he too watched Falon carefully. But where were Caissir and Ashre? He hadn't seen them since those last moments before the rout of the mrem.

Rhow hissed, startling Falon, who jumped back a few steps.

The lord laughed.

Yes, I've got to concentrate, can't be caught not paying attention . . . can't be too edgy.

No . . . It can't be like the last time.

Of course, there had just been a small group of villagers watching him then, a couple of dozen, watching him fall into the trap so carefully placed by Tramin. He too had smiled and hissed, watching Falon grow more nervous, until he reacted to Tramin's feint and snatched up the weapon.

This was another chance. Another try. There was more than his throne at stake, he thought.

There was his honor.

Rhow took a step inside the large circle.

Falon moved closer.

And then another step.

He's getting ready, Falon thought. Then Rhow paused, stepping carefully onto one foot, letting his claws emerge, threatening, long and shiny in the brilliant morning light.

The crowd was pressed flush against the metal gate.

Rhow began to circle again.

Easy, Falon told himself. He felt so tired. Just keep moving . . . keep watching. His body felt drained—from his wounds, from the battle—and suddenly he felt as though he were about to lose this duel.

Rhow looked in his eyes . . . and he saw it too.

"You're tired, Falon," Rhow whispered, breaking the unwritten rule against talking to an opponent. "Too many battles . . . too little rest. I wished it had not—" he took a step closer to his weapon "—had not come to this. In the end—" another step "—I would have served you faithfully."

"After I was dead," Falon answered, also sliding closer to the swords. They were only two small steps away. The Dance was drawing to a close. The crowd was perfectly still . . . awaiting the end.

Then Falon saw Rhow's gaze rise, leaving his for the first time, going up behind Falon to the great entranceway to the palace.

"No . . ." Rhow said.

Falon suspected a trick, but the twisted look on Rhow's face seemed all too genuine. He turned.

It was Taline, standing on the steps, calling out to both of them. She leaned against the wall for support.

Falon turned quickly back to Rhow.

"Now—" the old lord said and he took a large step toward the weapons.

And more, he reached down grabbing for his delicately inlaid sword.

Falon moved quickly, shocked by the lord's bold act. If Falon did not move, Lord Rhow would lose the duel in disgrace. But he could also kill Falon. Such a sudden move didn't seem to make sense.

Unless—and yes, Falon saw it then, as Rhow raised his weapon high enough for the entire crowd to see.

He wanted it this way. He wanted the crowd to see him attack first . . . taking on the shame. . . .

Falon picked up his own weapon.

"Very well, Rhow . . . we can fight. . . ."

And Rhow smiled, just as Taline's screams filled the courtyard.

They matched blow for blow, Rhow artfully dodging Falon's best-aimed shots, and then hurtling him back.

"They'll get—" Rhow spit out as he smashed his blade against Falon's, "a new king, Falon. This will leave them no doubt that you"—another blow—"deserve"—and again—"the throne!"

Falon stretched out, bringing his sword around in a clumsily executed swing. So easy to avoid.

Rhow lowered his weapon—looked at him—at Taline.

"Your servant . . ." he whispered as Falon's blade struck home.

Rhow fell to his knees. The crowd cheered, the terrible tension of the Dance ended.

Elezar ran over to Rhow.

Falon turned, and looked over at the palace steps.

Taline collapsed on the steps, her cries still carrying above the cheers of the crowd.

Falon let his sword fall to the ground.

Chapter 26

▲————————————————————————————————————▲

Plans for Falon's coronation began almost from the moment the invaders fled to their desert hideouts.

The court functionaries and sycophants who had served Mineir with perfect loyalty were soon hovering around Falon, offering possible menus for the gala dinner, preparing an extensive guest list (pending, of course, a quick check of who may not be alive), and desiring Falon's choice of wardrobe.

It all would have swamped Falon had he not had other concerns.

Taline was, according to the nurses and herbalists who attended her, beginning to heal, thank the All-Mother. But she had made one request of her attendants.

King or not, she didn't want Falon admitted to her chambers.

So Falon was often found pacing outside her door, waiting news of her recovery, hoping to be admitted to see her . . . to explain.

But it was an explanation that she didn't want to hear.

Then there was Elezar.

Falon thought this loyal captain of Rhow's might prove a formidable, perhaps even a deadly adversary. But Elezar had understood enough of what he saw in the courtyard to know that his master had provoked the duel with Falon. While the courtiers were buzzing around Falon, trying to ingratiate themselves and their services, Elezar pulled him aside and swore loyalty to him.

He even offered to explain it all to Taline . . . when she permitted such talk.

And so, the days of jubilant preparation went on, with a morose Falon stalking the wide, empty halls of the palace, strolling outside Taline's door, hoping to be admitted.

It was the night before the actual ceremony when he decided what he was going to do.

Tomorrow I shall be king . . . and tomorrow I will enter her room and tell her everything.

And even though he'd be king, the thought of storming her chambers filled him with dread.

Perhaps he could cajole Elezar into joining him.

The festivities began at dawn with the various guilds staging parades that wound their way through the streets of Tizare. Whole clusters of metalworkers, brick makers, and tradesmrem marched through the early morning streets at dawn, while street bands played horribly raucous music.

An enormous platform had been erected in the center of the courtyard, with rows of seats surrounding it for the very wealthy of Tizare and the visiting dignitaries from other cities who dared travel with so many stories of invading bands.

The three inns of the city opened their doors early to a booming business, and those pursuing more energetic pleasure found the boulevards filled with wide-eyed and eager she-mrem.

And Falon, dressed in layers and layers of a heavy material, watched all the excitement build outside the palace.

Soon, the plaza would fill with all the onlookers, the special guests would take their seats, and then some fat, taffy-colored mrem would run in and tell Falon it was time.

And when that happens, he told himself, *I will enter Taline's room and demand that she hear my story.*

Falon stood there, enjoying the feel of the early morning sun on his body. The royal musicians, dressed in garish outfits of bright orange, took their places and began playing brassy music with fanfares and great rattling drumrolls.

Street vendors gathered at the gate, selling simple fare to those not invited to the gala ball inside the palace itself.

The White Dancers, Falon noticed, had taken their position by the platform, ready to observe and add the story of this day to their repertoire.

Falon heard the steady pad of hurrying feet running into his bedroom.

"They're ready, Your Highness," the perpetually nervous councilor sputtered.

Falon turned. "Not 'Your Highness' yet," he said with a smile. Then he grabbed his ceremonial sword off the bed and strapped it on.

"Should I tell—"

"Tell them I'll be there presently. Have Elezar seat the dignitaries."

And Falon walked out of the room. He walked down the long corridor, down to where Taline lay, hidden away, unwilling to talk with him.

He knocked on the door. Once, then again.

Perhaps she was asleep.

He gave it one last knock. And then . . .

"Taline," he said, throwing the heavy door open.

The room was empty. The bed was made, and shafts of light from the windows caught the tiny specks of dust swirling in the air.

He spun around and started running down the corridor as fast as he could.

The nurse's room was a small alcove near where the chambermaids and other servants slept. He ran through the door.

The nurse was sitting on the bed, packing her things into a small cloth bag.

"Where's Taline?" Falon demanded.

She looked up slowly, as if she had expected Falon's question.

"She left," the she-mrem said in a thick Southern accent. "In the middle of the night. She said to give you this. . . ."

The nurse went to a small table and picked up a small dagger. She handed it to Falon.

The blade was completely black, as if it had been left in the fireplace.

"What does this mean?" he asked. The old nurse shrugged.

"I don't know . . . I just said I would deliver it."

The door pushed open behind Falon. It was Elezar.

"Falon, everyone awaits . . . the crowd is gathered. Come, why do you—"

Elezar saw the blade in Falon's hand.

"Where did you get that?" he said quietly. Falon pointed at the nurse.

"Taline's gone . . . she told the nurse to give it to me." Falon looked at Elezar. "What does it mean?"

Elezar took the blade.

"It's an old symbol, Falon. It means 'I will come back.'"

"Come back?"

"'For my revenge—for your death.' It's called the knife of sleeplessness. You're never supposed to know when your enemy will appear." He handed the knife back to Falon. "Look, Falon, I'm sorry. . . ."

Falon turned the ugly blade over and over in his hand.

"Falon, everyone is waiting. . . ."

Yes, thought Falon. *And now I will get to wait too.*

He nodded, and followed Elezar out to the cheering mrem of Tizare.

After three full days of celebration, the city gradually returned to its normal day-to-day functioning, with a new and untried king ruling over it.

The city, Falon found out rather quickly, tended to run itself.

There were layers and layers of officials who carefully controlled every aspect of life in the city. All dealings, whether they were commercial, social, or political, went through a convoluted, and well-financed, seine of bureaucrats.

The system probably was long overdue for change, but until Falon felt he understood how the whole massive operation worked, he thought he'd just watch it operate.

Elezar was an invaluable help, guiding Falon through the diplomatic niceties, explaining why this or that well-padded official might actually be important to the city. He discovered, as all kings do, that they are as much a prisoner of their kingdom as a ruler.

It should all change, he knew.

Except he was constantly preoccupied with another matter.

Taline!

He was afraid, though Elezar told him that when she came it would be for a duel, not to simply kill him in the dark. But every day he crawled out of the royal bed, feeling like an interloper, expecting to see her standing there, her hands squarely on her hips, the look of death in her eyes.

And so the days passed in Tizare, the citizens apparently happy with their ruler, the surrounding villages eager for protection from the city's army, and the tradesmrem prospering.

Falon devoted his time to reading the old parchments in the library of the palace. It was a dusty, musty-smelling room at the very bottom of the building.

When he had appeared, the custodian, a wizened mrem named Patriorr who looked more like a prisoner from some dungeon, at first seemed scared to see Falon there.

"Rest easy," Falon told the old mrem. "I'm here to learn about my predecessors, the rulers of the great cities."

Then the chunky old fellow bustled about, chuckling to himself, pleased as could be to have a visitor.

"Why yes, Your Highness. I mean it's all here," he said, gesturing to the stacks and stacks of parchments. "The battles, the first wars for the land, the establishment of the new cities."

"My father," Falon said quietly. "I want to learn about my father."

The old librarian seemed embarrassed. "Yes . . . well, there is material about Talwe, though he is not, if Your Highness will pardon me, part of the royal lineage." Patriorr seemed embarrassed. He tried to recover. "I believe there is some recent scholarship about your mother, before she left for Pleir. But everything afterwards is gone—" He cut through the air, as if slicing the old documents away. "Gone, destroyed." He looked up at Falon. "A terrible thing to do to important historical documents."

Falon nodded. "Let's start with the ancient kings and their wars then, until we get to more recent eras."

Patriorr nodded. "You should start with the Black King, if I may be so bold to suggest to Your Highness. The city was not such a good place to be then."

Falon followed the old librarian as he walked down a dim corridor lined with wax tablets and scrolls. Two small windows near the top of the large room sent a dull diffuse light spilling down. It would be next to impossible to read anything down here.

"Yes . . . just give me some time. . . ." Patriorr took an old ladder and carried it to some shelves near the back. Falon watched him climb up, muttering to himself, shaking his head, before fiddling through a great batch of the wax tablets. "Some are, of course, mostly illegible. I try to inspect them, save them from fading away. It's not easy, though, Your Highness, not when it's just me."

"Well, I'll see what I can do about that," Falon called up to him.

"Ah, here we are," Patriorr said. "It's very old but it appears in quite good condition. These will make excellent reading, Your Highness." Patriorr stacked the fragile tablets on his burly arms and climbed down, grumbling to himself all the way. When he reached the ground he said, "Will you read them in your chambers or—"

"No," Falon said, grabbing a rough chair that sat in front of a table filled with tablets and well-chewed chunks of trumpeter fowl.

He pushed them aside, gently, to make room for Patriorr's load.

"Well, I didn't expect—" the librarian said.

"Just go about your business," Falon told him, "and pretend that I'm not here."

Patriorr shrugged and put down the tablets.

Falon picked up the first one.

And slowly, with a growing sense of wonder, he began reading.

Every day, at the same time, Falon made his way down to the library. He did, though, make a few changes.

Torches would be dangerous around the tablets, but he had extra windows cut into the thick walls, putting in great panes of the clearest glass that Tizarian artisans could fashion. He also ordered more tables for Patriorr, and part of a storeroom was taken over to be used for storage of the more fragile records.

So after dealing with the remarkably small number of decisions required of him, most of them regarding business matters and citywide festivals, Falon could wallow in the richness of the history preserved on the tablets.

One day was spent learning of the founding of Tizare, the bloody feuding between three families for control of the wealthy area. And there were stories of the other cities, most of them secondhand and rich with an overlay of myth and exaggeration. Was Ar really founded on a spot where a dragon was killed? Did all the mrem really come from two small islands in the Southern seas?

Then whole cycles of the moon were spent reading the flat, brutal account of the first great war between the mrem and the liskash.

It had been so close, and only intervention from some magical, mysterious force had turned the tide in the great battle for the Western cities.

Most of the kings considered it the end of the threat from the Eastern Lords.

But we know better than that now, thought Falon.

Soon, a year had gone by, and still Patriorr kept the tablets piled on Falon's desk. He learned what little he could of his mother—just another palace worker save for her extraordinary beauty . . . and her headstrong, stubborn nature—

He smiled when he read *that.* . . .

He learned of the Black King's mysterious death, surrounded by his 'most loyal' ministers, one of whom had poisoned the corrupt old king.

Such was the foundation of Tizare.

Finally, Falon came to the end of the tablets he had asked for. There were still thousands of others, detailing events big and small in the history of the western cities. But he had learned enough of his history to have a sense of who he was to be, the mistakes to be avoided, the traps and perils of kingship.

It was simpler, he thought fondly, tending the herd-beasts on top the windy peak of Mount Zaynir.

And it was as he sat there, staring at the tablets, that Elezar came rushing down to the library with news that would shake Falon out of his lethargy.

"Falon—" Elezar said, having been told enough times to call him by name and not title, "I have news that concerns you."

Falon looked up, rubbing his eyes and scratching his whiskers. He felt gritty and in need of grooming. (There were always fetching she-mrem eager to groom the royal fur, he thought, not without pleasure.)

"Yes, what can this news of yours be?"

"I have spies," Elezar said slowly, "both in the villages and with the merchants who travel north and south. A runner brought me a message. A young warrior, a female who talks openly of removing the 'traitor' from the throne of Tizare."

Falon stood up. "And what does this warrior look like?"

"Golden fur, cool green eyes, and accompanied by a small but powerful band of soldiers."

"Taline . . ." Falon said quietly.

"I think it must be, Falon. We must take action. I'll start organizing an army to meet hers and—"

Falon raised a hand.

"No. There's been enough blood," he said, gesturing at the tablets. "Enough. She's coming for me, Elezar, for her promised revenge. Her army is simply to see that she doesn't get stopped."

"You don't mean that you'll let her enter the city? At least let me—"

"She wants me . . . and she can have me. But not here. This poor city," he said with a half-smile, "has had enough drama and spectacle." He walked over to Elezar. "You may let her inside the gates—No, *welcome* her and her band. You can, if you wish, try to explain to her what I did."

"And if she still wants to see you . . . to fight you . . ."

"Why then, you may tell her where I am." Falon laughed. "Tell her that I await her pleasure. . . ."

It was night, and Taline's soldiers had spread out, searching the city wall for any sign of an alert.

But it looked, she saw, totally quiet and peaceful. A few large torches burned at the great gate, and a few sleepy-looking guards walked the ramparts.

Very well, then, she said to herself. *We will try entering the city just as any other band of wanderers might.*

She gave the order to her soldiers to begin marching down to the gate. She took the lead, letting the strange wave of feeling wash over her. The city seemed alien to her now. Once it had been her home, a place she would fight to keep free. Now, it felt like some hostile camp.

She thought of Paralan . . . his last moments, and Ashre and Caissir, vanished. And Falon.

He would die. He had lived with the knowledge of her return and now she was ready to serve him her vengeance.

Her hand closed around the sword . . . her father's sword.

The guards noticed her party's approach and began stirring, signaling to the gatekeepers. More guards started appearing, edgy looks in their eyes.

"Should we draw our weapons?" her disheveled-looking captain asked her. She smiled at him. He and his mrem were used to raiding merchant caravans in the dead of night, or attacking other villages. The niceties of the Dance of Death would surely be lost on them.

"No," she said. "Have your mrem ready, but they should keep their hands off their weapons."

The burly captain nodded, then walked back to his soldiers, shaking his head disagreeably.

They reached the gate.

One of the guards took a step out, past the new wooden portcullis that was half raised.

"Your business?" the guard asked, not altogether masking his fear.

Taline spoke strongly, with authority. "I am here to meet with Falon."

The guards muttered among themselves, noticing that she didn't use Falon's title. "And who are you to demand to see the king?"

She took another step closer, and the guards began to spread out.

"I am Taline, daughter of Lord Rhow." Her soldiers were now clustered behind her.

"Welcome, Taline." It was a voice from inside the gate. The guards turned to see who it might be.

"Elezar," she said, not with any pleasure.

"Let them enter," Elezar said to the guards, and they quickly moved aside.

Taline moved past them, her soldiers snarling at the guards, enjoying their frightened looks. A few of her soldiers had their tails out, exposed, with the fur cut in a strange pattern.

Taline walked up to Elezar.

"I am here to meet Falon—"

Elezar nodded. "I know that. But first I want to explain to you—"

"You can explain nothing!" she hissed. "Nothing. You are just another opportunistic traitor—like him. Perhaps you too should die. . . ."

Her soldiers muttered eagerly at this.

"You can listen, Taline. Your father was the traitor, not Falon. He—"

"No!" she screamed. "I'll not hear that. Just bring me to Falon."

"I can't bring you to him, Taline. He's not here—he's gone—"

"Coward . . ." one of her soldiers laughed.

"No," Elezar said giving him a threatening look. Then he turned back to Taline. "He waits for you, Taline. Alone. Not in the city."

"Where?"

Now she saw Elezar smile, enjoying her frustration.

"He waits for you on Mount Zaynir."

Chapter 27

He sat on a cold outcrop of blackish curarr stone. A few drops of rain fell, wetting the tips of his whiskers, the furry hollows of his cheek.

Falon pulled his heavy cape closer, hoping that the icy rain didn't get stronger.

Below him, the herd stirred uneasily, feeling the unpleasant drops of water fall on them. The young mrem tending the herd-beasts had already taken refuge in a small cave.

The lead uxan kept raising its great head, looking up at Falon, remembering him from earlier days. It looked at him, expecting him to move them to some shelter.

Sorry, Falon thought, *it's not my job anymore.*

The rain started to pick up, big heavy droplets splattering on the black stone, beginning to soak his cape.

The herd-beasts started clustering together, their mournful moaning adding to the eeriness of the mist-shrouded mountain.

I could close my eyes, he thought, *and it could almost be as if it never happened. No Plano—the sly renegade—no Fahl, no Ashre, no Caissir, no Rhow, no king.*

And no Taline.

But the changes he felt were more than the expensive weight of the heavy cloth wrapped around him. Falon the highlander was gone. Forever.

And if Taline had her way, Falon the king would soon be gone also.

And still, at night, he dreamed of her . . . not wielding a black blade, but slipping off her kilt, coming to him. . . .

The rain fell harder, and now he was starting to feel cold and miserable. He tucked his head under his cape, but that was already sopping, and it felt clammy pressing against his fur.

He was ready to go in search of a cave.

When the uxen let out a terrific howl.

Falon stood up.

The lead uxan moved from side to side, then began pushing the herd off to the side . . . clearing a path.

Someone was coming.

The rain was so thick, and the mist so dense, that Falon could barely see the herd. But then, just barely visible through the fog, he saw something moving steadily up the mountain towards him.

And he didn't need any hints of beast magic to know who it was.

So this is how it ends, he thought. *Another duel, not far from my village.*

And this time he knew he'd lose.

She moved steadily up the hill, all alone, just as he knew she would come. She too wore a heavy cape, her head under a cloak.

He thought of going down to meet her. But he had no interest in hastening the moment.

If only there was something he could say . . . some words that she would believe. But if Elezar—her father's trusted captain—had failed to convince her, what chance would he have?

The beasts watched the stranger's approach with unusual interest, standing perfectly still.

He saw her eyes, sparkling even in this gloom.

"Taline . . ." he said quietly. "I wanted to tell you . . . to explain—"

She shrugged her cape off.

"There was no other way. Your father . . . he tried to kill—"

She undid her kilt, and Falon saw that her body looked leaner, tougher than ever.

"It was a way for him to die with honor . . . he knew that, he—"

She threw her weapon down onto the wet sporass.

"Your weapon," she demanded, in a voice colder than the icy rain.

He took a step closer to her.

"Won't you try to understand?"

"Your weapon!" she yelled at him, her voice causing a few of the herd-beasts to scamper away, giving Falon and Taline nervous looks over their broad brown shoulders.

Falon undid his cape, the water immediately soaking his fur. Then his kilt.

And what have I been doing? he thought. *Reading wax tablets while whatever combat skills I had became a distant memory.*

No, he had no doubt who would win the dance.

He unsheathed his sword—it was the same one he had used to fight her father—and he laid it on the ground, next to Taline's, facing the opposite direction.

Tiny rivulets of water streamed into his mouth.

"Are you ready?" she said.

He nodded. And she took some steps away from the weapons and went into position for the Dance of Death.

He moved to his position, slowly, sluggishly.

Taline started circling the weapons. With every step she hissed, and her claws pawed at the air, as if she was just about to pick up her weapon. A few times he nearly fell for her feint, rushing close to his weapon, ready to pick it up—only to see her standing there, sneering at him.

"You've grown slow, Falon, very slow. It's too bad the loyal citizens of Tizare aren't here to see this splendid performance by their 'king.' "

It was true. He felt out of touch with the steps. Her moves surprised him.

"Perhaps," she said, "I will make this easy for you. . . ."

She took a step toward the weapon, then another, until she seemed poised to pick up her sword. He scurried to catch up—and slipped on the grass.

He looked up. Following the ritual steps of the dance, Taline gracefully lowered herself to her weapon. Falon tried to scramble to his feet.

But he was too late.

Taline stood there with her weapon, ready to carry out the remaining steps.

Falon tried to come close to his sword.

Taline swung her sword through the air, while spinning around on one foot.

The blow nearly sliced his arm off.

He backed away.

"You struck my father when his weapon was down, didn't you, Falon?" she yelled, spinning again, sending her blade flying through the air while he ducked under it just in time.

"No," he gasped, wondering, *how many blows before she catches me?* "He lowered his weapon . . . knew that I gave him an honorable—"

She broke her step and brought the sword straight down, digging into the wet grass.

Falon rolled away.

Now he had a chance—if he wanted it. He ran to his weapon, hoping he could get it before she sent her sword crashing into his back.

He snatched the weapon, his claws closing securely around the hilt. He turned.

Taline smashed her blade against his, cursing now, her golden fur a drab brown from all the rain. She smashed again, and this time the blow sent Falon reeling backwards.

But he couldn't bring himself to attack her.

She made a movement as if she was going to jab him. He brought his blade close to him, ready to parry.

And then she brought her sword back for a surprise swing at Falon.

There was no time for him to protect himself.

"Stop—Taline—Falon—"

She held her blade in midair.

In the rain, the water streaming into his eye sockets, Falon couldn't see who it was. Then the voice spoke again, and he knew.

"Caissir . . ." he said.

He saw Taline still holding her blade above her head, her face still desperately grim.

"And Ashre," another voice said—a younger voice, but not the voice of a kit.

"Ash?" Falon said.

"Stay back!" Taline ordered. "We're not finished here. Not until I kill Falon—"

Then Ashre stepped between them . . . but not the kit

that Falon remembered. He was taller, his grayish fur darkening. And though there was still a youthful gleam in his clear eyes, there was something else.

"Put down your weapon, Taline," Ashre said to her.

"Step aside, Ashre. This is my dance with Falon . . . and I'll finish it—"

Ashre shook his head. "He's not the traitor," Ashre said gently. He took a step closer to her. He raised a hand to her.

And then they could all see the images . . . inside their minds. Rhow talking with Plano . . . Anarra's attempt on Falon's life . . . the assassin at the western wall . . . Each one of them saw the images, images Falon knew had to be conjured by Ashre.

Slowly Taline started to lower her blade.

"But—" she sputtered. "I didn't know—"

"None of us did, my dear," Caissir said, stepping up to the rock.

Taline let her blade fall to the ground.

"I've been a fool. . . ."

"No," Falon said, coming close to her. "Your father regretted his actions. He faced his deeds bravely . . . with honor."

She fell against him then, crying, digging her claws into Falon's fur. "I almost killed you—killed *you*, when it was my father who was the traitor."

"He fought bravely for the city, Taline. Without his leadership, it could have been lost."

"Yes," Caissir said, "that's quite right." He looked up at the sky. "Do you think we could find someplace dry to continue this discussion?"

Falon smiled, still holding Taline close. "Yes, a cave . . . just up a bit."

"A cave, eh?" Caissir said, making a funny frown. "Well, I guess we can't be too choosy. . . ."

Falon led them up.

The fire made a thick smudgy smoke that rose straight up to the top of the cave, before being sucked out by the cold winds rolling off the mountain.

"He's been an exemplary student, Falon. Absolutely the best."

"And you want to come back to Tizare with me?" Falon asked Ashre, still not used to seeing him older, no longer just a little kit.

"Yes," Ashre said sneaking a glance at Caissir. "I'd also like it if Caissir could come too."

Falon laughed aloud, trying not to stir Taline. She was curled beside him, close to the fire. Her head rested on his knee and she slept peacefully. She admitted that she had been hunting him, without rest, for days.

"Caissir? Why not? We have room for plenty of scoundrels in the city."

"It was Elezar," Caissir said quietly. "He's the one who sent a messenger to us that you might need some help."

"A loyal friend. . . ."

Falon saw Ashre look at Caissir.

There's more here than meets the eye, he thought. *It may be that I'll never know what the two of them are up to.*

"Well," said Caissir, "I guess I'll turn in. It's a long trip back to Tizare." He moved to the corner and curled up, facing away from the fire.

Ashre slid closer to Falon.

"I thought I should tell you . . ." he started to say, "though Caissir didn't want me to say anything."

"What, Ash?"

"There are dark days ahead for mrem . . . and not just in Tizare . . . in all the cities."

"I thought as much. I've been reading the old tablets."

Ashre stole a glance at Caissir. "Caissir believes some things are best kept among . . . among us. But there are battles and treachery ahead that will be very difficult . . . very."

Falon laughed. "You're beginning to sound like an old mrem, Ash."

But Ashre shook his head. "It's why we want to go with you. Others will be with the other kings, in their cities. But you must know this, Falon. There's pain ahead for you . . . and loss. . . ."

Falon watched the young mrem's eyes water, sparkling in the firelight.

"But Falon," Ashre said, finally, a smile breaking out on his face, "there will also be great, great joy."

Falon reached out and for the last time he thought—

recognizing that things had indeed changed—he ruffled Ashre's pointy ears.

"Now go to sleep . . . it's an early start in the morning."

Ashre grinned, and crawled to a spot well away from the fire.

And Falon sat there, his fur just about dry now, thinking of what Ashre had said.

He felt Taline stir, stretching slowly, reaching out into the air, before her eyes popped open.

"And what about me?" she said, looking at him.

"Eh? What do you mean?" Falon said.

She looked up at him, her eyes soft, sleepy now. "Do I get to go back to Tizare with you?"

"You mean you want to?" he said, smiling.

She looked thoughtful, then nodded.

"I heard what Ashre said . . . I'd like to be there . . . to help you."

He reached down, and let his hand trail the taut curves of her body.

"So beautiful . . ." he whispered, "even when angry."

She stretched out, and he saw her take a quick look at Caissir and Ashre. Their snores, a good octave apart, filled the cave.

"Yes," he said, letting her guide him on top of her, "you can come back with us." He brought his hands to her cheek, stroking the soft fur.

"After all," he laughed, nuzzling her neck, rubbing his nose against hers, "if you didn't, what would I do for a queen?"

EPILOGUE

The noise of the two bands, both of them playing at the same time, competing for the attention of the great crowds, was almost too much for Falon to bear.

He had asked Taline to take the newborn kits away, convinced that such a racket had to be unhealthy for them. But she laughed out loud, and swirled away, enjoying the pomp and partying that went with a royal birth. . . .

Especially when the birth is quadruplets, two males and two females, each one friskier than the next.

A small squad of nayas hovered near the large play crib, pulling this one off the back of the other, making sure one of the females with a penchant for climbing didn't use her tiny claws to escape the netted enclosure.

Of course the guests *oohed* and *aahed* over the four kits —that is, when they weren't stuffing themselves with fangle eggs from the north sea or pusto cheese spread on crisp green parra leaves. The wine flowed like water, and already some of the highlander clansmrem were dancing energetically around the grand ballroom.

It was a great party, but it was not one that Falon was enjoying.

Since assuming the throne, he had discovered a number of things about himself.

He liked his solitude. Whether from the habit of sitting on top of a forlorn mountaintop, or from the loneliness of ruling, he liked being by himself, or with just Taline and the newborns.

He even found himself staying apart from Caissir and Ashre. Caissir occupied a number of posts in his royal cabinet, none of which he seemed to care about. Mostly, Caissir was there to give some thoughtful advice or voice some ancient witticism that only convinced Falon to proceed in the direction he had already planned.

Ashre always seemed too busy to stay with him for long. One week the kit was learning all the maneuvers of the Tizarian army, the next he was discovering hidden passageways and corridors that even Taline knew nothing about.

And when he wasn't running around, Falon would spy Ashre and Caissir, talking quietly, secretly. . . .

And there was something else Falon discovered.

He took his ruling very seriously.

At first he introduced no changes to the way Tizare ran. The citizens appreciated that.

But before long he started tinkering with the old way things were done. He remembered how easy it had been for him to enter the palace, and he took steps to make it more secure. The great numbers of swindlers, cheats, liars, and mountebanks were forced from their prime position in front of the palace. Instead, a new park was created.

Classes were set up to train the soldiers in fighting the liskash, classes that taught the weak points, and the strength of the Eastern Lords.

While not officially approved, magic was removed from the list of unlawful activities, and Caissir helped set up a body to examine the claims of any magicians.

And as those first days stretched into the first year, he found himself continually preoccupied with thoughts of the East. Tizare was an exposed city . . . it would be the first to go, well before Ar.

It was something Falon wanted to prevent.

One of the servants carrying a heavy metal flagon of wine came by and started to fill his half-empty goblet. He shook his head.

"No, I've—"

"Why so pensive, Falon? You don't seem to be having a good time."

Falon turned around and faced Caissir.

"Oh, just lost . . . to my thoughts. . . ."

"What?" The wizard beamed. "No dancing at your own kits' party?"

"Perhaps later. . . ."

"I see," Caissir said, looking over at the swirling mrem on the dance floor, "that Taline has been wasting no time. You're acting more like her father than her husband, Falon. . . ."

And that's how I feel, Falon wanted to say. *I've changed, without wanting it or knowing it.*

"Perhaps you're right, Caissir," Falon said finally, watching Taline spin gracefully on the floor, her crimson and silver robes brilliant in the candlelight.

He handed Caissir his goblet. "Watch this for me," he said, walking out onto the floor.

The dancers parted as he came, his aura already a presence that he couldn't control. Many bowed their heads, while others just backed away a few steps.

Taline went on dancing madly, oblivious to his stalking of her.

Until he was there, as she spun on the arm of some effete-looking noble from Ar. The noble froze instantly.

"What's wrong?" Taline asked, laughing merrily, and then she turned and saw Falon.

"Falon—what is it? Is there anything—"

Falon shook his head. "I'd like the pleasure of a dance with my queen."

She grinned at him. "Why, certainly." And she curtsied before him.

The noble vanished to the buffet table.

Now he held her close, his movements stilted, almost clumsy. But her eyes radiated complete pleasure in their dance together.

"I'm so terrible," he said quietly. "I dance like a herd-tender—"

"Shush," she said, bringing a finger up to his lips. "Your dancing has gotten much better. And I'd much rather be led by you than some powdered dandy from Ar."

He gave her a warm smile. "You had better say that."

"But we should stop soon," she said, looking over to a table near the back wall of the great hall. It was piled high with gifts from the hundreds of guests. "Everyone will want to see their gifts opened and properly acknowledged."

Now Falon looked at the pile. *"That* will take forever."

"The nayas will help . . . besides, it is the custom."

He brought her close and squeezed her hard to him. "It is not a custom that interests me."

"Still," she said laughing, "it must be done."

"Then let's get it over with."

She led him over to the table, signaling to the two bands to stop their playing. The crowd, knowing what was coming, pressed close to the gift table. Falon looked around for Caissir, and saw him lingering near the back of the crowd, talking to Ashre.

Taline proved master of the situation, making a pleasant speech thanking their hundreds of guests, and arranging for the kits to make one last appearance before being whisked away to their nursery.

Falon saw that Taline, despite her engorged teats, was drawing some highly appreciative glances from some of the young mrem.

And then the gifts were opened. Quickly, smoothly, each one was unwrapped, held aloft, its giver acknowledged while the next in line was already being prepared.

Falon wondered whether he could slip away . . . perhaps to the library . . . or maybe even to his bed. Enough partying for one day! he thought.

Then the nayas had trouble with one of the presents.

It was a large crate, almost the size of a table.

Everyone grew greatly interested as it was hauled out onto the floor.

Even Falon took a few steps closer.

"They need some tools . . ." Taline said, gesturing at the wooden crate, its rough slats all close together.

Within moments, a few of the palace servants were prying open the crate, digging their metal bars into the edges.

Slowly the wood started to separate, and everyone came close to see what wonder might be in the crate.

"No! Don't open it!"

Falon turned. It was Ashre screaming from across the room.

He started running towards Falon.

Taline looked confused, and the crowd lost some of their happy smiles.

But it was too late.

Just as he screamed one end popped open, and the whole crate fell apart, like some kit's puzzle.

The crowd yelled, a high shriek that made Falon turn around, looking to see what might be wrong.

It was in the crate.

An animal unlike anything he'd ever seen.

And he wondered, how could it have rested so silently . . . so long, inside the crate?

It crawled out on four stumpy legs. Its bumpy head hid egg-white eyes that seemed incapable of vision.

"Taline!" Falon yelled, blocked completely from reaching her.

The monster was right there.

He started to push through the crowd, throwing some of the guests to the side, some to the floor, fighting to reach Taline.

He watched Taline's hand reach to her side, for her sword—that wasn't there.

"Taline!" he screamed again, fighting to get to her.

The creature moved sluggishly too, slowly, as if it had just awakened.

"By the All-Mother, move!" Falon yelled at the guests in his way.

Then Caissir was there beside him.

"Careful, Falon . . . It's a demon . . . a magical creature. I don't know how strong it is."

But Falon barely listened, and just kept fighting his way to Taline.

The creature turned, cutting Taline off. She climbed on top of the table.

"No!" Falon yelled.

Then the creature, growing more agile by the moment, raised itself up and rested its two front legs on the table.

Taline was back against the wall, with no escape.

Her eyes locked on Falon and told him one simple fact.

I need help.

"Well, if I'm going to try it I might as well . . ." Caissir muttered to himself.

Falon didn't see him raise his hand, mumbling to the sky.

All he knew was that all of a sudden the crowd wasn't there . . . Falon was somehow above the crowd, moving straight for the demon, soaring over their heads.

The screaming grew even more ear-piercing.

Then he landed at the foot of the table.

The demon took no note of him, just concentrated on inching closer to Taline.

"Thanks for hurrying," she called down to him.

"I had help," he said.

He brought his sword—the one from the battle for Tizare—straight up into the air. And then, down, aiming for whatever spine the creature might have.

It howled out its protest, turning, standing on two legs. It looked down at Falon, and then reached out.

"Your sword!" Taline called to him.

He flipped his weapon through the air, watching Taline catch it neatly.

The demon reached out for Falon.

Just as Taline drove Falon's sword right through its back.

It moaned, greenish blood gurgling from its throat, and then collapsed, kneeling before Falon.

Taline jumped off the table.

"Thank you for letting me finish that up."

"My pleasure." He smiled, wrapping an arm around her. "Next time just be sure to wear a sword under your gown. . . ."

"It says," Caissir said, fingering the tablet that came with the demon-gift, " 'In Honor of the New Ruler of Tizare.' " He handed the small wax tablet to Falon.

"Any idea where it might have come from?" Falon asked.

Caissir shook his head. "Not really. Except that I'm sure the Eastern Lords are eager to take their revenge on you."

Ashre was sitting at their feet.

"And you, Ash. Any idea where this came from?"

The kit shook his head.

And when Falon looked back at Caissir, he could see that he wanted to say something. "What is it, Caissir?"

"You had a close call, Falon, and there will be more . . . and we may not be able to help you. And that's why—well—"

"Caissir, you never were any good at spitting anything out. Just tell me what you want to say."

They were in the great hall, empty and cavernous now,

with the carcasses of a dozen trumpeter fowl and a couple of uxen lying like corpses at the end of a battle.

"We don't know enough, Falon, about the Eastern Lords. I want to leave . . . to go East. Perhaps pose as a renegade. What I learn might save you . . . your kits . . . Tizare."

"It's much too dangerous—"

"No more so than going on without knowing the power of the Eastern Lords."

But there was more, Falon thought, studying the chubby old mrem. "And?"

"I want to take Ashre. He's young, and he can carry the information we find throughout the Western cities. And, Falon, I may need his help . . . his power. . . ."

Falon nodded, and crouched down next to Ashre. "So what do you say, Ash?"

"Caissir saved my life . . . saved us all," Ashre said. "If he needs me, it's what I should do."

Falon put a hand on the kit—and a strange, painful feeling seemed to run into his fingertips.

He stood up. "When would you leave?"

Caissir looked at Ashre. "Tomorrow, I guess. The sooner, the better."

"And the sooner you leave, the sooner the day of your return will arrive," Falon said. He paused, looking at them now, Ashre rising to stand next to Caissir.

"I will miss you both."

And feeling more alone than ever, Falon turned and walked out of the great hall.

But he didn't walk up to the nursery to look at his kits, or to the royal chambers to be with Taline.

Instead, he walked out on the massive porch that overlooked all of Tizare.

And he stood in the cool night air and breathed deeply.

As he watched his city glowing like some rare and wonderful jewel.

His jewel, to guard and protect. . . .

THE END

Matthew J. Costello is a Feature Editor at *Analog* and *Isaac Asimov's Science Fiction Magazine,* covering film, video, comics, computer software and games. He's a Contributing Editor at *GAMES Magazine,* and he writes regularly for *Amazing Stories* and *The Los Angeles Times.* He is the author of **The Greatest Puzzles of All Time, Beneath Still Waters** and **Midsummer,** and is presently at work on a series of time travel novels.

A special preview of
Guardians of the Three, Volume 4

Defenders of Ar
by
Jack Lovejoy

A new king rules in the city of Ar, Talwe's grand-
son Tristwyn. Young, inexperienced and—unknown to him—under constant manipulation by
the Queen Mother Rhenowla, the king has not yet
realized that the threat shadowing the walls of his
city could mean the destruction not only of Ar, but
of all the mrem as well. In a desperate attempt to
save her beloved city and her people, Tristwyn's
grandmother Sruss finds herself once more rising to
the defense of Ar by mobilizing the one force she
knows can fight the most powerful evil Ar has ever
faced.

Sruss did not have to glance over her shoulder to know she was being followed—if not by the pair she had spotted by the peddler's cart, then by others, everywhere she went these days. No matter. They could not harm her, and she ignored them. It may have rankled the jealous vanity of Rhenowla to see another more revered than herself, but she was too cunning to harass Sruss, a senior White Dancer, the legendary queen and queen mother during Ar's ascendency, in public. If Rhenowla gnashed her teeth, she did it in private.

Sruss was more concerned for the wizards of The Three. They were not sacrosanct, certainly not revered, in a land where all magicians were distrusted. Especially now, when a confused and frightened people were beginning to look for scapegoats. She had already heard dark rumors about the fate of magicians in those borderlands threatened with invasion. It was well that The Three were now rallying to Ar—while they still could.

No thanks to Rhenowla, who was suspicious of any kind of unity as a challenge to her supremacy. There were other dark rumors that she was goading her son, the young king Tristwyn, with hints about a plot to seize his throne. So far she had succeeded only in an official ban on all public and private meetings of wizards—at the very time when their unity was most desperately needed. She had also let it be known, unofficially, that any meeting with the old queen mother would offend her—and set spies to watch.

That these spies should still call themselves H'satic, the Silent Ones, was perhaps Rhenowla's most baleful perversion of all. Insidiously she had turned what was once the eyes and ears of justice, the first defense against wickedness, into her personal secret police. Those with scruples resigned; those unwilling to do her dirty work lost their jobs. Yet in so vast and teeming a city, if one had friends—the Silent Ones no longer had any—there were always ways of evading them. Not too obviously, though; for Rhenowla might construe that as proof of conspiracies against the throne, a pretext for more stringent measures.

Turning a corner where yet another auction was in progress, Sruss strolled through the deferential crowds into a mercer's shop, which she was long known to have patronized. In fact, she needed some precious silkwares, if she was going to don once more the regal trappings of a queen mother. But first things first, and she exchanged a meaningful look with the old mercer and his wife, and stepped through a sliding panel into the fitting room.

The seamstresses had been dismissed for the night; the shop itself would normally be closing at this hour, but Sruss was a very special customer, and she was here for a very special reason. The old wizard rose as she entered, and bowed.

"My lady." He came straight to the point. "The news is even worse than we anticipated. All that we have feared so long has come to pass. The Evil One has somehow regained possession of the Third Eye."

"Are you strong enough to challenge him?"

He frowned. "By uniting the powers of The Three we may just be able to neutralize him, but no more. As you well know, true wizards tend to be solitary. Getting a whole council of wizards to agree on any common purpose, without endless wrangling, is seldom easy. But it must be done, and done before our very deliberations become known. It was only by taking the Evil One unawares that we were able to overcome him the first time." He hesitated. "You seem troubled, my lady. Have I spoken too bluntly?"

"You were ever blunt, Dollavier," she said. "Ever forthright and worthy of trust, and I appreciate those qualities now more than ever. What troubles me is the vengeance of the Evil One, for one I love may have fallen into his hands."

"Indeed something to be troubled about, my lady. For all of us have friends and loved ones similarly endangered. It has become dangerous even to contact them."

"How so?"

"Long entombment has left the Evil One wary of our united power, although he surely knows that not one of us dares face him alone. Thus far he has avoided open confrontation. Instead he's placed himself strategically to probe our dreams, to interfere with all attempts at telepathy, perhaps to render teleportation a trap."

"Where?"

"Cragsclaw. Do you know it?"

Her reaction startled him, and for a moment he was afraid she had been taken ill. She had no expression on her face, her mouth fell slack, and her eyes stared blankly past him as if in shock. Then she sighed and hung her head.

"Alas, I know Cragsclaw all too well. Too well to hear of its being so befouled without a wrench at my heart." With an effort, she at last regained her composure, and by a natural association of ideas turned to one who had shared many of her youthful adventures at Cragsclaw, even the very rebuilding of the city. "And what of dear Mithmid? Why hasn't he answered my summons?"

"He is even now on his way to Ar, my lady. But, as I say, teleportation would leave him dangerously vulnerable to the Evil One. His capture would incite an orgy of vengeance indeed, for no one was more decisive in entombing Khal beneath the Kazerclaw, or so vigorous in questing for the Third Eye. Alas, even he will be able to do little to unify us, when at last he arrives here."

"So I fear." She remained silent for the next several minutes, rapt in thought. The blunt old wizard was for once too tactful to interrupt. "It has long been my policy never to interfere in the administration of the kingdom," she said at last. "But there may soon be no kingdom, if I do not. Just as The Three must stand united against the Evil One, so too must all the kingdoms of the land unite before the hosts of the Eastern Lords. We have been accustomed to meet in this place every third day. Let our next meeting instead be on the fourth day from today, for on the third day hence I go to the palace."

"Very well, my lady. All the power I wield is at your disposal, even should you reclaim the throne."

"No, my good Dollavier," she said. "That is something I must never do. Though there were questions at the time about her true lineage, Rhenowla was accepted in law as a princess royal, and hence the king inherits his throne through her. Unity is all in all to us now, and few kings would form ranks behind a usurper. Difficult enough just to get them into the same room together . . . ."

It was in fact unlikely that anyone but Sruss herself could have done it. At least, not without brawls and challenges to combat.

Her gardens were all that remained of the old palace, in the oldest quarter of the Old City. They were now crowded with the tents of refugees—all the White Dancers who had fled the devastated city of Kazerclaw were here— for tonight's gathering. The humble pavilion, converted from the servants' wing of the old palace, hardly seemed adequate to contain so many kings. But not one of them felt his grandeur slighted, not one of them squabbled over rank of precedence, for the renown and moral authority of the legendary Sruss transcended even the vanity of kings. They stood deferentially before the armless wooden chair on which she sat facing them as if it were a jeweled throne, with their sons and chief retainers.

"My lords and gentlemrem," she addressed them, "you who have suffered invasion, and you whose realms now lie open to attack, know full well the evil that threatens us. Us, I say. All of us. For it is only through unity, only by leaguing personal interests in a common cause, for the common good, that we may hope to prevail. In peace, independence is a glory to the land. In war, it is folly. Old feuds must be resolved in a new spirit of cooperation. No matter who is to blame, or where the fault lies," she added quickly, as she noticed hostile looks being exchanged by two kings. "No matter what scores remain to be settled. We must all stand together, shoulder to shoulder, every sword pointed against the common enemy, or one by one we shall all perish. Be assured that, although the armies of the Eastern Lords seek only plunder and vengeance, the Eastern Lords themselves seek nothing less than our annihilation . . . ."

Resolving accusations, calming old hostilities, encouraging the withdrawal of challenges and the free return of hostages, she at last achieved what no other peacemaker in all the history of the mrem had ever been able to achieve. Even those who most resented the aggrandizement of Ar over their own kingdoms recognized its importance to their survival. All supplies and matériel must now be concentrated here, and the land scorched before the advancing enemy, denying him sustenance. That much was obvious.

Many decisions still had to be resolved; many concessions yielded, with varying degrees of reluctance; many sacrifices made. But the mighty walls of Ar were the one obstacle that could yet discourage such cruel and barbarous hordes—so long as they were vigorously defended. The city was a rich temptation to plunder, but such hordes were unlikely to endure the hardships of a prolonged siege. Once they began to straggle homeward with such booty as they had ravished elsewhere from the land, they would be vulnerable to counterattacks. Meanwhile Ar must be preserved, and that meant a sacred unity.

The All-Mother was the sole diety worshipped universally among the welter of cults, temples, priesthoods, and local gods and goddesses of the mrem. Her invocation in tonight's oath, consecrating the League of Ar, was thus symbolic of the vows of universal cooperation among the kings of the land. But Sruss knew that her work had only begun, for not a single king had mentioned The Three in regard to the invasion. A portentous omission, for nothing remained so urgently needed as the unity of The Three, both among themselves and with the warrior kings of the new League of Ar.

The evil that now looked down from Cragsclaw would seek by any means to shatter such unity, which it feared above all things. And its evil reached beyond this world, into dimensions that were themselves evil, whence sprang its ultimate source of power.

The refugee tents left little room for dancing in the gardens, but the White Dancers found space enough in which to celebrate tonight's consecration. Sruss herself joined in the complex figures with a grace and dignity that no king or princeling who witnessed it ever forgot.

These dances alone were visible to surrounding tenements, and hence all that could be reported to anyone keenly interested in everything that happened here.

"The throne is yours, my darling," Rhenowla whispered in her son's ear, as she groomed him with sensual, comforting hands. "Yours by maternal right, and by law. Never forget that. You know she's jealous of your power, and would take the throne back if she could."

"I know you've often told me that, Mother," said young Tristwyn, soothed by the grooming that was more than maternal. He was in early adulthood, although small and immature for his years. His face would have been childishly innocent, except for a telltale slackness about the mouth and fevered eyes, which gave him at times, and particularly after one of the orgies that had lately become so notorious throughout the city, the look of a depraved kit. "Does anyone else know about this?"

"How could they? The H'satic came straight to me with the news, and I naturally came straight to you. Within the hour."

In fact two whole days had passed since the meeting of kings, while Rhenowla brooded over the information. It could certainly be turned to account, but how she would use it and when—timing was everything with a mrem of her son's temperament—needed close calculation. She had been the great beauty of her generation, and was still attractive; her high amber coloring was variegated in such a way that it accented the curves of her voluptuous figure, and her dark piercing eyes were bewitchingly slanted. Her beauty alone ravished beholders; enhanced by a magical attractiveness, she became irresistible.

"I couldn't very well have refused her, Mother," pleaded Tristwyn. "I mean, with so many kings, and everything. They're all coming here tomorrow. After all, it's a public audience day, so I could, well, hardly turn them away. You know how the people feel about Sruss." He felt his mother tense, and knew he had again said the wrong thing. "Besides, you have no idea how big and fierce-looking the retainers were who came to the palace, requesting the audience. I meant to follow your advice, Mother, really I did. But I just kind of blurted out yes, and now I can't very well go back on my word, can I?"

"A king can do anything he chooses, my darling." Rhenowla continued to groom him. Despite the feebleness of his protests, she sensed in him signs of independence. Had he granted the audience for reasons other than those he claimed? And what did Sruss really intend? Was it possible that she in fact wanted the throne? Everyone took as much power as he could, and the time might just be ripe for a popular uprising. "Since you've disregarded my advice about granting an audience, at least have the audience chamber well guarded tomorrow."

"Yes, I certainly shall, Mother." He felt himself to be in a false position, as he always did with her; guilty about acting behind her back, uncomfortable about the very decor of his private quarters.

The drapes and furnishings of the secluded apartment were silkily voluptuous; the paintings and statuary crudely erotic. Incense burned in a copper thurible, perfuming the air with an aphrodisiac musk. His special friends would probably return here with him after tonight's orgy. He also felt guilty about his mother's exclusion from all such fun and indulgence, and listened obediently to her advice about how best to cope with Sruss and her entourage of kings tomorrow.

There was a spicing of old voluptuaries among the hundred or so wanton young mrem who crowded the banquet hall just after dark. The lighting was garish, the music wild and sensual, the dancing she-mrem skilled and abandoned, their lasciviousness increasing with each garment they stripped away. But though the food and drink were lavish, the service was plain crockery, at least for the most dissolute of all the courtiers. That they were so served had become a mark of distinction among them. They were the courtiers who from time to time had been caught red-handed trying to steal jeweled goblets or service of precious metal. Their punishment was to dine at subsequent banquets from plain crockery. The "Crockercups," as they were sportingly called, were young Tristwyn's most influential courtiers, and the most active in enriching themselves at the auctions, or in buying priceless heirlooms from refugees for a fraction of their true value.

It was their common boast that if the war lasted just a few months longer they would all be rich for life.

They pressed the king tonight for a strict law against dueling within the city, with heavy fines levied against violators. It would not be difficult to foment duels among the refugee noblemrem, who carried old feuds and enmities to Ar with their few salvaged heirlooms. The fines would be a new source of revenue for the court—and the courtiers.

The king was unusually thoughtful as he suffered their blandishments, but for once did not succumb, merely putting them off with vague promises to consider the matter. To their wonder, he remained thoughtful for the rest of the night, sipping his wine with unusual temperance, scarcely nibbling the lavish fare set before him, course after course. His moodiness disappointed both his special friends and his favorite dancing she-mrem, for he left the banquet alone.

His balcony overlooked the New City, crowded as never before with thousands upon thousands of refugees. Two of the three moons shone in the night sky. His mother assured him that the danger would soon pass; his friends all told him to enjoy himself and not to worry. All had warned him against ever letting The Three become too powerful, and now he was also warned against plots to seize the throne. The possibility that this was true was as disturbing as the suspicion that it was not.

He had always trusted his mother in all things, but what if she now proved untrustworthy? That his own grandmother, the legendary Sruss, could ever mean him harm was inconceivable.

These thoughts, more than the prospect of facing angry kings tomorrow, caused him a sleepless night. Even more daunting was the likelihood of making his mother still angrier with him than she already was. But, really, how could he possibly have refused an audience to his grandmother? A senior White Dancer? Sruss? Dawn found him dull and headachy—with nothing resolved.

He still felt less than prepared, hours later, in the audience chamber. The Crockercups also looked dull and headachy, although for other reasons. They stood at a discreet distance from the throne, brilliant as always in their court regalia, useless as always regarding counsel or advice—except where it tended toward their personal profit or aggrandizement. Behind the throne and to its right hung a curtain, behind which stood his mother. She was never officially present at public audiences, although in fact she was always there, and—until today—the decisions were always hers.

He wished for once that she were even more prominent. After all, he was the one who had to face this terrifying assembly, with every king standing before the throne glaring at him like a dragon. They were unarmed, and outnumbered twenty to one by his personal bodyguard, but still he felt uncomfortable. They looked so fierce! His mother often nagged him about sitting up straight on the throne, but it was now an effort to keep his shoulders from slumping, and himself from sliding forward.

"Your Majesty." Sruss seemed to understand his plight, and spoke with maternal kindness, as if to a beloved child, something his real mother never did. "We are here today, by your leave, to petition you to accept the leadership of a great league to be formed for the defense of Ar." She outlined the same arguments that had been so persuasive in the meeting at her gardens a few nights before. "All the resources that can still be salvaged from the kingdoms of the land, and all the mrempower, shall be concentrated here at Ar. All under Your Majesty's leadership."

There was a narrowing of eyes among the assembled kings, and more than one caught himself reaching unconsciously to his side for a weapon he did not bear today; but such was the influence of Sruss that even the most irascible held his peace.

The king braced himself, and sat up on the throne straighter than he ever had in his life. "I accept!" he cried.

There was a strangled cry from behind the curtain to his right, and again he felt himself sliding forward. But the kindness with which Sruss continued to address him again stiffened his backbone. The wizards of The Three had only bored or amused him in the past; he had issued the mandate proscribing their free association within the walls and territories of Ar to please his mother—the reason he issued most mandates. Now he withdrew the mandate to please his grandmother.

Then he immediately regretted it, for there was anger in the second strangled cry behind the curtain. These public audiences bored him more than wizards, but he decided to string this one out as long as there was anybody in the kingdom with a petition. If a stormy interview with his mother was now unavoidable, he wanted to avoid it until she was cooler.

How she could argue against a league of kings for the

defense of Ar, he did not know, or against a few old wizards meeting at times. Except that it was not her idea . . . .

In his nervousness and indecision his fevered eyes swept into every corner of the crowded audience chamber: armed soldiers at attention along the brightly painted walls; courtiers straggling deferentially before them in brilliant regalia (some of the Crockercups were so shaky from last night's orgy that they looked ready to keel over); flags, statuary, armorial pennons, and glittering mosaics. And directly before him the fierce warrior kings. At last, as if drawn by magic, he found himself gazing hypnotically into the eyes of Sruss herself.

"Be the king you were born to be, Your Majesty," she said. "Be true to yourself, and to the people who look to you for protection and guidance. Nothing more is expected of you—and nothing less."

Nor did he vacillate or go back on his word after she and the kings had departed. There were whispered instructions from behind the curtain, but for the first time in his life he did not heed them. Though he showed unprecedented patience with the weary parade of shopkeepers, farmers, merchants, and craftsmen petitioning for the redress of wrongs, real or imaginary. And if his decisions were sometimes callow, they were at least his own decisions.

There was now only deathly silence behind the curtain.

Tristwyn will need all his newfound strength and courage to fight the battle that lies ahead. He, together with Sruss, her protegé Srana, the orphan Branwe, and many others will all join forces to fight not just the treacherous Rhenowla, but the all-powerful wizard Kahl and the forces that empower his assault upon the mrem—the black sorcery of the Eastern Lords.

Guardians of the Three, Volume 4

Defenders of Ar
by
Jack Lovejoy
Coming in March, 1990
Don't miss it!